"For too l_____ secrets. He_____ _____ ___ __ ___ world know what some of us have known for a long time: Pati Nagle has an incredibly original voice. She takes us places that no one else can."
—KRISTINE KATHRYN RUSCH,
bestselling author of *Diving into the Wreck*

"In *The Betrayal*, Pati Nagle creates a magical world where the bright elves and their peaceful society are threatened by a darkly twisted new breed of elves who are as tragic as they are dangerous. Hope lies with a pair of young lovers joined by a powerful and unsettling magical bond. Lyrical and deeply romantic, *The Betrayal* is an enthralling read."
—MARY JO PUTNEY, author of *A Distant Magic*

"An enticing, solid debut fantasy . . . a fast-paced read."
—*Albuquerque Journal*, on *The Betrayal*

"Pati Nagle has created a world and culture that play with elvish and vampiric themes in a fresh way. That freshness, combined with interesting characters and a fast-paced story, makes *The Betrayal* an entertaining read."
—ANNE BISHOP, author of *Tangled Webs*

"A rich, intriguing novel, *The Betrayal* presents a multifaceted tale loaded with everything a dedicated fantasy reader could desire. The complex political and social dynamic that binds the sylvan ælven to their tainted alben kin introduces a conflict of truly epic proportions."
—JANE LINDSKOLD,
bestselling author of *Through Wolf's Eyes*

"Readers of fantasy romance will love this new addition to the genre."
—Romance Reviews Today, on *The Betrayal*

"Vivid . . . will complete any fantasy reader's shelves."
—Coffee Time Romance, on *The Betrayal*

By Pati Nagle

BLOOD OF THE KINDRED
Heart of the Exiled
The Betrayal

HEART
OF THE
EXILED

PATI
NAGLE

BALLANTINE BOOKS • NEW YORK

A Del Rey Books Mass Market Original

Copyright © 2011 by Patricia G. Nagle

Published in the United States by Del Rey, an imprint of The Random House Publishing Group, a division of Random House, Inc., New York.

DEL REY is a registered trademark and the Del Rey colophon is a trademark of Random House, Inc.

ISBN 978-0-345-50386-2

Printed in the United States of America

www.delreybooks.com

9 8 7 6 5 4 3 2 1

To Jane and Jim
faithful friends these many years

Acknowledgments

Heartfelt thanks to all who helped bring the ælven to life: my editors Liz Scheier and Kaitlin Heller; Betsy Mitchell (ældar of publishing); readers Peggy Whitmore, Sally Gwylan, D. Lynn Smith, Pari Noskin Taichert, and Jerry Weinberg; my beloved spouse Chris; and all the folks who came to the ælven photo shoot. You are the magic.

Share with your kindred, for kindness serves also the giver.
Always remember the power we hold in our hands.
Keep to your path though the storm of disaster may threaten.
Find your way back, when you falter, and seek to atone.

—Creed of the Ælven, second stave

⚜ Southfæld ⚜

Eliani gazed at the snow-capped peaks to the north-west, though she knew that one day's travel was not enough to bring her within sight of Midrange Peak. Riding as swiftly as the horses could bear, they might hope to reach Midrange on the third or fourth day.

Her thoughts flew to the pass there, where not long since she had stood looking down at an army of kobalen gathering on the plains west of the mountains. Remembered dread at that discovery filled her heart.

Only once before had kobalen massed in such great numbers: the Midrange War, five centuries since. A battle loomed, one that Eliani must take care to avoid.

She frowned, torn between a wish to raise her sword in defense of ælven lands and the knowledge that she had a more important task. Only she could perform it, and so she must avoid being caught in the fighting. She must hasten north as swiftly as possible, hoping to get beyond Midrange before the kobalen came through the pass.

Her mare balked, catching her anxious mood. She stroked its neck to soothe it, then turned to the captain of her escort.

"A gallop, Vanorin? Let them stretch their legs before nightfall?"

The captain gazed back, his dark Greenglen eyes and pale hair reminding her of her newly handfasted partner, Turisan. "A brief gallop. These mounts must last us to Highstone."

Eliani's mare tossed its head, and she tightened the rein a little to curb it. "The outpost at Midrange might be able to give us fresh horses."

"We cannot rely on that."

Eliani shrugged. "A gallop will not ruin them. It is not long until sunset."

The sun was indeed westering, and deep blue shadows were rising up the slopes of the Ebon Mountains to their left. The party would soon have to stop for the night.

Having heard no outright objection from Vanorin, Eliani drew her mount to the outside of the road and with a loose rein invited it to run. The mare obliged eagerly, and the others followed.

Twenty-one horses thundered northward behind her. Eliani grinned, reveling in the wind that whipped at her hair, the sharp chill of winter in her nostrils.

For a short time she held the lead; then Vanorin and two others of the Southfæld Guard passed her. She felt an urge to race them, to fight her way to the fore again, but she knew they had moved ahead only to protect her.

A roan gelding drew up beside her. She risked a glance at its rider, Luruthin: her clan-brother, onetime playfellow, first lover. His green eyes flashed at her in glee. She shifted her gaze back to the road ahead, her heart uneasy. She knew Luruthin had been disappointed by her handfasting with Turisan, though he seemed to bear it well. A part of her felt regret for ending his hopes. Granted, she had done nothing to encourage them for two decades, but Luruthin was her kin, and she still cared for him very much.

Eliani, I am going—

Startled, she jerked upright, unintentionally tightening her reins. Her mount reared, nearly colliding with Luruthin's. Shouts of alarm rose behind them, and Eliani's horse, nervous already, chose to bolt.

Eliani?

Wait!

The mare left the road, running instead on the verge that banked the Silverwash, passing Vanorin and the other guardians as if fleeing from attack. The animal's hooves flew over the dry grass. The river flashed by on her right, much too near for comfort.

The horse had its neck stretched nearly flat, ignoring Eliani's attempts to rein it in. She kept low over its withers, clinging with her knees.

Khi. Use khi to calm it.

She dared not loosen her hold on the reins but pressed her fisted hands against the horse's neck and concentrated on blending her own khi with the animal's. As she opened her awareness, she felt its terror, the blind fear that told it to run, and had to calm her own response.

Focusing on her soul's center, she brought her khi forward, filling her mind with a white-gold glow of peace. Gently, she sent this into the animal's thoughts, turning them to comfort, to safety, warm pasture, and the company of other horses. Safe in the herd, no danger. The mare's panic ebbed, and Eliani breathed relief as it slowed to an easier lope.

Hoofbeats pounded behind her. She took the reins in one hand and held up the other hand in warning; she had no wish for the mare to be startled again.

Vanorin's voice called out, and the riders behind her dropped back, allowing her room to bring her wayward mount to a halt.

"Easy, now. Gently, gently."

The mare slowed to a trot, then a walk, then stopped, its sides heaving. Eliani found she was breathing nearly as hard.

She patted the animal's neck. "That was a better run than I expected of you. I should enter you in the festival races next spring."

The horse blew and turned its head toward the river. Eliani dismounted, seeking the comfort of standing on the ground. Her hands shook a little as she drew the reins over the mare's head. She stroked the satiny neck, feeling the heat beneath the mare's golden coat.

Vanorin and a handful of guardians rode up to her at a walk. The mare greeted the other horses with a whinny, then nuzzled one of them.

"What happened?"

The captain's tone was not quite accusing. Eliani bit back a sharp reply.

"I was distracted."

"My lady, you must be more cautious—"

"It was not lack of caution."

"The Council has charged me with your safety, Lady Eliani. I dare not risk losing you to some accident—"

"Yes, yes. I will make certain they know that you are all solicitude."

"—or to a raider's dart. We do not know if there might be kobalen nearby."

She raised an eyebrow. Vanorin served in Southfæld's Guard. He should know better than she how likely they were to encounter kobalen in this realm, but she was skeptical.

In her own realm of Alpinon, attacks of kobalen against remote villages or travelers dropped sharply in winter. The creatures disliked the cold, so she ordinarily would assume that they were seen even less often in the south. Of course, these were not ordinary times.

She drew a careful breath. "I will be more cautious."

When he did not answer at once, she turned and led her horse toward the river, as much to get away from the captain as to calm the animal. Vanorin did not deserve her temper—he was only performing his duty—but she chafed at the unfamiliar constraint of being escorted by twenty of Southfæld's Guard. She was a guardian herself and accustomed to freedom of action.

She found an eddy where the horse could drink safely and sat on the riverbank watching it, willing her pulse to slow. Greenleaf trees surrounded her, their gray branches all but bare in early winter. A few traces of green remained in the grass at the water's edge, but the land was falling quiet.

After a moment she ran a hand through her hair, then closed her eyes. She drew deep breaths, quelling the fear of her still-new gift that lingered in her heart. This was why she was here; it was who she now was. A mindspeaker.

Turisan.

Immediately his khi filled her mind, his presence, his love nearly overwhelming her.

Eliani—I was worried. Why would you not speak to me?

I was riding. You startled me, and my horse bolted. My love, forgive me!

She felt his alarm and chagrin and wished she had been less abrupt. *No harm done. What did you wish to tell me?*

She sensed hesitation on his part, a slight withdrawal. When he spoke, he seemed guarded.

That I am going to the garrison before the Council convenes. Does Vanorin have any message for Berephan?

I am not near him at the moment. I will ask him shortly.

She waited, but Turisan said no more. She could still feel him at the edges of her mind, the tingle of his khi blending with her own. Amazing that she sensed him as though they were together, when he had remained in Glenhallow. So far their gift had not diminished with distance. It seemed their mindspeech would prove as powerful as the Ælven Council had hoped.

Silence stretched between them, more awkward by the moment. Eliani could think of nothing to say. They were still strangers in some ways. Lovers, yes, but only newly so. Handfasted a night ago and now parted because of the gift that had brought them together.

She rode north, carrying urgent messages to the governor of Fireshore. Their mindspeech would allow the answer to be returned in an instant instead of in another thirty-odd days of riding.

This was but the first day of her journey. The first day, also, of her formal partnership with Turisan. Not the most comfortable beginning.

She opened her eyes and saw her horse standing by the riverbank, nibbling at the long grasses that overhung it. Rising, she caught its reins and coaxed it out of the water, leading it to where Vanorin and the others waited.

Luruthin was beside the captain, his nut-brown hair

standing out against the sea of pale-haired Greenglens. He crooked an eyebrow at her but said nothing. Eliani gave him a brief smile, then went to Vanorin.

"Turisan is on his way to the garrison in Glenhallow. He asks if you have any message for Lord Berephan."

Vanorin blinked, then shook his head. "No, my lady. Please give him my thanks, though."

She nodded, then turned away to gaze toward the river. *Turisan—Vanorin thanks you, but he has no message for Berephan.*

Very well. Will you be riding on?

Until nightfall, I expect. We are anxious to make good progress.

I will not disturb you again, then. Speak to me when you have halted for the night, if you would.

I will.

She caught herself nodding and glanced over her shoulder, self-conscious. No one seemed to be watching, though. Luruthin was searching for something in his saddle packs.

Turisan . . .

Yes?

Nothing.

She flinched, angry with herself. She was behaving like a moonstruck child.

A gentle warmth filled her: Turisan's love, easing her heart and making it ache at the same time. *Spirits watch over you, my love.*

Thank you.

He was gone. The warmth, the delicious disturbance of his khi, withdrawn. Suddenly she felt colder.

She turned and mounted her horse. The guardians made haste to do likewise. Eliani guided her mount toward Vanorin's.

"Do we ride on?"

He swung easily into his own saddle and bowed slightly. "If my lady is not tired."

She stifled a laugh and gravely returned his bow. "Lead on, then."

◄ Small Sleeper Farm ►

Shalár paced in the small bedroom of a stone farmhouse, awaiting Yaras, her subcaptain, whom she had sent to fetch a kobalen. The farmhouse was poor accommodation by comparison to her home in the Cliff Hollows at Nightsand but better than the trees and makeshift shelters where her hunters, now training as warriors, rested by day.

Neither farmhouse nor Cliff Hollows could compare with Darkwood Hall. The governor's manse in Fireshore was a sprawling palace, built all of darkwood, the most coveted wood in all the ælven realms. Shalár's youth had been spent playing in the hall's extensive gardens. Soon she would reclaim it as her home.

She looked southward, as if she could see through the stone wall and across the leagues to Midrange. For several days now she had expected word from Ciris, another of her captains, who was there at her behest. Until she knew that her plans had gone forward at Midrange, she could not strike for Fireshore. She chafed at the delay, though the additional practice was honing her small army's skill.

She had brought her hunters here so that they might be a little closer to Fireshore when they were ready to march, and also so that the comforts of Nightsand would not distract them. Some of them had never lived without shelter, and she was teaching them how to survive in the woods and avoid being sun-poisoned, as well as training them to fight.

While Shalár trained her small army, Ciris was training the kobalen she had summoned to Midrange, over a thousand of the creatures at last word. They had agreed to fight for Shalár in exchange for her promise of immunity from being hunted, a promise she could make only because kobalen bred so swiftly and easily, unlike her own people.

The kobalen force was not nearly as skilled as the elite army she was training here, but then, it need not be. The kobalen need only pour themselves across the Ebons in sufficient numbers to hold the ælven's attention at Midrange while Shalár moved upon Fireshore.

She stepped to the drapery covering the doorway that separated the bedroom from the main room of the farmhouse. Mehir and Vashakh, the farmers, glanced up from a pallet near the hearth. Mehir smiled slightly; Vashakh looked away.

Seeing them together made her heart ache of a sudden. Her own consort and steward, Dareth, had yielded up his flesh and gone back to the spirit realm but a few nights since. She shut away the pain of it; she had too much else to do, too many others to oversee.

Shalár tapped her fingers along her thigh, frowning as she watched Mehir murmur something to his partner and Vashakh shake her head in response. The female looked up, casting a sullen glance at Shalár.

Vashakh had come to Nightsand not long since to beg for a kobalen with which to feed her family, theirs having died. Shalár had given another to her in exchange for twenty years of service from the young daughter she had brought with her. Vashakh still resented that demand, though she had agreed to it, knowing it to be the best choice both for Mehir and for their daughter, who would have many more advantages in Nightsand than on Small Sleeper Farm.

Shalár did not fault Vashakh's feelings. Indeed, she felt only respect for the farmer. To have borne a child and survived was a high achievement, one Shalár envied and wanted for herself.

Footfalls outside drew her notice, a light tread accompanied by a heavier shuffling. Shalár raised her head and scented the pungent odor of kobalen. It was not the one belonging to the farmers; they kept that in a small stone shed a little distance from the house, and Vashakh harvested blood from it there. This was one of the catch that Shalár and her hunters had recently made, one of the hundred kobalen she had brought with her to the farm.

The door of the house opened. Vashakh and Mehir flinched away from the sunlight, though it was gone again in a moment as Yaras hastened in, prodding a female kobalen before him. The kobalen's face was slack, its eyes unseeing. Yaras had it firmly controlled. He shut the door, pushed back his leather hood, and unwrapped the protective cloth from his face.

"Bright Lady. I came as quickly as I could."

Shalár nodded. Yaras's brows drew together in concentration as he turned his attention to the kobalen. It shuffled toward where Shalár stood, and Yaras followed.

Mehir's eyes sharpened as they passed, but he said nothing. Shalár stood aside for Yaras to bring the creature into her room, then lowered the curtain over the doorway.

Kobalen were smaller than her people, and stockier.

Blessed with the ability to breed as soon as look at one another, they also aged and died rapidly, a fact to which their slightness of intelligence was generally attributed. They had enough wit, though, to have devised a simple language and to use primitive tools, primarily weapons. It was the kobalen who had taught the ælven the meaning of war.

More important than any of that was their khi. Save that of the ælven, kobalen had the strongest khi of any living creature. It was this that made them of value, made them worth hunting and keeping despite their repulsiveness.

Nostrils pinching at the creature's strong odor of earth, sweat, and sharp fear, Shalár walked slowly around it. It looked mature yet strong. Covered all over with fine, dark hair, it was graceless, with clumsy hands and heavy feet.

Shalár glanced at Yaras, who stood impassive, waiting for her command. She had shared a kobalen with him once before, at the conclusion of the last Grand Hunt. They had coupled as she made Yaras yield to her his memories of his own child's conception. She thought her flesh had come close to opening to Yaras then, close to conceiving the child she wanted. It had brought her a better understanding of the mystery. She hoped to use the knowledge to her advantage, though so far she had not succeeded.

Time, then, to remind herself. Yaras would yield to her again, in flesh and in mind.

As if he sensed her thought, he looked up at her suddenly. She saw the muscles of his throat move in a swallow.

"Bright Lady, I have a boon to ask."

"Oh?"

"I saw Islir in Nightsand while we were gathering the army."

"Oh?"

Shalár felt a twinge of anger but hid it. Islir was the mother of Yaras's daughter. She had declined to hunt again, preferring to stay at home on her own farm, where she grew flax and cordweed and watched over their daughter.

"We have decided to handfast."

Shalár frowned. "That is an ælven custom. We have left all such behind us."

Yaras's lips tightened briefly. Though his expression remained neutral, she could see a hint of dismay in his eyes.

"Some customs have merit."

"That one puts us at a disadvantage, however. A variety of partners improves the chance of conception."

"But partners who have conceived once may likely do so again." She sensed the anxiety in his khi flare more strongly.

"Perhaps."

Yaras looked at her, his eyes pleading as he whispered. "Bright Lady, I would ask your blessing."

"My blessing for a practice I do not condone?"

He was silent, his brow creased. Shalár resumed her slow pacing, circling Yaras now instead of the kobalen. He stood still, not meeting her gaze as she looked over the clean, strong lines of his flesh, remembering their feel, their taste. His hair was as white as her own, as white as any of her people's. His eyes stared at nothing, and the color in his cheeks grew brighter.

A small shifting sound diverted Shalár's attention to the kobalen. Only a tiny movement of its feet, but it should not have been capable of that. Yaras had let his guard drop.

Shalár sent a stab of khi toward the creature, seizing control of it herself. It let out a sharp whimper and its eyes grew wide, but it did not move again. She turned to Yaras, holding back her annoyance.

"You cannot handfast. You have no ribbons."

Handfasting ribbons were made with magecraft, woven especially for the couple, with blessings and symbols of personal meaning. Magecraft, however, was one of the many talents lost to Clan Darkshore. No mages had survived their flight from Fireshore, nor had any with talent been born to the clan since.

Yaras's eyes closed briefly. "We will do without. A pledge is a pledge."

Shalár was displeased but forbore to express her annoyance. The hunger was partly to blame for her mood. She stepped up to the kobalen, drawing the hunting knife she wore at her hip, and made a neat slice on either side of its neck. The hot tang of blood, rich with khi, filled her nostrils.

"You are not pledged yet." She wiped her knife and restored it to its sheath. "Feed with me."

Yaras hesitated. Her patience at an end, Shalár wrapped a warning pulse of khi around him, a shadowed demonstration of her strength. At the same time she drew a little of his khi to herself. His cheeks paled, and he moved toward the kobalen without further resistance. Having one's khi fed upon was not a pleasant sensation.

Shalár hid a small smile as she set her mouth to the creature's throat. The hot sting of khi on her tongue made her forget all else.

She had not realized how tightly her stomach was clenched until it relaxed as the flood of warmth entered it. She drank deeply, conscious at first only of the heady richness of khi flowing through her, restoring her full strength, making her feel alive. It tingled through her flesh, to her fingertips and every part of her.

She became aware of Yaras, very close, feeding on the kobalen's other side. She reached up a hand and stroked his head, letting warm khi flow around him, gentle now. Memories of their coupling at the hunt flashed into her thought. As their khi began to blend, she felt the shadow of trouble in his mind fall back before rising arousal.

The kobalen sagged, its legs no longer capable of supporting it. Sated, Shalár drew back, her lips wet and sticky. Yaras raised his head and looked at her, eyes glowing in the rising light of dawn that slid in around the edges of the window curtain.

"Give it to the farmers. Then come back."

Yaras took hold of the kobalen, both its khi and its flesh, and started it stumbling toward the main room. Shalár held back the curtain and watched while he dropped the creature at the farmers' feet. Mehir fell upon it at once. Vashakh glanced up, need and resentment warring in her eyes, then bent to join her partner.

Yaras stood looking down for a moment, watching them feed. Shalár wondered if he would dare to defy her, but he returned. She let the curtain fall behind him.

She felt a sudden pang of sorrow, remembering Dareth. He had done his best to fulfill her wishes, though they had not been favored with a child. One of the original survivors from Fireshore, Dareth had understood her goals better than anyone. Her people showed her respect, gave her obedience, but she doubted that any but Dareth loved her.

Realizing that she was staring at the floor, she glanced

up to find Yaras watching her. As their gazes met, his expression of curiosity fell blank, then a flicker of wariness crossed his face.

"Come here."

He obeyed, saying nothing as he came to stand before her. His face showed resignation. Was it such a dreadful prospect, then, coupling with her? There were others who would not see it so, she thought, remembering Ciris's jealousy when she had chosen Yaras for this command.

She put her hands on Yaras's shoulders and leaned her brow against his chest, fighting a desire to weep. That she could not afford to do. After a moment his arms came up to hold her gently, bringing her even closer to tears.

"I want a child."

"I know."

Her hands clenched at his shoulders through the leather armor. She doubted he could feel it much, but his arms tightened around her all the same.

"Help me. You know how it happens."

"I have told you all I know."

"Tell me again."

She felt him draw a breath and let it out slowly, and then a sudden soft glow filled her awareness, as if a door had opened to a room lit with torchlight. Yaras had opened himself, yielding his soul to her as freely as Dareth had ever done. Surprised, Shalár felt a tear drip along her nose and fall away.

Memories washed over her, fragmented and filled with a jumble of feelings: passion, weariness after hunting, relief at having escaped injury, the flush of strength from feeding, and joy—sheer joy in touching each other as closely as two could touch. The last was

quickly followed by amazement as Islir's flesh opened
suddenly, swallowing Yaras more deeply, trapping him
in an unfamiliar and unbreakable grip as the throes of
passion sent them both into helpless frenzy. Then
something Shalár had not recalled—a quiet, ecstatic
peacefulness as they lay locked together in the deep embrace of conception, hearing the greeting of their child.

Shalár swallowed, aching to experience it herself. She
could feel the heat in her loins, roused by Yaras's vivid
memories. She pressed herself against him and felt the
readiness of his flesh. With a gasp that was dangerously
near a sob, she pushed away from him and began stripping off her tunic and legs.

Yaras silently removed his leathers and the clothing
he wore beneath. Shalár took his hand and pulled him
to the bed. His skin was slightly damp, cool to the
touch. She ran her hands over him, then lay back and
spread her legs, gaze fixed on his face, silently commanding him to come to her.

He did, holding her gaze as he leaned forward to
enter her. There was no love in his eyes, but there was
understanding. Shalár shuddered and wrapped her legs
around him, wanting to swallow him completely.

His hands moved to her shoulders and gripped them.
He moved gently, pressing slowly against her inner self,
frowning now in concentration. She closed her eyes
and wordlessly demanded the memories again.

He obliged, but the recollections were confused now
by the sensation of their present coupling. It was Islir's
memories she needed, memories of how it felt to open
the knot of inner flesh that was normally furled as tight
as a new-budded flower. She swallowed, trying to center
herself in that tiny portion of her flesh, willing her
body to yield.

He moved faster now, stabbing at her as his recollections swept him into heightened passion. Shalár thrust back, wanting him to batter her open.

With a stifled cry he spilled himself into her. Shalár felt her own flesh spasm in response, a delicious sensation but not what she had wanted. Angry, she dug her fingernails into his back and beat herself against him until they were both spent and slowly fell still.

"I am sorry."

His voice was a hoarse whisper. She felt a hint of bitterness wash through his khi.

"It is not your failure. You did your best."

She ran a hand through his hair and clasped her arms about him lightly, relaxing. She felt the warm ooze of his seed sliding out of her as he softened. Gone to waste.

Never mind. They would try again.

❦ Glenhallow ❧

"You gave him *what*?!"

Turisan watched his father's face, usually serene, take on an expression of outrage. He caught himself reaching defensively toward his right arm, where a tiny cut lay bandaged beneath the sleeve, and lowered his hand again.

"Only a small amount."

Jharan stood abruptly from his chair at the center of the curved council table. Rich tapestries depicting Southfæld's history softened the walls behind him, but his mood was far from soft. He was so angry that spots of red flew high in his fair cheeks.

The other councillors stirred uneasily. Turisan saw Lady Pashani and Lord Berephan exchange a glance and wondered whether he should have waited until he and Jharan were alone before explaining what he had done. He had thought what he had learned from the traitor Kelevon too important to wait, though, and the news should certainly be shared with all the Ælven Council.

Jharan frowned. "How could you think of doing such a thing? Violating your own flesh—"

"He was suffering." Turisan kept his voice calm. "It

gained us answers. No one else has had a word out of
him. Forgive me, Lord Berephan, but is that not true?"

Berephan, who as commander of the city's guardians
had been given the unpleasant task of keeping watch
over Kelevon, nodded. "True enough."

Turisan looked at his father. "Will you hear what I
have learned?"

Governor Jharan stood silent for a moment, his
breathing short and sharp beneath his formal robe of
sage embroidered with silver. At last he resumed his
seat.

"Very well. Tell us."

Turisan looked around the table at the councillors,
governors of all the ælven realms or their represen-
tatives except Fireshore, which had not answered
Jharan's summons to Council. Even now Turisan's
lady, Eliani, was riding to that northernmost realm to
try to contact its governor.

"I think Lord Ehranan's surmise is correct." Turisan
nodded to the warrior from Eastfæld who had been
named commander of the gathering ælven army. "I
think the alben's curse is indeed a sickness. Kelevon
acquired it—the hunger, he called it—while being held
by the alben. He was with our first envoy to Fireshore
when they were all captured."

He paused, glancing at Pashani. As governor of the
Steppe Wilds, she was the head of Kelevon's clan. Her
sun-bronzed hair, swept back from her face by a silver
circlet of state, curled every bit as wildly as Kelevon's.
Turisan wondered if she held any sympathy for her
former citizen. He could see none in her face.

Jharan's frown became thoughtful. "So that is
what became of them. My invitation never reached
Fireshore."

"No, it fell into the hands of the alben leader, and it

was she who wrote the false reply that Kelevon brought to us. Shalár, he called her, though he said her folk call her the Bright Lady."

"Shalár? That is no proper name."

Pashani gave a scornful laugh. "She deserves no proper name. She is not ælven."

"Is the envoy still alive?" Jharan's voice was steady, but anxiety showed in his eyes.

Turisan nodded. "The last Kelevon knew, they were alive, held captive in the alben's city, far to the west."

"They have a city?" Pashani's eyes widened. "There were only a handful of them left after the Bitter Wars!"

Turisan turned to her. "But that was twenty-seven centuries ago. Apparently, Shalár gathered that handful and kept them alive, and they have increased. Kelevon says the city rivals Highstone in size."

Pashani looked at Jharan. "Mayhap we shall have to cross the mountains and deal with this city."

"First we must deal with the kobalen at Midrange." Jharan picked up a battered note from the table before him. "A courier arrived from our outpost there today. So far the kobalen have not moved to cross the mountains, but there is no telling how soon they will."

Turisan nodded. "Shalár may have something to do with what is happening at Midrange. Kelevon said that he parted from her there."

Pashani turned to him, frowning. "Did he say what she was doing there?"

"I did not ask, but I could question him again."

"No."

Jharan's voice was hard. Turisan met his stern gaze.

"You are not to go near him. You are a mindspeaker. If he has a sickness, you must not risk the contagion."

"I did not touch him. I gave him the blood in a cup—"

"And you will not do it again!"

Jharan's eyes blazed with fresh anger. Turisan pressed his lips together and laid his hands against the polished whitewood of the council table, willing himself to be calm before he spoke again.

"What do you intend to do with him, Father? Do you plan to release him?"

"No!"

"Then we must make provision for him."

All were still for a moment. Ehranan's whisper broke the silence.

"Shades on water!"

Pashani leaned back in her chair. "Violators of the creed do not deserve its protection."

Turisan faced her. "I disagree. The creed is for our benefit as much as for that of—other beings. If we do not keep it faithfully, it does us no good." He turned again to Jharan. "I think Kelevon will not need much blood, nor very often. The change in him was remarkable, even with half a cup. It might be best if he did not regain his full strength."

"Is that harming none?" Pashani's voice was sly.

"He may not find it comfortable to remain hungry, but it should do him no harm. We could try to capture a kobalen or two to feed him on, though they will be much farther north at this season."

"No!" Pashani smote the arm of her chair with a fist. "If we hold kobalen captive to feed that worm, we are no better than the alben, and the Bitter Wars were for nought!"

"Then we must give him our own blood."

An uncomfortable silence followed. Berephan shifted in his chair. "I will contribute. And I will pass the word among the Guard for volunteers."

Jharan nodded slowly, his frown easing. "Very well.

Give him as little as needed to keep him alive. Observe him closely."

The governor gazed distantly at the mosaic floor within the circle described by the council table, his face strained. At last he looked up.

"Lord Ehranan, how many new guardians have been recruited?"

The councillors relaxed as the discussion turned to the training and equipment of the new recruits who were flooding into Glenhallow. Turisan leaned back in his seat and reached for the silver-chased goblet before him. He wished he dared to speak to Eliani, but he would not risk endangering her again.

Thinking of his partner made him catch his breath. His fingers brushed the handfasting ribbons bound on his left forearm and tingled with the khi with which they were woven. He loved Eliani beyond all reason, though in some ways they were still strangers. He yearned to see her, though she had departed only that morning.

No doubt that was the cause of the restlessness that haunted him. It was hard to be obliged to wait here in the safety of Hallowhall while his lady hastened north toward unknown dangers.

❧ Willow Bend ❧

Eliani dismounted, saddle-weary after a long day's riding. Her escort was settling into the camp at Willow Bend, guardians clearing ground, obeying soft instructions from Vanorin.

Luruthin knelt to build a fire circle with rocks that had been scattered against the cliff. Eliani watched him, marveling at his cheerful energy despite their hard pace and the uncertainty of what lay ahead. She had not seen him look so happy in many a day, though that morning she had noticed him smiling as he bade farewell to Lady Jhinani in Glenhallow's public circle. They had stood quite close, as she recalled—surprisingly close.

Eliani's mount butted its head against her shoulder. She led the horse to join the other animals at the stream below the camp—an icy rill that trickled down from the mountains and through the clearing on its way to join the Silverwash—and stood watching while it drank.

The sun was sliding behind the peaks of the Ebons, and with its disappearance the air quickly chilled. Sighing wearily, she stretched her aching muscles.

Turisan?

I am here.

Her heart swelled with pride. This was the farthest distance from which she had spoken to him, yet he answered with no more difficulty than if they had been in the same room. She began to believe that their gift truly was limitless, a thought that left her a little in awe.

We have stopped for the night.

Good. Where are you?

Willow Bend.

You have made good speed, then. That is often a second-day camp.

The horse lifted its head, and Eliani led it away from the stream, not wanting it to chill itself with too much of the cold water. She found some dry grass for it to nibble in the shelter of the trees and began to untack it.

Is the Council still in session?

No, we have recessed for now. I have some matters to discuss with you.

She paused, her heart twinging with alarm. She felt just as she had in her youth when caught in some mischief by her father.

Matters?

We have questioned the traitor sent by the alben and learned somewhat from him.

Kelevon. He meant Kelevon. Why did he not just say the name? Did he fear that she still cared for that betrayer?

She closed her eyes, overwhelmed by weariness and a wish to avoid talking of Kelevon. It seemed she would never escape her wretched past. She pulled up a handful of grass and brushed at the matted hair on her horse's back.

May we talk of it when I am rested?

A sharp pang of disappointment, and something else, too quickly hidden for her to identify. She swallowed, regretting her request.

Of course. Speak to me when you are ready.

Thank you. Turisan?

Yes?

How to say all she was feeling. Apologize? That seemed too strong, and she was terrible at apologies.

I miss you.

The wave of warmth that washed through her in response took her breath away. Wordless love, a hint of the passion they had shared only last night, enough to leave her aching with a strange emptiness as Turisan released her.

"My lady?"

She started, blinking, and realized that her horse had moved away to find sweeter fodder, leaving her standing numbly with her mouth agape, a swatch of grass in her hand. Vanorin stood before her, his expression doubtful. She dropped the grass and brushed her hands, shooting a sharp glance at him.

"What is it?"

"I thought you might care to choose where you will rest."

Surprised, Eliani blinked. Her first instinct was to be offended, but she realized he meant to honor her and so shaped a civil answer.

"I care not, so long as it is out of the wind."

"Perhaps you wish for privacy—"

Eliani barked a laugh. "I have been a guardian too long to care for that. Please, Vanorin, do not think I require special treatment."

The captain bowed, looking slightly awkward, and moved to withdraw. Eliani was surprised to realize that he must indeed see her as an oddity now, something other than a fellow guardian. That hurt.

"Vanorin?"

"My lady?"

"Please call me by my name. You were not loath to do so when last we rode together."

Eliani summoned a weary smile and offered to clasp arms. Vanorin hesitated, looking at the arm she offered, and Eliani realized he was shy of touching the handfasting ribbon that bound it.

"Go ahead." She nodded to encourage him.

He met her gaze with a rueful smile, then clasped arms lightly, pausing to peer at the ribbon. For a moment he seemed absorbed in the woven images. Then, recalling himself, he let her go and took a step back.

"I witnessed your handfasting, my l—Eliani. I found the ceremony quite moving."

"Thank you. I found it so as well."

His deep eyes grew sober. "I have never before seen a sword employed as a craft emblem on such an occasion."

Eliani gave a soft, ironic laugh. "These are dark times."

She glanced at her horse and, seeing that it was content, looked back at Vanorin. "What may I do to help make camp? Mind, I am a wretched cook, so for all our sakes let it be something else."

Vanorin grinned. "Firewood? I have a woodcutter's blade I can lend you."

"Good."

Eliani accepted the blade and a sling and started through the willows, following rising ground between the stream and the base of the cliff until she reached a part of the wood that had not been cleared. Briars tangled beneath the trees. She hacked her way through them with the heavy blade, making for a thicket where young trees fought each other for a glimpse of light. A few had lost the battle, standing brittle and forlorn.

Eliani chose a sapling and reached a hand to it, confirming that no khi remained. She felled it with a few blows, then set to work cutting it into lengths that would fit in her sling.

What are you doing?

She jumped and missed the log, the blade thumping into the ground beside it. She muttered an oath and pulled it free.

Cutting firewood. Why?

I sensed your exertion.

Did you? Come and help, idle one.

His amusement filled her mind. She stopped, sharply lonely for him. To distract herself she took a draught of water from her skin, then capped it.

Where are you, Turisan?

In the Star Tower.

Eliani stood still, her thoughts flying back to the tower and the previous night, when all her trepidation had burned away in the forge of white-hot passion. She closed her eyes, trying to escape the yearning to be back there.

I have decided to stay here for a few days. I told Pheran to let nothing be touched.

Eliani opened her eyes, blinking in the soft light beneath the willow branches. *Why?*

The pillows smell of you, my love.

She drew a sharp breath, then laid her blade to the dead tree, chopping the last of it into fire lengths. She stacked them in her sling and judged it would hold more, so she sought another casualty and began to cut it up.

Are you angry?

Eliani paused in her work. *No. Frustrated.*

She reached her thoughts out to him as for an embrace, which he gave her. For a moment she stood locked in the comfort of his love, their thoughts blending almost as deeply as they had done in the Star Tower, until a movement nearby startled her into abruptly withdrawing.

Her eyes flew open and her heart gave a sudden lurch of fear, for she had been nearly oblivious to her surroundings. A blur of gray-brown fur bounced away through the underbrush.

What is it?

Nothing. A rabbit.

An echo of wordless concern enfolded her. She swallowed, her heart still pounding.

Are we going to torment ourselves like this every day?

He did not answer immediately. When he did, the tone of his thought was quiet, contrite.

No. I am going to rest a while, love. Speak to me when you are ready to hear our news.

Turisan—

A wave of warmth swept through her, then was gone. She stood still, frowning, regretting her impatient words. After a moment she bent to her work, collecting the rest of the firewood and scattering the brush she had cleared so that the only sign of her activity was the absence of two dead willows and a bit of the tangled undergrowth.

Hefting her sling, she started downhill toward the camp. Dusk was falling, dimming the light within the wood. She was angry with herself, and troubled that the gift she and Turisan shared enabled her to hurt him even though they were leagues apart.

⊲ Magehall ⊳

Rephanin gazed at his circle of adepts, seated in the magehall's largest chamber, where they met each evening shortly after sunset. The room was round and windowless, its walls of golden stone minimally adorned. Chairs and small tables comprised its furnishings, and a large open hearth at the north side was the main source of light.

Golden fireglow washed the fair Greenglen faces of the adepts. Rephanin felt a deep pride in them. They were skilled mages, most having studied with him for several decades.

"I am afraid our studies will be interrupted for a time. Instead, you will have intensive practice at focus-building."

Jholóran, a rather serious male who was among the longest-standing members of the circle, looked at him. "What sort of focuses, my lord?"

"Those that will benefit the army being raised. Weapons blessed for accuracy, cloaks for protection. We will review the technique—"

The door opened, and Rephanin was surprised to see Lady Heléri enter softly. She had come to Glenhallow to attend the Council, having once governed Alpinon. She was dressed in violet with her long black hair loose over her shoulders, still every bit as lovely as when he had first seen her many centuries ago in Hollirued, the first city of Eastfæld.

They had met there shortly after the Bitter Wars, both having come thither to study magecraft. Soft-spoken and filled with wonder at the grandeur of Hollirued, Heléri had made little impression at first, though she had caught Rephanin's eye. He had flirted with her and even considered paying serious court to her, but he had found her reserve tiresome and at last dismissed her as pretty but simple, one whose admiration he would accept but who merited little more of his attention.

How bitterly he had come to regret that choice. He had wasted decades indulging himself with more openly appreciative companions until the Council of Governors had convened again in Hollirued. At that Council, Alpinon was represented by a new governor, Davharin. Not long after his arrival, Heléri had come to Rephanin asking advice on how to understand and manage mindspeech, and he had begun to realize what had slipped through his grasp.

Her smile was every bit as entrancing now as it had been then. "One of the magehall attendants told me you would begin work tonight. I wish to contribute, if I may."

"Of course." Rephanin swallowed and turned to address the circle. "Some of you may have met Lady Heléri. Please make her welcome."

A murmur, a shifting as Heléri joined the adepts. Stepping forward, Rephanin gestured for the mages to rise and set the circle. They moved closer until all were in arm's reach of their neighbors.

Rephanin held out his hands toward the mages on either side, right palm up, left down. His neighbors placed their own hands a handspan apart from his, close enough to feel the khi between them.

When the whole circle stood thus, he sent khi flowing from his left hand. In a moment he felt the pulse return through his right hand, augmented by the khi of the others. Silently asking for guidance from whatever spirits might be watching over the circle, he let it continue a little longer, then inhaled and released the contact.

"Good. Resume your seats, please."

He picked up a quiver of arrows and withdrew one, holding it before him. "These arrows represent an exercise in focus-building. You have all done this sort of work before; the difference is that now we must do it quickly. There will be hundreds of guardians to equip. Help has been requested, but for now it falls to us to bless as many items as we can in as short a time as possible.

"I caution you that though the work must be done swiftly it must yet be done thoroughly. This hall has never produced inferior work, and we shall not begin now."

The mages nodded agreement. Rephanin distributed the arrows, one to each. Greenglen colors marked the shafts, the fletchings were white, and the points new-made bronze.

As he handed one to Heléri he felt a whisper of her khi along the shaft until it left his fingers. She glanced up at him, smiling softly in a way that woke several distracting memories. He returned to his worktable, setting the quiver down as he kept one arrow in hand.

"The qualities to be focused are trueness, accuracy in flight, and penetration of the point. The denser the material, the more attention is required, so the metal point will require the greatest effort. Lay the khi *into* the arrow's fibre. A laying on of khi is not sufficient.

"Remember always to draw on prime khi. Do not use your own khi. And do not let the point of a weapon aim at anyone else in the chamber. Questions?"

Several of the mages were already preparing to work, aiming their arrows toward the fire, a good source of prime khi, especially for work with fire-forged weaponry. Rephanin moved away from the hearth to a table on which stood a timekeeper—a basin of water and several metal bowls. Selecting the smallest, he held it above the water in which it would float, slowly filling through a tiny hole in its base until it sank.

"You will have one cycle to complete the focus. Begin."

Releasing the bowl, Rephanin seated himself and turned his attention away from the surprised shifting of some in the circle. One cycle was little enough time; a quiver of arrows could take as much as half a day, though they were all blessed at once, not individually.

The arrow lay across his palms. Gazing at it with half-lidded eyes, he was briefly aware of small sounds in the chamber, then slipped past them to the place of calm from which he performed focus work. The sounds were still there—if he gave them his attention he would perceive them—but he kept his concentration on the arrow.

First he explored the faint echoes of khi within it: the life of the wood, that of the bird whose feathers had become the fletching, the fiery shaping of the bronze tip and the honing of its point. Rephanin decided to lay in this section of the focus first.

Closing his eyes, he shifted his awareness to the khi

within the chamber—a sparkling vivid cloud of energy swirling about the working mages—then beyond to prime khi, which pervaded all things. Khi moved fastest through air, so it was from air that he drew it and focused it within himself before directing it through his hands into the arrow.

Sharpness, strength, penetration. These qualities he held in his mind and laid into the dense fibre of the point. His perception narrowed to the tiny inner structure of the bronze—orderly for the most part, with some imperfections—and he set khi flowing through the pathways of this structure. Occasionally he would correct a flaw in the crystalline form of the metal, but he passed by all but the worst defects.

He moved on to the arrow's shaft, laying in trueness, strength, flexibility to withstand the shock of impact. Working through the lighter fibre of the wood was easier, though the material was also less well organized. Again he left most flaws alone.

Lastly, he shifted his attention to the fletching. Balance and steadiness in flight, suppleness, and durability; he layered them each in turn and had just finished when he heard the small sound of the timekeeper bowl contacting the bottom of the basin.

Rephanin withdrew his focus from the arrow and opened his eyes. "Cease working."

The mages stirred, some blinking as they returned their awareness to the chamber. Rephanin gathered the arrows, shifted them around in his hands to disturb their order, then laid them out across the table and ran his hand through the air just above them.

He chose one that felt dark, as if little khi had gone into it. His hand paused above another that emitted such brightness as to seem almost hot, but he thought he sensed Heléri's khi upon it, so he passed it by and selected an arrow that was nearly as vivid.

"These two arrows are quite different. Pass them around the circle and observe their state."

He handed them to Valani—a female of arresting beauty with large, dark eyes that missed little—who was seated at one end of the circle. She held them briefly, a slight frown of concentration on her face, then her brows rose. She handed the arrows to her neighbor and glanced at Rephanin.

He watched as each mage compared the arrows, and paid close attention when they were handed to Sulithan, the newest member of the circle, who he suspected had built the weak focus in the dark arrow. If the mage recognized his own work, he did not show it or give any sign of embarrassment. If this was modesty, Rephanin approved; if not, it boded ill for Sulithan's ability to understand the work.

When the arrows had passed around the circle, he took them back. "What differences did you perceive?"

Jholóran answered at once. "One arrow lacked khi."

Others in the circle nodded, and a discussion ensued in which Rephanin occasionally asked a question aimed at causing the adepts to reiterate the principles of focus-building. He hoped the restatements would help Sulithan grasp the ideas, for he could not accept work so poor as the dark arrow.

Heléri refrained from joining the discussion. Rephanin saw that she was watching him and took care to keep his gaze from straying toward her. At length he ended the discussion and went to a large wooden chest that stood near the door. It contained guardians' cloaks, finely woven and lined, clasped with silver Greenglen falcons. Rephanin took one from the chest and shook it out, pale green with a soft silvery lining, the colors warmed by firelight.

"The principles here are the same. The qualities to focus are protection, concealment, warmth. Take two cloaks each, though you might only complete the focus in one by tomorrow evening. Remember, it is better to work thoroughly than in haste." He folded the cloak in his hands and took out another, offering both to the nearest mage, who stood to receive them.

"You are welcome to work in this chamber at any time. I will be here most of the night."

Working in the same chamber tended to enhance the effectiveness of the khi in use, even if each mage was creating an independent focus. For this reason Rephanin kept the magehall's main chamber open at all times, available to any of the circle who wished to work there.

When the rest had collected their work, Heléri came forward. Rephanin handed her two of the cloaks. "It is good of you to assist us."

She smiled softly. "I am glad to be of service."

Rephanin watched her go to a table near the back of the chamber. He returned to the timekeeper and removed the metal bowl from the basin, carefully drying it with a soft cloth before setting it with its fellows.

The arrows lay loosely scattered over the table where he had left them. He could sense the intensity of the khi focused in a certain arrow and let his fingers brush the fletching as he moved away. The tingle of khi in the feathers was unmistakably Heléri's.

He returned to where he had left his two cloaks. Heléri was sitting with a cloak spilling in silvery folds over her lap, hands pressed together about a corner of it, eyes closed in deep concentration. Though he rarely saw khi, he thought he sensed a pale glow in the air around her head and hands. It made her appear even more beautiful. Turning away from this distraction, he took his seat and reached for a cloak, preparing for a long night's work.

⊲

Turisan arose early, partly because the sunrise coming through the Star Tower's glass dome disturbed his rest, partly because Eliani also rose with the dawn. He was glad, for it gave him time before the Council would convene, and he wished to visit the city garrison. He would stay away from Kelevon as he had promised, but he wanted to ensure that the Steppegard was being well treated.

He sent Pheran, his attendant, to fetch clothing for him and quickly donned the tunic and legs, grateful for their warmth in the chill morning.

"A cloak? I am going down into the city."

"Yes, my lord. The broidered wool or the velvet?"

Turisan was about to say "neither," then remembered that he had given his guardian's cloak to Eliani. He would have to request another.

"The velvet."

At least it was not covered with ornament. Turisan smiled at himself, acknowledging that his distaste for ostentation—not new, by any means—had increased significantly since he had met Eliani. Pheran had been clever enough to realize this was not a temporary state and had given up trying to dress him in grand style.

He drew a deep breath of chill air as he left Hallowhall to cross the public circle. Few others were abroad this early, only a handful of folk in the marketplace, trading early. Turisan sensed them watching him as he walked toward the magehall, paused briefly to collect himself, and went in to inquire for Rephanin.

The magehall was steeped in silence and shadow, its hearthroom vaguely lit by a single hanging lamp and a bank of coals on the welcoming hearth. Turisan paused to let his eyes adjust to the dimness, relieved to be out of the wind.

The attendant who greeted him—a slender female whose cool air suggested that no one's importance was greater, at least here in the magehall, than that of the magelord himself—deigned to lead Turisan to the hall's main chamber. She stopped outside its door and turned to him, speaking softly.

"Lord Rephanin may yet be inside with some of his circle. If they are at work, we must not disturb them."

Turisan waited silently while she opened the door a little way and peered in. A moment later she pushed it wide and invited him to enter.

The chamber, which Turisan had never seen before, was windowless, roughly circular, and furnished with more practicality than elegance. It was clearly a room for working rather than ceremony, and that surprised him somewhat. Ten chairs sat empty in a half circle before a dying fire, small worktables scattered behind them.

Rephanin stood near the hearth, dressed in a simple long tunic of dark gold, talking quietly with one of his mages. On a table that had been pushed against the wall between hearth and door was a small pile of cloaks. They were all sage lined with silver, the colors of Clan Greenglen, worn by Southfæld's Guard. The sight pleased Turisan, who had come in hopes of acquiring one. He waited until Rephanin's conversation ended and the other mage departed, then approached the magelord with a bow.

"Greetings, Lord Rephanin."

"Greetings, Lord Turisan. How may I serve you?"

Turisan gestured toward the cloaks. "I have given my cloak to my lady, and the garrison's stores have all been issued to recruits. By chance, have you one ready that I could take?"

Rephanin nodded and turned to the table, passing his hands through the air above the cloaks before selecting one and handing it to Turisan. "This is the best of what I have here."

Turisan accepted it with a small bow and ran his hands over the soft, pale green weave. It seemed warm to the touch, but perhaps that was from sitting near the hearth.

"Your work?"

"Heléri's."

Surprised, Turisan looked up at Rephanin, whose face told him nothing save that the magelord seemed tired, a small crease showing between his brows. Probably he had been at work all night and was ready to retire.

Turisan folded the cloak over his arm. "I thank you, and I will not keep you now, but I have another request."

One dark brow rose. Rephanin waited silently as was his wont, but Turisan felt none of the vague menace he had often known in the magelord's presence. Perhaps he had misjudged Rephanin. He hoped so, for he was about to ask his help and, by asking, perhaps learn whether Rephanin's gift was real or merely legend. He glanced toward the open door to make sure no one else was present, then spoke quietly.

"I have questions about mindspeech. I—we are both finding it distracting—sometimes even dangerous, I think. I would like to discuss it when you are at leisure."

Rephanin's gray eyes held his for a moment, then

looked down, hidden by dark lashes. "My gift is unlike yours. You would do better to ask Heléri's advice."

"I will, but I would value your counsel as well."

"Very well. Come tomorrow at sunset."

Turisan nodded. "Thank you, my lord."

He withdrew and followed the magehall attendant to the colonnade that connected the magehall with Hallowhall. Even here the wind was bitter, and Turisan cast his new cloak around his shoulders over the velvet, sighing as its warmth enfolded him.

Heléri's work again, like the ribbon on his arm. She was his kindred now, being Eliani's eldermother. Smiling at the thought, he hastened into the palace and down to the council chamber, hoping he was not late for the session.

⚛

Rephanin sat musing by the hearth in his private chamber. The dim light cast by a bed of glowing coals fell on an untouched meal on the low table beside him. He should eat, but he was too tense to do so, and he would not rest if he retired now. Too many troubling thoughts revolved in his mind.

Turisan wanted his advice about mindspeech. He found that rather ironic. How different this day might have been had he been the first to discover Turisan's potential, or Lady Eliani's.

He sighed, remembering his shock when Heléri had told him that the young couple had bonded in Alpinon—not here in Glenhallow—and the relief that had followed after he had taken time to reflect on this. It should not have mattered to him where they had found their gift, but strangely, it did. A chance missed by a wider margin was somehow less painful.

It maddened him that Turisan and Eliani had stumbled upon the gift he himself had actively sought for so long, the gift of distance speech. He was certain that either of them would have been a responsive distance partner for him, but chance had not brought them together.

Few understood his desire. Folk assumed that since he could share mindspeech with anyone in his presence, he must be satisfied. The fact that distance—even obstacles as simple as a door—could interfere with his gift seemed unimportant to them, but to him it was a source of infinite frustration.

Not that he had known such interference of late. It had been centuries since he had employed his gift.

Flinching away from painful memories, he rose and added a log to the fire. It flared brightly for a moment before settling to burn.

A quiet knock fell on his door. He almost chose to ignore it, and when finally he answered, his tone was sullen.

"Who is there?"

"An old friend."

The voice he knew at once, for he had first heard it centuries ago and had recalled it often. Indeed, it had haunted him for a time, though that was long ago. He closed his eyes briefly, taking a moment to compose himself, then rose and opened the door to Lady Heléri.

She stood cloaked in the color of the midnight sky, a color that was reflected in her eyes. Alone with her for the first time in hundreds of years, with no one to watch, he now dared to look at her more closely than he had since her arrival at Glenhallow. She seemed almost unchanged from when he had first known her in Eastfæld. It was only a deeper quality about her blue gaze, a greater steadiness in her, that told the difference made by the centuries.

"A gift from Alpinon."

In her hands was a small carved whitewood box, which she extended toward him with a soft smile. He glanced at it but preferred to gaze at her face, drinking in the features that for so long had only been a memory.

Heléri's smile opened into soft laughter. "May I come in?"

Rephanin stepped back and swung wide the door, accepting the box she pressed into his hands. It contained tea, the fragrances of leaf and petal rising richly when he opened it. Very likely she had blended it with her own hands. He carefully shut the box and stepped to a shelf to set it aside.

"Such a comfort to visit a fellow night-bider." Heléri removed her cloak and hung it by the door, next to his. "My kin all prefer more light than I enjoy."

"You used to love the day."

"Long ago, yes. I find I have changed."

"I have not." It was a challenge of sorts; he knew it as he said it.

Heléri walked to the hearth, then turned to face him, her form outlined in its fiery glow. "But you have, my friend. That is why I am here."

Rephanin waited for her to explain her meaning. A long moment passed in silence as she gazed intently at him, then she stepped toward him.

"Why do you no longer use your gift?"

Scowling, he looked away and stared into the coals. "Why use a tool that gives no advantage?"

"You are a trainer of mages—"

"And I can learn nothing through mindspeech that a student of any worth will not tell me openly."

Hearthlight glinted from her eyes. "You could use it to teach. That young mage who did not lay khi into his arrow—if you had shown him the technique through mindspeech, it would have been more effective than any explanation."

Rephanin turned from her, angry that she was right. Anger was a large part of why he no longer used mindspeech: anger, resentment, misunderstanding . . .

"Rephanin, you can give your circle the experience of mindspeech, show them what it is like. No one else in flesh can do that. Some of them may have aptitude—"

"Do you not think I have been searching for *aptitude*?" The words fell much more bitterly than he had intended. He stared at her, old hungers awakening to intolerable strength.

"Oh, Rephanin." Heléri's voice was filled with whispered sadness. "Still?"

He moved away, unable to bear her pity. Ancient jealousy twisted inside him.

He had realized too late that he wanted her. She had already met her Stonereach lord, had already found mindspeech with Davharin, by the time he knew it.

Perhaps it was only the gift she shared with Davharin that he truly wanted; he no longer knew. He had spent centuries searching for a similar bond without success. In the beginning he had confided his hope to her, but it was long since they had ceased to correspond.

He heard Heléri's step, felt the warmth of her khi beside him. He could not resist looking at her.

"Speak to me, Rephanin. Speak to me as you once did."

The blue depths of her eyes offered an open path to her heart, dizzying to contemplate. He held back from it.

"Perhaps you could speak to me. Have you tried since you came to Glenhallow?"

A wistful smile curved her lips. "Every time we have met."

Disappointment stabbed him. He closed his eyes briefly, his answer rasping in a throat suddenly gone tight.

"Well. That is not surprising. You are a distance speaker, and you have a partner. What would Davharin think of your being here?"

"He knows I am here."

So it was true that the bond outlasted death. She could still speak to Davharin though he dwelt in spirit. Perhaps she spoke to him even now.

"He does not mind? Were I he, this is the last place I would want you to be."

"No, he does not mind." She ran her hand along the back of a chair, her face distant, her voice soft. "I cannot explain, for I do not really understand why, but . . . many things that matter to us are unimportant to those in spirit."

Rephanin's bitter mood vanished, replaced by a tenderness he had not allowed himself to feel for centuries. "Why did you not follow him? You and he are the only mindspeakers I know of who have not crossed in the same season, if not the same day."

She fixed him with a steady gaze. "I have not done all I wished to do here."

Rephanin did not dare ponder her meaning. He drew a ragged breath, weary with heartache. Gazing down at her, he yielded and reached out to her as he had not done to anyone for centuries.

Heléri.

Her face lit with happiness, the way to answer opened by his thought. *Ah, my dear friend. Thank you.*

Her voice in thought was strong, much stronger than he remembered. Centuries of mindspeech with Davharin had honed her gift. Rephanin felt a visceral thrill at her strength and also an inevitable stirring of desire.

He moved away, hoping to hide it. Would that he could separate his feelings from the act of mindspeech. He had never succeeded.

So your gift is not lost, as some have feared.

He turned, gazing at her in surprise. *Lost?*

She nodded. *Many have begun to doubt its existence. Turisan told me he had never witnessed you using it.*

True enough. There has been no need.

There is need now.

He was too weary to argue. If he gave her all his reasons, explained all his past follies and transgressions, perhaps she would understand, but he had no wish to relive such memories.

Heléri approached him, looking up with concern once again. *Our forces need mage-blessed protections. Your circle needs all possible help to provide them. Will you not do all you can for your people when we are facing war?*

He rubbed at his temple, remembering the last war, also begun at Midrange. It seemed only a short while ago, though it had been more than five centuries. There had been no urgent call for his services then, but that had been a small conflict. Though it had its place in song and history, he always thought of the Midrange War as a minor crisis, compared with the travesty of the Bitter Wars.

Heléri was watching him, waiting. He sighed.

Of course I will do all I can.

She smiled and caught his hands in hers, clasping

them briefly. Her khi made his skin shiver with desire.

Thank you, Rephanin. I will see you at the Council session this evening.

She let him go and went toward the door, pausing to don her cloak. He watched her, admiring her graceful movements, the perfection of her flesh. She smiled at him over her shoulder and quietly slipped out.

He went to the closed door, leaning his hands upon it, and also his brow. He strove to follow her khi, to find a hint of it beyond the door, but as always, the barrier stopped him. Sighing, he turned back to his chamber.

She had just made him promise to use mindspeech in his circle. He had been avoiding that for centuries.

Perhaps she was right and it was time to let go of precaution. The needs of their people outweighed his scruples. He might even have gained greater control of his gift.

He hoped so. He would need it.

◄

Lord Berephan received Turisan in his work chamber, which took up the entire top floor of the garrison's gatehouse. Shelves upon shelves of bound records lined the walls, and a large table in the center of the chamber was scattered with maps. A window looked eastward over the city walls, giving a wide view of the plains, their grasses now dry and golden, that fell gently toward the Silverwash. Turisan saw a company of guardians practicing there.

Berephan stood frowning over the maps. He was tall, his fair hair coarser than usual for a Greenglen, showing a slight tendency to wave that suggested some ancient alliance between one of his ancestors and a Steppegard. He glanced up as Turisan approached.

"Greetings, Lord Turisan. You are abroad early this day."

"I wished to consult you before the Council convenes."

Berephan's mouth curved in a wry smile. He had been absent from the Council sessions for the most part. Southfæld's Guard was several hundred strong, the demands of their daily operations would not wait, and Berephan, as he put it, preferred to leave planning and philosophizing to the governors.

"Have you learned anything more from Kelevon?"

Berephan shook his head. "He claims to have told you everything. You have the knack of questioning him, it seems."

Turisan joined him, frowning. He glanced down at a map of Midrange Pass on the warden's worktable. "Have the recruits started arriving?"

"We had sixty volunteers by sunset yesterday, and another thirty-odd were waiting at dawn. That is who you see practicing out there, with a few experienced guardians in among them to keep them from falling on their faces."

"All from Southfæld?"

"All from the city, except one ardent Ælvanen who is here with Lady Rheneri's delegation and volunteered on a wave of sentiment. He will likely regret it before the day is out."

"You are working them hard."

"I have no choice if they are to be ready to march in time to defend Midrange."

"How may I assist?"

Berephan fixed him with a silent, steady gaze. Turisan

bore it with a certain fondness, for Berephan had been his captain when he had served a term in the Guard. His service had been mostly border watch and had involved no more adventure than an occasional chase after a small band of kobalen who had wandered too close to Glenhallow.

That was true of most of the Guard, even the most experienced. Every guardian skirmished with kobalen raiders sooner or later, but there were few among them who had ever seen a true battle. Berephan, who had been at Skyruach in the Midrange War, was one of those few.

The warden tilted his head toward the window. "Go out to the field."

Turisan drew a breath. "I will be glad to help, but I have never trained others. I would need instruction."

"You will remember easily enough, and in any case, that is not why I want you to go." A corner of Berephan's mouth turned up in the suggestion of a smile. "Your presence will inspire them."

Turisan gave a surprised laugh. "I have no reputation as a warrior."

"You are already a legend, Turisan. A mindspeaker, something most have only heard of in stories."

Turisan shook his head. "Lord Rephanin—"

"Rephanin keeps to his magehall. He is said to be a mindspeaker, but I know of no one who has seen him use the gift."

Turisan could not contradict him. Frowning, he let his fingers drift over the map, tracing the main ascent through Midrange Pass.

"Even those who once served with you, and may be presumed to have few illusions about you, now speak

reverently of your gift and of the sacrifice you and
Lady Eliani have made. Little else is now talked of in
the garrison or in the taverns." Berephan paused to
look out of the window. "Most of those recruits came
because of you."

Startled by that thought, Turisan looked out at
the guardians in training. He was not sure he could
live up to such expectations, but it seemed his duty
was to try.

"Shall I go now, or do you wish me to make a more
impressive appearance?"

Berephan smiled. "Appearance is unimportant. You
are cloaked as a guardian; that is enough."

"Do you ride with me?"

"Beside you?" The commander's eyebrows rose.
"They would not even see me, and I have matters to
attend to."

Turisan bit his lip. He was conscious of Berephan's
far greater experience, which he thought more deserv-
ing of the guardians' reverence than his own chance-
discovered gift.

"What should I say to them?"

Berephan gazed at him for a moment, then broke
into a grin. "Lad, I don't think it would matter if you
recited cradle rhymes. Just show them your face."

Feeling his cheeks grow warm, Turisan turned to
go. Berephan hastened to join him, walking with him
to the door.

"Captain Dirovon is training the recruits. You will
remember him, I think. We have two other experienced companies in the garrison, Phaniron's and—"

*We are riding out. Vanorin hopes to make Mid-
range by—*

Not now, love.

Turisan abruptly stopped walking, disoriented. Looking up, he saw Berephan watching him with raised brows.

"Forgive me—I was distracted for a moment. Phaniron's company and—?"

"Sivhani's. I think you do not know her."

"No."

The warden gazed at him thoughtfully. "Come and break bread with me and my captains tonight, if you can stomach a discussion of tactics with your evening meal."

"Gladly."

Turisan clasped arms with him, then went out, two guardians accompanying him at Berephan's insistence. They were purely for show, but Turisan accepted them, trusting that Berephan knew best how to make an impression on the recruits.

The morning air was yet brisk, and the sun still low enough to make him squint as he rode out of the city and onto the plains. His escort showed no inclination to talk, so he sent a tentative thought toward his lady.

Eliani?

Yes. Did I interrupt something crucial?

No harm was done. I was talking with our warden, Berephan. What were you telling me about Vanorin?

Only that he hopes to make Midrange by nightfall. You are traveling swiftly.

Yes.

A sharp, raised voice reached him through the chill air as he and his escort approached the practice ground, though he could not distinguish the commands at that distance. He glanced up to see the company abandoning their drill.

I will be in Council later this morning. Speak to me when you make a halt.

Yes.

She sent wordless love roaring through his being, then withdrew. Turisan beat back the sudden physical longing he felt and turned his attention to the recruits.

By the time he reached them, the company stood formed and silent, awaiting him. He rode up to the holder of the pennanted commander's spear and dismounted, handing his reins to one of his escorts. The commander dipped his spear in salute, and Turisan recognized him as Dirovon, with whom he had stood border guard a time or two.

Dirovon had continued service in the Guard, which had evidently resulted in his promotion to captain. His fair hair was caught back from his face in a hunter's braid. A few strands had escaped to whip about his cheeks in the morning breeze, even as the pennant whipped about his spear.

Turisan stepped toward him, acknowledging their past association with a nod and a small smile. "How do they look?"

"Rough, of course, but they will improve."

Dirovon's eyes glinted with a hint of humor that sent Turisan's memory back to congenial campfires. The captain gestured to his two subordinates, who in unison shouted the command for a sword salute, which the guardians executed with more enthusiasm than precision. Dirovon's gaze dropped briefly toward the ground at his feet and the corner of his mouth twitched, but he said nothing.

Turisan looked at the recruits, a small sea of pale-haired heads and the one dark-haired Ælvanen Berephan had mentioned. He saw inexperience in the faces turned to him. He drew a deep breath.

"In forty days or thereabouts, you will march north to Midrange. That is little time to prepare. We must turn all our efforts toward making ourselves ready. We have much to learn—all of us. I as well as you."

They stood silent, but he sensed a shifting, saw a nod here and there. They watched him intently, eager to be inspired.

"My father stood at Skyruach. Lord Felisan, my lady's father, did as well."

He paused, for something like a sigh had swept through the ranks. So it was true: He and Eliani had become a legend to them. He felt unremarkable alone, but his bond with Eliani was wondrous—indeed, he still marveled at it himself.

"We have not the benefit of their experience, but we have their wisdom and guidance. My lady, Eliani, and I have pledged ourselves to the defense of Southfæld, of Alpinon, and of all ælven lands. We ask that you serve in this effort as well, that you add your devotion to ours."

A couple of voices shouted agreement. The guardians stirred.

"Though Eliani rides north, she is with me in my thoughts and in my heart, and so she is also with you. Both of us have pledged all our strength to opposing the enemies of our people."

This time the shouts grew into a cheer that rolled through the company. A strong male voice cut through the noise.

"All hail Turisan and Eliani!"

"All hail! All hail!"

He glanced at Dirovon, whose face was still, though his eyes seemed a bit wide. Turisan doubted he could improve on what he had said. Inside, he was almost inclined to laugh, so unlike a hero he felt. He would not so dishonor the guardians' admiration, though.

Summoning his father's most dignified manner, he clasped arms with Dirovon, relinquishing the company's attention to him, and returned to his borrowed horse. His escorts bowed to him, and he had to stifle another laugh.

He mounted, raising a hand to the guardians in farewell. The handfasting ribbon on his arm glinted in the sun, and the guardians' cheers increased as he turned toward the city.

He returned his horse to the garrison, bade his escort a friendly and relieved farewell, and pulled his cloak closer as he made his way back to Hallowhall through a flurry of snow. The peaks above the city were already capped with white, the passes already closed by deep drifts. He wondered if storms would affect the kobalen at Midrange. They did not love cold weather and generally migrated to warmer northern regions in winter. He supposed it too much to hope that weather would prevent them from crossing the pass.

He wished suddenly that he was riding with Eliani. Folly; he must stay here or her journey was for nought.

Hallowhall's great front doors stood open, the warmth from the massive fire in its welcoming hearth reaching out into the public circle. Turisan hastened to the council chamber and reached it just as the Council was gathering. He took his place beside his father and soon found himself listening to a lengthy discussion of plans to establish a network of couriers linking all the seats of government of the ælven realms: Glenhallow, Hollirued, Highstone, and Watersmeet.

And what of Ghlanhras? No mention was made of Fireshore's greatest city. Until Eliani sent them news of it, the Council seemed to be ignoring its existence.

At last, impatient with the lack of progress, Turisan showed his hand to indicate his wish to speak. Jharan acknowledged him, and he stood.

"I understand the desire to improve our communications, but I believe that High Holding is equally crucial. We must send a force to occupy it in advance of the army and to make it ready to hold."

Jharan responded quietly. "That is not in question, but we do not have the resources ready."

"There are new recruits pouring into the garrison. Surely a company of guardians and a handful of stonemasons can be spared now."

Parishan, Pashani's son, responded. "The masons, yes, but I question that the guardians can be spared. Perhaps some of the recruits—"

Turisan shook his head. "To stand in defense of the pass we need experienced guardians. The recruits would be better fit for courier duty."

Pashani's amber eyes flashed. "If you think it is wise to throw them untrained onto horses bred for speed, I wish you joy of the effort!"

Jharan held out a placating hand. "I am sure that was not Turisan's meaning."

Heeding the warning in his father's glance, Turisan swallowed his impatience. "No, my lady governor, it was not. I meant only that they would be less at risk. Of course they must be trained."

Pashani's eyes narrowed. "A pity we cannot summon more mindspeakers to assist us. There would be no need of couriers then."

Refusing to respond to what he expected she meant as provocation, Turisan merely nodded. "Very true."

Beyond her, Parishan met Turisan's gaze with a small, apologetic smile. Turisan felt a sudden kinship with him; they were both nextkin to their parents, who were governors. Some day it might be they who led their Council delegations.

Pashani turned away and began to reiterate her reasons for insisting that the couriers be given priority. Turisan fell quiet, giving up for the present, though he was not deterred.

High Holding needed defenders. The garrison at the outpost was only a handful, enough to give warning should the kobalen begin coming through the pass, but no more. They would have to abandon the outpost to avoid being slain.

And they would offer little protection to Eliani as she traveled past Midrange. Turisan closed his eyes, acknowledging that concern for her was one of his reasons for urging that High Holding be garrisoned immediately. Was it wrong to want to place a few hundred guardians between his love and the kobalen threat? He knew that she would be beyond Midrange before a garrison ever reached it even if they set out immediately, but still he wanted the comfort of sending them. They might be able to help her if there was need. If only he could go himself.

He opened his eyes, turning to look at his father. Would Jharan permit him to lead a force to High Holding? A thrill filled him at the thought, though he heard his father's objections at once: too dangerous, defeating the purpose of Eliani's journey.

But if he could convince Jharan that his going would benefit the army's morale—would attract more recruits and inspire the experienced guardians with greater courage—Berephan might help him persuade the governor that the benefits outweighed the risks. He wished the warden had been present this afternoon, but Berephan had little patience for the Council's debates.

Turisan gazed at the table before him, thinking, the councillors' voices washing over him unheard. He would have to pledge to return at once, of course. There was no possibility of his remaining away from Glenhallow for more than the few days it would take to ride to Midrange and back. He would go despite this if he could.

A call for a vote dragged his attention back to the chamber. The Council had agreed on a plan to deploy the couriers, and in a formal vote by delegation, the plan was approved. Governor Pashani's mood was consequently jovial; she even smiled at Turisan as the councillors left the chamber.

"Do you go to the feasthall? You may escort me if you wish."

Turisan smiled politely, making a slight bow. "Alas, I am committed elsewhere, though I will be glad to see you in before I must leave."

She gave him a wry look. "Committed elsewhere? Does your lady know of this?"

"I hide nothing from my lady, Governor Pashani."

He escorted her to the feasthall, then took leave of her and of his father and hastened back to the garrison. The sun was just setting, making the golden stones of the avenue gleam beneath his boots. He was once again glad of his new guardian's cloak and hoped the other was keeping his lady warm.

Eliani? Have you made camp?

Not yet.

Two days' hard ride apart, and he had noticed no diminishment of Eliani's voice. Each day proved the greater worth of their gift. Turisan smiled to himself, delighted and still in awe.

I will be in company for a while. Berephan has asked me to sup with him and his captains.

Drink a flagon of wine for me. I shall be feasting on dried meat and apples.

My poor love. The outpost at Midrange will have some comforts for you in another day or two.

I have fixed my hopes on Highstone.

He smiled, then sent love and farewell as he reached the garrison and turned to Lord Berephan's house. A guardian showed him to Berephan's hall, where high narrow windows to the west let in the last of the sun. On the walls were the Guard's banners and pennants, lit by torches and fading sunlight.

Berephan and his guests were already at table and passing around platters of food. As Turisan entered, they fell silent and turned to look at him, rather more intently than he had expected.

The warden rose from his chair to greet him. Another movement caught his eye: Dirovon, nodding. Turisan smiled back, then clasped the arm offered by his host.

"Good evening, Lord Berephan. I am late and crave your pardon."

Berephan dismissed it. "The Council have been talking your ears numb, no doubt. Have a seat; we have only begun."

Turisan took an empty place between Berephan and another he recognized, Captain Hothanen, who commanded a company of the city's guardians. Hothanen nodded to him and lifted a wine pitcher, offering to fill his cup while Berephan made introductions.

"Lord Turisan, may I make you known to Captains Phaniron and Sivhani?"

Turisan nodded to each of them. "Well met."

Phaniron, a slender, fine-boned male who sat beside Dirovon, seemed shyly pleased to meet him, but Sivhani looked as if she feared he would do something alarming at any moment. Grow wings, perhaps, Turisan thought, concealing a smile by sipping his wine.

Berephan offered him a platter of meat. "What news from the Council?"

"They spent the day discussing equipments for the army—which realms can contribute weapons, horses, and so on. And they have decided to set up courier relays among the capitals of the realms. Both the Steppes and Eastfæld have pledged horses and riders."

Hothanen accepted the meat platter in turn and helped himself. "It will take away riders who could serve in the army."

"The Council thought faster communication would be worth the sacrifice."

Sivhani spoke up from beyond Hothanen, her tone disbelieving. "Does Lord Jharan really expect to have an army assembled in less than forty days?"

Turisan looked at her, saw her eyes widen with the realization that she was addressing Jharan's son, and answered patiently. "He holds to that hope. I cannot say what he expects. We must all do our best."

A moment's silence was broken by Phaniron. "Your lady is well, I hope, Lord Turisan?"

"Please, do not be formal with me here." Turisan looked around the table. "Berephan, you do not mind?"

"Of course not. This is not the high court."

Dirovon chuckled, and Turisan grinned at him before answering Phaniron. "My lady is well, thank you, though a bit tired. They are still riding."

Phaniron's face showed surprise. "You have spoken to her today?"

"Several times. We must keep testing our gift. If it is limited, we must know as soon as possible."

Dirovon picked up a piece of soft flat bread and tore it in half. "What will happen if you lose contact?"

"She will retrace her movements until we can speak again."

Berephan handed him a platter of roasted root vegetables. "Rather late for them still to be in the saddle."

"They wish to make all possible speed." Turisan helped himself, then passed the platter to Dirovon. "How long did you spend working those recruits? They looked promising."

Dirovon grinned. "We had them out all morning, until the wind began to freeze their wits. The afternoon was spent getting them into barracks."

"Which are now full." Berephan poured more wine for himself. "We shall have to begin issuing tents."

Turisan ate as he listened to the captains discuss the Guard's ordinary business, which was fast becoming extraordinary as the preparations for war began. The mood at the table grew more relaxed, and soon the discussion turned to the tactics of mounting a defense at Midrange.

Berephan turned to him. "Has the Council discussed High Holding? We shall have to occupy it."

"I mentioned it today. Lord Ehranan wishes to inspect it."

"Have you been there in recent years?"

Turisan shook his head. "I have ridden through Midrange, but I have not gone up to the work since I stood guard duty at the outpost."

He glanced at Dirovon, with whom he had explored the stone barrier that Lord Jharan had built after the Midrange War. The massive wall—the first public work Jharan had ordered in his new role as South-fæld's governor—stood on a plateau at the foot of the mountains, guarding the eastern egress of Midrange Pass.

High Holding had been occupied by guardians for three centuries after Skyruach, but kobalen had not come through the pass again in large numbers, and the holding had at last been abandoned. Now only a few guardians stood watch at the more accessible outpost, which lay at the southward turning of the Silverwash.

Dirovon gave a grimacing smile. "I was up there this past summer. Much work is needed before the holding can be used again. The work is overgrown with brush and crumbling at either end. The spring failed a few decades ago."

Turisan frowned. "I will raise this again in Council."

"Do. Tell Lord Ehranan I am at his service whenever he wishes to inspect the holding."

Nodding, Turisan reached for his cup. As he picked it up, a stab of terror struck him. He felt the wine splash over his fingers as the cup fell back to the table and his attention left the hall, flying northward.

Eliani?

We are under attack!

꧁

"Ride! Forward!"

Vanorin's shout was harsh and his eyes blazed as he moved his horse to Eliani's left, placing himself between her and the darts that were flying out of the twilit shadows to the west. Turisan's panic added to her distress.

What is happening?
Kobalen!

No time for more; a dart whipped past Eliani's head as she urged her tired mount to a gallop and gave her attention to staying in the saddle. A horse shrieked behind her. She glanced back and saw the rider clinging to his rearing mount, a black-fletched dart sunk in the animal's flank.

Breathing in short, sharp gasps, she leaned low over her horse's neck and stared at the river ahead. By chance, they were near a bend where the water spread out, shallow enough to ford. Vanorin guided the party into the water at full speed, making for the woods on the far side.

Cold water slapped against Eliani's leather-clad legs, splashing up onto her hands and face as the horses plunged across the ford. The horses surged out of the river and up the far bank, slowing as they entered the wood.

Not until they were deep within the wood, out of sight of the river, did Vanorin call them to a halt. The horses stamped and blew, their sides heaving. Vanorin, his face reddened by the cold wind, turned to face the valley, raising his hands.

Reaching out with khi, he searched the valley for sign of more kobalen. Eliani could feel it tingle in the air between them. Vanorin remained thus for a moment, then lowered his arms.

"It is only a small band. There are no others nearby."

Eliani steadied her mount. "What if they are a scout from Midrange?"

Vanorin looked at her, then glanced around at the guardians. "Then they will not return there. I need ten to remain here with Lady Eliani; the rest will come with me. Theyn Luruthin, stay with her if you would. If we do not return by dark, make for High-stone."

Eliani felt a stir of anger and moved her horse closer to Vanorin's. "Why diminish your numbers? I can fight!"

"My lady, I dare not risk you. You are not merely a guardian."

She felt a touch on her arm and turned to see Luruthin beside her. "Your gift. Fireshore."

He was right, of course. Swallowing frustration, Eliani looked at Vanorin, then nodded.

"Spirits guard you."

The captain gave her a grim smile and started back toward the river, leaving Eliani with her handful of protectors. The others departed in a tumult of hooves thudding on fallen leaves, and in their wake the wood was strangely quiet.

◌

Turisan became aware of tense silence as his focus returned to the room. His hand lay in a puddle of wine on the table. He righted his cup, blinking, and glanced around at the captains, who were all staring at him.

"I . . . forgive me."

Berephan offered him a cloth, which he used to dry his hand. Trying to steady his breathing, he looked at the warden.

"Eliani's party has been attacked."

Several of the others exclaimed at once. Berephan gestured for silence.

"Is it over? Are they safe?"

"I—I do not know. Give me a moment." Turisan in-haled and closed his eyes.

Eliani? What happened?

He sensed woodlands in dusk, similar to those he

had caught a wild glimpse of earlier. Eliani's khi no longer rang with fear, but she was alert, listening to the breath of the forest.

Kobalen threw a volley of darts at us. It is just a stray band—Vanorin has gone to hunt them down.

Where are you?

East of the river. Sheltering in a wood.

Not alone?

No, with Luruthin and ten others.

Turisan relaxed somewhat. Opening his eyes, he repeated what Eliani had told him.

Berephan's brow creased with a frown. "Were there wounded?"

Turisan passed the question to Eliani and returned her answer. "One horse was struck. The rider's fate is not known."

Berephan summoned an attendant and sent him to fetch paper, pen, and ink. He turned to Turisan, offering a cloth. "You will want to inform Lord Jharan."

"Yes. Thank you." Turisan pressed the cloth into the spilled wine, watching the liquid darken the fabric.

"I will send twenty guardians north at once to reinforce the outpost at Midrange."

"I volunteer to lead them!"

Turisan glanced up and saw Phaniron's eyes shining with excitement. Berephan paused before answering.

"Thank you, Phaniron, but I need you here."

Hothanen looked at Berephan. "Can the kobalen army be moving so soon?"

"I doubt it, but this is all the more reason to occupy High Holding at once. Step downstairs, if you will, Hothanen, and ask a courier to come up."

Turisan gave Berephan a rueful glance as the captain departed. "I fear I have disrupted your evening."

Dirovon's crack of laughter silenced the others' soft-spoken protests. "Nothing like! We should all be grateful to you. I know I will sup well for a week on the tale of tonight's doings!"

He picked up a pitcher of wine and grinned. "Pass your cup, brother. You look as if you could use a draught—if you can manage to hold on to it."

Turisan looked at him sharply, then reluctantly returned the grin. He pushed his cup toward Dirovon, holding its foot against the table.

"I make no promises."

⚘

Eliani paced beneath the trees, impatient for Vanorin's return. Dark was falling swiftly, but she did not want to ride north without knowing his fate, the fate of half of her escort.

A new presence caught her attention, and she ceased her restless walking. The guardians all turned southward to listen, and she could taste the edge of fear in their khi. A moment later she placed the approaching khi as ælven and horse, and relaxed.

A lone guardian. Eliani watched and listened as he dismounted and greeted his compatriots, then came toward her and made a formal salute.

"My lady, Captain Vanorin sent me to inform you that the kobalen attackers have been dispersed. Many were slain, but not all—some escaped into the canyon. The party is hunting them down."

Eliani nodded. "Were any hurt?"

"Two wounded, neither dangerously. They will be returning here shortly. The rest should be back before the moon rises."

Eliani glanced at Luruthin. "We had best make camp, then. Our mounts need a rest, and so do we."

Drawing her horse's reins over its head, she led it toward the river. The guardians followed, save for one who gave his mount to a friend and stayed to build a fire.

At the river's edge Eliani stood listening and scenting while the horses drank. Stars were beginning to gleam out above the dark shoulders of the mountains, even where the sky still glowed slightly with blue. All was quiet under the deepening night. She felt a wild tremor of khi to the south and west—too distant to read—and nearer from a smaller, uneasy presence that she soon identified as the two wounded guardians, slowly returning.

She saw them come onto the road a short distance to the south, their tired horses walking with heads low. One was hunched forward in the saddle—Eliani could see a dart's fletching protruding from one shoulder—the other's left arm was bound with a makeshift bandage. Two of the guardians went to meet them and lead their mounts through the ford.

The horses having drunk their fill, Eliani and the others followed their wounded companions back to the camp, where golden firelight glinted between the trees to guide them.

My love? Turisan's touch was gentle.

Yes?

You have been quiet for a time.

Oh—not much has changed. Vanorin sent a message, and two wounded have returned.

She gave him what little news she had while she unsaddled her horse and hobbled it near the camp, where it could graze on the dry grasses beneath the trees. Turning to the fire circle, she found a courteous welcome and a cup of hot tea awaiting her. She sat near the fire and held the cup close to her face, inhaling the spiced aroma while its warmth spread through her fingers.

Berephan recommends you continue north. The kobalen are not likely to follow in darkness.

The horses need rest.

The wounded came to the fire, helped by their friends. Eliani felt a stab of loneliness, for these guardians showed one another the care of longtime compatriots. She had known such friendships in Alpinon's Guard, but these all were Southfæld guardians, strangers to her.

The one was having the dart drawn from his shoulder, his face set in grim endurance while a fellow guard carefully worked to free the wicked barb. Eliani winced in sympathy.

The wounded will need rest as well.

Turisan's concern rippled through her. *Perhaps some from the Midrange outpost can replace them.*

Perhaps, but we are probably two days from there. Shall I ride to join you?

She smiled despite the sharp longing caused by this suggestion. *There is nothing I want more, but you know you must not.*

I know.

She sensed an echo of her own loneliness, a hollow yearning. To resist it, she sent forth her love, closing her eyes briefly as she reached for Turisan, then as quickly drawing back.

You are still in company.

Yes.

She opened her eyes and glanced at the strained and weary faces around the fire. *I had better get the others to eat something. I will let you know when Vanorin returns.*

All right. Berephan means to send twenty guardians to reinforce the Midrange outpost.

Excellent. I will tell the guardians there when we reach it.

Eliani finished her tea with one deep swallow and rose to return the cup. She suggested to the others that they eat, then turned to the two wounded guardians.

Both were bandaged now, leaning against tree trunks. The one with the shoulder wound had his eyes closed; the other was sipping at a cup of the hot tea.

Eliani addressed them gently. "I am sorry you were hurt. You should probably not ride farther with us."

The second guardian nodded, regret in her eyes. She held out her newly bandaged arm. "Will you bless me, my lady?"

Eliani hesitated, discomfited by the request. "I am not a healer."

The guardian smiled a bit crookedly. "Indulge me?"

With a shrug, Eliani sat beside her. If she could offer comfort thus, she would gladly do it. Taking the guard's hand in one of hers, she gently laid her other over the wound.

At once she felt a strong stirring of khi in her hands and an answering glow from the ribbon on her arm. She drew a sharp breath and heard the guardian do the same.

Yielding to what she assumed must be an echo of Heléri's power, she closed her eyes and allowed the khi to flow through her. It rose warm and tingling in her arm and on her scalp and grew hot in the palms of her hands.

Eliani? What are you doing?

I am not sure.

The ribbons—

I know. Wait.

For some moments the sensation continued, then it gradually faded. When it was gone, Eliani opened her eyes and drew a deep breath, releasing the guardian, who looked dumbfounded.

"Thank you, my lady." The guardian's voice was a whisper. She gazed at Eliani in awe.

"It was the ribbon."

The guardian's eyes—dark Greenglen eyes—glanced at Eliani's handfasting ribbon, then strayed to her wounded comrade. "Perhaps—?"

Eliani swallowed, then nodded. She did not fully understand what had happened, but if blessings were coming through her to others in need, she could scarcely refuse.

"Sirinan." The guardian touched her friend, who opened his eyes.

Love? What was that?

A healing, I think. I will explain later. You will probably feel it again in a moment.

The female guard was murmuring to the other, Sirinan. He looked doubtfully at her, then somewhat anxiously at Eliani. She could see the pain etched in lines of tension on his face, no longer sharp but still present.

Eliani moved to sit beside him, careful not to jostle his injured arm. His dark eyes followed her. She looked at his bandaged shoulder, then realized she was gnawing the back of her thumb. She folded her hands and met his gaze.

"Do you want me to try?"

After an instant's hesitation, he nodded. Eliani gently took his hand and slowly reached toward his shoulder. Heat leapt into her palm even before she touched it. She did so lightly, scarcely feeling the cloth of the bandage against her skin.

Sirinan made a small, startled sound, then sighed deeply and closed his eyes. Eliani did likewise and again felt powerful khi flowing through her.

Her breathing slowed, and that of the wounded guardian matched it. She had little sense of time passing, though she thought the heat remained in her hands longer this time before fading. She could feel it flowing between her palms, through the guardian's arm and his wound. At last it ebbed, and she drew back, opening her eyes to find Sirinan gazing at her in amazement. She sat back on her heels.

"It was the ribbon. Not me."

Sirinan looked at his comrade. "You had better get a ribbon like that one, Kiravhi."

Both guardians laughed, and Eliani joined them. Turning her head, she saw all the others around the fire circle watching intently. At once she felt uncomfortable, and to hide it she looked away, back at Sirinan.

"Can you eat a little, do you think?"

He nodded. Kiravhi stood up, leaning her good hand against a tree for balance. "I will fetch your pack."

Eliani would have followed, but Sirinan touched her arm. "I do not know how to thank you, my lady."

"Recover your strength; that is how you can best thank me." She squeezed his wrist and gave him a smile that she hoped was less awkward than it felt, then got to her feet.

"The others are returning!"

Glad of the distraction, Eliani hastened to the river to meet Vanorin and the others. She was relieved to be away from the fire circle and those dark, intense Greenglen eyes. Her people now, she reminded herself, feeling a stray pang of homesickness. It was not that they were Greenglens—she liked Greenglens perfectly well,

one in particular—but that they stared so. Even Luruthin had looked astonished at the healing. Well, so
was she astonished.

Spirits guide me, she thought. Even resting in camp,
I am moving too fast.

◈ Magehall ◈

Rephanin stood before his circle of mages, nervous for the first time in centuries. More cloaks yet to be blessed waited in chests by the door. He had already set the circle for the evening, and there was no need for him to delay their work with further discussion, except that he had agreed to do so.

His gaze flicked to Heléri, who was sitting at one end of the row, gowned in Clan Stonereach's blue and violet. He wondered if Davharin was with her now.

Annoyed with himself, he straightened his shoulders and swept the circle with his glance. "It has been brought to my attention that it might benefit you all to be introduced to mindspeech."

The mages stirred, and some exchanged looks with their neighbors. He did not know or particularly care what rumors were in circulation about his ability. What he was about to do would no doubt give rise to a whole new crop of them.

"Because this form of contact is . . . somewhat intimate . . . anyone who does not wish to experience it is free to decline. There are new cloaks by the door if you prefer to take them away and continue your work."

Rephanin walked to the table that held the time-keeper, averting his attention from the circle so as not to discomfit anyone who chose to leave. The arrows still lay scattered there. He reached a hand toward them, feeling their varying levels of focus, slightly jarring, a chorus out of harmony. Gathering them into both hands, he swept them clear with a single white wave of prime khi. Time to begin their focus anew, as he was about to do with his circle.

He looked up at the mages. Not a soul had moved. They sat watching him, some ill at ease, some excited, all expectant. He laid the arrows down and moved to stand before the fire.

"Once I have addressed you in mindspeech, you will be able to answer in like fashion. I will speak to all of you together and ask that you signal your desire to respond. If several of you speak at once, your voices will be indistinguishable.

"We will be able to communicate thus as long as we remain together. Once we are separated by any sort of barrier—a door, a wall—the contact will be broken."

He paused, glancing at the hearth, where the flames had retreated, leaving a bed of coals glowing orange-hot. He licked his lips.

"I encourage you to attempt to contact me after we leave this session, when you will have a better understanding of mindspeech. The ability is very rare, but it is possible that any of you may possess it. Some mindspeakers do not discover their gift for decades, even centuries. Certainly it is worth the attempt."

He glanced across the circle of faces. Valani showed her palm, and he acknowledged her with a nod.

"Will we all be able to speak to one another?"

"That will be possible, yes, but please allow me to guide the discussion. My purpose is to demonstrate my technique of laying in khi to a focus. Are there further questions?"

Silence answered him, a palpable tension in the circle. Time, then, for it to be dispelled.

The warden of the Guard—

A collective gasp swept the circle before he finished the thought. At the same time Rephanin was suddenly acutely aware of each of them, the brilliance of their khi almost overwhelming. He paused to allow himself and the mages to recover composure. Heléri kept her eyes lowered, but he saw her lips curve in a smile.

The warden of the Guard has asked me to extend to you his thanks for your work on the cloaks.

He looked around the circle, searching each face for any sign of distress. Finding none, he continued as he moved to the chests of cloaks and withdrew one.

A number of new recruits are waiting for cloaks, so I will not take up much of your time this evening. Have you any questions before I proceed to demonstrate focus-building?

Jholóran showed a hesitant hand. Rephanin nodded to him.

Have you ever been unable to speak to someone?

A good question. No, I have never met anyone to whom I could not speak, though not all choose to answer.

A nervous laugh ran through the circle. It broke the tension somewhat, which was what Rephanin had hoped. Valani signaled for recognition, and he gave it.

Now that you have spoken to us all, will we all hear everything you say?

Another good question. I can speak to all of you at once or to any of you alone, as I choose. Speaking to a selection of you is more difficult but also possible.

What makes that so difficult? Valani's eyes were brilliant with curiosity.

Picture yourself as a weaver, with many strands to

manage. Moving any one is simple; moving some but not others requires more attention. The analogy is not perfect, but it will serve.

Valani responded, her enthusiasm plain in her voice. *Or a harper, choosing which strings to play!*

Yes, a harper is a better example. To play one string is easy, to play all is simple, but to select those which harmonize requires skill. More questions?

He waited only a brief moment, knowing the questions could continue indefinitely if he allowed it. *Very well. We will have time to discuss this again in future sessions. For now I will proceed with the focus-building.*

He drew a chair forward and sat in it, draping the cloak over his lap and taking one corner of it between his hands. Daring a glance at Heléri, he saw that she was watching him, still softly smiling. Her khi was the brightest in the room, drawing him to her. He resisted and turned his gaze to the others.

For this I must ask you all to give me your full attention. You may feel an increase of khi through the circle.

He closed his eyes and centered his own awareness, noting the mages' varying brightness of khi, especially that of Sulithan, the mage whose work had been flawed. When he was certain of their attention, he moved his thought into the fabric of the cloak, bidding them to follow.

He drew upon prime khi to build the focus of protection, warmth, and concealment into the cloak. *Follow the pattern of the weaving. No need to take one strand at a time; the gridwork will serve you well as a pathway.*

Khi flowed in a slow tide outward from his hands, spreading through the twisted fibers, filling the spaces between, binding all with the blessing. He moved his hands to another part of the cloak while maintaining the focus, then built it further. At last he ceased and withdrew.

The mages stirred, some sighing, some still with eyes closed, as if holding on to the moment. Rephanin smoothed the fabric of the cloak and waited, watching them.

The nervous tension had vanished. The circle was calm—unusually so, he thought. The sole exception was Sulithan, who sat gazing downward, frowning slightly.

Rephanin rose, left the cloak on his chair, and quietly walked to the chest. When he reached it, he turned; seeing the circle all watching once more, he picked up another cloak.

Thank you all for your attention. Those who wish to stay and work now may do so; the others may take cloaks and return when you will.

The mages gathered to accept their work, some murmuring words of thanks, others silent. Valani stepped up to him, her khi fairly radiating excitement.

Thank you, my lord! I look forward to learning more.

Rephanin smiled as he handed her two cloaks. *You are welcome.*

She stayed a moment, smiling back, then moved to a worktable and took up one of the cloaks. Rephanin was surprised at this, for she was a day-bider. She glanced up at him and flashed another smile, and he sensed the first faint stirring of a familiar danger. Turning his attention to the next mage, he avoided looking Valani's way again.

Sulithan had kept to the back of the line, waiting until all the others had left or settled in to work.

When Rephanin held out a cloak to him he hesitated, frowning.

Your demonstration—I have not been doing anything like that.

Rephanin smiled gently as he placed the cloak in the mage's hands. *You will do better now.*

Sulithan drew himself up. *Yes. I will.*

If you ever have questions—

I will not hesitate to ask. Thank you, Lord Rephanin.

Sulithan left the chamber, brushing a shoulder against the door frame in his haste. Rephanin hoped that he would not be discouraged, that he would build upon what he had learned this night.

Two other day-biders had chosen to remain and work, leaving six gathered in the hall. Rephanin walked back to his chair, relieved at the smaller group. With six the circle's khi was less intense, though still strong. Rephanin could have shut the others out of his awareness but knew that Heléri would disapprove. Shared khi was stronger khi; their work was improved by being together and would be even more so by retaining the contact of mindspeech. Rephanin shifted his attention to his work while allowing the contact to continue. Before long he was deep into focus-building.

The work went swiftly. He completed two cloaks and was well into enhancing a third by the time he sensed a new presence in the chamber. Opening his eyes, he saw his attendant, Tivhari, carrying a tray bearing fruit and bread, cups, and an ewer of steaming tea. He knew by this signal that it was morning.

He set aside his work and acknowledged Tivhari with a smile. She smiled back, then placed the tray on his worktable and slipped out of the chamber.

Looking at the mages, he saw them deep in concentration and was hesitant to disturb them. Heléri's eyes opened and met his gaze. Feeling her khi shift to him along with her glance, he was swept by a wave of desire. He hastily drew back, shielding his emotions from the circle. After a moment he felt calm enough to speak.

Gentles. Keep working if you wish, but know that it is morning. Refreshment is here for you.

Jholóran stirred, then roused and stretched. The others came back to awareness. Rephanin gently withdrew his khi from the circle, maintaining only the slightest contact, enough for all to hear if someone spoke, but no more. He rose and went to the table, pouring himself a cup of tea.

Valani hurried forward, eyes shining. He offered the tea to her. Her fingers brushed his as she accepted the cup, and in his heightened state of awareness he sensed her unmistakable admiration. At that moment she would, he knew, accept any invitation he cared to make. He shifted his gaze to the ewer and poured out tea for the others who came to join them.

Jholóran's face was filled with quiet elation. "That was extraordinary! Thank you, Lord Rephanin, for sharing this with us."

Valani turned a brilliant smile upon Rephanin. *Yes. Thank you.*

"You are all welcome. I am glad this night enhanced your work."

While the mages helped themselves to fruit and bread, Rephanin retreated to his chair, picked up the cloak that he had yet to finish, and folded it, setting it on a shelf. He then went to the table by the door and gathered the finished cloaks into an empty chest. The Guard would collect them during the day.

The mages began comparing their experiences, talking eagerly about not only the mindspeech but also the improvement the night had made in their focus-building skills. Seeing them thus occupied, Rephanin quietly slipped out of the room and walked the curving corridor to his chambers. Though it was morning outside, the magehall remained dark, lit with gentle lamplight. Rephanin reached his rooms, went in, and closed the outer door, breathing silent relief.

It had not been as bad as he had feared. No one had overreacted to the mindspeech, but a shadow of dread still troubled him. He knew how easily it might have gone differently.

Tivhari had left a small lamp burning in his outer chamber and had banked the coals on the hearth. Rephanin sat before it and held his hands out to the warmth, then rubbed them over his face. He felt shaken despite the night having gone well. He had no confidence, he realized, that resuming the use of his gift would cause no harm. Ill effects might yet manifest. He had sensed the seed of them this night.

A quiet knock on the door made him freeze. It was not Tivhari; her knock was different. He considered ignoring the visitor. He had done enough for one night, had he not? And he felt unsteady, unsafe.

"Rephanin?"

Heléri's voice. Relief washed through him. He rose quickly and went to the door, glancing down the corridor as he welcomed her in. No one else was near.

She carried two teacups and offered one to him. "You left this."

"Oh. Thank you."

She smiled up at him, her blue eyes deep with experience, with kindness. It was kindness that had brought her here, that had made her urge him to speak to the mages. That and concern that their people have all possible aid in this troubled time.

He sipped the tea, which had cooled to a gentle warmth. He should offer Heléri a chair, though it would be safer for them both if she left.

He gazed at her in awkward silence. She smelled faintly of starflowers, a sweet fragrance that reminded him of Eastfæld. They did not grow in Southfæld, nor in Alpinon as far as he knew.

She raised a hand to touch his cheek, her khi tingling on his skin, enhancing the ache in his heart and awakening his body's desire. He caught her hand and held it away.

"You are yet bound in spirit."

"But no longer in flesh." She smiled softly. "And I have my lord's blessing."

Rephanin swallowed, thinking of Davharin. "I do not want your pity. Nor his."

"Pity did not bring me here."

Her fingers turned in his hand to slide between his. All his senses seemed on fire, a white-hot tingling spreading from her hand to his and throughout his flesh.

You are more beautiful than when I first saw you. I cannot bear it.

For answer she drew his hand to her lips, her kiss sending pleasure stinging through his senses. They had played at love long ago but had not gone beyond flirtation. Rephanin doubted he was capable of such lightness any longer.

If you do not leave now—

Let me stay.

Her free hand came up to brush his neck, fingers sliding through his hair. Rephanin closed his eyes, and a soft moan—half pleasure, half remorse—escaped him.

I should have claimed you then. I was a fool.

Never mind. I am here now, and it is cold without.

He looked at her through heavy-lidded eyes, his desire awakened beyond restraint.

Yes. Cold without.

His hand moved up, tracing her hip and waist before embracing her. He kissed her, his pent passion flowing forth as their thoughts entwined and moved beyond language. They joined as he had dreamed for centuries of joining, and as their khi merged so that their very souls became indistinguishable, his doubts burned away in the fire of her love.

Much later, they lay drifting in warmth and contentment. Thoughts still deeply mingled began to separate—awareness of the self to coalesce—acknowledging the differences between self and other. Rephanin; the name recalled became identity, donned like a garment.

Heléri.

Gratitude and fondness expressed without words, as color, as music, through shaded swirling khi. Her response a shimmer of gladness, washing through his being in waves, shadowed with violet and blue, laced with a whisper of ancient gold and white.

He became aware of his bed beneath him, of the physical warmth beside him, a weak echo of her soul's fire. He had a body as well, he recalled. He drew a deep breath into it, reminding himself where he lived.

His eyes opened and in the gentle darkness beheld the strange shapes that made up his private chamber, shapes he took for granted most times. He gazed at them in lazy curiosity, then turned his head to look at Heléri. She lay on her side, dark hair flowing over pearly flesh, the taste of her still hovering in his senses.

Thank you.

She stirred, a smile brushing her lips. Her eyes opened, and a shade of concern fleeted through the deep blue.

I was worried when I heard it said that you had lost your gift.

He allowed himself a wry smile. *No such good fortune for ælvenkind.*

What do you mean? Yours is perhaps the greatest gift we have ever been given.

Think you so? A pity it was not entrusted to one who would make better use of it.

That is harsh.

He gazed up at the ceiling again. *Not harsh enough.*

She raised herself onto an elbow and brushed a strand of his hair back from his shoulder. He shifted his gaze to her and could not help smiling.

She tilted her head. *This is not the confident magelord I once knew—the one who struck whole rooms full of people speechless with awe. What has happened?*

His smile faded. *No.*

She could seize the answer if she wished to; their khi was still entwined, and he doubted he could deny her anything she sought in his heart. He knew she would not try, though. Such a misuse of khi, such an invasion of privacy, was against the creed, for it could not but do harm. Khi misused brought its own punishment, as he knew from sad experience.

She moved her hand across his chest, fingertips brushing his skin. He caught it and carried it to his lips.

I should not have let you stay.

Why? Davharin does not mind.

I was not thinking of Davharin, though I hope you will extend my gratitude to him.

Her eyes lit as with a new thought. *Would you not prefer to tell him yourself?*

Rephanin laughed. *I have done many things, but I have never spoken to the spirit realm.*

You could speak to him through me.

Startled, he let go her hand and sat up. *Is he here?*

Heléri laughed softly. *He is in spirit—he is everywhere and nowhere. Yes, he is with me, and he would like to speak to you.*

She reached for his hand, pressing it between both of hers. He could feel the sudden heat of her khi in his palm.

Wait—

Even as he formed the thought, a new presence flooded his awareness, immensely powerful yet gentle, unlike anything he had experienced yet vaguely familiar. It was pure khi overlaid with the slightest echo of an ælven soul. Rephanin felt his breathing become short and quick.

Davharin?

A feeling of confirmation—unformed, a mere ripple through the brilliant khi—was followed by a confusion of ideas Rephanin could not interpret. Heléri sat up beside him, still clasping his hand, her palm hot against his.

He seldom uses language anymore.

He saw her close her eyes, felt her wordless request for clarity. Agreement swept through Davharin's brightness, then Rephanin sensed a drawing in, a contraction that intensified power rather than lessened it. Closing his own eyes, he waited. At last a single word rolled over him like thunder across the mountains.

Speech.

Rephanin frowned. *I do not—*

An image leapt into brilliance in his mind, a perfect

circle of glowing whiteness. It became irregular, varying in thickness, and now he saw that khi was flowing endlessly around it. With a shock Rephanin recognized it as his mage circle, as if he were looking down on it from above and seeing only the khi of the mages who formed it.

He applauds your use of speech with your circle.

Rephanin knew that Heléri's interpretation was correct. The thought rang within him with the clarity of a deep chime. If a spirit considered the matter important enough to tell him so, he had better pay attention.

Thank you, Davharin. I—thank you.

Warm amusement flowed around him. He thought he sensed an echo of the ælven shape Davharin had once worn. It sparked memories of a sober-eyed mountain lord whom Rephanin had never troubled to know. Regret swept through him—his own, for an opportunity lost—and was answered gently.

Deferred. Not lost.

Rephanin smiled at the promise of this thought, feeling his body relax, tension suddenly flowing away. Opening his eyes, he saw Heléri watching him and felt a rush of gratitude.

Yet another gift you have given me.

He brought her hand to his lips and on impulse began to kiss her fingertips one by one. She stiffened, and he glanced up, seeing shock in her eyes.

Davharin used to do that.

Did he?

He bent his head to finish what he had begun, at the same time sending a wordless query toward Davharin and receiving instant confirmation. A sense of dizziness went through him as he became aware of a possibility he had never considered. He looked up at

Heléri, who was gazing at him with an expression of wonder.

Rephanin drew a deep breath. *Davharin?*

His invitation was enthusiastically accepted, and a wave of powerful khi moved through him or, rather, into him. Bits of memory sparked past too quickly to be caught.

He had shared his mind and his body with countless companions in flesh, but this differed. Davharin was overwhelming, and Rephanin could only trust that the spirit would not consume him completely.

Even as that thought fleeted through his awareness, he knew he was himself, though also some small part of Davharin. Smiling at Heléri, he reached up to brush the concern from her face. His hand then slid to the back of her neck and drew her toward him, and he found himself gently kissing her forehead, then each of her eyelids, as Davharin's voice whispered in his soul.

She likes this, also.

❧ Small Sleeper Farm ❧

Shalár gazed at the black peak of the Great Sleeper rising sharply into the night. In the distance, the Ebon Mountains were a shaded wall. Beyond them lay Fireshore, calling to her.

A faint clang of metal on metal reached her, rare enough on this field, for only a few of her hunters carried swords. She glanced down again at the dark forms surging amid the tall grasses below, clad in the full weight of their leathers. Their khi told her they were weary but not spent. They had improved much in the few days they had been here.

She shifted her gaze to the farmhouse, thinking of the labor it had taken the farmers to clear the field where her warriors now practiced. It had been allowed to go fallow, there being insufficient hands to farm it. Doubtless the trampling feet of her army were doing it little good.

Two other fields were given over to fleececod. A small orchard of no more than ten trees—apples and stonefruits—looked in reasonably good order, though tangles of brambles were encroaching on its edges. Such foods would not sustain her people, but they were necessary for the digestion of the blood that was their true food. They were also needed by the very young to whom the hunger had not yet come.

Vashakh was at work harvesting fleececod, the sack over her shoulder bulging with the fluffy blooms. As Shalár watched, she emptied the sack into a cart that stood nearby. Her head turned toward Shalár, and she stood still for a moment, then went on with her work.

Shalár looked away, back to her hunters. Perhaps she would send a few of them to assist Vashakh for a night or two, help her harvest the fleececod. Compensation for the damage to her field.

Yaras called out an order, drawing her attention. At his command the hunters fell still, standing silent in the field, their weapons in hand. Their pale hair gleamed in the starlight. Shalár was moved by the sight: her people's hope, their future. They must not fail.

She left her vantage place and strode among the ranks of her warriors, looking at each face in turn, seeking any sign of weakness or fear. Some met her glance or nodded greeting as she passed. Many had been with her on the recent Grand Hunt, when they had rounded up kobalen to fill the pens in Nightsand so that her people would have food while she made her way to Fireshore.

She permitted herself a slight smile, remembering the feast at that hunt's conclusion and the wild coupling that had followed. That night had bound all those hunters more surely than any spoken oath.

She glanced at Yaras, recalling the heat of his hands on her flesh. He had not been merely dutiful then. She walked to where he stood, catching his gaze.

"A melee."

Yaras stepped forward at once, shouting orders. The warriors divided into two forces and took up positions on either end of the field. At Yaras's command, they rushed toward one another, crossing the flattened grass of the field like the wind, nearly silent until the first blows fell.

Shalár watched and listened, tasting the khi that sang in the night air. Confidence was the dominant note. They were ready.

A spark of khi approaching from the west drew her attention. She looked away from the melee, searching the woods for the intruder. It was not Vashakh. Shalár reached out with khi to sound the newcomer.

A runner, come from the direction of Nightsand, but come from much farther. News from Ciris at last!

The runner's breath rasped slightly as he bowed before her. He must have left Nightsand at sunset and run all the way. It was Ranad, who had been a novice on the recent Grand Hunt.

"Bright Lady, I bring you greeting from Midrange. Ciris and Welir send you their obedience."

He proffered a letter. Shalár broke open the seal and swiftly scanned the few lines.

The news was good. More than three thousand kobalen had come to Midrange at her summons, and still more were arriving.

Shalár smiled grimly. She would have to have additional rings made, small rings in the ear that marked the kobalen who wore them as protected from her hunters. Convincing the kobalen of her sincerity had been difficult, but now it appeared they wholeheartedly embraced the bargain. Fortunately, kobalen roamed the wastes in such numbers that her people would not go hungry even when a few hundred were held immune from the hunt.

She glanced at Ranad, who stood waiting. "Come with me."

Yaras looked up sharply, and a frown drew his brows together. Shalár paused, staring at him.

Jealous? No, disapproving. He thought she intended to drag poor Ranad into her bed, did he? She had not had such an intention, though she doubted Ranad would protest.

She turned to the runner. "Are you hungry?"

She could feel that he was. He swallowed and gave a single nod. Hiding a smile, she turned to Yaras.

"Halt the melee and set them to single combat practice. And send a kobalen to the house."

She brushed past him without waiting for an answer. Let him think what he chose. She did not mind unsettling his exasperating state of calm.

As they walked, she questioned Ranad about the kobalen at Midrange, as much to learn about his attitudes as to compare his information with that given by Ciris. He seemed enthusiastic about the effort to mold an army out of the kobalen and described to her his attempts at captaining them.

Ciris had only a handful of hunters with him at Midrange, and Shalár's greatest concern had been that the kobalen might turn on them. So far, though, the creatures had listened and obeyed to the best of their ability.

She heard voices as she approached the farmhouse: Vashakh and Mehir, talking in low, urgent tones. A pebble grated beneath Shalár's foot, and they stopped abruptly. She entered the house, nodding at the male farmer as she led Ranad through toward her room. At her gesture Ranad sat on the bed while she seated herself at the small table, took out paper and ink, then picked up a quill, mending it with a small bone-handled knife before dipping it in the ink.

She wrote first to Farnath, the metalsmith in

Nightsand who had created the kobalen earrings for her, telling him to make another thousand of them and send them at once to Ciris. As she was sealing the letter, a hunter sought admittance, bringing with her a kobalen.

Shalár stood and took hold of the creature with khi, thanking the hunter, who glanced at Ranad with mild interest before retiring. Shalár went to the doorway and lowered the curtain, then turned to Ranad. He was staring fixedly at the kobalen. She made the creature sit on the floor and knelt beside it, drawing her knife.

"Come here."

Ranad joined her on the floor. Palpable waves of hunger shook his khi. He had not fed in Fireshore, then.

"Take hold of it."

Ranad was still fairly new as a hunter, but he showed no hesitation in seizing the kobalen's khi. Shalár released it to him, then made a cut on the creature's throat and leaned forward to take the first mouthful.

The hot blood combined with the singing of Ranad's hunger raised excitement in her, but she took only one swallow, then sat back and gave the kobalen to Ranad. He fell on it with a grunt. She left him feeding and went back to the table.

She drew a page toward her, then sat pondering what to write to Ciris. It seemed the kobalen army was as ready as it could be, ready enough for her plans. She did not need that force to be honed to sharpness. Kobalen were limited in their understanding; they would never be a precise weapon.

Soon winter would grip most of the ælven lands. Nightsand, lying well to the north, would merely be covered in cloud and rain, a respite from the punishing sun. And Fireshore would be as it ever was, lush and green, though the rains would cool it somewhat. A pang of homesickness smote her, longing for the once familiar forests of Fireshore, the looming presence of Firethroat by the sea.

Now was the time to move. Ciris had reported that Midrange was still passable, but the snows had already begun. Soon the kobalen would not be able to get through.

She dipped her pen and wrote a few brief lines of instruction, then set the quill down and gazed at the drying ink on the page. Once this message was sent, she could not turn back.

She never asked for help or guidance, either from unseen spirits or from the ældar who the ælven believed watched over each form of life. Not since she had been driven from Fireshore. She did not ask it now, but she thought of Dareth.

He had grown weary of life and especially of dependence on the blood of kobalen. He had given up, and that had wounded her. Toward the end he had seemed inclined to go back to the ways of the ælven, ways that she had deliberately abandoned.

Was his spirit watching her now? Would he approve her actions? Her heart ached with those questions.

Folly. Dareth was gone and no longer had a say in her life. She must rely upon her own wits.

She glanced at the letter to Ciris; nearly dry now. The lives of many of her people hung on those lines. Gazing at the words without seeing them, she acknowledged that she had already committed to this course of action. The only question that had remained was when. The answer was now.

A sigh behind her made her look at Ranad. He had finished feeding and was sitting up, turning eyes drunk with satisfaction toward her. The kobalen lay on the floor, the wound at its neck seeping a little, eyes glazed and staring sightless at the ceiling. Ranad had drained it. He must have been extremely hungry. Perhaps he had not taken time to hunt on his way here.

"Are you ready to return to Ciris?"

"As you will, Bright Lady. I thank you." He gestured toward the kobalen.

She nodded, then turned back to the table. Picking up the letter, she waved it to dry the last of the ink, then carefully folded it.

On impulse, she took two small coils of precious ribbon from her writing box, one red and one black. They had been made in Eastfæld, taken by kobalen in a raid on a trade caravan some few decades since. Her watchers in the mountains observed such raids and went through what goods the kobalen left behind, culling treasures such as these.

The ribbons were becoming fragile with age. She wound both once around her hand and cut them with her knife, then held them up.

Clan Darkshore's colors. Her colors. Colors that had once signified Fireshore and soon would again. She wrapped them tightly around the letter, poured heated wax over the ribbons' ends, then pressed her ring into it.

"Take this to Ciris." She handed the letter to Ranad. "And this other goes to Farnath in Nightsand."

Ranad bowed and slipped both letters into his tunic. Shalár went to the doorway and pulled back the curtain, following Ranad out.

Mehir glanced up from his place at the hearth.

Shalár met the farmer's anxious gaze with a small smile and jerked her head toward her room, inviting him to take what was left of the kobalen.

Striding out to the field with Ranad, she felt her heart lifting. The decision made, its weight was no longer of concern.

Yaras stood watching the warriors. He glanced up at her approach, frowning slightly as his gaze flicked to Ranad. Shalár murmured a farewell to the runner, who sprinted off westward, disappearing into the woods.

"What do you think of them?" Shalár nodded toward the warriors. "Are they ready?"

"They are, Bright Lady. As ready as they can be."

"Bring them to stand, then."

He stepped forward, shouting orders to halt the mock fighting. The hunter-warriors gathered again, looking toward Shalár, waiting for her command. She pushed back a fleeting, fearful doubt. Ranad was on his way to Ciris with her letter. There was no turning back.

"You are fit." Her voice rang across the field. "You are ready, and Fireshore is waiting. Break your camp, prepare to march, then return here."

An excited murmur rose as the hunters dispersed. Shalár turned to Yaras, who was about to follow them to the camp.

"Bring the kobalen to this field."

He looked at her in surprise. "All of them?"

"All that are left. There are not many, are there?"

"Perhaps fifty."

"We cannot march them with us; they will slow us down. Nor can Vashakh and Mehir make use of them all."

Yaras nodded his understanding. "As you will, Bright Lady."

She watched him go, then walked over to the rock outcrop from which she had often watched the training. Climbing it one last time, she sat hugging her knees and gazing at the night sky.

A shred of cloud drifted past, floating eastward toward the Great Sleeper. Soon the rains would arrive. It was well that she had decided to march before then. Perhaps they could reach Fireshore by the time winter set in.

A small thrill lifted her heart at the thought. Fireshore at last. After all these lonely centuries.

The warriors began to gather in the field again, leaving their packs at its edge. Yaras returned along with those who had been set to guard the kobalen, bringing the huddled, shuffling mass of creatures with them. The hunters surrounded them, their quick exchange of sharp glances indicating they had guessed Shalár's purpose. Part of it, at any rate.

Shalár came down from the rock and strode into the field, joining Yaras near the kobalen. Her nostrils twitched at the powerful stench given off by fifty of the creatures together. She waited until all the warriors had returned, then turned to Yaras.

"Summon your captains."

He called them forward, a male and two females, each in command of a hundred warriors. They bowed before Shalár and stood waiting. She acknowledged them, then addressed all the army once more.

"You have done well here. You have honed yourselves into a weapon to pierce the heart of Fireshore. Tonight we march, but first we feast. From this night on we are a pack, and our prey is the city of Ghlanhras!"

A cheer rose up from the hunters, an eerie keening that made the kobalen tremble where they stood. Shalár felt deeply moved, and to hide it she turned to the kobalen. Selecting a large male, she took hold of its khi and moved it forward from the rest. With her knife she opened its throat and took a mouthful of blood, then handed it on to Yaras. He took a mouthful and gave it to one of the captains, who in turn would give it to three warriors to share. Shalár hoped this feast would last them well on their way to Fireshore.

She kept back one small kobalen, scarcely grown, for herself and Yaras. When all the warriors were feeding, she came to stand beside him.

"I have been thinking of your future."

Yaras looked surprised. "Mine, Bright Lady?"

"Yes." She reached out a hand to smooth a stray strand of hair back from his face. A tremor went through his khi and rippled out through the army. Some who were feeding paused to look up.

"I am in need of a new steward. Nihlan is managing for now, but the pens alone are plenty of work for her."

A flash of dismay crossed Yaras's face. He glanced down, not meeting her gaze. She smiled softly, eyes narrowed.

"Serve me well on this venture and you shall be steward in Nightsand."

His face was blank. Shalár admired his self-control and was also amused by it, for it did not extend to his khi. She could feel his consternation in the air between them.

"But Islir—"

"She may join you in Nightsand. You may both reside in the Cliff Hollows."

He swallowed, brows twitching into a slight frown.

No doubt he thought Islir would dislike the suggestion. Shalár was enjoying herself but deemed it time to relent.

"After all, you will want company there, as I will be in Ghlanhras."

The relief that flooded his face nearly made her laugh. He looked up at her, then fell to his knees.

"Bright Lady! I thank you."

"Thank me when you are in Nightsand." She reached a hand down to him. "First we must win Fireshore."

He took her hand and stood. Smiling, she brought the young kobalen forward and opened cuts on either side of its throat.

"Feed with me."

Neither of them was acutely hungry, having fed recently together, but Shalár enjoyed the sensation of sharing the kobalen. She let her khi mingle with Yaras's and with that of the creature whose life they were consuming. The strength that flowed into her brought a hint of arousal, and she fed it, reaching out to touch Yaras.

Her fingers brushed his face, then down his arm to find his hand, khi sharp in his palm as she pressed hers to it. She felt his lingering relief and gratitude and, more immediate, his response to her touch. She wanted him but would not waste the kobalen. Not until they had drunk all its life did she abandon it and move toward Yaras.

His khi ran with myriad feelings: gratitude, wariness, anticipation of the struggle in Fireshore, arousal. She fixed on the last and echoed it with her own. She felt the moment when he yielded, abandoning caution and concerns to revel in pure physical lust.

The army felt it as well. Shalár sensed their khi shift from the satisfaction of feeding to the arousal of desire.

They followed her in this, as in all things. She smiled and kissed Yaras deeply, enjoying the urgent grip of his hands on her flesh. She let him strip her, there in the midst of her army, and felt the tingle of their attention as Yaras knelt before her once more.

The warriors began to abandon their feeding, finding partners, shedding armor and clothing. The field they had trampled to dust was already stained with the blood of kobalen; now the heady scent of lust overlay other smells. For a fleeting moment Shalár wondered if any would conceive this night, then abandoned the thought and gave herself wholly to the pleasure of Yaras's touch.

She pulled him to her and fumbled at the straps of his leathers. He helped her remove them and stood before her, naked and proud in the starlight. She ran a hand down the whiteness of his flesh, feeling his strength.

Someone nearby gave a gasp. Shalár reached her khi toward the sound, tasting the rising urgency of the army's coupling, and could wait no longer. She pulled Yaras to her, and together they sank to the ground.

His hands pushed roughly at her legs. She caught her fingers in his hair and gave it one sharp pull, claiming his attention. He waited, breathing deeply and fast, eyes fixed on her face. At last she released him, and he at once shoved into her fiercely, making her grunt in surprise. He was more urgent than he had been since their arrival here.

Pleased, Shalár thrust herself against him and slid her khi around him, caressing, urging him to higher passion. She did not seek his memories now, for she had felt them often enough. Instead she focused her khi on their coupling, feeding the heat of their flesh, heightening the sensation of their contact almost beyond bearing.

She felt herself begin to melt, to turn to molten fire like the spew of Firethroat. Yaras reared up and stared into her eyes, his khi rising in a silent, urgent agreement.

She peaked in that moment, crying out in frustration, for she knew it was a breath too soon. She lost hold of Yaras's khi, though she could feel him hammering against her, trying still to find his way into her deepest self, but it was too late. At last he poured out his seed with a strangled groan and lay gasping on top of her.

So close! So very close.

She knew she would find her way there. It was only a matter of persistence.

She lay staring up at the stars, her fingers playing in Yaras's pale hair. Around her the hunters were relaxing, some shifting and talking in quiet tones, others yet finishing their passion. Their khi lay soft and weighty on the field, mingled and sated. They were one now, a pack that had shared the deepest bond and would ever know a silent understanding. Shalár smiled, satisfied.

Some little distance away the sound of a scythe began anew, rhythmically cutting grain. Shalár had not heard it during the pack's bonding. Perhaps Vashakh and Mehir had found their own passion renewed this night.

She closed her eyes, wishing for a moment that she could drift away in the gentle gratification that washed through her. That luxury was not open to her, though. This night was a beginning, not an end. Not until she was in Ghlanhras would she be able to lie at ease.

Pushing Yaras away, she sat up and brushed her hair out of her eyes. She could feel his dark gaze upon her and turned her head to meet it, the hint of a challenge in her eyes. He was silent, watching her, waiting for her next command.

She stretched her arms skyward, then ran her hands over her naked torso, savoring the feel of the night air on her flesh, knowing she would not feel it again for some time. She must hasten her army to Fireshore now.

Standing up, she hunted out her tunic and legs from the tangle of clothes and leathers on the ground. Tossing Yaras's tunic to him, she pulled on her own.

"Ready them for the march." She turned to go to the farmhouse and collect her belongings.

Yaras caught her hand, staying her. She looked back, questioning, and saw the anxious hope in his eyes.

"Did you mean it?"

Brushing aside annoyance at his doubt, she squeezed his hand and held his gaze. "If we win Fireshore and we both survive, you shall be my steward in Nightsand."

He pressed his brow to her hand, and she saw his throat move in a swallow. She stood still for a moment, then gave his hand a final squeeze and pulled away.

⊰ Glenhallow ⊱

"An advance force could go forward now to occupy High Holding." Turisan drew a breath. "I offer to lead it."

The gazes of the councillors all turned to him, some surprised, others approving.

Jharan frowned. "No."

Ehranan stood. "Your pardon, Lord Jharan, but I think it a good idea. Turisan's presence will inspire the army."

"Turisan is needed here. The Council must maintain communication with Lady Eliani. That is the whole point of her journey, that their gift of mindspeech shall tell us more quickly what is happening in Fireshore."

"Eliani is many days from Fireshore as yet. I could take a company to High Holding and then return within a tenday."

Jharan fixed him with a gaze Turisan knew well; his father had reached the limit of his patience. "We will discuss it later. Lord Ehranan, what are the numbers of your recruits?"

Ehranan cast Turisan a glance that spoke of resignation, then proceeded to answer at length. Turisan picked up the cup before him and drank a deep swallow of cool water, concealing his disappointment.

He wished more of the councillors were present. Some of those who might have supported him were not. Heléri was among them, and Rephanin's chair was empty as well. None of the night-biders were in attendance today.

Governor Felisan, Eliani's father, seemed deeply absorbed in examining the broidered cuff of his sleeve. Alpinon's governor disliked what he called prosaic brangles, as he had confided to Turisan.

Turisan leaned over to murmur in his father's ear. "I must depart soon. I am pledged to meet with Rephanin at sunset."

Jharan turned a look of inquiry on him and answered quietly. "About equipping the Guard?"

Turisan gave a small shake of his head. "To ask his advice."

A slight frown creased his father's brow. Turisan stayed to listen a while longer, then quietly left his seat. He felt Jharan's gaze follow him.

Stepping onto the colonnade, Turisan saw that the sun was nearing the snowy peaks to the west. He paused, looking out at the fountain court, inhaling the fountains' moist breath, then followed colonnades to cross from the palace to the magehall.

Rephanin's attendant greeted him and led him down a curving hallway lit by sparse torchlight. She stopped before a door and knocked softly.

"Lord Turisan is here to see you, my lord."

"He may enter."

The attendant opened the door and stepped aside. Turisan went in, glancing around a room he had never seen before as the door closed quietly behind him.

Rephanin's taste seemed a combination of lavish

and spare. What ornaments he possessed were rich, but they were few: a pair of carved chairs with cushions covered in thick gold velvet, a small table between them of finest darkwood, a single tapestry that was plainly the work of Clan Ælvanen's best weavers. The room was lit only by the freshly built fire upon the hearth.

Rephanin came forward, adjusting the fall of a tunic he had apparently just donned. He stepped to a set of shelves along one wall and picked up a flagon.

"Would you care for a cup of wine?"

"Thank you, yes. The Council was tiresome today."

Rephanin's lip curved in a smile as he handed Turisan a finely wrought silver cup. "Tell me."

Turisan sighed, settling into his chair. "It would not interest you, I fear. An argument over whether to occupy High Holding."

Rephanin took the other chair and sipped his own wine. "And the result?"

"It was left undecided."

"Never let it be said that the Ælven Council makes decisions lightly."

Turisan laughed. "Or swiftly."

He took another mouthful of wine, enjoying its subtle flavors of fruit and wood. Looking up, he saw that the magelord was watching him. He swallowed, pondering how to raise the subject that had brought him there.

Rephanin spared him the trouble. "So you feel mind-speech is a dangerous distraction."

"Sometimes, yes."

"You are not the first to tell me so."

Turisan raised an eyebrow. "Oh?"

Rephanin placed his cup on the table, then leaned back and laced his fingers together. "You are distracted when in company, sometimes embarrassingly so. When walking or otherwise moving, you may lose sense of where you are. At any time you may be taken off guard by physical sensations that are disorienting."

"Yes." Turisan nodded, impressed. "Can we avoid any of this?"

A small smile crossed Rephanin's face. "Most of it. You and your lady must establish some customs between you."

"What do you suggest?"

"The single most helpful thing is to agree upon a signal that you will use when you wish to make contact. It is far less distracting than beginning with speech, and gives your partner the opportunity to refuse or to find privacy."

"What sort of signal?"

Rephanin hesitated, gazing down at his hands. "With your permission, it would be easier to demonstrate than to explain."

Turisan felt an echo of past wariness, but with an effort he dismissed it. He had come for Rephanin's help and had no cause to mistrust him.

"Very well."

Are you ready?

Startled at the magelord's voice, Turisan nearly spilled his wine. A cold tingle washed through him as he realized that what he had hitherto shared only with Eliani was no longer exclusively theirs.

It had never been that, he knew. Rephanin could speak with anyone in his presence, though Turisan had never heard him speak before. He set down his cup and drew a breath to steady himself.

Yes.

Rephanin sat up straight in his chair, and his eyes closed. In a moment Turisan sensed a slight pressure on his brow and a warmth, as if someone had rested a hand there. Behind the sensation he caught a whisper of Rephanin's khi—powerful yet restrained—that struck him with awe.

The pressure vanished as the magelord opened his eyes. Turisan nodded slowly.

"I see. How is it done?"

Easiest to show you. Follow me.

At once Turisan was again aware of Rephanin's khi, but this time it was open to him, vast and potent, inviting him into a closeness he had shared only with Eliani. He hesitated, and immediately his attention was directed to a soft grayness, a barrier concealing part of the magelord's khi from him, which he found reassuring.

Accepting the contact, he was drawn in and for a moment experienced the sort of double awareness that often disturbed him—his own body and Rephanin's at once. He closed his eyes, and the feeling quickly passed.

He found his thoughts trailing the magelord's, reaching through the khi of his body, finding the point of focus, and applying a gentle brightness of khi to it. The signal's sensation returned, then faded in the next moment as Rephanin withdrew.

Turisan opened his eyes, inhaled, and reached for his cup, feeling slightly stunned. A sip of wine served to calm him.

"Thank you. That will help a great deal, I think."

Rephanin leaned back in his chair. "Choose a different point to signal that you are not in a position to speak—the back of a hand, for example."

"Would it not be as easy to speak?"

"When you are accustomed to it, you will find the signal is faster and less obtrusive."

Turisan nodded. "What else?"

"You and Lady Eliani should agree upon when to avoid intruding upon each other. It may be difficult, given how swiftly she is traveling."

"I will discuss it with her, thank you. I have another question. Last night two of her party were wounded, and Eliani blessed them with healing. I felt it through my ribbon." He ran his hand along the woven ribbon and looked up at the magelord, who seemed astonished.

"A healing? I did not know Lady Eliani was a healer."

"She is not. She tried only because the wounded requested it. Can you tell me why I felt it?"

Rephanin slowly shook his head, his expression unreadable. "You will have to ask Heléri. I have never heard of such an occurrence."

"I will consult her, then."

Rephanin reached for his wine and took a deep swallow, turning the cup around in his hands as he stared into the fire. Turisan waited, not wishing to intrude on his thoughts. At last Rephanin stirred and glanced up at him.

"You have further questions?"

"Only one. Did Dejharin and Dironen have such difficulties?"

Rephanin gave a soft laugh. "I do not know. I was acquainted with them, but only slightly. I was fairly young at that time and not nearly as important as they."

Turisan nodded and took another sip of wine. "Like me, compared with you."

"Oh, no."

The magelord's gray eyes fixed on him intently. Turisan shifted in his chair, uncomfortable under that gaze.

Rephanin spoke softly. "You are far more important than I. You are a distance speaker; you and your lady are the only such partners we have at present."

Turisan paused before answering. "And your gift of speaking with anyone nearby is the only such we have had in all ælven history. Is that not so?"

Rephanin's gaze dropped. "In recorded history, yes. I am—a curiosity." A corner of his mouth curved wryly.

Turisan frowned, surprised that Rephanin, who by all reports was well aware of his worth, would so underrate himself. He gazed thoughtfully at the magelord.

"And all the mages you have trained, all the work you have done—that adds nothing to your importance?"

Rephanin's expression hardened as he stared into the fire. "If someday it can be said that I did more good than harm, I will have lived a useful life."

He drew a breath, then seemed to cast off the somber mood, favoring Turisan with a smile as he rose from his chair. "And now it is time for me to meet with my circle. I hope you will find my suggestions helpful."

Turisan stood as well, leaving his cup on the table. "Most helpful. Thank you again."

Without thinking, he extended an arm, and after a slight hesitation the magelord clasped it. Turisan felt again the hint of controlled power in Rephanin's khi.

They parted, Rephanin going to his circle and Turisan returning across the colonnade to Hallowhall. The sun had set, and the blue of twilight was fast deepening under a quarter moon.

Turisan paused at the balustrade overlooking the fountain court. Another formal banquet awaited him—one he dared not miss if he wished to escape his father's displeasure—but he was not ready to face the councillors yet and allowed the fountains' whisper to lure him into the courtyard.

The evening was chill enough that he found himself alone in the gardens. He strolled along the paths, listening to the water's music and thinking over his encounter with Rephanin.

All his life he had held the magelord in awe. Since childhood Rephanin had been to him a figure of mystery and undetermined threat. Now that he had shared khi with the magelord, he wondered why he had felt so intimidated. He had not felt threatened, save when the strange hunger touched the magelord's gaze. He was beginning to think it was merely envy, though why Rephanin should envy him he could not guess.

Eliani. He envies the gift.

A stray breeze blew a fountain's mist into his face. He blinked, recalling that until today he had known of Rephanin's gift only by report. Indeed, until today he had seen no proof of the magelord's mindspeech nor heard of any who claimed to have experienced it. Something had changed.

Turisan?

Distracted by Eliani's voice, he smiled. *Yes, my heart?*

We are coming into Highstone. We will spend the night, replenish our supplies, and set out in the morning.

Enjoy your rest. I must go and feast with the councillors.

Speak to me when you are finished.

I will do better than that. Harken to this.

Drawing a breath, he closed his eyes and reached out to send her the signal Rephanin had taught him. He sensed her surprise.

What is that?

A gentle request for your attention. Rephanin showed me how.

Rephanin!

Yes—he had good advice for us. I will explain it to you when we both have leisure.

He sensed her skepticism. *Very well. Enjoy your feast.*

Turisan smiled, sending his love to enfold her, catching his breath at her swift, fierce response. She slipped away, and he opened his eyes, staying for a moment in the courtyard before returning to the palace and his duty.

◅ Highstone ▻

Luruthin watched the white-gold rays of the sun's farewell stretch upward from the peaks of the Ebons as the party entered Highstone's public circle. They were greeted with joy by the citizens, who instantly surrounded Eliani, pelting her with questions. Luruthin dismounted and gratefully gave his reins over to a groom who hurried out from the stables.

Gharinan, who was serving as temporary governor in Felisan and Eliani's absence, came to greet them, and Eliani at once led him back to the Hall, talking intently of supplies, horses, and riders. Ten of the Southfæld Guard who had ridden this far were to be replaced by ten from Alpinon's Guard, the Southfælders to return to reinforce the outpost at Midrange.

Luruthin shouldered his saddle packs and turned gratefully to the warm lights burning in Highstone's windows. The door of the public lodge stood wide, revealing a large fire on the welcoming hearth and the lodge keeper chattering brightly to the guardians who were already crowding inside the house. Guessing that it would take some while to settle twenty guardians, Luruthin turned to Vanorin.

"There will likely be a vacant bed in the theyns' lodge, if that would suit you."

Vanorin's brows rose. "Must one be a theyn to stop there?"

"A theyn or a theyn's guest. I hereby invite you."

The Greenglen returned a weary smile. "Is it very far? I should stay near my guardians."

Luruthin grinned and gestured toward the lodge. "Nothing is far from anything in Highstone. It is just the other side of the circle."

Vanorin shouldered his packs. "Lead on, then."

The theyns' lodge was smaller than the public lodge, and the fire in its hearthroom was banked. Strains of hesitant lute music came from deep within the house. Luruthin rang the guest chime, smiling an apology to Vanorin.

"Bithanan is sometimes slow to answer. Never fear; his table makes up for it."

The music ceased, and the lodge keeper appeared after a few more moments. Slender almost to thinness, with his russet hair caught back in a simple clasp, he blinked at them in surprise.

"Theyn Luruthin! Has the Council ended?"

"Not nearly. Eliani and I are riding northward on an errand at their behest and will only be stopping the night. This is Vanorin of the Southfæld Guard. I trust you can accommodate him?"

"Of course! Let me show you to rooms. When you are refreshed, come down again and I will have a meal ready for you."

Bithanan led them up a flight of stairs and down a hallway, opening a door to either side. "Be at home, my lords. I will send hot water for you presently."

He bowed and withdrew, leaving them standing in the hall. Luruthin gestured to one of the doors.

"Perhaps you would like the room overlooking the circle. You can keep an eye on your guardians."

Vanorin stepped into the room and across to the window to pull back the tapestry. Luruthin could see the windows of the public lodge ablaze with light. Vanorin looked over his shoulder.

"Thank you."

Smiling, Luruthin crossed the hall to his own room and set his packs on a chest at the foot of the bed. He rummaged in them for his comb and untied the thong that secured his braid, sitting on the bed with a sigh of pleasure.

A bed for the night. Sheer luxury.

The last bed he had been in was Jhinani's. He closed his eyes as he worked the knots from his hair, remembering his departure from Glenhallow.

While Governor Jharan was making speeches to a throng of cheering citizens in Glenhallow's public circle, Luruthin had drawn Jhinani aside, reached into his tunic, and pulled out a slender crystal, half a finger's length, clear and perfect and set in a silver mounting hanging from a matching chain. A short time earlier he had pulled apart all his luggage—thoughtfully packed for him by one of Hallowhall's many attendants—to find it. Now he pressed it into Jhinani's hand.

Her fair skin flushed pink with pleasure and surprise. Luruthin smiled as he watched her hold the stone up to the sunlight.

"Mined and wrought in Clerestone."

"It is beautiful. Thank you." She glanced at her attire, a gown of silver cloth, unadorned, needing no jewels to augment it. "I have no gift to offer in return."

"You have given me enough."

The roughness of his own voice surprised him; he felt an urge to catch her in his arms. Instead he helped her don the crystal, relishing the feel of her silken hair in his fingers as he held it clear, the soft skin of her neck as he laid the silver chain against it. Her scent came to him on a breeze, and he inhaled deeply, thinking of the previous night.

The memory of that scent stayed with him even now. He had not thought so much could change in a single evening. He had watched the celebration of Turisan and Eliani's handfasting, feeling rather sorry for himself, until Jhinani had invited him to share a private cup of wine. They had shared much more than that, and what had begun as a casual encounter had ended, to their mutual surprise and delight, with their conceiving a child.

No one knew. There had been no time to tell anyone in Glenhallow, what with the fuss surrounding Eliani's departure, and since then he had not found a comfortable opportunity to mention it. He was glad, actually, to have this secret to treasure to himself for a while. A child was a rare gift among the ælven, and conception the rarest and most remarkable of experiences.

He remembered lying close to Jhinani afterward, gazing into her warm brown eyes. Their khi still flowed together, and he could just sense the lighter tone of their child's khi. The spirit of their child had greeted them at the moment of conception and would remain near Jhinani until the body she would build for it was ready to be inhabited. Male or female? The child had not informed them.

A fateful evening, that last in Glenhallow. For Eliani, also. His love for her had not diminished but had somehow transformed. He no longer felt desperation or hopelessness. He loved her as the cousin she was and had no need for more. This he owed to Jhinani, to whom he had pledged himself for a year and a day. With a silent thought of thanks to his Greenglen lady, he smiled.

◈

Eliani stood in her father's study with Luruthin, Vanorin, and Gharinan, drinking mead as they discussed the map spread on the table around which they stood. Vanorin's fingers followed the North Road from Highstone.

"Is this the route? It looks mountainous."

Eliani nodded. "There are roads on the plains, but they are well to the east. To use them would add to the length of the journey."

"Unless the weather becomes inclement."

Eliani turned to Gharinan. "How were the roads on your journey hither?"

"Clear, but that was more than a moon ago."

"And when did you last hear from Heahrued?"

Gharinan smiled wryly, acknowledging her deduction. He was not one to ignore his village even when called upon to serve as temporary governor.

"Four days ago. The road was then clear, though snowy in places."

"We will take the mountain road, then. We start at dawn. Will the provisions be ready?"

"I cannot swear that all will be ready by dawn. More likely by midday."

Gharinan offered to pour more wine for her. She nodded but indicated a small measure.

"Very well. Dawn if possible, midday otherwise. I thank you, all of you, for your help and support." She took a last swallow, sweet and mellow on the tongue, then set down her cup. "Time for the Guardian's Reward."

Luruthin's eyes lit up. "Cousin, you are brilliant! Gharinan, do you join us?"

"Absolutely."

Eliani smiled mischievously at Vanorin, who looked bewildered. "Shall you accompany us as well?"

"If it is something a stranger may share, my lady."

Luruthin laughed. "You are no stranger—we have been under attack together! You are entitled to the reward."

Eliani held up a chastening finger. "But only if you cease calling me 'my lady.' I am never addressed so by those with whom I have gone unclad."

Vanorin's eyes widened, and Luruthin laughed again. "It is a hot spring. Do you not have them in Glenhallow?"

The Greenglen looked relieved. "Oh. Yes, there are springs above the city. I have not visited them in years."

Eliani chuckled. "Then you shall refresh your memory as well as your body. You may tell us which are better—Glenhallow's springs or the Guardian's Reward."

She sent him off with Luruthin to collect a change of clothing while she fetched a fresh tunic and legs from her own room. Spotting a small jar of Heléri's sage-scented soap on her shelves, she caught it up and went out.

The night air was bracing as they left the city, climbing north and west on the main road from Highstone. Above, a half moon was already riding westward. The breeze sharpened as they rounded a bluff, then dropped as they turned from the road to follow a trickling, sulfurous stream up into the woods.

The path ascended a wide, pine-filled canyon, then

ran beside the stream up a steep, rocky wall. Stripes of moonlight filtered through the dense branches, dappling the ground and flashing over Vanorin's pale hair as he passed through them. The sight made Eliani wish it was Turisan who walked before her, but she swiftly dismissed that. Someday she would bring him here, she decided as they reached the small clearing surrounding the spring.

The pool looked fathomless in the moonlight, a trick of the black sand that covered its base. In fact it was little more than knee-deep. The surface was still except for tiny ripples spreading out from the spring's source in the face of the rocky hillside.

Drifts of steam rose from the water into the night, pale against the black boulders that surrounded the pool. Eliani piled her belongings on one of them and pulled off her boots, tunic, and legs, then stepped into the hot water with a hiss of pleasure.

Leaning her back against a rock whose edges had been worn smooth by ælven bodies over the centuries, she slid down until the water reached her chin. Her sigh was echoed by her companions as they entered the pool. She closed her eyes, enjoying the grittiness of the sand beneath her and the sharp pine scent of the woods.

Slowly her muscles yielded up their aches and stiffness to the water's heat. She rubbed her hands along her legs, then with a start sat up and pulled her arm from the pool, staring in dismay at the handfasting ribbon.

She had forgotten she was wearing it! Peering at it in the moonlight, she wondered if she had ruined it.

Luruthin had seen her reaction and drifted toward her across the pool. "It does not appear to have taken any harm."

Annoyed with herself, Eliani frowned as she squeezed the ribbon about her wrist. Though she could not see the colors well at night, the images seemed unchanged, and the trickle of water that ran across her fingers was clear. The ribbon still tingled slightly with khi, though the water inhibited her sense of it.

"Well, if it shrinks and my hand drops off by morning, we shall know."

Luruthin laughed softly. "I think Heléri's craft is better than that."

"I suppose they are not usually worn while bathing."

The ribbon still felt firm and secure on her arm. It was meant to come unbound once its wearer and her partner had arrived at their new home.

Spirits knew when that would be. Eliani felt a pang of loneliness and wondered if Turisan was still feasting. As he had not spoken to her or sent the strange calling he had shown her, she assumed that he was.

She submerged her chilled arm again. If water could harm the ribbon, the harm was already done.

She ducked her head underwater, reached for her soap, and rubbed some vigorously into her scalp, then offered the jar to the others. Their ablutions sent clusters of bubbles floating across the pool, eventually to slide out between two of the boulders and spill down the hillside with the escaping stream.

Vanorin leaned against the rocks, fair hair drifting about his shoulders in the water as he turned his head to look at Eliani. "Please tell me there are such springs all along the road we are to travel."

She chuckled. "Not as many as we would like, but there are a few. Gharinan, does Heahrued have a spring? I misremember."

"Not within a league of the village, alas."

Luruthin stirred the water before him with his hands.

"There is a very hot one near Althill, though it is reached by a bit of a climb."

Eliani grinned. "We shall see how badly we want it by the time we are there."

"We may have to make camp at that spring if Theyn Mirithan is feeling unfriendly."

Eliani sent a splash of water toward Luruthin's grinning face, then stood and moved closer to the spring's source, where the water was hottest, enjoying the momentary sting of the night air on her wet flesh before she sank back into the pool. She was aware that the males were watching, but their regard did not trouble her.

That was part of the Guardian's Reward, the chance to admire one another's flesh. She had often taken advantage of it during her years riding scout with the Guard and knew Gharinan's and Luruthin's forms well enough to tell them apart at a glance.

Vanorin she did not know. She looked his way and saw him avert his eyes. She smiled, letting her gaze linger on the strong, lean lines of his body, pale against the dark floor of the pool. He was her clan-brother, she thought, still surprised to remember that she was now a Greenglen.

Luruthin moved to join her, reaching his hands toward the place where the heat welled from deep within the mountain. "Ah. The best spot. You are willing to share it, cousin?"

"Of course."

"I did not wish to crowd you."

There was curiosity in his eyes, and the faintest shadow of something else—she could not read his khi here in the water. Perhaps he thought she had moved away so as to speak to Turisan. She moved a little to one side, allowing him a better share of the spring.

"You do not like Turisan, do you?"

Luruthin hesitated for an instant before answering. "How can I like or dislike him? I scarcely know him." He looked away, down at his hands in the water and spoke again in a lower voice. "If I had thought him unworthy of you, I would not have participated in your handfasting."

"My father obliged you to. I regret that; I would never have placed you in such a position—"

"Hush. Let it go, Eliani. I have." He looked up, smiling. "I am happy for you."

She frowned, concerned for him. He had never given up hoping to resume their past romance, she had recently learned, much to her chagrin.

"Truly?"

"Truly." His smile widened. "I have something to tell you."

"What?"

"I have sired a child."

Eliani gasped. "Luruthin!"

He shushed her with a gesture, chuckling as he glanced at the others. She lowered her voice.

"When?"

"The night of your handfasting!" He looked down again, still smiling. "I was not in the best of moods. A lady offered me consolation, and—well, we were both surprised. Both delighted."

"What lady?"

"Lady Jhinani."

Luruthin looked up at her, his expression a mixture of pride, humor, and a touch of chagrin. She felt a weight of worry fall from her and reached toward him without considering their unclad state. She hastily changed the offered embrace to a clasp of arms.

"Congratulations! What a blessing, cousin!"

He gripped her arm, soaked ribbon and all. "Thank you. I am still amazed."

"The child spoke to you?"

"Yes. I think that was the best moment of my life."

His voice and expression were so tender that Eliani felt a twinge of jealousy. She was glad for him, though, and infinitely relieved. Now he had someone to live for and cherish without reserve—a child, and Lady Jhinani as well.

"Do you think you may handfast?"

"I do not know. We did cup-bond before I left."

"Lady Jhinani is Governor Jharan's sister?"

"Kin-sister. Yes."

Eliani nodded, remembering now what her father had told her. Jhinani was sister to Jharan's lady, Turisan's mother, who had died bearing Jharan's second child. Sadly, the child had also perished.

A new thought occurred to Eliani, and she turned to Luruthin. "You should not go to Fireshore."

He smiled. "I discussed that with Jhinani. She felt I could best serve by going."

"You should be with her!"

"Eliani, we will be back by midwinter, spirits willing. If I had stayed, I would only have ended up at Midrange, serving in the defense. I would not be with her either way."

His words were gentle, but they fell heavily, reminding her of the dangers drawing nigh. She swallowed, thinking of what might happen if kobalen came through Midrange Pass in force before she returned from Fireshore. She had not wanted to acknowledge that this was possible. She drew a breath.

"Well, we shall have to bring you back swiftly, that is all."

Luruthin smiled, nodding agreement. Neither of

them voiced the thought Eliani suspected they shared—that he might yet serve at Midrange, as might they all. She shivered despite the warmth of the pool and leaned her head back, looking up at the stars and reaching for happier thoughts.

❧ Magehall ❧

"From the palace, my lord."

Rephanin accepted the folded note from Tivhari and returned to the work chamber, where Heléri and Valani had finished their cloaks and were placing them on the table. Valani smiled up at him, then looked disconcerted. Plainly she was trying to speak to him, but his leaving the chamber had broken their contact. She smiled again, as plainly hoping he would engage her in mindspeech. Instead he nodded.

"Thank you for your work."

She hid her disappointment with a jest. "I will soon become a night-bider at this pace."

"Keep to what is comfortable for you." Softening the dismissal with a smile, he stepped past her and opened his message.

Heléri spent a moment straightening the cloaks on the table, then came toward him. "An invitation?"

"More a summons, I think. It is from Jharan. Very brief and very formal. I wonder if he is displeased."

"What about?"

Rephanin glanced up and, seeing that Valani had left, smiled at Heléri. *Perhaps he dislikes my monopolizing one of his guests.*

He heard me offer to work with the circle. He

cannot object to that and has no claim on my time of rest.

Rephanin could not help smiling. *I was going to offer you refreshment, but I had better see what Jharan wants.*

Come to my chamber afterward.

Is that wise? Perhaps others have noticed the time we are spending together. Certainly our attendants have.

Heléri's smile lit a fire in his heart. *Misani is the soul of discretion, my dear friend, and I am sure Tivhari is of the same temper.*

True.

I will see you shortly. She started toward the door, then paused and looked back. *Valani is much taken with you.*

I know. More with the mindspeech, I think, than with myself.

Heléri gazed at him for a long moment, then softly smiled and left the chamber. Rephanin stood listening to her footsteps, wondering why she had brought up Valani. When he could no longer hear her, he glanced at the page in his hand and sighed.

"Tivhari, I am going across to the palace." He came out of the work chamber and closed the door.

"Yes, my lord. Do you wish for your cloak?"

She held it out to him, and he smiled, grateful for her anticipation. Thanking her, he donned it, drew up its hood to shield his face from the light, and went across the colonnade.

The sun was just rising, and Rephanin hastened to get under shelter before its full force struck the city. Hallowhall was too open to the daylight for his taste. He kept his hood up and his back to the windows as he entered the gallery outside the governor's chambers.

This long, airy room looked out on the fountain court through wide windows open to the colonnade and was filled with morning light despite its facing westward. Two attendants greeted Rephanin, one of whom went to apprise the governor of his arrival and a moment later returned to usher him in.

The governor's suite comprised a large outer chamber and two smaller rooms, one where records and correspondence were kept, the other a workroom. Much of the governor's business was conducted here, and the furnishings of the outer chamber—rich ornaments, heavy carved chairs with thick cushions, and many sconces blazing with light—reflected this. Rephanin paused a little way inside, gazing at a set of hanging tapestries that depicted the Midrange War. With a small shock he realized that he had never seen them before.

He had not entered this room in centuries—not since before Midrange, when Turon had occupied these chambers. For a moment the past swirled around him, memories and regrets haunting him.

"Thank you for your prompt response, Lord Rephanin."

Jharan's voice was quiet as he came forward from the doorway of the smallest chamber. He was dressed in a long tunic of pale green with silver embroidery at the throat and cuffs, wearing no other ornament than his circlet of state. Rephanin faced him, put back the hood of his cloak, and made a formal bow.

"How may I serve you, my lord governor?"

Jharan gazed at him for a moment, then turned aside, picking up a small wooden sculpture of a falcon from a table that stood behind a grouping of chairs. "How goes your work?"

Rephanin was certain that this could not be why Jha-ran had summoned him but answered respectfully. "Very well. We are now completing better than twenty cloaks a day and will soon be finished with what was provided to us. Berephan has weapons to bring us when we are ready for them."

Jharan nodded, still gazing at the falcon in his hands. "I hear you have begun to use mindspeech with your circle."

Rephanin blinked. "News travels swiftly."

"Is it starting all over again?"

Jharan's words were soft, but they froze Rephanin's heart for an instant. He closed his eyes briefly.

"Not if I can help it."

The governor put down the falcon and turned to gaze at him. "I had hoped for something more defi-nite, Rephanin."

A heaviness settled in Rephanin's heart. "I will not make you a promise I am not certain I can keep. That is the best faith I can give you."

Jharan walked a few steps toward the tapestries, frowning as if in thought. Rephanin wondered ex-actly how much the governor knew of the years be-fore the Midrange War, years when the magehall's reputation for magecraft had nearly been exceeded by its reputation for sensual excess. Jharan had been young then—a guardian, a minor connection of Governor Turon—uninvolved, or so Rephanin had thought. Now he was governor, and the face he turned toward Rephanin was stern.

"I left you in charge of the magehall after Midrange because of the quality of your work. That is the pur-pose of your circle, not your personal entertainment."

"I agree." Rephanin swallowed, misliking the

conversation's trend. "But mindspeech complicates that. It is very intimate and often becomes emotional. I cannot control the emotions of my circle—"

"Can you at least control your own?"

The edge in Jharan's voice sparked resentment. Rephanin paused before answering in a careful tone.

"I do not know. I wish I could assure you that I can."

Jharan leaned his hands against the table, flanked by elegant ornaments. "This is not an idle matter, Rephanin. We have mages coming here from other realms. They *must* be treated honorably."

"What is it that you want me to do? Renounce my gift?"

He was half-angry but also half-serious. Such a command from the governor would make his life simpler and safer, though he believed it would ultimately be a loss to his people.

"I have spent five centuries that way, Jharan. Heléri has convinced me it was wrong. In the past two days my circle has accomplished more—"

"I do not want you to renounce your gift. I want you to use it in a responsible manner!"

"I never intend otherwise."

"Why do I not believe you?"

Rephanin inhaled sharply. "You accuse me of deceit?" He stared at the governor, his anger rising. "If I gave you the promises you want, I would perhaps be guilty of that. Believe me, it gives me no joy to confess my failings to you."

Jharan's eyes were hard, and one finger tapped the polished wood beneath his hands. At last he withdrew the insult.

"I accept that your intentions are honorable. But I want more than that, Rephanin. I want some assurance—"

"I do not demand your trust."

"But I do!" Jharan slapped his hands against the table with a force that made Rephanin start, then rounded it and strode toward the magelord, his eyes blazing with anger. "I demand that I can trust you! My son came to you for advice! In the past he has always come to me. Always!"

Caught off guard by this shift, Rephanin took a step backward. "He wanted advice about mindspeech."

"And is that all you gave him?"

Their gazes met and held. Beyond the wrath radiating from Jharan's eyes, Rephanin sensed a trace of fear.

"I have not harmed your son, Jharan. I *will* not harm him."

The governor's lip curved in a mirthless smile. "Not if you can help it!"

Rephanin's anger flared. "Do you think me a fool? He is handfasted!"

"That did not stop you before!"

The words smote him like a physical blow, recalling all the worst memories of his life, memories he had tried to leave behind. He spun away, seeing a face he had tried to forget—young and fair—

Soshari.

Delighted with her first visit to the city, breathless with wonder and excitement, open to any adventure. Come to visit the magehall at the behest of some friend, who had not bothered to explain to her what magehall gatherings were like . . .

Rephanin took a few steps and blindly stumbled against a chair, caught at it, and gripped it with both hands, feeling sick. "I did not know she was handfasted."

Jharan pursued. "How could you not have known?"

A bitter laugh escaped him. "She did not tell me."

"Ah! So the blame lies with her!"

"No!"

Rephanin turned to face him, furious with grief though he managed to control his voice. "I accept the responsibility. Do not think I will ever forget it. Two are dead because of me."

Jharan stood silent, watching him. Rephanin looked away, unable to bear the accusation in those dark eyes.

"I did not think you knew."

A moment passed before Jharan answered. "Turon spoke of it."

Rephanin swallowed, then smiled wryly. "Turon. I think he would have cast me out had the Midrange War not . . . intervened."

"Had he survived, do you mean?" Jharan's voice was quiet. Rephanin heard him step closer and glanced up. The governor's anger was gone; now he merely looked weary. "His death was a great loss to us. His and all the others."

Behind Jharan, a tapestry of Skyruach depicted his younger self fighting the desperate defense of that place where so many had perished. Rephanin wondered how he could bear to be reminded of it every day.

Jharan sighed and ran a hand across his face as if warding off his own bad memories. He moved to one of the chairs, sat down, and gestured to Rephanin to join him.

"You gave good service during that war. I want to believe that you will always give good service, Rephanin."

"So do I." Rephanin sat across from him, feeling numb. "Talk to my circle if you wish, though I doubt that will reassure you. There is one among them who is already . . . showing a personal interest."

"Someone other than Heléri?"

Rephanin looked up sharply to meet Jharan's gaze but saw no censure there. "Heléri is a visitor. I do not count her among my circle." He sighed and spoke in a softer tone. "She is an old friend, Jharan."

The governor shook his head slightly, making a dismissive gesture. "I do not mean to intrude on your privacy. Only where does it end, Rephanin? Where does your privacy end and the good of your circle begin?"

The brown eyes he raised were filled with concern. Rephanin rubbed his forehead with one hand.

"I wish I could tell you. It would give me peace as well."

They sat together in silence for a moment, then Jharan spoke, almost in a whisper. "What did you say to Turisan?"

Rephanin drew a slow breath. "I made some suggestions to help him and his lady avoid being distracted by mindspeech."

"Distracted?"

"Distance speakers must agree on when and how to make contact, or they can distract each other at inopportune moments. Suppose Turisan was addressing the Council, and Eliani began speaking to him. It would jar him."

"Oh. I see."

Jharan looked troubled, and Rephanin's instinct prompted him to be more specific about his meeting with Turisan. If Jharan should question his son and learn that they had shared khi, he might well think Rephanin had tried to mislead him.

"I also showed him a technique for signaling a desire to make contact." He met Jharan's nonplussed gaze and continued carefully. "I used mindspeech to demonstrate for him, as I have lately done with the mage circle."

The fair eyebrows twitched together. "You spoke to him."

"Yes."

Jharan looked away and rested his chin against his clasped hands, frowning. Rephanin watched him for a moment, then spoke again, softly.

"Jharan, he is perhaps the one individual in Southfæld who is least in danger from me."

The governor closed his eyes. "Have I your word on that?"

"Yes. On that I will give you my word."

A wry smile touched Jharan's lips. "I should not be satisfied with that. I should hold the well-being of all as equally important."

Rephanin was silent, knowing he was seeing a side of Jharan few were shown. He was reminded of Jharan's installation as governor of Southfæld—a ceremony in which Rephanin had played a minor part—and the dread that had resounded through Jharan's khi at that time. The young governor-elect had been aghast at the authority to be placed in his hands, intimidated by the circle of officials and advisors seeking to influence him, and clearly overwhelmed by his new responsibilities.

Some echo of those feelings showed in Jharan's face now, though he had risen to every challenge, had restored Southfæld's prosperity and increased its security tenfold. It was no accident that Southfæld had the largest and best-equipped guard of any ælven realm.

"Well." Jharan inhaled deeply and sat up straight in his chair. "I suppose I must take your five centuries of self-imposed abstinence as a sign of good faith."

Rephanin made no answer. Jharan met his gaze.

"If it begins to get out of control . . . at least give me warning. Come to me, and I will help if I can."

"Agreed."

Rephanin nodded, though he was not sure what help Jharan could give. The smoothing of ruffled feathers, perhaps. He preferred not to envision the problems that might arise.

The governor rubbed a hand idly along the arm of his chair, staring at the floor. "I have a reputation for excessive formality, for a love of pomp and ceremony. It is in some ways undeserved." He frowned slightly in thought. "Perhaps excess is not necessarily wrong, as long as it causes no harm."

"It is my ardent wish to avoid causing harm."

Jharan met his gaze. "I see that. Hold to it, Rephanin."

The outer door opened, and an attendant looked in with an apologetic cough. "Your pardon, Lord Jharan. Governor Pashani is without."

"I will see her in a moment."

The door closed again, and Jharan turned to Rephanin with a sigh. "The day moves forward, and I am keeping you from your rest. Thank you for being open with me, Lord Rephanin."

"I am grateful for your understanding. Also for your forbearance."

Jharan regarded him for a moment, then gave a small nod, smiling slightly as he extended an arm. Rephanin could not remember when Jharan had last offered him this courtesy. He clasped arms, feeling a whisper of the governor's khi: controlled and vigilant, with a surprising underlay of gentleness and an echo that reminded him of Turisan.

The governor rose, and Rephanin did likewise. He made another formal bow, then turned and left the chamber, pulling up his hood as he reached the door.

Daylight smote him, and he felt inclined to retreat to the magehall at once. Heléri deserved greater courtesy, however, so he hastened up a broad flight of steps to the upper colonnade and sought her chambers. Her attendant admitted him to the comforting darkness of the outer room, where he stood still just inside the door, realizing how much tension had invaded his flesh.

Heléri came toward him with a smile. "Welcome, my friend." One dark brow rose slightly.

He met her gaze but could not bring himself to use mindspeech at that moment. He stood looking out at her from the depths of his hood, unwilling to forsake its shelter. Swallowing, he spoke slowly.

"Perhaps I should not stay. I doubt I am very good company just now."

Concern flitted through her eyes, but then she smiled. "Then come and sit by the fire a little while before you must go out into the day."

She moved toward the hearth, where a bed of coals glowed softly. After a moment he followed, sighing as he removed his cloak. Misani, the attendant, took it from his hands and exchanged a glance with Heléri.

Rephanin sat in one of the chairs—less ornate and more comfortable than those in the governor's suite—and gazed at the coals, feeling drained. A part of him was tense, waiting for questions, but Heléri raised none. She sat opposite him in companionable silence while her attendant brought forward a small table and placed it between them.

The attendant, a russet-haired Stonereach, was quiet and efficient as she set out tea, fruit, and fresh bread, then left the room. The door closed with a soft click of the latch, and silence descended.

Rephanin was still. He should speak, in voice or in thought, but felt disinclined to do it. He should eat, but his stomach rebelled at the idea. Jharan's anger and suspicion had troubled him, but it was more the knowledge that they were justified that weighed on him. He closed his eyes.

The past would not be repeated, not if he was vigilant. There would be no more salacious gatherings in the magehall, no explorations of arousal through mindspeech. The very thought made him sick at heart for what it had cost.

He would have only his circle to cope with, and the new circle that was forming, and the visitors when they arrived. Just a few mages, never all at once. He would speak to them in groups as seldom as possible, only when their work would plainly benefit by it. In this way he would avoid being swept away by their emotions. He would stand vigilant, and thus the mage circles' work would be worth the risk.

How ironic, when he considered that the greater part of his life had been spent reveling in just the sort of indulgences he now hoped to avoid. Doubly ironic, for beneath the heartache and regret, he still wanted them.

He drew a sharp breath and opened his eyes. Heléri remained unmoving in her chair, her eyes closed and her hands clasped lightly in her lap. Around her head and shoulders he again saw a soft light, faintly golden, glowing against the darkened room behind her. He watched for a moment, then broke the silence with a murmur.

"What are you doing?"

Heléri opened her eyes. "Praying for healing."

"For whom?"

A whisper of a smile touched her lips. "For you."

Rephanin's brow drew into a frown, and he rubbed at it with one hand. That she should pray for him thus made him uncomfortable.

"I am not wounded."

"No?"

The subject of healing teased at him; there was something he needed to say about it. He looked back at Heléri and saw that the golden light had faded.

"You studied healing at Hollirued, did you not?"

"Yes, for a short time. I practiced the art now and then after I removed to Alpinon. It has been useful."

The bothersome memory crystallized as Rephanin remembered his conversation with Turisan. He turned in his chair to face Heléri, watching her intently.

"Did you put a healing focus into the handfasting ribbon you made for Turisan and Eliani?"

She raised her eyebrows. "I put every blessing I could think of into that ribbon. They have a hard road before them."

"But a focus to enhance healing? Specifically?"

Heléri frowned in thought for a moment, then shook her head. "Not specifically."

Rephanin leaned toward her. "Eliani has performed a healing. Did Turisan tell you?"

"No!"

He repeated Turisan's description of how Eliani had healed the two wounded guardians. Heléri seemed as mystified as he. Her blue eyes widened as she listened.

"That child has never shown an interest in any craft calling for the manipulation of khi!"

"Could Turisan have been the source? He mentioned that he felt it."

She gazed thoughtfully at the coals on the hearth. "I do not think so. I will speak with him of this, for I must seek him out to give him messages for mages in Highstone. How extraordinary!"

"Extraordinary indeed." Remembering his prior mood, he looked at Heléri's face, faintly lit by the glow of the embers before her. "And your prayer seems to have worked. You have set me at ease without my being aware of it."

Heléri smiled, then turned to the table and picked up the ewer of tea. "Some for you?"

He nodded, watching her fill both cups, enjoying the tea's fragrance as it drifted toward him. Knowing his body needed food, he picked up a slice of bread and took a bite. It was sweet and tasted slightly of nuts.

They talked as they shared the meal, but only of innocuous subjects. He mentioned that a second mage circle was forming and asked if Heléri would help him oversee it.

"I would be glad to as long as Felisan remains here. When he departs, I must go with him."

Rephanin nodded, feeling a stab of unhappiness. He would miss her in a hundred ways when she left. Dismissing that pain to the future, he finished his tea and set the cup down.

"I should go."

Trouble brought a crease to her brow. He wanted to reach out and smooth it away. Instead he stood up and summoned a smile.

"Thank you. My mood is much improved, but I still do not wish to inflict it on you, hard as it is to forsake your company."

"We could both do with a little solitude, I suppose."

She smiled as she rose, but the trouble remained in her eyes as she reached up to touch his face. He caught her hand and leaned his cheek into it, then pressed a kiss against her fingers, a silent promise.

"I will see you at sunset."

"The Council meets this evening."

"I know. Once the circle has its work in hand, I will attend."

She nodded and went with him to the door, handing him his cloak. Grateful for her patient understanding, he turned to her once he had donned it.

Thank you, my friend.

The concern he had seen on her face instantly filled the air between them, abated by relief, tempered with solicitude. He was tempted to stay now, but he put up his hood and opened the door, flinching a little at the daylight.

Rephanin—

Not now, dear one.

Stepping out into the light, he shut the door, severing their brief contact. He paused, leaning against the door for a moment and closing his eyes. How weak he was to be so sorely tempted by one gentle touch. He would have to do better than that if he was to survive the coming test of his will.

◅ The Three Shades ▻

Luruthin pointed across the Asurindel's valley and down toward the foot of the triple waterfall, where the conic tips of three small stone pillars were just visible amid shrouds of drifting mist. "You can see the conces there, at the foot. They honor those for whom the falls are named."

"The Three Shades." The Greenglen turned to him, dark eyes lit with curiosity. "Who were they?"

"Three females who were handfasted to warriors killed in the Bitter Wars. Their names are forgotten, or at least I have never heard them."

"And they died there?"

"They watched there, and when their loves did not return . . ."

Vanorin drew his cloak closer to him. Though dawn was not far off, the night's chill clung to the mountains. "So now their shades haunt the place?"

"So it is believed. I used to haunt the place myself, hoping to see one."

Vanorin looked at him, raising an eyebrow. "And did you?"

"I might have, once."

Vanorin gazed at the falls again. "May we walk down and look at the conces?"

"If that is your will, though the falls have worn away whatever markings they bore. The water is relentless."

Vanorin nodded thoughtfully. "I would like to stand there."

They made their way down the road through Highstone and across the public circle, where the day's market was already beginning. Folk from nearby holdings were laying out their goods of carved wood and stone, berries and nuts. A few farmers had come up from the eastern plains with carts full of roots and onions.

Two of the onion growers, females, paused to watch Luruthin and Vanorin cross the circle. Vanorin smiled at them, then spoke under his breath.

"I am a curiosity here."

Luruthin nodded. "It was the same when Turisan was here. A Greenglen is an uncommon sight in Highstone."

"And a Stonereach is rare in Glenhallow. We have a little more diversity, perhaps, but Greenglen and its kin-clans make up most of Southfæld's people."

A grin crept onto Luruthin's face as he remembered the sea of fair heads at the first feast he had attended at Hallowhall. The Council delegates from other realms had been easy to discern.

"Well, there must have been a Greenglen or two among Stonereach's forebears. We are lighter in coloring than Ælvanen, though we began as their kin-clan."

Vanorin gave a laughing nod. "Perhaps some of those who went to settle Fireshore fell out in Alpinon along the journey."

Luruthin stopped walking, staring in astonishment at Vanorin, who halted and turned a questioning gaze at him, his smile fading. Was Clan Darkshore so casually spoken of in Southfæld? Had the Greenglen intended an insult by implying that traitors' blood ran through Clan Stonereach?

As if his thoughts had followed the same trend, Vanorin flung up a hand in defense. "I meant the new settlers, those who went to join Clan Sunriding after the Bitter Wars."

"Oh." Luruthin gave an embarrassed laugh as they both relaxed. "I do not know why I thought otherwise."

"We always mean Sunriding when we talk of those who left Southfæld for the north." A hint of bitterness sounded in Vanorin's tone.

Luruthin could understand his feeling. All ælven were bitter against the alben, but as it was Greenglen from whom Clan Darkshore had sprung, theirs was the greatest fury at Darkshore's violation of the creed.

They walked on in silence, leaving the city behind, and soon reached the bridge over the river Asurindel. Luruthin glanced at Vanorin to see if he took note of the bridge—made all of darkwood brought from Fireshore with considerable trouble. Darkwood resisted weathering far longer than any other wood and was coveted for works such as this bridge.

Vanorin seemed not to notice it, however. He stood gazing westward, listening to the muffled roar of the falls.

Luruthin crossed to the far side and waited for Vanorin at the narrow trail that led toward the Three Shades. As the Greenglen joined him, Luruthin cautioned him, here where they could still hear without shouting.

"Go carefully. The rocks around the falls are always wet and slick."

Vanorin nodded, and Luruthin led him up the trail. The sky was lightening to a jewel blue, cut by knife-edged dark cliffs above them. Before long they reached the last sharp ridge, beyond which were the falls. Luruthin paused to glance back at Vanorin.

The Greenglen raised his voice over the sound of the falls. "What a roar!"

Luruthin grinned. "Only wait."

He stepped around the edge and waited for Vanorin to join him, watching his expression of awe as the thunder of the Shades smote them both. Cold spray dashed their faces as billows of mist rose from the foot of the triple cascade, instantly painting their exposed skin with a layer of wetness.

Vanorin moved toward the conces, near the edge of the pool at the base of the falls. In the deep canyon it still seemed night, with dense mist obscuring the sky.

The three conces were grouped an armspan apart. Vanorin stood in their midst, closed his eyes, and stood motionless, as though reaching for the khi of the place. Having done this himself many times, Luruthin knew that the effort would be fruitless: The Shades overwhelmed any other power that might chance to be near. He doubted that Vanorin could even sense his khi so close to the falls.

He glanced at the pool, where he had once thought he saw a glimmer of a shade, then let his gaze trace the plummeting water back up to the clifftop. A drift of mist revealed a figure there, glowing white in the growing dawn. He caught his breath and squinted, trying to determine if the light was playing tricks on his vision.

Vanorin stirred, drawing Luruthin's attention. He called something, but his words were drowned in the water's roar. Luruthin pointed toward the cliff, and Vanorin looked up.

The pale figure was still there, standing motionless just by the head of the falls—a lady clad in a white gown that looked far too light for this season. Her dark hair spilled down her back beneath a veil of blue, and for a moment Luruthin thought she was Heléri, but she could not be; Heléri was yet in Glenhallow. Even as this thought passed through his mind, the figure moved, stepping calmly forward, off the cliff's edge.

She plummeted down, her gown whipping and rippling round her, the veil trailing as she disappeared into the roiling mist of the falls. Luruthin felt more than heard his own cry of horror.

Vanorin bounded toward the water. Luruthin caught his arm to hold him back.

Even at a distance from the churning foot of the falls, the pool was filled with currents of deadly strength. He had not thought to mention it because there was no question of anyone wanting to bathe in the frigid water of the Shades, certainly not at this season.

The Greenglen turned an angry, frightened face toward him. Luruthin leaned closer to shout an explanation, then paused, his gaze fixed on the pool where the white-gowned woman now drifted slowly and gently as if she lay in the hot spring far above them instead of the maelstrom at the foot of the Shades.

Vanorin's hand grasped at his arm as he also saw her. The two of them stood frozen, unable to look away from the lady in the water.

She floated on her back just beneath the pool's surface, her face fixed with a sadness that froze the heart. Luruthin felt as if the warmth was draining from his blood, leaving snowmelt to run in his veins.

A shade. She was a shade.

She seemed unmoved by the turbulent waters. Long

dark hair twined about her white fingers, her ice-blue eyes gazed skyward, and the gown glowed softly white though no glint of sun penetrated the mist. She drifted there briefly, then vanished, fading slowly into the black depths of the pool.

For one moment they were still, then Vanorin clutched convulsively at Luruthin's arm. The Greenglen's eyes were wide, his face nearly as white as the shade's gown.

Luruthin jerked his head toward the eastward path, and they scrambled to it, clinging together. Not until they had rounded the cliff's edge and gone down the trail a good way did they let go and stop to lean against the canyon walls.

They were still close enough that the Shades shook the earth beneath their feet. Even the cliffs seemed to tremble.

Vanorin coughed. "W-was that—?"

"A shade. One of the three."

Vanorin's expression was of mingled disbelief and accusation. "And you have seen this before?"

Luruthin shook his head. "No. Nothing like that. What I saw before—it must have been nothing."

He pushed away from the wall, running a hand through his damp hair. His fingers were shaking.

Vanorin sank to the ground with his back against the rock. Luruthin watched him for a moment, then staggered over and leaned a hand against the cliff.

"Come, it is too cold to stay here. Back to Highstone. The public lodge serves a good cup of mulled wine. You look as if you could do with some, and I know I could."

Vanorin nodded. Luruthin helped him to his feet, and they made their way back to the bridge.

Luruthin kept seeing the white-clad figure jump, again and again, and each time his heart contracted painfully. The roar of the falls, usually a welcome sound, now taunted him with memories of the pale lady drifting in the pool.

On the bridge, Vanorin paused. The Asurindel glided beneath them, nearly silent now. The Greenglen looked back toward the falls, though they were not visible from this place.

"Do—do many see this vision?"

Luruthin his head. "I have not heard anyone describe what we just saw. I do not think anyone living has seen it, or if they have, they did not speak of it."

"Why us?" Vanorin's voice was a hoarse whisper. "What can it mean?"

Luruthin looked upstream, dread riding on his heart as he watched mist billow above the cliffs. He swallowed and turned away, toward Highstone.

"Maybe nothing."

−

Rephanin arose, though he knew it was scarcely past midday. He had tried to meditate but found no peace. Too many memories had been awakened this day. He put on his cloak, paused to take a length of ribbon from a shelf in his chamber, and went out into the city.

His cloak, in which he had constructed a shielding focus that was several days in the making, had not often been tested so severely. By the time he had walked to the city gates, his eyes ached from the day's brightness despite its protection. He went on, though, passing both gates and walking along the road that led to the Silverwash.

On the plain outside the city walls, many guardians

were in training. He could hear the shouts of their
commanders and turned his gaze away from the bright
glint of light on their weapons.

Ahead was the first bridge over the Evrindel as it
flowed around Glenhallow on its way to join the Silverwash. He left the road before it crossed the bridge,
turning aside to walk down to the riverbank.

A solitary conce stood there, just outside the
shadow of the bridge. He recoiled a little on seeing it
despite having known what he would find. He had
never come here before.

Slowly he approached the monument. He had selected
the stone himself—contributed it anonymously—
and had even made himself watch while the mason
cleaved it in twain. One half had gone south to Cold
Crossing, to mark the place where Soshari's partner
had taken his life. The other stood here, bearing only
her name, carved into the broken face of the stone
with deep strokes like those she had used to open her
veins here on the riverbank.

Rephanin glanced up, looking above the brush on
the far bank where small birds argued over seeds and
long grasses stood dry and yellow, northeastward to
where the foothills faded into the plain. The river's
murmur could not fill that vast openness.

Soshari had chosen a pretty place to die. He wondered if the view had brought her any peace as she sat
here, letting her blood flow down into the water, her
khi drift away on the wind.

He looked at the conce again. Her family had
placed no words of commemoration on its surface,
no hint of her life or her crossing, save that which the
conce itself told—that she had died here, through violence, comfortless and alone.

He reached out a hand to the stone's pointed tip, hesitating briefly before touching it. There was nothing of Soshari in it, of course, but he thought he sensed an echo of her family's grief. They had mourned here, though as far as he knew they then had returned home and made no pilgrimages to keep their grief alive.

He drew the ribbon he had brought with him from his sleeve—a length of white with a single thread of gold—remembrance from an Ælvanen, a foreigner. He looped it around the conce and through itself, letting the ends fall free to stir in the restless breeze.

"It shall not happen again." Though alone, he whispered, uncertain whether it was a promise or a plea.

The river drew him, and he stepped forward to crouch at its edge, peering at the grasses and reeds, watching the water's endless progress. Pushing aside a fear of what he might find, he slowly opened his awareness to the khi of the place. He sensed only the small urgencies of creatures hurrying about their lives, readying themselves by instinct for winter's trial. The clay beneath him had long since been washed clean of Soshari's blood.

He breathed relief. He had half feared, through the centuries, that a shade might have formed here and had kept an ear to the city's tavern gossip for any tale of such an apparition. None had surfaced, and having now seen this place, he felt confident no shade existed.

Soshari had not been troubled by unresolved problems, only by the unresolvable mortification of having broken her handfasting vow. Death had been her solution to a life irretrievably damaged, honor lost and unrecoverable. No ælven pledge could be recanted in good faith, but the vow of handfasting was the most sacred. She had broken it, and though the fault had not truly been hers, she had chosen the customary atonement.

Rephanin closed his eyes. Davharin's assurance that those in spirit were present with those in flesh prompted him to address the soul that had walked as Soshari.

I will not forget.

No answer came. He had expected none. She had scarcely known him; why should she make any extraordinary effort to speak to him? Perhaps she could not do so even if she wished to.

The irony of his responsibility for her death was that he had not himself touched her, not until he had understood her situation and removed her from the magehall, taking her at once to the healing hall. By then, of course, it had been too late.

His only comfort—a small one, at best—was that few knew of Soshari's suicide. He had spent several days in agonized suspense, wondering if any who had been at the magehall that evening would deduce what had happened, if more deaths would follow as others realized their roles in Soshari's doom.

That had not occurred, and he was grateful to Aliari, mistress of the healing hall, for her discretion. Turon had been told, and word had been sent to Soshari's kin in Cold Crossing, but few others had known—and then the war had come.

Rephanin rested his chin on his knees. Saved by a war, an ignoble preservation. With another war looming, he was prey to uncomfortable reflections.

He was far from alone in this. Many were frightened without understanding what they feared, including a fair number of the newly recruited guardians.

He glanced toward the plain where they practiced,

the rumble of their footfalls now intruding on his thoughts. Most were younger than he and had never faced a war. He did not envy them. Their courage, however born of inexperience, humbled him.

❧

Turisan stood and addressed the Council in formal tones. "The latest word from Midrange is that there are now more than three thousand kobalen massed beyond the pass. I ask for the honor of organizing an advance force and leading it to occupy High Holding."

He looked at his father as he spoke, expecting resistance. The rest of the Council fell silent.

"You cannot command High Holding." Jharan's voice was quiet. "You are needed here."

"I will return once the garrison is established."

Turisan met his father's gaze, and what he saw was rather more complex than flat denial. He did not understand all the tones in Jharan's expression, but he thought pride—pride in him, his son—was among them.

Jharan turned to Ehranan. "How many guardians would you recommend?"

"To occupy High Holding? A company of a hundred at the least. Better four or five."

Lord Berephan, who at Turisan's urging had come to the Council session to support his request, pressed his lips together. "We do not have that many ready to march."

Jharan turned to him. "Can three companies be spared?"

Southfæld's commander nodded. "If a third or a half may be recruits."

"Half."

Jharan looked back at Turisan, eyes challenging.

Turisan was too astonished that his father now seemed willing to let him leave Glenhallow to resent the terms.

"Agreed."

Jharan's mouth curved slightly upward. An attendant stepped toward him, murmuring words Turisan did not hear, for his growing excitement distracted him. He was going to Midrange!

An advance force that was half raw recruits. He would have to continue their training on the journey north and make certain he left them in the hands of a competent commander at High Holding.

Jharan looked up at the Council. "Gentles, evening has fallen, and refreshment awaits. Let us pause for now."

The chime was sounded, and the councillors rose, eagerly seeking the promised repast. Turisan hastened around the table to Berephan.

"A word with you, Lord Berephan?"

Berephan smiled and nodded toward the colonnade. Turisan followed him out of the chamber and into the evening's chill.

A bright sky shone above the mountains, glowing blue with twilight, pierced by one gleaming star. The warden lounged against a tree-carved pillar on the balustrade, regarding Turisan with a bemused expression.

"Was I too bold?"

"No, but you have set yourself a hard task."

"My father has not made it easier."

"No. He sensed your purpose."

Turisan looked at him sharply. The Guard commander smiled.

"Why do you think he asked Ehranan how many guards to put into the garrison? Jharan *built* High

Holding; he was the first to occupy it. He needed no advice, but he honored Ehranan by asking it. He honors you by making demands of you. Jharan knows you wish to prove yourself."

"Will you advise me?"

"Of course. Come to my house in the morning—break your fast with me, if you wish—then we will assemble the Guard on the plain and you may select your three hundred."

"Thank you, I will. I—"

Approaching footsteps stayed Turisan from continuing. He turned to see Rephanin coming toward them along the colonnade, cloaked in dark gold, his black hair spilling across his shoulders. The magelord slowed as he neared them and nodded in greeting.

Berephan returned the nod. "Lord Rephanin. I scarce expected to see you today."

A flicker of emotion crossed the magelord's face, gone before Turisan could identify it. "I fear I must have missed most of the session."

The warden laughed and nodded toward Turisan. "You missed our young lord's bid for glory! He is off for High Holding and will suffer no more of the Council's tedium."

Rephanin raised an eyebrow. "So the occupation of High Holding has been authorized? Good news."

Turisan gave a soft laugh. "If I can pull three raw companies together."

"Half raw, not fully raw." Berephan chuckled. "You will manage. All you must do is command their attention, and I doubt our valiant mindspeaker will have trouble doing that."

Turisan's eyes met Rephanin's, an idea striking him. He held the magelord's gaze, sensing the powerful khi behind the gray eyes, and spoke quietly.

"If I had your skill, I could easily claim the attention of my guardians."

Rephanin's eyes narrowed. He held silent, watchful. Turisan continued quietly, though he could not wholly suppress his excitement.

"It would draw them together, give them a common ground, a bond that could otherwise take days to form. Rephanin, would you be willing to come to the training ground tomorrow morning and speak to my recruits?"

Rephanin frowned. Turisan saw Berephan shift restlessly, but he kept his attention on the magelord, hastening to elaborate upon his idea.

"A short message—a welcome, perhaps a statement of our task."

Rephanin raised his chin. "I have recently had to explain to some fifty magehall candidates that mindspeech is not an idle pursuit." His voice was temperate, but Turisan sensed his frustration.

"My purpose is not idle. This will help me focus them and help them understand the nature of mindspeech. Is that not an aim of yours?"

Rephanin paused, and when he did answer, his voice was low. "It is."

Berephan stepped away from the balustrade. "Well, if I want anything to eat, I had best go in. I will see you anon, my lords."

He strode into the palace without waiting for an answer. Turisan glanced after him, wondering at his abrupt departure, then turned back to Rephanin.

"Please consider this."

A curious smile touched the magelord's lips. He seemed to relax, and something like excitement shone out suddenly in his face.

"I need no time for consideration. If I can be of help

to you, I am happy to serve, but I think it would be best if you spoke to them yourself."

Turisan laughed softly. "Would that I could."

"You can. Through me."

Astonished, Turisan stared at him. Rephanin's smile widened.

"I have not tried this with—with very large groups, but as long as your message is for everyone present, it should not be difficult."

Turisan blinked, amazed. "I did not know it was possible! I can speak to others through you?"

"As long as we are all together."

Turisan inhaled deeply. "Thank you!"

He held out an arm. Rephanin hesitated to clasp it. His dark brows drew together, and he shook his head, one hand rising briefly as if to ward away the gesture.

"We should go in."

He turned and went into the palace with much the same haste Berephan had shown. Turisan watched him go, puzzled that Rephanin would so generously agree to his request—even better it as he had done—and then would not take his arm. Something more than what had been said lay between them.

⦥

Rephanin excused himself from the rest of the Council session, pleading the need for his presence in the magchall. He was far more comfortable there despite the potential complications of using mindspeech with his circle.

Heléri did not join the circle that evening. Rephanin hid his disappointment and spent the night concentrating on his work, completing the focus in a fourth cloak just as the dawn was breaking.

Setting the cloak in the stack of finished work, he left

the chamber, nerving himself to don his own cloak and face another day. He was ready to rest, but he had pledged to speak to Turisan's recruits this morning.

He entered his private chambers, permitting himself a small sigh of weariness as he closed the door. Looking toward the hearth, where Tivhari would have left him a meal, he was startled to see Heléri sitting there, quietly awaiting him. A wistful smile crossed her lips as he sat down beside her.

"Felisan is preparing to return to Highstone."

Rephanin froze, heart going numb. "When do you leave?"

"Tomorrow morning."

He closed his eyes. He had known this was coming, but knowing did not ease the pain.

"I shall miss you."

"And I you."

Silence enveloped them, filled with memories, some ancient, many new. Rephanin felt the return of emptiness looming before him. He shook his head.

"You were never mine."

"Never and always."

He met her gaze, and her soft smile seemed both warm and sad at once. He was tempted to reach for her in thought to learn her meaning, but he hesitated. It would make parting all the more grievous.

A moment passed, then she reached a hand out and laid it over the back of his. The warmth of her khi sent shivers through him. When she spoke, it was almost in a whisper.

"You always seemed to know how fascinating you were, so I never told you I found you so as well. From the very first."

Her words rang in his soul, carrying him back to Hollirued, where she had not paid him the homage he had expected and he had hence dismissed her. He closed his eyes.

"I was the greatest fool walking."

"You knew your path."

He laughed softly and turned his hand to clasp hers, yielding to her touch, knowing he would also yield to her wishes. She alone could command him, and she did so by demanding nothing.

My heart.

Oh, thank you, love. I worry so when you will not speak to me.

I am trying to learn discipline. So far I have fared rather poorly.

Discipline?

He hesitated, guarding his feelings from her, not wishing to explain in full. He chose what to tell her carefully—truth, but not all the truth.

I wasted much time in Hollirued and caused pain where it was not deserved. I have done the same here—spent centuries treating mindspeech as a game. I must never use it so idly again. We face war, and our gifts must go to serve our people.

A flicker of remembrance passed through him, gone before he could grasp it. Something to do with the war—it had almost felt as if Davharin were the source of the thought.

So you are doing. Heléri's expression was earnest. *You have enhanced your circle's understanding tenfold—*

And endangered one heart among them, at least. He smiled ruefully. *Fascination, you called it. It is the mindspeech that fascinates, not me, but I become the focus for it. I must not be tempted to take advantage of that.*

Valani is not so weak as to be hurt.

No? Yet I dare not risk hurting her and losing her service to the circle. She is a gifted mage.

Heléri took his other hand, holding both tightly. *You are too strict toward yourself.*

He could only laugh. "No." He raised her hands to his lips, one after the other.

I want to ask when I will see you again. I know there is no answer.

Come to Alpinon.

He felt his heart lift at the words, though he doubted he would soon be at liberty to leave Glenhallow. He sensed that she knew this as well, yet he answered.

I will.

He looked up at her, smiling, then remembered Turisan and the Guard. "I have an obligation this morning."

Heléri dropped her gaze to their hands. He squeezed her fingers to reassure her.

It will not take long. Please stay.

Her smile as she looked up caught at his heart. He stood and lifted her from her chair into his arms, kissing her passionately, then at last drawing back. As he did so, a powerful warmth—unmistakably Davharin's—flooded his awareness.

Remember.

Still clasping Heléri's arms, Rephanin swayed slightly, disoriented by the spirit's sudden presence. *Yes, Davharin?*

Remember your path. The search will be worthwhile.

As suddenly as he had arrived, Davharin withdrew. Rephanin saw Heléri watching him with concern in her eyes.

Do you know what he meant?

Rephanin was about to shake his head, when suddenly he did know—the guardians. Three hundred guardians he had never met, might never meet again. He was pledged to speak to them already. What difference would a small assayance make? He might find a mindspeaker among them. His heart beat a bit faster.

Yes, I know what he meant. Rephanin smiled and kissed Heléri's brow. *He was wishing me luck.*

⚘

Eliani was trying to cram an extra tunic into her saddle packs when an insistent knocking sounded on her chamber door. She glanced toward her window, where the predawn light was creeping in around the tapestry, and went to answer.

Luruthin and Vanorin stood outside. A faint scent of mulled wine accompanied them.

She grinned. "Did the lodge keeper chase you out? You were not singing, were you, Luruthin?"

Luruthin shook his head, and Vanorin dropped his gaze. Her jest unsuccessful, Eliani felt a jab of concern. She opened the door wider.

"Come in. What is wrong?"

The two males exchanged a somber glance. Eliani pulled chairs away from her table for her guests and sat across from them on her bed.

Luruthin cleared his throat. "We went to the Three Shades."

She nodded. It was common to share the falls with visitors, and Vanorin had expressed interest.

"We saw a shade."

Luruthin's voice dropped to a whisper on the words, and his face paled. Remembering her own fear at seeing a shade beside the waterfall not long since, Eliani bit back the teasing remark that rose to her lips and answered gently.

"You had seen one before, I recall."

"Not like this."

She listened as he described the apparition they both had seen. It sounded horrifying, much more so than the shade she had seen, which had only stood at the foot of the falls and then walked across the pool. Vanorin added little to what Luruthin said; he seemed stunned.

"I know we must depart today, but—Eliani, would you send a message to Heléri for us, asking her advice? She might know what it means."

"Of course. Give me a moment to contact Turisan."

She drew her legs up beneath her and closed her eyes, sending the signal of warmth to Turisan's brow. It took some concentration, for she was not yet practiced, but he answered.

Yes, love? I am going to the training field—

Could you visit Heléri on the way? Luruthin and Vanorin wish to ask her advice.

Very well.

She explained about the shade as he made his way to Heléri's chambers and waited while he knocked on the chamber door. A moment later he spoke.

Heléri's attendant informs me she is not here.

Not there? Is the Council in session?

Not until midday. I can try to see her then.

Yes, please do. Thank you, love.

Turisan gave her a warm farewell, then their contact faded as both released it. Eliani opened her eyes.

"I am sorry, Heléri is not in her chamber. Turisan will try again later in the day."

Luruthin looked disappointed but nodded. She wanted to catch him in a hug but refrained, only touching his arm.

"Luruthin? It was just a shade. They cannot harm us."

He gave a fleeting smile and nodded before rising to go. Eliani caught up her cloak and followed him and Vanorin out, knowing that they shared an unspoken thought.

Shades were considered portents of ill. The appearance of this one was not auspicious for Eliani's journey.

❧ Glenhallow ❧

Turisan gazed at the guardians assembled east of the city, standing mutely with their backs to a brisk breeze off the plains. The fifty he had seen only a few days ago had been joined by hundreds more. Six companies stood there, as well as a rabble of unattached recruits so fresh that they had difficulty holding still.

Berephan shifted in his saddle and gestured toward the rabble. "Those are the newest. Have your pick of them or take the whole lot."

Turisan raised a hand to shade his eyes against the morning sun. "If I take a hundred and fifty of them, may I fill out my companies with experienced guardians?"

"As long as you understand that 'experienced' in this case means those who have been training these few days. The seasoned guardians are scattered among all the companies, and I cannot let you have a hundred and fifty of those. Fifty, perhaps—enough to command your patrols."

"I will need a capable commander to leave with them at High Holding. May I take Dirovon?"

"If he is willing."

None of the newest recruits had a guardian's cloak

yet. Some stood shivering in the morning's chill with no cloaks at all.

"One hundred and fifty of these, then, and I ask that all the remaining cloaks in the city be held for my companies until they are all equipped."

"Done." Berephan's gaze shifted, and he frowned. "Your magelord is arrived."

Turisan turned to see a figure on foot approaching from the city. The hood of the cloak was drawn well forward, but by its golden color he knew it was Rephanin's.

"You are displeased?"

"I do not see what benefit it will yield. Such mysteries belong to the magehall, not to us."

"They belong to me, also."

Turisan spoke quietly, but Berephan's head snapped toward him, and he saw to his surprise that the warden was afraid. It had not occurred to him that a soul of Berephan's experience—six centuries and more a guardian—could be frightened of mindspeech. Rephanin was right; mindspeech was sorely misunderstood, and that must be corrected.

Turisan dismounted and strode out to meet the magelord. They turned to walk back, the early sun bright in their faces.

"Greetings, Rephanin. Thank you for coming."

"Forgive my late arrival. Which of the guardians are yours?"

"Some hundred and fifty of these." Turisan gestured toward the recruits. "The rest will come from the established companies."

"Let me speak to them."

Turisan could just see the glint of Rephanin's eyes in the shadow of the golden hood. The air between them tingled with khi, and Rephanin's voice was low and intense.

"I have never tried to speak to so many at once. Let me address them, call for your volunteers, and we will know by the response whether they have all heard."

"Very well."

The magelord turned to the assembled guardians. Turisan gazed at them as well, wondering which of them would be willing to go with him. High Holding was not an enviable post.

If any . . . hear . . . now.

Turisan glanced sharply at Rephanin. He had heard a whisper, the words mostly indistinguishable.

Rephanin seemed not to notice his reaction. He spoke again, slightly louder than before.

If any of you can hear me, answer now.

Frowning, Turisan looked back at the guardians. Why this request instead of the call for volunteers? He had scarcely heard the message himself, so faintly had it been given, and he stood immediately beside Rephanin.

No response came from the guardians. The magelord's shoulders dropped slightly, then he drew himself up.

Greetings, guardians of Southfæld.

This time Rephanin's voice was strong, and the Guard's reaction was immediate. A shiver seemed to pass through the ranks—all of them, even the farthest—accompanied by a murmur of wonder and fright.

I am Rephanin, master of the magehall in Glenhallow. I have been asked by Lord Turisan to assist him in addressing you. Pray give him your attention.

Rephanin turned toward him, and Turisan realized he was being invited to speak. Swallowing sudden nervousness, he looked at the guardians.

I am Turisan of Jharanin—

As he spoke, he became conscious of the khi of hundreds of listeners and caught his breath. The sensation was muted—perhaps because Rephanin stood between him and his audience—but palpable nonetheless. He continued.

Today I am forming an advance to occupy High Holding. I will take one hundred fifty from the new recruits, another hundred and fifty from the established companies. All who are willing, step forward.

For a long moment no one moved, and Turisan felt an awful dread that none of the guardians would voluntarily join his advance. Perhaps he had judged wrongly. Perhaps the mindspeech had frightened them off.

A guardian from the company nearest him—serious and bright-eyed, a seasoned campaigner by the dust ground into his boots—took a step forward, gazing steadily at Turisan. Another joined him, then several more.

The ranks sprang alive with movement, and Turisan watched in growing wonder as nearly every guardian present stepped up to volunteer. He looked to Berephan. The warden gazed back at him from the saddle, his expression unreadable.

"Well, make your choice of them."

Turisan glanced at Rephanin. The magelord nodded.

I will wait.

Smiling his thanks, Turisan hastened to his horse, mounted, and rode along the ranks, selecting guardians. He made sure to include the one who had been first to volunteer.

Dirovon, mounted on an elderly mare whose head was lowered in a manner expressive of stoic endurance, waited at the head of a company in the rear of the assembly, one that had come from the camps in the foothills. Turisan smiled as he came abreast of his old friend. "I need a commander for the advance. Do you wish for the honor?"

"The honor of freezing my soul on the plains before Midrange?" Dirovon laughed. "Well, it is better than freezing out here. Aye, I will have it, but only for the sake of your companionship."

"A poor reason to accept. My companionship will not be yours for long, as I must return to Glenhallow once you are established at High Holding."

"Why, then, I accept because I tremble before you, Mindspeaker!"

Turisan grimaced, but Dirovon's grin set him at ease. The captain handed his pennanted spear to his second and, leaving his company under her command, rode with Turisan back to where the new companies stood gathered in rough ranks, some still making their way forward.

Leaving Dirovon to organize them, Turisan returned to Berephan and made a formal bow from the saddle. "Thank you, Lord Berephan. With your approval, I have chosen my guardians."

The warden looked at him long, in silence. Turisan sensed his discomfort but could not tell whether he was angry. He waited, and at last Berephan moved, nudging his horse toward the force that Dirovon was cajoling into order.

"You did not tell me what you meant to do."

Turisan followed. "Did I not? I thought you had been present last night when I talked with Rephanin."

"About his speaking to your companies, not the whole Guard. And I did not know you meant to speak to them as well."

"If I have erred, I crave your pardon."

Berephan's brow creased in a frown. "I do not know whether you have erred."

Berephan turned and summoned his herald with a gesture. The musician raised a silver-chased ram's horn to his lips and blew the signal for dismissal. The Guard began filing away, back toward the training grounds to the east.

Turisan returned to where Rephanin stood and dismounted. "Many thanks, Rephanin. You have been a great help. May I offer you my horse to speed your return?"

Rephanin started to shake his head, then hesitated. "I—yes, if it is not a great inconvenience."

"None at all. I will have my hands full here all the morning."

Turisan offered the reins to Rephanin. "Give him over to the palace stable hands and ask them to send him back out to me."

Rephanin took the reins. "Thank you. I am *most* grateful!"

Turisan laughed. "You could command a much better reward."

"At this moment, you could give me no better."

Rephanin mounted the horse, and Turisan thought he glimpsed fire in the gray eyes hidden within the hood's shadow. Almost before Turisan could raise a hand in farewell, the magelord was off toward the city gates. Turisan watched him go, then turned to the shaping of his raw command.

◈

Rephanin lay in Heléri's bed, his fingers entwined with hers, his soul steeped in her essence, from the scent of her body to the lambent glow of her khi. At dawn she had invited him to join her for a meal in her guest chambers at Hallowhall, and the rest had followed, to his great delight. He half suspected that Davharin had suggested the invitation. Heléri's partner in spirit had joined their lovemaking again; Rephanin still sensed him, though distantly.

Davharin?

A suggestion of attentiveness washed through the peaceful drifting of his thoughts. Rephanin moved a little nearer to alertness, recalling a question that had been in his mind earlier but that he had not dared to voice.

Do you know what is in our future?

Rephanin sensed the contraction of khi that he now knew was Davharin's focusing in order to use language, more necessary for the discussion of abstractions than of matters that could be expressed in symbol. He was becoming accustomed to Davharin's methods of communication and thought the spirit showed an increased ease with language.

Nothing is certain. Davharin's voice was no longer overwhelming, though Rephanin suspected controlling it thus required considerable concentration on Davharin's part. *Paths are planned but may change.*

Rephanin swallowed disappointment. *Can you give us no help? What of the kobalen—will we defeat them?*

I cannot tell you. We do help you in many ways. We are always near you, though you do not normally perceive us.

Heléri stirred, shifting her position slightly, then sighed. She offered no comment, though Rephanin had a fleeting sense that she and Davharin had discussed these questions many times.

I confess I had hoped for a more informative answer.

A warm wave of sympathy came from Davharin. *The future is fluid, and its course can easily shift. If I*

*were to define answers to your questions, they could
be false by the time the events took shape. They could
actually mislead you and cause you to alter your path
for the worse.*

I fear I do not understand.

*Yes. I have also tried to explain to Heléri, but the
concept does not translate well.*

Rephanin turned his head to gaze at the beauty beside him, dark and pale, elusive yet unbending as stone
when she chose. He delighted in her company and had
found deep satisfaction—even healing—in their intimacy, but he knew their paths ultimately lay apart. She
belonged to Alpinon, her lord's realm. She had pledged
herself to it when she had handfasted with Davharin
and would return there when the Council was ended.
Rephanin's work, however, was here.

*Davharin, can you tell me if I will find a distance
partner?*

That would not serve you.

So you do know!

Rephanin pressed his eyes shut, swallowing impatience. Perhaps the spirit realm's guidance should not
be spent on his own selfish interests.

Davharin's voice came to him gently, almost a whisper. *I know only one thing for certain: Your search
will be worth the effort.*

Rephanin's eyes flickered open. A chill of hope
washed through him, stealing his breath. Abruptly he
sensed the spirit's retreat. The conversation was ended.
He closed his eyes again with a sigh.

Thank you, Davharin.

A shimmer went through the khi in the chamber, a
moment's effervescence, swiftly gone. Rephanin recognized it as the spirit's form of a smile.

Turisan worked the new companies until sundown, then returned to Hallowhall. Learning that the Council had dispersed, he sought his father's private chambers, far less elaborate and far more comfortable than the governor's public chambers. There he found Jharan enjoying a light meal with Lord Felisan, which they at once invited him to share.

Jharan passed him a plate of cheeses. "The feast of leave-taking will be in the morning. I hope you will attend."

"Leave-taking?"

Felisan sighed, a glint of laughter in his eyes belying his sorrowful tone. "Yes. It is time for me to return to Highstone, though it wrings my heart to go. Such good company, such excellent wine."

He held out his empty goblet to Jharan, who reached for an ewer. "Mayhap the three barrels you take with you will be of some comfort."

"Mayhap." Felisan's smile widened as he sipped.

Jharan filled a cup for Turisan as well. "The Council concluded today."

Turisan felt suddenly breathless. With the Council ended, the war seemed closer, a reality, not a mere theory.

"Forgive me for being absent."

"No need. Several were absent. But do come to the leave-taking if you are able."

"Of course." Turisan looked to Felisan. "Do all of Alpinon's delegation go with you?"

"Aye. Pashani and hers are leaving as well. She is anxious to return to the Steppes." He glanced at Jharan, raising an eyebrow. "We have not so much concluded as recessed. We will convene again in Highstone on the first of spring. By then we shall have much more to discuss, I warrant."

Turisan's heart clenched. Eliani would have returned by then. Would he join her in Highstone for Midwinter?

Thinking of her reminded him of the request she had made that morning, that he visit Heléri. He swallowed the rest of his wine in two gulps, evoking a frown of disapproval from Felisan.

"I have just remembered an errand. Will you excuse me?"

Jharan nodded, pushing a plate of food into his hands as he stood. "Eat something. We will see you in the morning."

Turisan walked to the guest suite that housed Alpinon's delegation, nibbling nuts and dried fruit along the way. He reached Heléri's door and knocked softly.

Heléri smiled as she opened the door. "Lord Turisan. I am glad you chose to visit before I depart."

"I am glad for the chance to visit, but in truth I am sent here. My lady has a message for you."

Heléri looked politely curious and invited him to join her by the hearth. With a gesture she offered a nearby tray holding goblets and wine. Turisan shook his head, setting down the plate he had brought. Heléri leaned back in her chair and folded her hands.

"What is the message?"

"Allow me a moment."

He closed his eyes, sending a signal to Eliani. She responded at once.

Greetings, love. We have just made camp.

I am with Heléri. She is ready for your message.

Very well. Let me find Luruthin.

A pause followed. When Eliani spoke again, her khi betrayed a hint of strain.

Do you remember the Three Shades?

Turisan smiled. *I could not soon forget.*

Luruthin and Vanorin claim they saw a shade there this morning.

He opened his eyes. *A shade?*

They believe so.

Turisan looked at Heléri, whose brow grew creased with concern as she watched him. He licked his lips.

"A shade appeared at the falls near Highstone."

He explained fully to her, passing along the details given to him by Eliani. As he did so, he felt a growing unease, which had to be at least in part from Eliani. He had no reason to fear the falls and had never seen a shade.

Heléri listened in silence, the trouble in her face diminishing. When Turisan had conveyed the entire account, she gazed into the fire and softly sighed.

"It must have been Josæli. Ghivahri did not leap."

Her tone was conversational and held no amazement at the subject of the apparition. Turisan gazed at her in surprise.

"Can you have known them?"

"No." She smiled sadly and glanced up at him. "Though my lord did. He shared their story with me. A sad tale."

"What does it mean?"

Heléri sighed, frowning slightly. "I cannot say. I believe the shades are aroused by great agitations of khi."

"Then they are an ill foretoken?"

"I would not say 'ill.' Shades have no awareness; they are mere echoes. They cannot judge but only respond, and only in their limited way." Heléri leaned toward him, laying a hand feather-light upon his wrist. "This visitation tells us what we already knew—that great movements are under way. Please tell Eliani there is no cause for alarm. The shades are harmless, though their appearance can be troubling."

Turisan nodded and closed his eyes to pass the message to his lady. She responded wryly.

Troubling is not how I would have put it. Luruthin is upset—I know his moods—and so is Vanorin. Love, will you ask Heléri if the shades ever appear away from the falls?

Heléri shook her head when the query was put to her. "I have never heard of their doing so."

A scratching at the door forestalled Turisan's response. Heléri rose and walked swiftly to it.

She says no, love, and someone has arrived now. Wait until I call to you.

Heléri returned with Rephanin. Turisan hastily stood. He was aware that the magelord and Heléri had been much in company of late. He bowed and made as if to leave.

"Rephanin. Good evening."

"Forgive my interruption."

"No, no. I am here only to deliver a message, and that is done."

He glanced from the magelord, who seemed restive, to Heléri, whose face betrayed nothing of her thoughts. Feeling his own presence was unwanted, he turned to Heléri.

"Thank you for your counsel, my lady. I will bid you both good night."

She smiled and saw him out. He stepped outside into the chill dark of the colonnade and glanced back as she closed the door, catching a glimpse of Rephanin, whose eyes were suddenly afire as he looked at Heléri.

Turisan felt a similar fire within himself despite the

cold and darkness. Following the whisper of the fountains, he walked to the balustrade and leaned against it, closing his eyes.

My love? I miss you.

Eliani's answer was wordless and strong. He let the feeling wash over him for a time, then bestirred himself, looking down at the fountain court. The moonlight was feeble and troubled by clouds. The fountains were restless, pale shadows in the night.

Are Luruthin and Vanorin at all comforted?

A little, I think. They have retired, and I am about to do so as well.

Show me where you are.

Turisan shut his eyes and let her take his senses. After a moment he perceived the flicker of a campfire, the resinous smell of pine. He sighed, wishing he were there with his lady.

Now where are you?

He showed her the night sky and the fountain court below, dizzy for a breathless moment as his sense of place shifted. He felt her momentary flash of fear in response.

Cold.

Yes.

Does a fire await you in the Star Tower?

He smiled. *I am certain it does.*

Why do you wait, then?

Without another word he left the balustrade and started for the stairs to what had become his private chamber. Eliani's wordless urging spurred him on, promising a night in her heart's embrace, which was second only to that of heart and flesh together.

◈ Westerlands ◈

Shalár walked across a meadow, the army strung out behind her. Their pace was no longer brisk.

She quested through the sparse woodlands ahead, seeking sign of kobalen, but found none. This terrain was not the sort where the creatures were likely to stop. It would be another day or two, if not more, before the army found kobalen again. They would last, but much longer than that and their strength would begin to fail.

Onward. They must cross this open land and get into the woods by morning. Already two of them had suffered slight sun poisoning from inadequate shelter. She must get them under good cover by daybreak.

She looked up at the Great Sleeper, whose northwest shoulder they were crossing. Deep in the mountain's heart there was fire, but it had slumbered since before her birth. She glanced skyward, hoping for a glimpse of stars, but gray cloud covered all the sky.

She pushed on, skirting a patch of fleececod growing wild at the edge of the meadow. Something odd caught her eye, and she paused, halting the hunters behind her with a gesture.

Some of the fleececod bushes were bare. Quite a few were, she realized, glancing over the patch. Fleececod did not normally drop its old cods until the new buds of spring pushed them away.

Shalár frowned. Kobalen did not make cloth; they would have no use for fleececod. Mayhap they had discovered it could stanch a wound.

"Yaras."

He joined her, and she pointed toward the bushes. "Have you ever known kobalen to harvest fleececod?"

"No, Bright Lady."

"Can you think of why Irith or Ciris might have done it? I assume you did not."

Yaras frowned, then shook his head. "We would have no reason."

Shalár took hold of a bare stem and closed her eyes, exploring the fleececod's khi, searching for a hint of the harvester. Something whispered of an awareness greater than the plant's, but beyond that she could detect nothing.

Kobalen would not have picked fleececod. Her watchers had no reason to do so. Who, then?

She shook her head. She had no leisure for such puzzles.

"Onward."

Yaras nodded and strode forward, the army following. Shalár gazed at the bushes as she walked after him. Finding one that had not been picked, she snapped the dry stem of a cod and cupped the white, fibrous bloom in her hand as she walked on. A question with no answer, an ideal focus for meditation.

◈

Shalár heard the footfalls of a hunter running toward her, light sounds scarcely different from the patter of falling leaves. She frowned and glanced up at the setting moon, clearly visible through barren branches as it sank toward a gray wall of cloud in the west. She and her army were in a greenleaf wood, climbing the flank of the Great Sleeper toward evergreens that would shade them for the morrow. It was too soon for the army to seek shelter, though. Yaras must know that.

"Why do you return now?"

She pushed her way through a stand of scrub oak even as he appeared out of the brush before her. Her temper was short owing to the hunger that had begun to grip her. Yaras seemed not to notice, for he dipped a bow and grinned.

"I have found something. Halt the pack."

Shalár glared at him, angered by his presumption. It was she who commanded here, not he. She felt an urge to strike him but mastered it. That was the hunger, and she would not let it rule her.

She closed her eyes to signal the army, the expense of khi making her gut clench with sudden need. They halted.

She glared at Yaras once more. He had his head up, listening and scenting. After a moment he looked at Shalár and smiled.

"They are still asleep. Kobalen. A small band, no more than thirty."

Shalár could have wept with relief. Hunger roared in her ears at the thought of food so near. She should have sensed them, but she was tired—so tired.

"Where?"

Yaras nodded toward the slope behind him. "Half a league to the east. Camped in a hollow by a spring. Five hunters should be enough to capture them."

"Take ten."

She would take no risk of losing this catch, for there might not be another before they reached Fireshore.

She ought to lead the hunt herself, but she was weary and weak from hunger. Yaras was not so afflicted yet, though she could sense his need. He had done right to come back, and she knew it must have cost him an effort to refrain from feeding at once.

She closed her eyes again to summon the army to her. She had been walking ahead of them, and now they came up quietly, gathering in a clearing carpeted with fallen leaves. Some sat down at once, and a few sprawled on the ground.

Shalár nodded to Yaras to choose his hunters. He quickly picked ten of those who seemed least weary and led them eastward up the slope, shadows fading into the scrub beneath the trees.

Shalár sat on a rock to await their return, sighing as she looked up at the sullen moon now half-hidden by cloud. Her face tingled slightly from its reflected light, a sign of her weakened state.

As she gazed westward, a dim glow of light seemed to shine through the brush beneath the trees. It was not moonlight, more like the flickering of a campfire, for it moved, glimmering, now shining out between branches, now fading almost to nothing. Shalár frowned as she watched it, the hair on her neck rising as she realized it was approaching.

Torchlight? Someone coming to the army? But her own hunters would not have made a light, and they were all here save those Yaras had taken to hunt. There were none of her people living this far from Nightsand. Kobalen could command fire, but they would never approach the army. That left ælven, though she doubted they would come near her hunters, either, even if they had dared to venture this far into the Westerlands.

She swallowed, wondering whether to call out a challenge. Glancing around the clearing, she saw that none of the army had taken notice of the light. With growing unease, she looked back at it.

It was closer. Not torchlight, too white for fire. It shimmered now, growing brighter as it came nearer. Shalár shifted, reaching for the knife at her hip, its solid hilt a comfort.

The light was moving along the ground, approaching as if cast by lantern or torch. At first she had thought it was dancing, but now it merely shifted from side to side, as if someone was walking through the wood, stepping around obstacles, between trees. Shalár glanced up toward the moon, but it was gone now, sunk behind the clouds, the only hint of its presence the outline of golden fire it cast around the edges of the cloud.

Cautiously, she reached out to taste the khi of the intruder. The moment she opened herself to it, she gasped at its brilliance and quickly pulled back, squeezing her eyes shut and closing all her senses.

Whatever cast that light was powerful, both strange and familiar. She tasted fear, tried to breathe more steadily, tried to calm her thundering heart.

After a moment she dared to look again and saw the glowing figure, now much closer. The army gave no sign of having noticed.

Her fingers gripped the knife hilt convulsively, though she knew now the weapon was useless. Warily she watched the silvery light take shape as the walker emerged from the woods. Tall, male, robed in white and carrying something—a child? Suddenly she knew him, and her heart clenched with cold fear as she whispered his name.

"Dareth?"

But it could not be he. Dareth was gone, crossed into spirit many days since.

Crossed into spirit. Shalár began to tremble.

He stopped at the edge of the clearing, no more than a rod away from her. It was Dareth, looking strong as he had not looked for centuries, looking as he had in Fireshore, before the hunger. His long, pale hair was loose over the shoulders of his robe, falling down to the middle of his back, waking a longing in Shalár to run her fingers through its silkiness. He stood silently gazing at her, eyes rich with love tinged with sorrow.

"What do you want?"

Dareth bent to set the child he carried on its feet. Shalár could not see its face, for it glowed with a light even brighter than that surrounding Dareth. He held its hands to steady it for a moment, then released them.

The child sped away at once, toward Shalár. Without thought she opened her arms, but the child spirit passed her by, so swiftly its brilliance sent a wave of tingling heat through her. There was no sound in its passing. She turned her head, but it had vanished.

A few of the army were watching her, mildly curious. They saw nothing of Dareth or the child, she knew. Swallowing, she looked back at Dareth.

"What does this mean?"

He merely gazed at her, softly smiling, giving her sympathy but no answers. Was this the spirit of the child they had tried and failed to conceive together? Or a child she might yet bear? Heartache smote her at the thought. Should she have said something, offered something?

She stood up and had to pause for a moment to steady herself. All the discomforts of her flesh returned to her attention: weariness, sore muscles, aching feet, weakness, and hunger. She turned resentful eyes toward Dareth.

What good was such a vision if it offered no comfort? Dareth had left her, chosen to leave his suffering flesh. He had abandoned the struggle to regain what they had lost, leaving her to fight on alone. Why did he now taunt her?

She took a step toward him, feeling her anger flare. As if her movement had disrupted his khi, the light around him rippled, distorting her perception of him, like a reflection on the surface of troubled water. She stopped, suddenly afraid of his departure. He was lost to her, yet she saw him now and wanted to see him still, wanted to gaze at him forever.

The ripples continued, waves of shadow damping the light, which grew dimmer moment by moment. He was leaving.

"Stay. Please stay."

He reached a hand toward her, his face now sad. Shalár gave a small gasp and stepped forward, reaching out to touch him. The light faded as her hand passed through the air where he had been.

Slowly she moved to the spot where he had stood. With an effort she opened her awareness once more, seeking for a whisper of him on the wind. There was nothing but darkness and the hollow rustle of dry leaves.

Her face was wet, she noticed. Wet with tears. She had not allowed herself that weakness in a very long time.

She stood a long while gazing into the empty wood, seeing Dareth in her mind's eye, trying to remember every subtle shift of his expression.

Why a child? Why here, now? She thought it through again and again but could find no answer.

"Bright Lady?"

She turned, surprised at the stiffness in her legs. One of the army, a female with a tattered armband over her leathers, a token of affection from some loved one, made a slight, hesitant bow.

"Your pardon, Bright Lady. The hunters have returned."

Shalár looked past her, startled. It did not seem long enough, yet there they were, Yaras and the others, herding a small band of subdued kobalen into the clearing. Shalár smelled the creatures' pungent scent, tasted their fear on the air. Her hunger woke anew, hot and angry.

Yaras glanced up and saw her. His face was pinched now, exertion and hunger sharpening his features. He nodded in greeting and glanced at the catch.

"One to every twelve hunters, by my reckoning. I wish there were more. We took them all; none escaped."

"You did well. Summon your captains."

Shalár laid a hand on his shoulder, a gesture meant to convey her approval. The shock of touching solid flesh surprised her. She gave herself a shake to dispel it.

"This one was too small to feed twelve." Yaras gestured toward a tiny kobalen sitting on the ground nearby. "I set it aside for you, Bright Lady."

A small, coarse face turned toward her, round eyes wide with fear and red-rimmed in contrast to the black fur. The kobalen was young, no more than a handful of years, though a child of Shalár's people would not grow so large in twenty. Kobalen matured swiftly in their short lives. This one was yet a child.

A child. Shalár frowned.

Dareth could not have meant this creature. The

child with him had shone with a light fiercer than his own—it must then have been something even mightier, not so feeble a thing as kobalen. She saw again the child running free, a flash of brilliance that burned her soul as it passed.

What if she set this child free? What if she chose to be merciful—that ælven ambition—and spare this small life?

The kobalen would die alone, then, of starvation most likely. Or if it had the good fortune to encounter another band of its kind, it would become a slave to them. It would warn them, also, of her army's presence.

"We are ready, Bright Lady."

She turned to look at Yaras, saw the captains beyond him waiting sharp-eyed with hunger. Yaras held a knife in his hand, which he offered to her. She shook her head, gesturing to him to begin sharing out the catch. He turned to the clustered kobalen and selected a large male.

Shalár went to the kobalen child, ignoring the frightened sounds behind her. The child stared at her warily and moved to scramble away, but she caught its mind and stilled it, holding it gently with khi.

There are other kinds of mercy. This creature shall not suffer.

She spent a little more khi to cloud the kobalen's mind, to blind it to the blade she raised to its throat, to numb the slight pain as she opened its vein. Gathering the small body to her, she fed gently, sending the creature into a dreamless sleep where no fear would ever trouble it again.

◈ Glenhallow ◈

Escorting Heléri to Glenhallow's public circle, Rephanin saw a large crowd gathered to see the delegations off on their homeward journeys. An honor guard of twenty Southfæld guardians waited to accompany Governor Felisan's small party northward. Rephanin kept his hood drawn well forward against the bright, cold dawn. He could feel the coming winter settling into his bones—a dull, lonely ache.

Jharan kept his words of farewell brief and informal, for which Rephanin was silently grateful. The idle thought came to him that he could speak to all here assembled; he could enable Jharan to speak into their thoughts if the governor so wished. Such possibilities had not occurred to him before. In all his centuries of mindspeech, he had never thought of it as a tool for public use.

He was changed—profoundly changed—from what he had been before this Council had commenced. He looked at Heléri, her own hood and veil deeply sheltering her from the biting sun.

I cannot resist tormenting us both a little more.

He felt her smile. *I am glad.*

He handed her into the chariot that had brought her to Glenhallow and stood silently watching the small cavalcade's departure. He could still feel the warmth of her in his heart. When she passed beyond the first gate, he expected to lose contact with her, but apparently the carriage wall was an insignificant barrier to him, or perhaps she had the window open.

Rephanin began to breathe a little faster. Could it be that outdoors he was a distance speaker? Why had he never thought to test this?

Are you with me, dear one?

Heléri's gentle laughter rippled through her response. *Anxious, beloved?*

I am wondering how long I will be able to speak to you. I can no longer see you.

Her silence bespoke her musing upon this question. Rephanin waited, straining to catch every whisper of her, every glimmer of her khi.

The crowd around and between them made this difficult. He sorted through many random currents, seeking Heléri's khi. Most of the others he could disregard, but he became aware of khi focused on himself from someone nearby. Glancing up, he saw Turisan beside him, watching him.

Rephanin made a small gesture to stay him, then stepped away from the center of the circle, still focused on the retreating Alpinon party. Behind him he heard Jharan making further farewells, heard the jingle of the harness bells with which the Steppegards were wont to adorn their horses on ceremonial occasions.

He walked to the circle's edge, gazing eastward. The sunlight stung his eyes now. He blinked fiercely and pulled his hood as far forward as it would go but continued to stare into the morning, eyes fixed on a distant banner of violet and blue above the receding cavalcade.

Heléri?

Yes?

You said you chose to remain in flesh because you had not done all you wished here. What did you stay to achieve?

No answer came. For a long, agonized moment he thought he had lost contact with her; then a wave of warmth flooded through him, tender and loving, making him ache to touch her. He shivered, the morning cold against his flesh at odds with the heat in his soul. His heart seemed to melt within him, all fear vanishing in the fire of her love. He returned his own to her, sending his khi flying out to wrap her tenderly about.

I—hope you mean to stay yet awhile.

A while, yes.

Of course, he thought in a small private corner of his mind. Like you, Rephanin, to assume you were her only reason for remaining.

Still, he was pleased beyond expression. He stood watching her with his mind more than his eyes, heedless of his surroundings save for a dim awareness of successive departures. He could see the Steppe Wilds party on the plain now, but he kept his gaze fixed on Alpinon's little column. The sun was well up by the time they neared the foothills, where the road drew away from the Silverwash to climb through a shallow pass.

The mountains may interfere between us.

He nodded. The heartache was returning.

I will come to Alpinon. Wait for me.

Warmth, a smile. Loving tenderness. He closed his eyes briefly, treasuring it, then opened them to catch a last glimpse of the banner as the column started into the pass.

I love you, Heléri. I love you, I love you, I love you—

A touch on his arm startled him. Reluctantly he gave part of his attention to his flesh, turning to look at Turisan.

Jharan's son smiled gently back at him, then tilted his head toward the magehall. Rephanin became aware that the gathered crowd was dispersing, taking up their daily business. The councillors who were leaving this day had all departed.

Rephanin looked back toward the foothills. Alpinon's banner had passed from view.

Heléri?

Gone. He swallowed, feeling emptiness soak into him, widening in his soul like a cold pool. His flesh was numb from standing overlong.

He inhaled slowly, turning to Turisan with a small nod of agreement. He took a step and was surprised at his unsteadiness. Turisan moved swiftly to help, grasping his upper arm. Normally this would have made Rephanin indignant, but just now he felt battered, bruised. Had Turisan felt so, he wondered, when Eliani had left?

No, for they could still speak. He swallowed a moment's bitter envy, knowing it was unworthy of him.

Turisan's khi hummed against his arm, muted by the sleeve of his robe. He withdrew from it, wanting to remember the tone of Heléri's khi, wanting only that in his mind.

He did allow Turisan to guide him to the magehall and sighed with relief when they entered the shelter of the hearthroom. Flames flickered overhead in two small hanging lanterns of golden glass, and the warmth from the banked coals on the welcoming hearth eased into his chilled flesh. He put back his hood and looked at Turisan.

"Thank you."

Turisan smiled. "Heléri did me the favor when Eliani departed. I could do no less for you."

Rephanin returned the smile weakly. "How fares your lady?"

Only an instant's hesitation, but it was there. Turisan tried to hide it with another smile.

"She is well, thank you. Shall I leave you to your rest?"

Rephanin blinked, finding his thoughts clouded. Fatigue, perhaps. And heartache.

He nodded. He did need rest. All his feelings were raw, and there was much to do. There was his circle—both circles, old and new—to attend to in the evening. Cloaks to deliver and weapons waiting to be blessed.

At least there were no more Council sessions to claim his attention. He turned toward the door into the magehall, pausing to look back at Turisan.

"Thank you again."

Turisan made a graceful motion, something between a nod and a bow. He stood watching, waiting until Rephanin went in before departing.

Kindness. Rephanin had grown unaccustomed to it, living for so long in sullen withdrawal. Now his shield of solitude had been torn away, and in his new vulnerability even kindness frightened him. Particularly coming from Jharan's son.

Shaking away those thoughts, he opened the door into the magehall. Its comforting darkness welcomed him, and he breathed a sigh as he closed the door on Glenhallow and sought the privacy of his chambers.

❧ Alpinon ❧

Eliani rolled her shoulders, trying vainly to ease their stiffness. She glanced up past the tops of tall pines to the blue mountain peaks beyond which the sun had sunk some time since.

Clouds were beginning to gather, and a sharp breeze from the south whispered of winter. Eliani shivered and drew her cloak across her, throwing one corner over the opposite shoulder. Glancing down at the pale green, she reminded herself, still with faint surprise, that she was now a Greenglen.

Walk many paths, the creed tells us. I am on a new path now.

She glanced at Luruthin and the other Stonereaches of her escort, glad of their familiar company. They were her friends and her kin, unlike the Greenglens, who seemed strangers still.

Eliani peered forward along the road, which was dappled now by the shadows of tall pines uphill. Dusky pools of shadow spread beneath the trees, and a stillness lay upon the wood.

Too still. Too quiet, even for dusk. Something was wrong.

The horses sidled, and one uttered a low nicker. Eliani put a hand to the neck of her mount, patting to reassure it. It raised its nose to the wind, tossing its mane. Unease spread swiftly to the other horses in the escort, and Eliani held up her hand to halt them.

Vanorin turned to her. "Wait here. I will go forward."

Eliani suppressed irritation and nodded. She murmured words of comfort to her mount as she watched Vanorin advance, a pale shadow in the darkness, soon hidden by the trees that marched close to the road. She quested through the woods with khi, her awareness brushing against the somnolent pillars of trees, a scurrying mouse, a pair of raccoons startled from feeding. They fled, and a moment later Vanorin's horse let out a high neigh of protest.

Galloping hoofbeats returned. Vanorin reined in, high color in his cheeks, eyes sharp with horror.

"A killing, just off the road. Southfæld Guard. I fear it is the envoy Governor Jharan sent to Fireshore."

Eliani's chest tightened. "How recent?"

"Not very. There is not much—left . . ." He paused to swallow, seemed unable to say more.

Eliani urged her mount to a trot, the others following. The smell of death assailed her, and her horse flung up its head, rolling its eyes in terror. She tugged at the reins, and the horse moved sideways, hindquarters colliding with Luruthin's mount, which screamed in anger and fear.

"Halt here!"

She dismounted and strode up the road, accompanied by Luruthin and Vanorin. She pulled a kerchief from inside her leathers and pressed it against her face. Vanorin led them a short way, then struck uphill to the west.

Despite the cold and the scraps of snow that glowed blue beneath the trees, the smell of decay was overpowering. They reached what had plainly been a campsite, with a fire circle over which the remains of two small animals hung on a spit, charred beyond recognition or the notice of carrion eaters.

The guardians had not fared so well. Only by counting the pale green cloaks and the swords that were scattered around them could Eliani tell that there had been five. The cloaks were rent and torn, covered with decaying remains that were gnawed to the bone in many places, and many of the bones were missing.

Long gouges in the earth led to a stand of bushes nearby, beneath which lay a sixth body, all its limbs torn asunder, lying in scattered disarray. Eliani's gorge rose at the sight of the slashed leathers, which looked as if they, too, had been partially eaten.

Luruthin joined her, grimacing. "Catamount."

Eliani nodded. "But why would it attack such a large party? I have never heard of such a thing!"

Vanorin approached. "There is one more, near where their horses were tied."

His voice was tight, and Eliani glanced at his face. He looked pale but seemed in control of himself, brows drawn together in a frown of grief.

"Do you know any of them? I mean, can you . . . ?"

"I have not looked closely. I will do so."

He gazed down at the mangled remains in the bushes, stepped nearer to the head, and knelt to touch a pale tangle of hair. The skull beneath now stared hollow-eyed at the pines above, shreds of flesh clinging to the bone. The hair had once been braided but was pulled into a snarled mess, as though some creature had tried to nest in it. Vanorin touched the leather thong that had secured the braid. A small green feather was tied into the knot.

"Mishali, I think. She was with the second envoy to Fireshore."

Eliani bit her lip. "I am sorry."

Vanorin rose, blinking fiercely. "I will go and look at the others."

He turned away and walked back to the fire circle. Eliani watched him go, breathing shallowly, her eyes stinging. She felt a touch on her arm and turned to look at Luruthin.

"We should burn them."

She pressed her lips together and nodded. It would take most of the night to tend to them properly, but the horses must be rested in any case, and she could do no less than to honor the dead.

"A conce. We must set one by the road. Luruthin, will you see to it?"

"Yes. We cannot carve it, though."

"That can be done later, but we must mark the place. I will send a message to Highstone."

She shivered. Luruthin laid a hand on her arm.

"Are you all right?"

She met his gaze, saw that he was pale. Suddenly the horror of the killing overwhelmed her.

She turned away, stumbling to a bush as her stomach heaved up its contents. Luruthin might at least have held her, she thought peevishly, but then she heard the sound of his own retching nearby.

Trembling, she straightened and wiped her mouth with her kerchief, wishing for the water flask tied to her saddle. She had seen death before, even violent death, but nothing like this.

Vanorin had knelt beside one of the corpses. Still weak, Eliani joined him. He held up a leather pouch.

"I found this."

The pouch was ornamented with broidery and beads. It had been clawed at and chewed but not successfully opened.

"It was Leharan's. I recognize the work; it is Kirilani's."

"Kirilani? Our Kirilani?"

Vanorin nodded, his eyes troubled. Kirilani was one of the Southfæld guardians in Eliani's escort.

"Was Leharan sent with the second envoy?"

Vanorin nodded and stood up. "And they were seven. These are they."

Eliani looked at the scattered remains, the torn cloaks, and swallowed. "I cannot believe that one catamount slew seven guardians. Could it have been kobalen?"

He shook his head. "Kobalen would have looted the dead. They would have taken this pouch and the cloak clasps and other things."

Eliani glanced at the swords scattered near the fire. One had been dragged a little distance, apparently by something that wanted to eat the leather belt from which it hung. They would have to be collected, carried home to the families of the dead, with the pouch and what little else could be saved. The cloak clasps. Mishali's feather.

Eliani's throat went tight all of a sudden. She looked at Vanorin, whose face was blank, as if he had closed his heart in order to cope with what must be done.

A keening wail rose on the cold air. Eliani turned toward the sound, as did Vanorin. Running footsteps came toward them, and Vanorin hastened to the road. Eliani followed but stopped at the edge of the trees, watching while he went to meet the guardian who approached.

"Leharan!" Kirilani stared past Eliani into the woods, eyes haunted with grief. "Leharan!"

Vanorin caught her, restrained her. She struggled to

get away, and he spoke urgently, quietly into her ear. Kirilani shook her head, straining against his hold.

"Leharan!"

Vanorin shook her briefly, then caught her hands and pressed the leather pouch into them. Eliani heard him speaking again, though she could not make out what he said. The guardian stared at the pouch in her hands, then dropped to her knees, sobbing. Vanorin knelt to comfort her.

Eliani turned away, knowing she must inform Turisan and Jharan of the envoy's fate. She walked down the road to get away from the stench of death, pulling her cloak tight around her.

She sank to the ground at the foot of a tree, leaning back against it with eyes closed. A few deep breaths to calm herself, then she carefully signaled Turisan by the means he had taught her.

His happiness flooded her like sudden sunlight. She caught her breath at its unexpected joy.

Yes, my love?

Turisan . . .

What is it?

Alarm edged his response. Eliani inhaled shakily.

Are you alone?

I am at Berephan's house, supping with the Guard captains, but I have stepped aside. Berephan said Kelevon sends you his apologies, by the way.

Eliani covered her face with her hands, frowning. She did not need the heartache of hearing from Kelevon just now.

Find a private place. I have bad news.

Wordless dismay replaced Turisan's happiness. Eliani waited, counting the heartbeats that pulsed in her throat. She looked up through the treetops to the western sky, where a single star gleamed down through the branches.

I am alone now. What is it?

She told him, as briefly as possible, the fate that had befallen the envoy. Turisan listened without interrupting. At last she fell silent and sat staring at the darkening sky, feeling numb.

I will go to my father at once.

Eliani nodded. *Tell him I am sorry. We are putting up a rough conce to mark the spot. Speak to me after you have seen Jharan.*

I will.

His love enfolded her fiercely, briefly. The next moment she was alone again.

She pulled her cloak about her as if she could feel Turisan's embrace in it and slowly walked back to the site of the killing. The wind had dropped, and the smell seemed even more horrible. She fumbled for her kerchief again.

Luruthin and two others had found a narrow pointed stone and hauled it down the hill to the road. All three had cloths tied around their faces as they dug a hole in which to set the stone at the roadside near the site of the killing.

An unshaped conce, a raw finger pointing skyward, unmarked save for a pale green ribbon tied about it, the color muted by moonlight. A humble token, but it must do for now. Others would carve the names of the fallen onto the stone, master carvers from Clerestone, perhaps. Eliani pressed her lips together and walked back down the road to where the escort waited.

She saw Kirilani sitting in the midst of the Greenglens, hunched over a sheathed sword, which she clutched to her, rocking slightly back and forth, the sword's hilt rising above her shoulder. Vanorin rose at Eliani's approach and came toward her.

"She insisted on taking Leharan's sword. I retrieved it for her, and thought I should bring the others down as well."

Eliani saw the rest of the swords lying piled beneath the trees. She nodded approval.

"With your permission, I would like to send Kirilani back to Highstone to take word of the—tragedy."

"Yes. Thank you, Vanorin. Choose one to go with her. She should not camp alone tonight."

"That reduces your escort by two."

"We shall manage."

He held her gaze for a moment, then nodded. "Thank you, Eliani."

She gave him a sad smile, then glanced toward Kirilani and lowered her voice. "Was she very close to him?"

Vanorin nodded. "They were not bonded, but yes, they were close."

They were lovers. Eliani was certain of it, seeing the grief on Kirilani's face. Her heart jumped in fear at the thought of losing a loved one so horribly. The very pain of the idea made her want to look away.

Instead she walked over to Kirilani. The Greenglens sitting near her looked up at Eliani's approach, but Kirilani merely stared at the ground, face fixed in a frown, slowly rocking back and forth.

Eliani crouched beside her and watched her for a moment. "I am sorry."

Kirilani stopped rocking. After a couple of breaths she looked up at Eliani, eyes dry of tears but deep with pain. On impulse Eliani reached out and laid a hand on her shoulder.

Kirilani closed her eyes and shuddered even as

Eliani felt the startling heat of khi rise in her hand again. She stayed still, and the heat quickly faded. Kirilani sighed, bent her head, and began to weep.

Eliani felt sorry for her and hoped her attempt at comfort had not made her feel worse. She stood up under the silent gaze of the other Greenglens and walked away to find her horse.

It was certain now that none of Jharan's messages had reached Fireshore. She felt as if she was riding toward a blank space, a vast unknown. The envoy's misfortune weighed upon her, and she had to fight a rising dread.

She silently asked the ældar of the wood to watch over the spirits of the dead, though by now those spirits were long gone, returned to the realm of light. The living needed protection more.

Eliani sent those of the Greenglens who appeared most disturbed by the gruesome attack away to make camp and look after the horses. She and the rest spent the night making a pyre for the dead in the clearing where the envoy had camped and been attacked. When all was ready, when the remains had been laid atop the pyre and the envoy's possessions set aside for their kindred, Eliani gathered the guardians who had stayed to finish the work in a circle around the pyre.

She should say something, she knew. She disliked making speeches and thought fleetingly of asking Turisan for help but decided not to trouble him. Instead she tried to imagine what he would say. She cleared her throat.

"These were our brethren. Spirits welcome them, and may the ældar bless them with freedom from fear and pain. They carry the sorrows of flesh no more."

Someone inhaled sharply, making her glance up. They were all watching her—Luruthin still somber,

Vanorin silent and pale. She had never seen the captain look so crushed and looked away from his pinched face, back at the pyre.

"What remains of their flesh, let it return now to light. Their lives will be remembered with honor and affection."

She raised her hands, palms toward the pyre, and the rest of the circle did likewise. Sending her khi out into the stacked wood, she sought for a dry place to set a spark.

The pyre burst into flame. Sparks rose into the night sky, golden flecks dancing toward the whiter stars. Eliani stepped back from the sudden heat and watched the golden light wash over the faces of her escort.

Weary faces, and the journey not half-done. The sorrow of this night would affect them, but she dared not let it slow their pace. Fireshore would not wait.

❧ Glenhallow ❧

"Father . . ."

Jharan turned to him—half questioning, half annoyed—and Turisan realized he had intruded upon a private conversation. He had walked into his father's chambers without pausing, thinking to find him alone, but Lady Rheneri was with him, radiant in an elegant gown of Ælvanen gold and white, making Turisan suddenly conscious of his simple attire.

She gave him a tolerant smile, then glanced at Jharan. "I believe I would like some more of this excellent wine. Will you excuse me?"

Jharan gazed after her as she strolled to a side table that bore an ewer and goblets. He turned back to Turisan with a wry look.

"Yes?"

"Father, come outside with me a moment."

Jharan's eyes sharpened. "What is it?"

Turisan lowered his voice. "News from Eliani."

"Is she in danger?"

"N-no. Please come away from here."

Turisan nodded slightly toward Rheneri. Jharan pressed his lips together, then turned and strode out into the corridor without further ado, the skirts of his silver-woven robe swaying about his feet.

The passage opened onto a balustrade overlooking the fountain court. Turisan's chambers opened off the same passage, though lately he had been residing in the Star Tower.

Jharan moved across to the balustrade and stopped there beside one of the great tree-shaped pillars. Turisan glanced along the colonnade to be sure that no one would overhear them.

"Eliani and her party have found the second envoy."

He gave Jharan what details Eliani had shared with him. Jharan's frown deepened as he listened.

"So Fireshore never did receive my message."

"No."

Jharan rubbed a hand across his face, looking weary of a sudden. "What can I do?"

The question caught Turisan off guard. "I cannot say. They have set a rough conce and sent messages to Highstone. I think there is no more to be done."

Jharan drew a deep breath. "Give Eliani my—my regrets. And my thanks for her care of our clan-kin."

Turisan nodded. For a moment he thought he saw grief, then Jharan drew himself up and calm settled upon his features. The glimpse of his father's heart was gone; it was the governor who stood before Turisan now.

Southfæld had cost Jharan a great deal, more than Turisan had realized until now. What might it cost him someday when Jharan stepped down and he assumed the governance of the realm?

He walked beside his father, their footsteps masked by the whisper of the fountains below. Pausing outside his chambers, Jharan turned to him.

"Thank you for bringing me this news."

"I am sorry the tidings are ill."

Jharan shook his head, half smiling. "In this alone, you and Eliani have already given great service. Tell her to be careful."

Turisan laughed softly. "I tell her that every day."

With a fleeting smile, Jharan held out his arm. Turisan clasped it, then watched his father return to his guest. He saw Lady Rheneri look up as Jharan went in, just before the door closed.

Turisan stood for a moment, frowning in thought. The slaughter of the second envoy made him feel the need to act, though he could not help Eliani in dealing with it. He had his own preparations to make and little enough time in which to make them.

Briefly he wished that Eliani were not engaged upon her mission. If she were free, they both could join the army at Midrange, offering Ehranan the advantage of mindspeakers on the field, which had led to victory in the Bitter Wars.

Perhaps it was a less important advantage when the enemy was kobalen, not alben. The ælven were unlikely to have need of coordinating complicated maneuvers against the kobalen. What would truly be of use at Midrange was a gift, like Rephanin's, that would enable the commander to speak to all the army at once.

Turisan drew a breath as a tingle of realization went through him. Why not have Rephanin upon the field?

It had not occurred to him before because Rephanin was not a warrior. He need not be, though. He could remain behind the lines . . .

Turisan hastened along the colonnade and crossed the arcing span that joined Hallowhall to the magehall. Rephanin would likely be at work with his circle, but

Turisan could leave a message for him. He sought the hall attendant's chamber and was surprised to find Rephanin there, talking with Tivhari.

The magelord glanced up, and Turisan made a slight bow. "I am glad to find you. I thought you would be closeted with your circle."

"The high circle has not yet convened. I have just finished instructing the new circle."

"More mages for more blessings?"

Rephanin nodded. "How may I serve you?"

Turisan paused, pressing his lips together. "Will you come with me to the garrison, briefly? It will not take long. Lord Ehranan is there, and I wish you to speak to him."

"We are acquainted."

Turisan hesitated. "I mean, I wish you to—if you will—"

"Ah." Rephanin's brows drew together. "Why?"

"I have an idea. I will explain as we walk."

Rephanin did not answer immediately, and Turisan feared he would refuse. His attendant knew better, apparently; she slipped away and returned a moment later with the magelord's cloak. As she handed it to him, he stirred as if roused from a trance.

"Thank you, Tivhari. Please tell the circle I will return shortly."

Turisan smiled his thanks to her as he hastened the magelord out into the night.

⊛

Rephanin felt acutely uncomfortable in the warden's hall, facing the stares of several captains gathered around a table scattered with maps and tallies. Berephan's stiff bow of welcome did nought to ease him.

Turisan crossed at once to Ehranan. The Ælvanen

warrior looked up, his gaze slightly skeptical as it fell upon Rephanin. He was dressed in tunic and legs of a serviceable cloth dyed a dark gold, with his black hair bound back in an unadorned hunter's braid. His face made Rephanin remember Hollirued, long ago.

Ehranan had fought in the Bitter Wars. He had been quite young then—as had Rephanin—but had acquitted himself well. More recently, Ehranan had led Eastfæld's hastily assembled force in the Midrange War. The memory of those battles had stamped itself into the lines of his face, and his blue eyes were coolly watchful.

Berephan picked up an ewer from a side table, offering to pour wine. Rephanin glanced at Ehranan and politely declined. Turisan accepted a goblet, then turned to Ehranan.

"Recently Lord Rephanin used his gift to allow me to speak to the assembled Guard."

Ehranan nodded, eyes narrowing. "Berephan told me."

"Have you considered the possible advantage of having such a gift on a battlefield?"

Ehranan's black brows twitched together in a frown. "You are suggesting that both yourself and Lord Rephanin be risked in battle?"

Turisan shook his head. "No, for my presence would not be needed. Rephanin can enable *you* to speak to every guardian on the field. Or you, Lord Berephan."

The two warriors exchanged a glance. Rephanin folded his hands together inside the long sleeves of his robe, clasping them tightly to keep himself still. He had not realized this was Turisan's intention; perhaps he had not listened carefully as they walked hither. He had assumed Turisan merely wanted more help with the advance force he was training.

Turisan's eyes lit with enthusiasm. "Imagine giving an order and having it instantly understood. Having immediate response from every guardian under your command."

Ehranan lifted his chin, then turned a sharp glance toward Rephanin. "Assuming the order was correctly passed. Forgive me, Lord Rephanin, but you have little experience of a guardian's work."

Rephanin coughed slightly. "It would not be a matter of my understanding what you say. You yourself would give the order. I would merely enable the guardians to hear you."

The Ælvanen's gaze narrowed. "Berephan said *you* spoke to the Guard."

"So I did, but I need not do so beyond establishing contact, as I did for Lord Turisan."

Rephanin glanced at Turisan, uncomfortable in having assumed the role of explaining what was, after all, Turisan's plan. Turisan merely nodded, however, with a slight encouraging smile. Rephanin began to wish that he had not refused the wine.

Berephan shook his head. "It would distract the guardians. Too many things can go wrong on a battlefield."

Turisan turned to him. "All the more need for the means to communicate swiftly. If things go badly, an order to retreat would have an instant response."

"Or one might shift the position of companies more quickly." Ehranan nodded slowly. "But Rephanin would have to leave the magehall for this, and I doubt that would please Jharan. Nor would it be wise to risk the injury of such a gifted mage."

"He could remain behind the lines, and guardians could be assigned to protect him."

Berephan's frown deepened, then all at once he

crossed the space between himself and Rephanin in two swift steps, frowning at him face to face. Rephanin drew back.

"Why do you wish this? Guardians' work is no part of your magecraft!"

Hostility and fear shivered through the warden's khi. Rephanin answered with careful calm.

"In truth, until I came here, I had no notion of what Turisan intended to suggest. I am willing to serve, but the plan is not of my making."

"What brought you here, then?"

Berephan's hostility was easy to understand. He feared the mindspeech he had inadvertently tasted and wanted no more of it. Rephanin stood his gaze for a long moment, then decided to lay his hopes bare. He glanced down, deliberately yielding to Berephan, and answered in a quiet voice.

"Setting aside Lord Turisan's suggestion, consider this: If I can find a partner with whom I am able to speak at distance, you would have another pair of mindspeakers at your service."

Berephan looked surprised, caught off guard by the change of subject. Ehranan seemed intrigued. Encouraged by his interest, Rephanin continued.

"Turisan and Eliani must remain as they are until she has reached Fireshore and told us how matters lie there. If you had another pair of distance speakers, you could place them as you wished. One here, one in Hollirued, perhaps."

Ehranan sipped his wine. "Is it not highly unlikely that you will find such a one? Mindspeakers are extraordinarily rare."

"It is unlikely, yes. But if I do not search, unlikelihood becomes impossibility."

"And what has this to do with us?"

Rephanin turned to face Berephan. "You have many new recruits for the Guard. Let me speak to them, as I did a few days ago. I may find one who is gifted."

Berephan frowned. "Why the Guard? You could ask Jharan to call the citizens out to the circle."

"I could, yes. Mayhap I will, but as your guardians will assemble anyway, why not take advantage of the opportunity?"

Berephan glared at him. "What of your mages? Are they not gifted?"

"For magecraft, yes, but I have found no mind-speakers among them. Believe me, I have sought in earnest."

Ehranan's eyes narrowed. "And will you wish to seek among the forces of Eastfæld? Of Alpinon and the Steppes?"

"Wherever I can."

Ehranan looked down at the table before him and shifted his empty goblet from the map to a tally. "So you would come to Midrange."

The full implications of Turisan's plan suddenly rose in Rephanin's mind. He would have to leave his circle—both circles—to another's guidance. Jholóran was capable . . . yet Rephanin felt reluctant to leave his work and the magehall where he had dwelt almost since his arrival at Glenhallow.

He swallowed. "If you think I might be of service. Perhaps you would like to try speaking to the army here to see if you think it worthwhile."

The Eastfæld warrior was still for a moment, then he nodded. "Yes. Tomorrow at dawn. Will that suit you?"

Rephanin bowed his head in acknowledgment. He would tolerate daylight for the sake of his search, as he had done before.

"Good. Now, to the matter of dispositions at Midrange . . ."

Ehranan turned back to the table, bending over the maps and tallies once more. Thus dismissed, Rephanin turned to leave and found Turisan walking with him to the stair.

Rephanin glanced back at the warriors and lowered his voice. "Turisan, may I ask a favor of you? The next time you form a plan that will completely disrupt my life, would you tell me of it before presenting it to others?"

Turisan had the grace to color. "Forgive me. I had not considered all the implications."

"Nor I. Never mind. You are right; it would offer a great advantage to our forces in battle. I will not grudge the cost if Ehranan asks me to go to Midrange."

Turisan gazed at him for a long moment, a smile slowly spreading on his lips. "Midrange is but a day's ride from Highstone."

Rephanin's heart skipped, and he drew a sharp breath. Turisan's smile widened into a grin, and with a nod of farewell he turned back to the warriors, leaving Rephanin to make his way home to the magehall in a state of bewildered anticipation.

&

With the morning sun again stinging his eyes, Rephanin looked out at the guardians gathering on the plain east of Glenhallow. Many were new, and many had no weapons or cloaks. Rephanin felt a pang over that lack, but the magehall could not bless items that did not yet exist. He imagined furious activity in the weavers' and sword-smiths' halls.

Today he had borrowed a horse from the palace stables, a sturdy brown mare that seemed to have no more regard for him than he for it. Never comfortable in the saddle, he made a conscious effort not to fidget while he waited beside Turisan for the guardians to assemble.

Ehranan circled his horse around to face Rephanin and Turisan, the guardians at his back. He wore golden-hued leathers and a cloak whose snowy whiteness must owe something to magecraft. His black braid lay against it like a rope; that and the black coat of his mount made him look exotic amidst the fair colors of hundreds of Greenglens.

"How is it done?" Ehranan's voice was commanding, but a hint of uncertainty showed in his blue eyes.

Rephanin glanced at the guardians. "When they are assembled, I will speak to all, beginning with a very quiet call that will only be heard by those with potential for mindspeech."

"Ah." Turisan nodded. "I heard that before. I wondered what you were doing."

Rephanin gazed at him, somewhat surprised. It made sense, he supposed, that one attuned to mindspeech would hear his call. He felt a pang of regret that he had never tried speaking to Turisan before Eliani had entered his life but dismissed it as unworthy and turned back to Ehranan.

"If none respond, I will then speak openly to all. You will hear me, after which you will be able to address them."

Ehranan's eyebrows twitched, then he sat back in his saddle, looking thoughtful. A horn rang out, calling the assembled guardians to attention.

Ranks upon ranks stood motionless on the plain. The shouts of the captains died down, leaving the sigh of the morning wind the only sound. Rephanin drew a deep breath, readying himself to speak with the quietest of thoughts.

If any of you can hear me, answer now.

I hear you.

Rephanin's heart leapt, instantly thundering as if he had just run a league. His horse reacted, sidling until his hands tightened on the reins to steady it. He looked at Turisan but knew it had not been his voice.

Who spoke? Where are you?

Here, my lord. Thorian.

A hand was raised several ranks back in the midst of the Guard. Rephanin knew the name, and though he could not be certain at this distance, he thought the face familiar. One of the new circle of mage candidates, he suddenly recalled.

Volunteers had flocked to the magehall in recent days, seeking training, seeking to help. Thorian had been among them and must have become accustomed enough to mindspeech to be sensitive to his call. Rephanin was somewhat disappointed at this realization, but still it bespoke promise on the guardian's part.

Well done, Thorian. We will talk of this before tonight's circle.

Yes, my lord. He seemed pleased.

I want you to try something. Before you come into the magehall, try speaking to me like this from outside. Do you understand?

Yes, my lord. Of course.

Good.

Rephanin glanced at Ehranan, who was watching him with an expression of curiosity. Facing the guardians, Rephanin opened his voice.

Greetings, guardians of Southfæld.

As it had before, the mindspeech caused a stir among the Guard. Rephanin continued quickly before they could begin to talk among themselves.

*I am Rephanin, master of Glenhallow's magehall.
Pray do not answer, but listen. I bring you greeting
from Lord Ehranan of Eastfæld, who is given command of the defense of Midrange.*

He turned his head to look at Ehranan and nodded.
The warrior's throat moved in a swallow, then he
straightened in the saddle.

Fellow guardians—

Ehranan paused, seeming surprised at his own
voice. The attention of the Guard shifted to him, the
change palpable in the thin morning air.

*You have pledged yourselves to the defense of
Midrange. What you learn in the next few days may
save your life or the life of the guardian beside you.
Display your weapons!*

The force of the command surprised Rephanin. He
laid a hand on the withers of his mount as the Guard
suddenly moved as one, drawing swords or raising
bows.

Sunlight glinted off metal in the farthest ranks, and
a sudden chill chased down Rephanin's spine. He
glanced toward Ehranan, saw him exchanging a look
with Berephan.

Rephanin swallowed. Yes, that was most effective.
Proof also that his voice had reached every guardian
on the field.

Be at ease.

The guardians lowered their arms. Rephanin found
that he was breathing rather swiftly and shallowly,
and made an effort to be calm. He felt as if the earth
had shifted subtly beneath him, as if the sun's angle
had suddenly altered.

Midrange. I am bound for Midrange. How soon?

A hundred tasks and obligations sprang to Rephanin's

mind. He would have to confer with Jholóran, find out whether he would accept charge of the magehall and both circles temporarily—indefinitely, perhaps. Jholóran must also be introduced to Jharan, for the governor would need access to the master of the mage-hall—

"Lord Rephanin?"

He looked up at Ehranan, startled by the warrior's physical voice. Ehranan's face was alight with sup-pressed excitement.

"Will you break bread with me this evening? I am housed at Hallowhall."

Rephanin bowed in the saddle. "You honor me."

"The honor is mine."

There was no longer any sign of doubt in Ehranan's face. Instead, smiling speculation.

This trial had changed everything. Ehranan would seize on it—had already seized on it—and would spare no application of mindspeech to better wield his army.

Rephanin turned his horse toward the city, ignoring Turisan's triumphant glance. If this was the path meant for him, he felt no enthusiasm for it.

Returning to the magehall, he at once addressed himself to his outstanding obligations, pausing only to ask Tivhari to carry a message for him. He did not stop to rest, knowing he would find no peace until he had arranged the magehall's future to his satisfaction.

Late in the afternoon, Tivhari ushered a visitor into his sitting room. Rephanin looked up from the tally book he had been perusing.

"Thank you for coming, Jholóran. Have you broken fast?"

Jholóran shook his head as he handed Rephanin his

cloak. "I came as soon as I arose and read your message. Did you wish to hear about the circle's work last night?"

"Yes, briefly. I trust all went well?"

Rephanin hung the cloak on a peg, then led Jholóran to the hearth and invited him to sit. He picked up an ewer of tea—Heléri's blend, fragrant with flowers—and poured for Jholóran, who settled himself and reached his hands toward the fire.

"There were several questions about the difficulty of laying khi into metal. It might be of benefit for you to demonstrate again—"

Lord Rephanin?

Rephanin sat up suddenly, spilling a drop of tea on his robe. With a gesture he silenced Jholóran. He half thought he had imagined what he had heard and was cautious in response.

Thorian?

Yes, my lord.

The answer was faint, but real. Rephanin felt his chest grow tense. He scarcely dared to breathe.

Where are you?

At the garrison. I have just been dismissed for the day. Shall I come to the magehall?

The garrison. Not the public circle just outside the magehall but fully as far as the city's inner gates. Rephanin glanced at the closed door of his chambers, his throat tightening.

Yes. Please do.

Jholóran looked at him, one brow raised in curiosity. "Are you all right?"

Exhilaration sang through Rephanin's veins. He drew a deep breath.

"Yes. Please forgive me. You were saying?"

"Laying focus into metal. I think you should give the circle another demonstration."

"Of course. Tell me, how did they respond to your guidance?"

"Well enough." Jholóran picked up a slice of bread thick with nuts and currants from a plate Tivhari had left on the table between their chairs and broke it in half with his fingers. "They spared no effort and accomplished a good deal. Everyone seems to work harder of late. I think they are anxious to please you."

"Their concern should be for the quality of their work, not for my opinion."

"So it should."

The mage calmly chewed his bread as he returned Rephanin's regard. Though reluctant to yield the place he had held for so many centuries, Rephanin knew he must not delay.

"Jholóran, I have a boon to ask of you. I expect to be called away from Glenhallow soon. Will you oversee the magehall in my absence? Guide the circles in their learning and their work?"

Jholóran looked surprised and somewhat alarmed. "Called away? Where?"

"To Midrange."

Rephanin explained briefly what had passed on the field that morning. Jholóran listened, frowning at the coals on the hearth.

"You are more than capable of guiding the work of this hall. Will you take my burdens for a while?"

Jholóran looked up to meet his gaze. "For how long?"

"I cannot say."

The dark eyes regarded him for a long moment. Unspoken understanding passed between them. There was a chance that this change would be permanent if any ill befell Rephanin at Midrange. Jholóran nodded slowly.

"Of course I will, if you ask it."

"Thank you. There are a few small matters of which you should be aware. Tivhari does an excellent job managing the magehall—"

A quiet knock on the door interrupted him. Rephanin rose to answer it and found Tivhari and Thorian outside.

A pang of excitement smote him at the sight of the guardian. Thorian smiled, an answering spark in his eye. Out in the corridor beyond, Rephanin heard voices. The new circle was gathering.

"Thank you, Tivhari. Jholóran, will you guide the new circle in their practice tonight? Thorian and I have a matter to discuss."

Jholóran raised an eyebrow as he glanced at Thorian. "Of course."

He left with Tivhari, and Rephanin looked at Thorian. One unassuming, rather inexperienced guardian. A small vessel to hold Rephanin's centuries-old hopes.

"Please, be at home." Rephanin gestured toward the hearth. "May I take your cloak?"

Thorian undid the clasp on his guardian's cloak and handed it to Rephanin with a shy smile. Rephanin found himself checking the quality of the blessings in the garment as he hung it up. Strong habit, born of the recent intensity of work in the magehall.

The focuses in the cloak were well laid. Jholóran's work, he thought.

Thorian sat down rather gingerly in one of the chairs near the hearth, as if he felt out of place. Rephanin regarded him for a moment, thinking he must not be older than a century or two. He showed little of the reserve that came of a long lifetime of disappointments.

Rephanin fought against the urge to question him through mindspeech. Thorian must be given the opportunity to choose this path himself, and he must first understand the consequences of that choice.

Setting aside Jholóran's cup, Rephanin took down a fresh one for Thorian. "I was surprised to hear you answer this morning. How long have you been in the Guard?"

Thorian shifted in his chair. "I joined only recently, when the call for volunteers went out. I was one of the last to receive a cloak." He glanced toward the pale garment now hanging by the door.

Rephanin handed Thorian a cup of tea and drew his chair around to face his guest. "You have done well today. You heard me when no other did this morning, and you spoke to me from the garrison. I believe that you possess the gift of mindspeech, that you may possibly be a distance speaker."

Thorian blinked once. His hands gripped the carved arms of the chair, and his brown eyes opened rather wide.

"What do you know of mindspeech, Thorian?"

"Only what you have shown us in the circle. I have heard stories of Dejharin and Dironen."

"They were distance speakers. My gift differs from theirs. Do you understand how?"

"I think so. Distance speakers can speak only to their partners, but across any distance. You can speak to anyone, but they must be in your presence."

"Yes. Physical barriers in particular interfere with my gift. Your being able to speak to me from the garrison is cause for hope that you are a distance speaker. If we work together to develop your ability, you and I may be able to speak regardless of barriers or distance."

Rephanin leaned back in his chair, resting his elbows on its arms and folding his hands lightly as he watched Thorian's face. The guardian seemed both excited and slightly apprehensive.

"Before we pursue this, you should know that it will mean our becoming quite familiar with one another."

Thorian looked bewildered. "You mean we will know each other's secrets?"

"Not quite that. Mindspeech is . . . intimate. Those who use it to any great extent cannot help becoming close. You might not know what I am thinking, but it is possible you will know my feelings at times, and I yours."

"Oh."

Thorian gazed at the hearth, absorbing this. Rephanin watched traces of doubt flicker across his features. Classic Greenglen features: the high cheekbones, the long jaw. Already Rephanin felt drawn to him. He paused, choosing his next words carefully.

"Take some time to think on this. If you decide not to pursue this path, I will understand."

Those had been hard words to say, and Rephanin was glad his voice had not wavered. He wanted, quite intently, to develop Thorian's gift.

The guardian looked up at him, his face serious. "If we do pursue it, will we be like Turisan and Eliani?"

"Perhaps. We must determine whether your gift is limited by distance. We know that mine is."

A fire of excitement lit Thorian's eyes, and he leaned forward in his chair. "I need no time to consider."

Rephanin could not help smiling but made an effort

to subdue the answering emotion in his heart. He wanted nothing more than to speak to Thorian in thought at once, to embrace his khi. He drew a steadying breath.

"Still, I ask you to do so. Go home tonight, talk of this with your family and friends. They may raise concerns that have not occurred to you."

And some may remember a time when I was less discriminating with mindspeech. A time when I ignored its risks or at least imperfectly understood them.

A pang of remorse struck Rephanin as he thought of Soshari's conce by the river. She had stumbled unwary into the seductive intimacy of mindspeech. He would never allow that to happen again. Thorian must understand the implications of this path before he chose to walk it.

"If we do this, we will be opening our hearts to each other. Do you see?"

The guardian blinked, and a swallow moved the long muscles of his throat. He nodded slowly.

"Yes. I will think on it."

"Take as long as you wish."

They sat in silence until Rephanin realized he was reluctant to see Thorian leave. He stood abruptly, breaking the moment, and went to fetch Thorian's cloak. Thorian followed, frowning in abstraction as he accepted the garment.

"Thank you, my lord."

"You need not be so formal, Thorian. Call me by my name."

Thorian's eyes widened, as if this were a great responsibility. His voice fell to a hushed whisper. "Rephanin."

Khi burned in the air between them. Rephanin nodded, then opened the door.

"Good night, Thorian. Take good counsel and rest well."

"Good night."

He watched the guardian go down the corridor, at first with slow steps, then faster. The Greenglen cloak swirled about his shoulders just before the curve of the corridor hid him from view.

It occurred to Rephanin only now that Thorian might have a lover and that she might be the one with the greatest objection to his pursuit of mindspeech. It would not be the first time Rephanin had been seen as a threat to such a relationship.

He closed the door and returned to the hearth. The choice was Thorian's, and he would have to make his own peace with it.

Heléri.

She could not hear him; no one was near to hear him. How he wished he could share this news with her! He would have to wait. Another reason to look forward to his journey to Midrange.

❧ Glenhallow ❧

Turisan lay upon his bed, watching swirls of snow through the glass dome overhead. The dome was fashioned with magecraft and did not admit the winter's cold. Heavy tapestries were drawn tight along the balustrades of the Star Tower, and fires burned in all the hearths, yet despite all, he felt chilled.

The journey to Midrange—to which he eagerly looked forward—would soon begin. All that delayed them now was the lack of equipment, and another day or two should remedy that.

Beyond that, the future was less certain. He wondered what might await Eliani in Fireshore and what course the war would take.

His musings were interrupted by the visitor's chime from below. He had sent his attendant away for the night, so he rose and hurried down the steps to the torchlit antechamber. When he opened the door, he saw his father outside, looking grim.

"Kelevon has escaped. I came to inform you so that you may warn Eliani."

Turisan's heart gave a thud of alarm. "Escaped?"

Jharan nodded. "He wounded a guardian. I am going to the garrison to learn what happened."

"I will come with you."

Turisan fetched his cloak and followed his father down the spiral stair to the palace. The rotunda was softly lit by torches and strangely quiet in the absence of the Council and all the additional visitors it had attracted to Glenhallow. Alone in the vast hall, they hastened down the grand stair and out into the city.

Turisan pulled his cloak tighter as a gust of snow blew into his face. "How long has the traitor been gone?"

"Since early evening was Berephan's best guess. The four guardians watching over him were changed at sundown, and the new guards were found dosed with essence of dreamflower."

"So he had help."

Jharan's face went stony. "Yes. The guardian who was wounded."

As they reached the garrison near the city's inner gate, Jharan turned toward Berephan's house, where the guardians at the door admitted them at once. They were guided to a small chamber on the ground floor.

Berephan joined them outside the door. "Her sister is with her, and a healer."

He knocked softly, and a moment later the door was opened by an anxious-looking female in a plain gown, her unbraided hair caught hastily back in a simple clasp. Her eyes widened as she stepped back to admit Jharan.

Turisan followed him in, and Berephan came after, softly closing the door. The female hastened back to the hearth, where a newly kindled fire roared brightly. Seated on a bench beside it were two others, male and female.

The male was lost in a trance of healing, his hands resting on one side of the female's neck. She was the guardian, then, though she wore only tunic and legs at present. Turisan noticed her Southfæld Guard's cloak on the floor nearby, bloodstained.

Jharan spoke quietly to Berephan. "What has she told you?"

"Little yet. I thought it best that she be tended first. Her sister arrived only a short time ago."

Turisan glanced at the sister, who had sat down beside the guardian and taken her hand. They were plainly kin, though the sister's face was softer, rounder. The guardian's was drawn with harsher lines, sharpened by care and weariness. She stared into the fire with dull, unseeing eyes.

"How badly is she hurt?"

"Two cuts, scraped hands, a few bruises. The wound to the throat is the worst."

Turisan looked at Berephan. "Knife wound?"

Berephan nodded. Turisan exchanged a glance with his father and saw that they were pondering the same question: Had Kelevon fed from that wound?

Berephan stepped toward the guardian. "Filari, Lord Jharan has come to see you."

The guardian's eyes flickered and she looked up, mild surprise on her face. She nodded, hampered by the hands of the healer.

"My lord governor."

Her words were a rough whisper. She cleared her throat, straightened her back, and gazed awkwardly at her visitors.

Jharan sat on the bench opposite her, and Turisan joined him. The healer stirred and withdrew his hands. Turisan winced at the sight of the long, angry gash showing red through a light dressing. The healer stood, glanced at the newcomers with a mild frown, and retired from the room.

Jharan leaned forward. "Do you feel able to tell us what happened?"

Filari gazed at him for a long moment, her face showing nothing. A slight crease between the brows was all the sign of distress she gave.

"It was my doing." Her voice was hard. "I helped him go free."

Jharan's lips pressed together briefly. "Were you compelled?"

She blinked, gazing at the fire. "No."

"Why, then?"

"He did not deserve to be held captive, nor to be killed."

Turisan's anger flared. "You do not know what he deserves!"

Jharan glanced at him in silent warning. Turisan gritted his teeth and was still.

He regretted his leniency with Kelevon, but despite his resentment, deep in his heart he knew that Filari was right. Kelevon's ill deeds—even the latest, his abuse of her—did not justify his being slain or kept confined indefinitely. Nothing justified such fates according to the creed, because the creed made no provision for the sort of behavior Kelevon had shown. An ælven living by the creed would have died before doing such harm.

"Did he feed upon you?" Jharan gestured to Filari's wound.

Pain clouded her eyes—the pain of affection betrayed. Impatient with Jharan's gentle questioning, Turisan caught her gaze and held it.

"How did he leave the city?"

"By the grottoes." Her voice fell to a whisper; her eyes pleaded that no pursuit be sent. Turisan could not help grimacing.

"Which trail did he take?"

"I do not know. West, perhaps. He asked about the pass."

Berephan stirred, shifting his feet. "It is snowing."

Jharan glanced at him, then nodded. "Send out trackers. No fewer than three together."

Berephan nodded and started toward the door. Filari stood up suddenly.

"Why can you not leave him alone? Let him cross the mountains and be away. He wishes no harm to any of us!"

"He is a danger to all of us, whether he wishes it or no." Jharan nodded at Berephan to go.

The warden left, and Filari slowly sat down again, looking bereft. A log popped on the hearth, sending a spark skittering across the stone floor. Jharan spoke gently once more, though his eyes were stern.

"What you have done has placed others in danger. Do you see that?"

Filari nodded, gazing at the floor. "I will atone."

Misliking the flatness of her voice, Turisan hastened to speak. "You are an experienced guardian. You cannot be spared."

He glanced at Jharan before continuing, wondering if his father's thoughts followed his own. Filari could not continue to serve in the garrison at Glenhallow. There were four guardians there, at least, who would never trust her again.

"Come and serve in my command. We march for Midrange soon, and more than half of my guardians are raw. I need help training them. Let that be your atonement."

Filari was still for a moment, then looked up at him with hopeless eyes. "If that is your wish, my lord."

"It is."

Turisan held Filari's gaze until she bowed her head, closing her eyes with a small sigh. Her sister threw an arm around her shoulders and glared at him.

"She should rest."

Turisan nodded. "Go home now. Report to me on the field at dawn."

"Yes, my lord."

"I am your captain now."

Her gaze flickered to his face. "Yes, Captain."

A warmth bloomed on Turisan's brow; he returned the signal asking Eliani to wait. He watched as Filari allowed her sister to urge her to her feet. When the door was shut behind them, Jharan looked up.

"She is at risk of the alben's curse."

Turisan nodded. "I will observe her closely."

"Not too closely."

"Father, we are all at risk to some degree."

Jharan was silent. After a moment he nodded. He looked weary as he stood.

"Come. Let us take what rest we can."

They met Berephan in the hearthroom. He stamped his feet, leaving tracks of hardened snow upon the rug, and shook the snow from his cloak.

"Four teams have gone out, though they will have a difficult task in this weather."

Jharan made a small, formal bow. "Thank you, Lord Berephan. Send word to Hallowhall when you have news."

"Aye." Berephan glanced at Turisan. "Keep warm. It grows bitter out."

Jharan and Turisan stepped out into a night swirling with snow. The wind had risen and now moaned among the houses and larger halls. Turisan had to raise his voice to address his father.

"He may have taken shelter from this."

"Or be gone beyond hope of finding already."

Jharan huddled deep in his cloak as they strode up the avenue toward Hallowhall. Turisan pulled his hood forward to protect his face from the stinging snow and sent the signal of query to Eliani.

Yes, love. What were you doing earlier? I thought you were troubled . . .

He told her, bluntly and in few words, what Kelevon had done. She said nothing at first, listening to his description of Filari's wounds and his concern for her.

I am taking her into my command.

To be part of the garrison at High Holding? One might call that a harsh duty, being posted so near to danger.

She should leave Glenhallow in any case, and I wish to keep an eye on her while I may. She faults herself for Kelevon's escape and spoke of atonement in a way that I misliked.

He felt the sudden heat of Eliani's wrath, so strong that he nearly flinched. His boot slipped on the snow-slickened stone of the avenue, and Jharan reached out a hand to steady him.

It is Kelevon who should atone! Has he charmed her into thinking she is responsible for his misdeeds? I hope your trackers drag him back to Glenhallow. Save him for me, if you will.

You will have to share the chance to discipline him with several others, I think.

I claim precedence.

Turisan smiled, bemused. *I believe my father precedes you.*

Precedence of grievance.

Her tone was grim, making him wish he could fold her in his arms. Kelevon had hurt her in more than one way. Her pain over their failed cup-bond had made her push Turisan away at first; he remembered it all too well.

He wondered briefly if he should have spared her the knowledge of the traitor's escape but knew that he could not have avoided telling her. At the least, she had to be warned that Kelevon was now at large.

Have a care, my love. He may pursue you.

He will have to make haste.

I would not be surprised if he made for the Steppes.

Turisan felt another flash of her anger, though this time it was quickly damped. In its place a brittle coldness filled her voice.

He is welcome to try.

◈ Alpinon ◈

Eliani pressed her party onward despite a chill evening breeze blowing down from the mountain peaks. They were nearing Heahrued, and she was anxious to reach it before halting for the night.

It was not only the prospect of a night in a bed or the urgency of her errand that drove her. The guardians of her escort were grief-stricken, especially the Greenglens. She hoped that coming into a village where they might talk with other folk, even if only to tell them what they had seen, would bring them some relief.

She herself looked forward to the comforts of the village—company, a hearth, a roof overhead—to drive away the horror of the slaughter in the wood. She would not be surprised to learn, some years hence, that shades had risen in that place.

Shades. Had the envoy's fate been what Luruthin and Vanorin's vision at the Three Shades had portended?

She looked at Luruthin, riding beside her to keep her company. Vanorin, whose mood continued dark, had insisted on placing her in the center of the party. She had yielded, though with ill grace.

Luruthin noticed her gaze and turned in the saddle

to look at her. His lips curved in a wan smile. "Tired, cousin?"

"Ready for a respite, yes. I think we can talk Gharinan's steward out of a few loaves of fresh bread."

"You could offer to perform healings in exchange."

She glanced sharply at him but had not the heart for banter, nor did Luruthin's voice hold the edge of humor she would have expected with such a quip. He dropped the attempt and instead looked at her seriously.

"What led you to heal those two back at Midrange? I did not think you had ever studied healing."

"The one asked me to bless her wound. I was as surprised as she when something happened." Eliani raised her forearm, the woven handfasting ribbon gleaming in the moonlight. "I think it was this. Heléri must have put some sort of healing into it."

"You do not think it may be your own gift?"

She scoffed. "You know I am far more likely to damage my own flesh than to heal another's."

"When you were younger, yes. But you have reached your majority now and left all such childish awkwardness behind you."

She shook her head. "Sometimes I feel I no longer know who I am."

"Then I shall have to remind you from time to time. You are Eliani, daughter of Felisan, governor-elect of Alpinon—"

"I have left my clan."

The words fell starkly into the twilight. Luruthin made no answer.

"Whenever I remember that, I feel frightened."

His voice was softer when he spoke again. "You march now with Greenglen, yes, but you are yet Stonereach. We are still kin, Eliani. We will stand by you."

A cry of alarm rose from ahead, and the horses plunged in fright. Luruthin held his mount with a stern grip, his face suddenly grim. Eliani pushed forward, heart pounding with fear. The mount of a Southfælder turned itself across her path, blocking her.

She stood in her stirrups, trying to see past the riders. Confused shouting filled the air. She saw a flash of golden fur and heard a spine-chilling howl.

Catamount!

The horse in front of her reared, nearly throwing its rider. The cat was suddenly before her, slashing at the frightened horse.

Eliani nocked an arrow to her bow. Beside her, Luruthin shouted a warning to a guardian who had dismounted and was brandishing his sword. Folly to close with a catamount, however long one's sword might be, but the guardians were reacting, not thinking.

Eliani's brow grew warm. She hastily returned the signal for "wait," then caught a clear view of a golden haunch and let her arrow fly. It struck, and an enraged scream filled the air as she reached for another.

Others were now using their bows. Several more arrows plunged into the cat's flesh, and it danced with rage, biting at those it could reach.

Eliani's heart ached for the poor maddened creature. She loosed an arrow at its eye, and it struck. A short shrieking cry rang out, then was stilled as the creature collapsed.

The guardians lowered their weapons. Eliani leapt from her mount and hastened forward. Others dismounted as well, still trying to calm their horses.

The cat lay still, its face fixed in a furious scowl, blood staining the golden fur dark below the ruined eye. Even in death, it made her heart pulse with fear. Why had it attacked so large a party?

She looked up the road, trying to discern where the attack had begun, and saw a cluster of dismounted guardians. Heart filling with dread, she hastened forward.

"Hanusan!"

She pushed her way through to the fallen Stonereach, dropping to her knees beside him. Her kindred and a good friend.

Hanusan lay on his face, blood seeping through dark punctures in his cloak at the back of his neck where the cat had bitten him. There were also deep wounds on his arms where claws had sliced through his leathers. He breathed but did not move when Eliani hesitantly touched him.

"Bandages!" She looked up at those standing near. "Quickly!"

Guardians hastened to respond, reaching for their saddle packs. Eliani bade one of them help her, and together they removed Hanusan's cloak and leather jerkin. She bandaged his arms while two guardians held him upright, then was suddenly overwhelmed with a need to grasp his shoulders.

She closed her eyes, her scalp tingling as the khi rose in her hands. Warmth poured into her head from above, flowing down through her arms to Hanusan. She caught her breath, frightened, and made an effort to relax and accept what was happening.

Again her brow grew warm with Turisan's calling. She dared to answer.

Not now, love. I am well.

Another healing.

Yes.

He said no more, though she could feel him with her, a distant comfort. For a long while she held still. Not until the murmur of someone's voice penetrated her awareness did she realize that the warmth of khi flowing through her was fading.

Sighing, she withdrew her hands and opened her eyes. The guardians stood around her, watching. Hanusan slowly raised his head.

"Eliani?"

His voice was weak, and he blinked several times, his brow tightening in a frown of pain. Eliani glanced at the nearest guardian, summoning her to assist.

"Hush. You must rest."

They moved Hanusan, gently resting his back against a pine tree, cushioning him with his bundled cloak. He closed his eyes and shivered. Eliani took off her own cloak and laid it over him, then walked over to Luruthin and Vanorin, who stood up to meet her. Both stared at her. She glared back.

"I was compelled. I understand it no better than you."

"Lady, it is a powerful gift." Vanorin bowed with the words. "We all felt it."

Eliani was startled, then embarrassed. She glanced at Luruthin, who nodded. She felt her cheeks go warm and looked away, toward Hanusan.

"He cannot ride. We must send for help from Heahrued."

"Is it far, my lady?"

"No, not far." She looked back at the guardians and summoned one with a gesture. "Mærani! Ride to Heahrued, fetch back a cart. Hurry!"

She saw the rider off, set two others to build a fire to keep Hanusan warm until Mærani returned, then went to find her horse. Luruthin accompanied her, leaning close to murmur to her.

"Back to 'my lady' again."

"I know. I did not want to chide him for it now."

As they passed the dead catamount, Eliani paused to look at it. "I wonder if this was the same cat that killed the envoy."

Luruthin frowned. "A catamount should never have attacked a party this size."

"It was enraged. Perhaps it was mad."

Luruthin squatted to examine the cat. "I see no sign of raving, no lathering at the mouth."

Eliani joined him, brushing her fingers against the cat's coarse coat. It was somewhat dull and matted with burrs, as if the animal had neglected to groom itself. She murmured a few words of regret to the catamount's ældar, then returned to her horse.

The sun had set, and the party was gathering near Hanusan's fire. Other horses were already grazing in a meadow to the east of the road. Eliani led her mount to join them and leaned against a tree to watch it paw dry grass free of the shallow snow.

Turisan?

I am here. What happened?

She told him, brushing her fingers along the ribbons woven on her arm as she described the extraordinary sensations of the healing. She could pick out the handfasting ribbon by touch, though its fabric was as smooth as that of the others. It was almost as though she could feel the images woven into it—here a firespear tree, there a fountain or a star. They came into her mind as she ran her fingers across them.

Could you ask Jhinani about this healing when next you see her? I believe I should seek some guidance from an experienced healer.

Of course. Speaking of Jhinani . . .

Yes?

Has Luruthin confided anything to you?

Eliani smiled. *She has told you. Good. Is it not wonderful?*

Wonderful, and surprising.

Well, they were surprised as well.

Were they? Jhinani did not mention the circumstances.

I should leave it to Luruthin to tell you, I suppose. You males enjoy sharing such triumphs.

Cruel. I must wait until your party's return to learn how my mother's sister was seduced?

She sensed Turisan's laughter and smiled. *As I understand it, she did the seducing. It was the night of our handfasting.*

It would have to have been.

They cup-bonded before we left.

Did they?

He seemed approving. Eliani hoped it would ease his mind to know Luruthin was so bound. She knew he trusted her—believed in her—probably more than she did herself, but Luruthin's vow to Jhinani should be an additional comfort to him.

She heard Vanorin's voice rise, calling out instructions, and glanced back toward the fire. Twilight was settling over the mountains.

I wish you were here, love.

So do I.

I—I need . . .

His answer came not in words but in pure love. It washed through her, easing her heartache but making her long all the more for Turisan's arms around her.

❧

Turisan stood at the eastern balustrade of the Star Tower, watching for the first sign of dawn. He held the heavy tapestry back in one hand, a cold breeze stinging his face and troubling the embers in the nearby hearth. The coals spat and sparked as if disturbed in slumber, making the mountain-shaped hearth seem like a waking volcano.

It was dark yet, the eastern sky barely showing a hint of blue and still strewn with stars, but Turisan was unable to rest. Today his company would march for Midrange.

He had considered moving out to camp with them but had not been able to bring himself to leave the Star Tower. In this place he and Eliani had consummated their union. One precious night, the night of their handfasting, they had spent together. The next day she had ridden for Fireshore.

He had dwelt here ever since, treasuring every reminder of that night, every pillow and drape of this chamber. Now, today, he must leave it at last.

He let the tapestry fall and put on the clothes Pheran had laid out for him, a soft fleececod tunic and legs to go beneath his leathers. He did not don the leathers yet. Instead he went barefoot down the short stair to the antechamber below and into the tiring room where Pheran kept his wardrobe.

The stone floor was cold. Turisan shivered a little as he crossed to where a small space was reserved for the single gown of Eliani's that was here, the gown she had worn for their handfasting. It was of silk from Eastfæld, all in blue and violet, with a veil that shimmered in both colors, its edge beaded with tiny bright crystals. Turisan touched the silk, catching up a double handful and burying his face in it. There, a whisper of her khi.

He wanted to take the gown with him, or even just the veil, only to look at it and remember Eliani's face as she wore it. The colors reminded him of her, though they were no longer hers. She was a Greenglen now.

He stepped back, letting the silks fall. He could not take them to Midrange. They would doubtless be damaged if he did, and he did not care to face Eliani's wrath when she learned he had ruined her father's gift. She had worn them only thrice.

He smiled, remembering the first time, when she had reached her majority on Evennight. They had danced in Highstone's public circle, which was bedecked with harvest fruits and strewn with golden leaves, Eliani a swirl of violet and blue and flashing green eyes. Little had they known then what their future paths would be.

Turning away, he ran his fingers over the ribbons woven on his left forearm. These were all the memento he needed. The blue and violet were there, along with silver and sage. Images of Alpinon and Glenhallow both. And hidden in the weave, part of the magecraft that bound the whole together, was Eliani's khi along with his own.

He returned to the Star Tower and saw through the dome that the sky was definitely growing lighter now. He put on his leathers, then took up his cloak and, draping it over his arm, hastened downstairs.

The rotunda was busy with murmuring voices as he made the last turn onto the gallery. He had asked his father not to keep his command standing in the cold dawn during a long farewell ceremony, and Jharan had honored his request by moving the ceremony indoors. Tables of fresh bread, roasted meats, and late autumn fruits stood to one side of the rotunda, and many of Glenhallow's important citizens were already enjoying the repast.

Turisan saw his father standing in a small knot of

dignitaries. Berephan, Ehranan, and Lady Rheneri turned to greet him as he came down the grand stairs and approached them. It occurred to him to wonder why Rheneri had not returned to Eastfæld after the Council disbanded, but this was not the occasion to ask. Perhaps she had stayed in support of Lord Ehranan.

Rheneri smiled, her black hair and blue eyes reminding him of Heléri though she wore Ælvanen's gold and white. "All honor to you, Lord Turisan, and may spirits guide you on your journey."

"My thanks to you, my lady."

He bowed over her hand, keeping to himself the thought that if he could not find his way to Midrange without the aid of spirits, he was not fit for his command. She had not meant it literally; he knew that. His mood was too brittle this morning. As atonement, he made an additional effort to be pleasant to all the guests.

He took little food and sipped a cup of hot tea rather than the wine and ale that were also offered. He was grateful when Jharan at last called the gathering to order. He loved his home and would miss its comforts, but he was eager to be gone now that the day of departure had arrived. Sooner gone, sooner returned, and the better for all ælven interests to have a garrison at High Holding.

Jharan addressed the assembled guests, praising the courage of those who had volunteered to go to Midrange in advance of the main army. No feast in a warm hall for them, though Turisan had asked Jharan to have the palace kitchens send them fresh bread and some of the same delicacies that were served here in honor of their last meal before the march.

Jhinani came up to stand beside him, smiling. She

had stood as his mother after her sister's death, and the affection in her eyes warmed his heart. He leaned close to whisper to her.

"Eliani wants your advice about healing."

"I am happy to give it, but perhaps it must wait until your return."

He nodded, and as Jharan turned to him at that moment, he fell silent. His father raised one eyebrow slightly, then proceeded.

"All Southfæld thanks you, Lord Turisan, for leading these companies to Midrange."

"All ælvenkind must thank you." Ehranan bowed as he said the words, and Turisan swallowed. To be honored thus by one who had stood at Westgard . . .

"You will have in your care not only these three hundred but also a mindspeaker." Jharan turned to Rephanin, who had joined the gathering unbeknownst to Turisan.

A mindspeaker? Rephanin, to come with the advance? It made no sense, and Turisan was about to protest when he saw that a guardian stood with the magelord—one of his force, if Turisan recalled correctly. His face shone with eagerness as he looked at Rephanin, and Turisan suddenly remembered the magelord's attempts to find a mindspeaker among the recruits.

Turisan's heart began to race. Another mindspeaker!

Rephanin laid his hands on the guardian's shoulders. "Thorian shows great promise as a distance speaker. His presence with your command will give a double advantage, that of testing his gift and that of providing Governor Jharan continuing contact with you."

Turisan bowed slightly to Thorian. "This is joyous news. May your gift prove limitless."

Thorian returned the bow with reverence. "Thank you, Lord Turisan."

"Hail the new mindspeaker!"

The assembly took up the cry, and Turisan watched Thorian's cheeks redden with surprised pleasure. Rephanin murmured something to the guardian—his partner now, apparently—and then stepped back.

Turisan's feelings were mixed, and he quickly smote down a trace of jealousy. Absolute folly to wish himself unique; another mindspeaker was a boon to the ælven in every way. He wished Thorian complete success.

He could not keep this news to himself. As the cheers continued, he queried Eliani.

Yes, love? Are you leaving already?

Not quite. Ceremonies.

He felt her mirth. *Dear Governor Jharan!*

Eliani, Rephanin has found another mindspeaker!

A mindspeaker? Tell me!

He gave her the details, such as he knew. The cheers dwindled meanwhile, and Jharan turned to address him again.

I must go, love.

Ceremonies. Speak to me when you are free; we are just now breaking fast.

I will.

Jharan offered his arm, and Turisan clasped it. "Lord Turisan, you take all our blessings with you. Ride swiftly and return swiftly."

"I will. Thank you, my lord governor."

Cheering rose again as Turisan made his way out of Hallowhall. Jharan, Thorian, and several others followed.

Horses stood waiting in the public circle, along with a small crowd of citizens who had braved the morning chill to see them off. Word of Rephanin's discovery must have already spread, for they called "Hail the mindspeakers!" and threw garlands of winterbloom to Thorian as well as to Turisan and Rephanin.

Jharan came to stand with Turisan beside his horse. "I will not go with you to the gates; I would only delay you."

Turisan smiled ruefully. "I did not mean that—"

"No, you were right. Jhinani has pointed out to me that when I do not wish to do something, I postpone it with speeches. I do not wish to bid you farewell, but I must."

He was frowning. Turisan knew it was a sign not of disapproval but of heartache. He offered his arm.

"Thank you, Father, for permitting me this."

Jharan pulled him into a brief, firm embrace, voice husky with emotion. "Spirits see you safely there and home, my son."

Squeezing his father's arms as they parted, Turisan could only hope that his smile said all that was in his heart. Here, in public, was not the place for lengthy demonstrations of affection.

Jharan stepped back, his expression returning to the governor's serene calm. Turisan mounted his horse, hoping his face was equally calm as he started toward the city gates, for his heart was full of thunder.

◈ Althill ◈

Luruthin's hopes rose as the party rounded a bend and the lights of Althill glimmered into view. Snow had fallen off and on all day, and now a heavy mist was gathering in the hollows and valleys. This high in the mountains the night promised a sharp freeze.

Luruthin gazed at the back of Eliani's cloak, its hood pulled up to keep the snow off her head. The pale green cloth seemed to shed water like a swan's feathers. He glanced around at the Southfælders, all warm and dry beneath their Greenglen cloaks. His own blue cloak from Clerestone, sadly lacking in mage-crafted blessings, was saturated, and the cold was starting to seep through his leathers.

Vanorin drew up beside him. "Does Althill have hot springs?"

Luruthin gestured westward, where the mountains loomed in the dark, shrouded in wisps of fog. "Up toward the peak. Half a day's ride."

"I suppose Eliani will not wish to take the time."

Vanorin looked disappointed, as well he might. The party had not had leisure to bathe in many days, though at Heahrued, Vanorin had stripped and plunged himself into the frigid Heahrindel to wash away the stench of death. He had then spent half the evening shivering by the fire.

A light shone out as a doorway opened, and a voice was raised in a friendly hail. "Eliani? Is that you?"

The party reined to a halt while a youth ran the short distance to meet them. Eliani grinned down at him from her saddle.

"Ghithlaran! How you have grown!"

Ghithlaran grinned back, brown hair tousled over the shoulders of his cloak, half of it caught beneath the garment. "My father says I may join the Guard next summer!"

"Does he? What makes him think the Guard will have you?"

Ghithlaran laughed, then peered at the party. A smile of recognition lit his lean face, and he poked a hand out of his cloak to wave to Luruthin, who waved back.

"How many are you? We thought it was a patrol."

Eliani dismounted. "A bit larger than that. We are nineteen."

"Nineteen! We cannot house you all!"

Luruthin slid from his saddle. "Is the meethall in use?"

"N-no. It is rather full of barrels, though. We just finished pressing the last of the cider. You would be crowded."

"Crowded is better than wet." Eliani assumed a formal tone, even sweeping a bow. "Pray tell Theyn Mirithan that I crave an audience with him."

Ghithlaran made no answer, his attention caught by the ribbons woven on Eliani's right arm. "You are handfasted!"

"Ah—yes."

"I thought you said you would never handfast!"

"Did I? Well, I changed my mind."

"Who made your ribbon? It is beautiful!"

"Heléri. You will be able to see the pictures better in the light."

Ghithlaran took the hint and dashed away to alert the village's theyn of their arrival. The rest of the party began to dismount, and the horses sighed and shook themselves, knowing their work was done for the nonce.

Vanorin glanced at Luruthin as he slid from his saddle. "Rather a formal gesture for Lady Eliani to stay waiting in the road."

Luruthin grinned. "She has good reason to flatter Mirithan's authority."

Ghithlaran returned, slightly out of breath, and reached for Eliani's reins. "Theyn Mirithan bids you welcome. You may visit him at his house if you wish."

Eliani cast a grimacing glance at Luruthin, then thanked the youth and walked toward the theyn's house. Ghithlaran led her horse and the party across the circle to the meethall.

The village's largest building, it was perhaps half the size of the feast hall at Felisanin Hall in Highstone. More folk came to help with the horses, and the friendly exchange of news began as the party carried their packs into the meethall.

Better than half of the meethall was crammed with barrels, as Ghithlaran had warned. They were stacked to the vaulted ceiling, with an aisle barely wide enough for passage between them. A dusty, fruity smell pervaded the hall as Luruthin edged his way through.

Beyond the barrels was an open space where two villagers were kindling a fire in a wide hearth. Luruthin allowed himself a grateful sigh as he stacked his packs against the wall and stretched out his hands, though the flames were too new to have much warmth.

One of the fire builders, a tall female with her rich red-brown hair caught in two long braids, stood up, brushing dust from her tunic and legs. Luruthin knew her well, for he had visited here on patrol and had once maintained a pleasant dalliance with Taeyani. A glint of laughter came into her green eyes as her gaze fell upon him.

"Welcome, Luruthin! Did you bring stags?"

He grinned. "Not this time. We have other business, I fear."

"Oh? What business?"

"We are escorting Lady Eliani to Fireshore." Vanorin's tone was formal, even cold.

Taeyani raised an eyebrow. Luruthin detected a bristling in her khi and hastened to make the introduction.

"Taeyani, this is Vanorin, who commands our party and is a captain in the Southfæld Guard. Taeyani is steward in Althill."

Vanorin bowed. Taeyani's brow remained high, but she returned the courtesy, then turned to Luruthin.

"We are gathering a meal for you. I should go to oversee it; Diriani can never organize anything. Oh, you may open a barrel of apples. You may have all the apples you wish!"

She showed them which barrels held apples and which cider, invited them to partake of both, then started toward the entrance, beckoning Luruthin to follow with a glance. Seeing Vanorin busy with an apple barrel, Luruthin walked after her down the narrow aisle. She paused inside the hearthroom, where a chill breeze from outside lifted sparks from the fire.

"Your captain is very formal. Are all Southfælders like that?"

"He has many cares."

"Hm." She glanced back into the meethall and spoke in a softer, warmer voice. "Your party will be crowded. You might be more comfortable in a bed."

A slight tingle went through Luruthin. He knew whose bed she meant.

"Thank you, but I am cup-bonded."

Her brows rose again, and for a moment she looked disappointed, then her eyes narrowed. "Do not tell me—a Southfælder?"

"Actually, yes."

She laughed. "They must not all be rigid, then. Well, joy to you."

"Thank you."

She brushed a kiss against his cheek and went out through the hearthroom. Luruthin returned to the back of the meethall, where by this time the fire was burning briskly. Taeyani was right; the party would be crowded. They would have to lie close tonight.

Eliani came in, looking as if she had just finished an unpleasant task. Luruthin ladled a cup of cider for her and grinned as he handed it to her.

"How does our good theyn?"

She pushed back her hood and grimaced. "Stiff as a board of darkwood. He is still offended. Made certain I was aware of the magnitude of his generosity in allowing us to sleep in their meethall."

Luruthin laughed. "Oh, dear."

"I should have sent you to talk to him, theyn to theyn."

"I would have fared no better."

Vanorin joined them, looking curious. "Perhaps Theyn Mirithan is not aware of your standing, Eliani."

"Oh, he is aware. It is not that."

Luruthin grinned. "We should have sent Vanorin to ask his charity and hidden ourselves among the trees."

Eliani cocked an eye at Vanorin, her lips twitching in a smile. "That might have served. But Ghithlaran had already seen me."

Vanorin looked bewildered. Luruthin chuckled, taking pity on him.

"We wasted a day of the villagers' time in running stag races some years ago. Mirithan had a cold supper and has not forgiven us since."

Eliani shook her head as she moved closer to the fire. "He never will forgive us."

Whether by chance or by design, the supper that was brought to the meethall was also cold. They did not mind, as it included buttery cheeses and soft bread along with the apples, wine, and ale, as well as a basket of carrots hastily pulled from winter beds. A cold haunch of roasted venison was also offered, and though there was only enough meat for a mouthful apiece, the guardians expressed their gratitude for their hosts' generosity.

The meethall became crowded with villagers as well as guardians. They milled together, everyone standing for lack of room, talking and eating from platters propped atop barrels and along the wide stone mantel of the hearth.

Taeyani came up to where Eliani, Luruthin, and Vanorin stood beside a cider barrel, offering a platter of cheese. "Accept my belated congratulations on your majority, Lady Eliani."

Eliani smiled as she helped herself to the cheese. "Thank you, Taeyani. You look well. Your brother is wonderfully grown."

"Next summer will mark his thirtieth year."

"Already? Spirits!"

Luruthin took a slice of cheese. "What news from the Steppes?"

"Very little. We have not seen a trade caravan since before Evennight. We did hear there was to be a Council in Glenhallow."

Vanorin nodded. "It was the Council that sent us. Have you heard any news from Fireshore?"

Taeyani regarded him thoughtfully. "We almost never hear from Fireshore. It is a thirty-day journey by caravan to the border, ten of them across a waterless plain, and we have little to offer in trade that they cannot make or grow themselves."

Luruthin nodded in sympathy. Althill's disadvantage was that it lay off the common trade route, the easier road that crossed the plains just east of the Ebons. They saw traders from the Steppes, mostly, horse breeders who valued the village's mountain wines and meads.

Vanorin frowned. "Thirty days by caravan. Twelve riding quickly, and that is only to the border. Ghlanhras is at least another six days beyond that. We are behind our pace."

Taeyani tilted her head. "You are in haste?"

Eliani traded a glance with Luruthin before answering in a lowered voice. "Governor Othanin never replied to Jharan's summons to the Council. A second envoy was sent but never reached him—we found them slain south of Heahrued."

"Slain!"

"Please do not speak of it other than to Mirithan. There is no sense in alarming your people. If you should see Kelevon, though, beware of him. He is a traitor. That much you should tell all your citizens."

Taeyani nodded, eyes wide. Kelevon had been known in Althill.

"So you ride to Fireshore. Do you plan to cross Twisted Pine Pass?"

Luruthin glanced at Eliani. The pass had not occurred to him. The last time any expedition of note had gone through it was before the Battle of Westgard many centuries ago.

Eliani looked as if she had not thought of it, either. "How many days would it save us?"

"With your horses you could cross the pass in four days and be in Fireshore in six or seven."

"Six days instead of twelve."

Eliani glanced at Luruthin, plainly weighing the risks. A harder path, and it meant going west of the Ebons, though only slightly. In this cold, there was little likelihood that kobalen would trouble them.

Luruthin turned to Taeyani. "Could you spare us a guide?"

"To the trailhead or all the way to the pass?"

"Whatever you can manage."

Taeyani smiled wryly, a glint of laughter in her eyes. "I imagine Ghithlaran would be thrilled to miss a few days of chores around the village."

Eliani looked surprised. "Mirithan will not object?"

"Oh, no. He finds Ghithlaran almost as annoying as he finds you."

Luruthin stifled his laughter. Vanorin cast him a disapproving look, then shook his head.

"I do not like crossing the Ebons."

Luruthin turned a lazy glance upon Taeyani. "The trail runs near the peak, does it not?"

"Yes, past the hot springs."

Vanorin's eyes lit with interest. Luruthin hid a smile as Eliani reached for the cider ladle.

"We shall take the pass."

⚭

Eliani peered westward into the fog, toward the pale glowing ghost of the sun. Shreds of thicker cloud, troubled by wind but not banished by it, curled around the feeble orb. She looked over her shoulder at her escort, strung out single file as they led their horses over the narrow, rocky track.

A loose stone lay in her path of a size and sharpness to threaten the horses' hooves. She kicked it off the trail. It clattered as it fell down the steep slope.

The barren rock of the Ebons' western face was depressing. What few plants grew there were weedy and gnarled, clinging stubbornly to the rock against the constant assault of bitter winds.

Eliani called to their guide, who walked before Vanorin a few paces ahead. "Ghithlaran—should we not begin to look for a camp?"

The youth paused and looked back at her. "It is only a little farther to the crest of the pass. There are springs beyond it; we can reach them by dusk, I think."

Springs. Yes, that comfort was worth trudging on a bit farther.

Thinking of it made Eliani thirsty. She shook the water skin at her hip, misliking the lightness of it. She left it closed and swallowed with a dry tongue. Her fingers were cold despite her gloves. She felt despair creeping into her heart, and to fight it she signaled Turisan.

Yes, my heart?

Where are you? Have you halted for the night?

Not yet. We are crossing one more ridge before we make camp. How goes your journey? Have you seen any kobalen?

Eliani scoffed aloud. *No kobalen with a scrap of wit would come near this place.*

She glanced up and saw that the sky above her head was shredding, drifts of mist swirling counter to one another. The wind rose in a sharp rush, shrieking around the rocks. Surprised, Eliani halted and leaned against her mount, turning her face from the sudden frigid blast. When the wind subsided, she looked up again and caught her breath.

The fog had broken, the last wisps of it twining away from sharp crags of gray rock. To the northwest a giant mountain towered high above the rest of the range, its peak bare, its slopes streaked with dark stands of pine and rivers of golden firespear. The sun emerged from its shroud to set them ablaze, and Eliani stood rapt. She heard Vanorin exclaim in wonder.

"What is that mountain, Ghithlaran?"

"The Great Sleeper. You can see the Small Sleeper off to the west."

"Yes."

The Small Sleeper stood well apart from the Ebons, jutting up from the plain in the distance, not as high but nearly as striking as its larger fellow. It was between those two peaks that Dejharin had taken his army, having brought them across the Ebons at Twisted Pine Pass. Eliani peered at the steep, broken slopes they must have descended to reach the plain, and her respect for Dejharin increased.

Vanorin started forward again, and Eliani followed slowly, her gaze still drawn to the looming mountain. The sun was near the horizon now, and a filmy haze began to dim its brightness once more. Fog clung in hollows of the cliffs below, ready to spread across the mountains again when evening fell.

Kobalen dwelt in those lands, but they were not the only danger there. The alben also dwelt west of the Ebons. They had a city, Kelevon had said—and a leader who had sent him to deceive the Ælven Council.

A sudden cry rang out from behind Eliani, echoing against the rocks as a rumbling, sliding sound followed. She turned and watched in horror as the trail collapsed beneath one of the horses toward the rear of the party, a frightened guardian sliding after it down the slope.

Shouts of alarm filled the air. Vanorin brushed past her. Eliani handed her reins to Ghithlaran, then followed the captain back along the trail, hastening past horses and guardians. She came near to losing her own footing in her haste to reach the collapse. Vanorin stood beside another Greenglen male—Sunahran—and called down the mountainside.

"Verashi!"

Sunahran peered down, frowning. "Do you see her?"

A frightened whinny rose from below, setting up a nervous answer among the rest of the horses. Eliani reached the collapse and leaned forward to stare down into the dust and shadow of the slope.

Hands caught her arms and pulled her back. She turned her head and saw it was Luruthin, his face pale and his brow furrowed with dismay.

Vanorin called out again. "Verashi!"

"Here."

The response was faint. Vanorin dropped to his knees beside the trail, peering down through the gathering dusk.

"Are you hurt?"

"A l-little. I turned my ankle."

"Do not move. We will lower a rope."

He stood and took a rope from the saddle of the nearest horse. With Sunahran's help he tied it to the saddle, then made a sling to send down to Verashi.

Eliani looked up at the trail beyond the collapse, where three guardians stood with their horses, staring helplessly back at her and their other companions. She glanced at the sun and saw its lower edge now flattened. She had never seen such a thing before, and it took her a moment to realize the sun was starting to pass below the western horizon. She turned to call to the guardians cut off by the collapse.

"Gælvanin, you three go back to Althill! Tell them what happened. Tell them Ghithlaran is safe. He will come with us and return by the North Road."

Gælvanin hesitated, looking at the two others with him, one a Greenglen and the other a Stonereach like himself. He took a step toward Eliani, and the ground a short way before him gave, sending another slide of pebbles and dirt down the mountain. All three hastily moved back. Looking unhappy, Gælvanin made a stiff bow.

"Yes, my lady."

She watched them turn away. Vanorin put a hand on her arm. She looked up at him and saw his brow knit with concern.

"I must ask you to move forward on the trail. The ground here is still unstable."

"Yes." She looked at Luruthin and the others crowded near. "All of us should move."

She led the party northward, slowly bringing the nervous horses away from the slide. When she reached Ghithlaran, she found him looking pale and alarmed.

"Did someone die?"

"No, no. The trail collapsed and one guardian fell, but Vanorin will bring her up again."

She said nothing of the horse, which most likely would have to be abandoned, killed out of mercy whether or not it was injured. Verashi would have to do it once she was secured with the rope.

"You are trapped with us for a little longer, I fear." She smiled at Ghithlaran, hoping to distract him. "Are we far from the crest of the pass?"

He shook his head. "Not far at all. See that crag where the two pines stand?"

Eliani nodded, though "stand" was not the word she would have used. The two trees were large, so they must be old, but they seemed to cling tenuously to the rocks, their limbs twisted back by years of punishing wind.

"Lead on, then. Show me these springs you promised. I hope they are hot."

"Very hot, mistress."

The glint in Ghithlaran's eyes and his sudden grin showed she had succeeded in distracting his thoughts. Young rogue. He was probably imagining her unclad.

When they reached the two pines, she looked west once more, in time to see the last misty glint of the sun sink below the strange, flat horizon. The trail had curved, and she could now see Vanorin and Sunahran slowly hauling Verashi up the slope.

The fallen guardian looked rather battered, covered with dust and a dark smear of blood here and there. Her saddle packs and fodder net were slung over her shoulders, and she used one foot and her free hand to steady herself against the slope, the other foot hanging limply as she held it away from anything that might touch it.

Eliani held her breath until Verashi was up, hauled the last armspan by the two males reaching down to grab her. They pulled her upright, and Verashi winced as her injured foot touched the ground.

A cheer rose up from the watching escort, but Eliani quickly hushed it. "Noise might set more of the slope to collapsing. Come, let us make room for them."

Vanorin and Sunahran lifted Verashi onto the waiting horse, then started forward to join the party. Breathing relief, Eliani turned away and stepped between the two gnarled pines.

Tall rocks closed in about her, cutting off the wind. The air was thin and cold, and with night falling she saw her breath misting before her.

The trail grew level, then began to descend. The narrow valley through which they walked opened out, and trees began to appear, pines standing tall, as they should, untroubled by the vicious winds to the west.

Ghithlaran looked back over his shoulder. "Not far now, mistress. There is a good camp near the springs."

Stars were glinting between the treetops by the time he led them into a large clearing against a wall of gray rock surrounded by forest. A trickle of running water sounded nearby. Eliani spied a small cascade, no more than a rod high, falling down the face of the rock.

Ghithlaran pointed northward along the foot of the bluff. "The hot springs are that way. A short walk."

"How many will they hold at once?"

"Oh, a good ten, mistress. Shall I lead you there?"

Eliani saw Vanorin coming toward her. "In a little while. Take some of the others first."

Vanorin looked worried as he stopped before her. "Will you come and look at Verashi's injuries?"

"Of course. She has more than one?"

"A few scrapes. It is the foot that concerns me. I fear it may be broken."

Eliani winced then nodded. Vanorin led her toward the waterfall. Verashi was sitting beside the small pool at its base, her back against the rock, huddled in her dusty cloak with her legs stretched out before her. Sunahran was nearby, building a fire from a scatter of kindling and pine cones.

Eliani knelt before the injured guardian, peering at her face. One cheek was scraped, and her hair was tangled and smeared with blood.

"You gave us a fright, Verashi."

Verashi smiled weakly. "Myself, also."

"I am sorry about your horse."

The guardian frowned and gulped, and sudden tears slid down her cheeks. She looked down, blinking.

"I do not know why I should be so upset. Its legs were broken; it would not have survived."

Eliani reached out a hand to grasp Verashi's left shoulder. Warmth leapt up within her palm. Verashi drew a shuddering breath, then grew calmer.

"May I look at your ankle?"

Verashi nodded and drew her left leg up out of the way, leaving the right lying limp along the ground. "It twisted when I fell. I cannot put weight on it."

Eliani folded her legs beneath her and peered at the injured ankle. It was swollen enough to make the soft leather of Verashi's boot taut. A bad sign.

Feeling awkward, Eliani held her hands out above the ankle, not touching it for fear of hurting Verashi. She might have a gift, but she had no training in the healer's art, which involved knowledge of the flesh as much as application of khi.

Spirits, help me. Give me guidance.

She lowered her hands to within a handspan of Verashi's foot, and heat bloomed in her palms. In her mind a phantom image of the foot began to take shape. Dull red surrounded it, with dark shards of pain leaping up at any small movement. Eliani's instinct was to draw away, but instead she shifted her attention past the darkness, closer to the flesh.

She sensed throbbing in Verashi's khi, a heartbeat with which the pain swelled and ebbed. The khi that moved through her own hands was steady, golden and warm. She watched it spread around the foot and begin to dissipate the cloud of pain.

Closer still, her attention focused down into the flesh itself, exploring structure, seeking damage. Eliani did not see so much as sense the swollen tissue, the strained tendon, and the bruised muscle. Bones seemed like pearly sculpture, columns and arches and other wondrous shapes, beautiful in their fragile strength. Those in the ankle were sound, but an angry red spike of trouble rose from one of the long bones in the foot.

Eliani focused her attention there and perceived a crack marring the ivory length of bone nearest the outside of the foot. She directed khi to it and saw the red soften.

She stayed there, observing as the khi that flowed through her hands blended with Verashi's khi, smoothing it, dissolving pain, easing fear. At length her hands grew cool again. She withdrew them and opened her eyes, blinking.

Golden firelight flickered against the stone cliff, glinting in the falling water and on the ripples of the pool. Eliani sat back, surprised at the stiffness in her shoulders and legs. She had been at this longer than she had realized.

"I think you have cracked a bone, just here." Eliani gestured to the outer side of Verashi's foot. "You will have to ride henceforth. One of the packhorses can carry you."

Verashi sighed and nodded. "Thank you, my lady."

"Please, not 'my lady.' Vanorin is spreading bad habits."

A chuckle behind her made her turn. Beyond the fire Vanorin sat watching, along with Sunahran, who appeared highly amused. His smile faded to seriousness under Eliani's gaze.

"Thank you, Eliani." Vanorin nodded gravely as he spoke.

She became aware of the others in the glen. It was fully dark now, but the stars glimmered in a clear sky. Two other fires had been built, and the guardians were gathered around them, talking in quiet voices, sharing food. A spit over one fire held a skinned coney, and several guardians had speared apples—the parting gift of Althill's folk—on sharpened twigs and propped them over the flames.

Eliani ignored her stomach's growl in response to the tang of roasting apples, for she had noticed that some of the guardians around the fires had wet hair. Thus reminded of the hot spring, she turned back to Verashi with a brisk smile.

"Well, now. You will feel better yet after bathing. Vanorin, perhaps you and Sunahran could help her to the springs? I believe it is not far."

Sunahran stood. "Not far at all. I walked up to see. I would be happy to help Verashi go there."

"And I will help you bathe."

Verashi glanced doubtfully at her injured foot. "I do not think I can get the boot off."

Eliani nodded. "It will have to be cut."

"I can fashion a lacing to bind it back together."

Sunahran's offer made Verashi smile. He and Vanorin together helped her stand and hop one-footed toward the springs. Eliani brought Verashi's saddle pack and also a pot of soap and a spare tunic and legs from her own pack.

Wisps of steam rose from the broad, shallow pool. Several guardians were relaxing there, but they moved to make room for the newcomers. Eliani smiled her thanks, then directed Vanorin and Sunahran to ease Verashi down beside the pool.

Vanorin drew a small knife, with which he made a long cut down the outside of Verashi's boot; then he carefully removed it from the injured foot. Verashi winced and gripped Sunahran's supporting arms rather fiercely but made no cry. Eliani shooed the males away and helped Verashi undress, then shucked her own leathers and clothes and carefully eased Verashi into the pool.

Verashi hissed as her foot went into the hot water, then gave a long sigh. "Thank you, my—Eliani."

Eliani smiled, reaching for the pot of soap she had left at the pool's edge. "You are welcome. Let me wash the dust out of your hair."

Dust and matted blood. Eliani eased her fingers through the tangles and gently sought for cuts as she rubbed the herbal soap into Verashi's scalp. She found one small one—Verashi winced when she touched it—but most of the guardian's injuries seemed to be bruises. Eliani was silently thankful it was not worse.

She looked across the pool, where Vanorin, Sunahran, and Luruthin all sat in the water, pretending not to watch. She called to them.

"I think it would be best if Verashi returned to Althill with Ghithlaran."

Verashi seemed relieved. "Yes. I fear I would not be of much use to you now."

"You will be of considerable use to me by going with Ghithlaran. Keep him out of mischief, see him home."

An injured guardian was not ideal protection for a youth of thirty, but Verashi could at least talk him out of doing anything idiotic. She was pretty enough that Ghithlaran probably would listen. He might even be inspired to a mood of protectiveness.

Eliani looked at Vanorin almost as an afterthought. "If this meets your approval, Captain."

"And if it does not?"

Eliani felt herself blushing but held on to her dignity. "I would hear your alternative suggestion, of course."

Vanorin chuckled. "I do approve."

Relieved, Eliani washed her own hair, then emerged from the water, quickly dressing. She helped Verashi out of the pool and into her clothes, then bundled the guardian's cloak around her. This time again it was Sunahran who supported Verashi, and he had found a branch for her to use as a crutch. By the time they reached camp, the two of them were talking in soft voices.

Eliani watched Sunahran tenderly help Verashi sit down by one of the fires. It was clear that the injured guardian would not lack a comforting embrace tonight.

Suddenly lonely, Eliani turned away and saw Luruthin also watching the two Greenglens, his damp hair loose about his shoulders. He met her gaze and smiled in commiseration. He was bound, too, and also far from his love.

Eliani went to her saddle pack to put away her jar of soap. A cloth-wrapped bundle, small and slim, caught her eye. She hesitated, then took it out and carried it to the nearest fire. Sitting across from Luruthin, she untied the ribbon and carefully unwrapped the blue cloth from a small reed flute.

"Turisan gave you that."

Eliani nodded as she draped the cloth around her shoulders to keep the cold air off her neck. The flute had been a gift on the day of her confirmation, when she had been acknowledged not only as a full adult but as nextkin to her father and governor-elect of Alpinon. It was for that occasion that Turisan had first come to Highstone, representing Governor Jharan, who had sent with him a rich gift for Eliani of a brooch in the shape of two stags, gilt and set with jewels in Stonereach colors.

The brooch was back in Glenhallow with the rest of her finery. The flute had been Turisan's own gift. She treasured it more, though she had not yet played it beyond trying a note or two.

She held it in her hands, feeling the quiet glow of khi within it. Turisan had made it, she knew. His khi suffused it. Once that had frightened her; now it was a comfort.

She raised the flute to her lips, knowing its smooth surface had rested on his own lips. Closing her eyes, she blew a note, low and soft. It seemed mournful.

She let a melody rise, her fingers moving without conscious thought, following something her heart wanted to say for which there were no words. She filled her lungs and breathed her love and loneliness into the flute. She had hope, which softened the song and kept it from becoming bitter. She had courage, drawn in part from Turisan and her awareness of his love. She let the tune build upon that, rise and become stronger, the clear notes ringing in the night air.

Behind them the little waterfall played counterpoint, quiet and constant. The last note of the melody seemed to hang in the air, ringing softly until it faded into the trees.

And Turisan was there. She felt him and offered a wordless welcome. His love enfolded her in return.

I heard your song, my love. It was beautiful.

She smiled softly and opened her eyes. Luruthin was watching, his expression tender. So were all the others, she saw. Dark eyes and green eyes gazed at her in silence. The only sounds were the water's murmur and the crackling of the fires.

She lowered the flute to her lap. As if released by her movement, the others looked away, began to speak in quiet tones, reached for cups, and wrapped their cloaks closer. Luruthin smiled at her, then glanced at the fire, picking up a twig to toy with the coals.

How is it that you heard?

I do not know. Perhaps because the music came from your heart.

Her fingers tightened on the flute. *I miss you.*

And I you, love. Did you reach the pass?

Oh. Yes, after a slight misadventure.

She told him of the trail's collapse, of Verashi's fall and her decision to send the guardian back to Althill. Somewhat shyly, she added a brief description of her effort to heal Verashi's injury and how she had sensed the damaged bone.

She wrapped the flute up again, tying it with the violet ribbon, wondering why she had chosen to cover it in Stonereach colors. Clinging to her past, perhaps? Or claiming Turisan's handiwork as her own?

She lay down beside the fire, pillowing her head on her pack, holding the bundled flute in her hands. As she watched the flames dance above the coals, her mind drifted in Turisan's warm embrace as her flesh rested from the day's efforts.

◈ Midrange ◈

Turisan stood with his back to the mountains, gazing up at the massive earthwork that had been his father's first accomplishment as governor of Southfæld. Though it had long been neglected, High Holding was still impressive.

Built of unmortared stone and earth, forbidding despite being overgrown with weeds and grass, High Holding spanned the width of a flat bluff at the foot of the mountains, straddling the trail that rose to Midrange Pass. Heavy iron gates in the center of the work—gates that had always stood open in Turisan's memory—had now, with some effort, been shut across the trail. Midrange Pass was closed to travelers.

To the west of High Holding a narrow, flat plain was bordered on the south by a steep drop to the valley floor and on the north by the Silverwash, falling in a cascade that was almost as high as the Three Shades. The ends of the work were crumbling but still barred passage. The gate was the only way through.

Turisan looked over his shoulder at Midrange Peak, its snowy slopes gilded by the westering sun, the trail through the pass a gray shadow against gold-white. His gaze dropped to the conces set in long arcs west of the earthwork, their line echoing its curve. Long shadows reached from them toward High Holding. They were for the warriors of Eastfæld who had fought in the Midrange War, those Ehranan had commanded. They had driven the kobalen back through the pass before going south to relieve the besieged guardians at Skyruach.

Dirovon appeared at the top of the work. Turisan climbed up the steep slope of the earthwork to join him. Loose stone shifted beneath his feet. It was an awkward climb even without archers raining arrows down from the top of the work.

Dirovon nodded in greeting as Turisan reached him. "Not so very bad, eh? We will have to shore up the ends. It would be simple to repair if it were not quite so . . . large."

"The masons have found the quarry and say there is plenty more stone to be taken from it. The recruits can help."

"Ah, yes. Good training for them." Dirovon chuckled. "Perhaps you will do me the favor of issuing the order yourself before you ride back to Glenhallow."

Turisan narrowed his eyes. "You anticipate a poor reaction when city-bred recruits are asked to haul stone?"

Dirovon shrugged, grinning. Turisan looked back at the peaks, his mood not suited to banter.

"I will give the order. It was my decision."

They were silent for a moment, then Dirovon gave a quiet cough. "Do you ride south at once?"

"In the morning."

"Aye. Get a good rest and start early." Dirovon nodded and shifted from foot to foot. "Are we finished here? There is a fire at the camp, and that Filari has a way with spiced wine."

Turisan glanced toward the camp and beyond it eastward. Across the river, situated in the woods at the foot of a lesser, hook-shaped bluff, was a small outpost maintained by Southfæld's Guard, overlooking the ford where the trade road crossed the Silverwash.

"Save a cup for me. I must go to the outpost and find Thorian to send my report on High Holding's condition to Glenhallow."

Turisan glanced up at the mountains once more, and his heart clenched. He squinted, unsure of what he had seen against the setting sun, hoping he was mistaken.

"Dirovon."

The subcaptain turned to follow his gaze upward. High on the shoulder of Midrange Peak, the gray trail had turned black. It was too distant to discern individuals, but there was movement. No Southfæld guardians appeared so dark, not with their light-colored cloaks, fair hair, and pale flesh.

Dirovon's mouth dropped open. "Sweet spirits. Kobalen."

&

Rephanin started up from his meditation, his heart filling with sudden dread. He opened his eyes, disoriented, searching his chamber for the threat.

Rephanin! Thorian's khi was sharp with alarm.

What is it?

They are coming! The kobalen are coming down!

Rephanin leapt from his bed and pulled on shoes, then went out to his sitting room. He caught up his cloak and flung it around his shoulders as he hurried down the corridor toward the colonnade to Hallowhall.

Where are you?

On the bluff above the outpost. I can see them—
Get to safety!

Sunlight blinded him as he opened the side door to the colonnade. He recoiled, then pulled his hood forward and went out, breaking into a run across the graceful stone walkway. He must find Jharan at once.

Into the shade of the palace colonnades overlooking the fountain court. Rephanin sighed with relief and slowed to a walk, heart pounding.

An attendant turned in surprise as he brushed past, calling out a question he did not hear. He ignored it. At the governor's public chambers he strode up to the chamber attendant, past the curious glances of the handful who were waiting to see Jharan.

"I must see the governor at once. News from Midrange."

The attendant's eyes widened, and he gave a frightened nod. "One moment, my lord."

Instead of waiting, Rephanin followed him into the audience chamber. Jharan was not there. The attendant shot a nervous glance over his shoulder as he hastened toward a closed door at the back of the chamber. Rephanin followed.

The attendant stopped to knock at the door. "My lord governor, Lord Rephanin is here—"

Rephanin pushed past him and opened the door, revealing a small chamber in which Jharan looked up from behind a worktable strewn with tallies. Berephan sat across from him, scowling as he twisted in his chair to look at Rephanin.

Rephanin met Jharan's gaze. "The kobalen are descending through Midrange Pass."

Jharan stood up, his face going pale.

"Where is my son?"

❦

Turisan's heart thundered with fear as he and Dirovon ran for the camp. It would take half a day for the kobalen to descend to the plain, by which time it would be dark. Kobalen disliked fighting at night.

He hoped they would wait until morning to attack, though that thought provided little comfort.

Reaching his tent, where the pennant of command stood planted in the sod, Turisan caught it up and swung it in a wide circle, the signal for assembly. A horn blew in response. His thoughts raced ahead, picturing what would happen when the kobalen reached the foot of the pass. Would they indeed wait until morning to attack?

"Get the command into the work and move the supplies there. Water! Send a patrol to haul water from the river—"

"Turisan, go to the outpost!"

Dirovon's manner had changed. There was nothing of humor in his face, only fierce determination. Behind him the garrison was already starting to gather.

Turisan swallowed. "Yes, I must send word to Glenhallow. I will return—"

"No, stay at the outpost. Better yet, ride for Glenhallow."

Dirovon glanced toward the mountains, his face gone grim. He looked back at Turisan and spoke in a lowered voice.

"Your work is done here. Take the other mindspeaker with you."

Turisan drew a breath, the cold air drying his mouth. Dirovon was right. He must not risk himself only because he wished to prove his courage.

He gave his spear to Dirovon. "You have command."

Dirovon strode away at once, shouting to the guardians. Filari came striding from the camp, bow in hand and a quiver slung over her shoulder, and paused to look toward Turisan with questioning eyes. He gestured toward Dirovon, then turned away, clenching his jaw as he hurried to the trail down from the bluff.

He ran, cold air burning his lungs and the cold water making him hiss as he splashed across the ford toward the outpost. He felt the warmth of Eliani's signal on his brow. Though he wanted her touch more than anything, he returned the signal to wait. He must first find Thorian.

The guardians at the outpost were already in motion, dousing fires and breaking camp. Turisan hurried to Josanan, the outpost's commander.

"Where is Thorian?"

"Behind the bluff, at the storage caves. I told him to wait there; it is safer."

"Has he contacted Glenhallow?"

Josanan nodded. "They have asked for you."

Turisan glanced toward High Holding, then beyond it to the dark line of kobalen at the top of the pass. The sun was setting now.

"Send a rider to Highstone at once to tell Governor Felisan we need arrows, as many as he can spare. If he can send guardians also, that would be well, but he should not leave Highstone undefended. The kobalen could turn north . . ."

If High Holding falls. He could not speak the words.

He coughed. "Have a rider make ready to go east. I have a message to send. Take the rest to High Holding and carry your supplies with you."

"Yes, my lord."

Josanan's face was grave. Turisan reached out to grip his shoulder, then moved on toward the bluff.

He found Thorian pacing in the woods. The guardian looked up at his approach and hastened toward him.

"Rephanin is at the palace. Governor Jharan is anxious to speak with you."

Turisan wished for a moment that Thorian's gift was like Rephanin's, that it would let him speak directly to his father. Instead, he had to entrust his words to Thorian. He described the situation, then asked which road the Eastfæld riders would take to Midrange.

Thorian's gaze grew distant. After a moment he answered.

"Ehranan says they will follow the Asurindel, then cut across the plains a day's journey from here. Not enough water on the trade roads for a large force."

"Tell him I am sending a rider out to hasten them."

Thorian paused, then nodded. "He says he is leaving Glenhallow at once with the Southfæld Guard. They will march without rest and be here by the third day hence."

Turisan felt a chill wash through him. It was beginning. It was war.

"I ask that some few be sent forward on horseback. A hundred, two—as many horses as can be spared. Riding hard, they can be here in a day or a day and a half."

And that might yet be too late. Three hundred were in High Holding, another two . . . five hundred at best, to hold the valley against countless kobalen.

Perhaps Felisan would send a few more. Still, it was not a question of whether High Holding would fall. It was a question of when.

He should be there with the garrison, not hiding here behind the outpost. His father would never have left his guardians to defend Skyruach alone.

But his father had been only a captain at Skyruach. Here, now, Turisan was the keeper of a gift of great worth to his people. He looked at Thorian and saw an echo of his struggle on the guardian's face.

"J-Jharan asks your word that you will not go back to High Holding."

Turisan pressed his lips together. His father knew him too well.

"I give my word. If High Holding falls, you and I will ride south."

He turned to go, but Thorian's hand caught his arm. "Rephanin is to ride with the Guard. Have you anything more to say to anyone in Glenhallow?"

With a start, Turisan realized this was his last chance to communicate with his father. How quickly he had taken Thorian's gift for granted! He thought for a moment, then spoke softly.

"My best regards to Lady Jhinani and my best obedience to Lord Jharan. Eliani expects to be at Bitterfield soon."

Thorian passed the message, keeping his gaze lowered as he added, "Your father sends you his love."

Turisan felt his throat tightening. Very rarely did Jharan make such expressions.

"Give him mine in return."

A small smile curved Thorian's lips as he nodded. He seemed extremely young in that moment, and Turisan felt a sudden protectiveness. He frowned, reconsidering his plan.

"Perhaps you should ride south now, while the kobalen are still far away. Jharan will want you back at Glenhallow if Rephanin is coming here."

Thorian looked up at him. "The governor did say I was to return there."

"Well, the sooner you go, the sooner he will have news. Let us find you a horse."

"You are not coming with me?"

"I will follow."

Thorian fetched his belongings and accompanied Turisan to the clearing where the outpost's horses were kept. They found Josanan talking urgently with

a guardian who stood beside a saddled horse, its reins
in her hand.

This was the rider Turisan had requested. He told
her where to search for the Eastfæld warriors and what
to say when she found them. She mounted and gal-
loped away, and Turisan turned to Josanan.

"Thorian is to ride back to Glenhallow. Can you
spare three to ride with him?"

"Yes, my lord."

He called to some of his guardians. Turisan turned
to Thorian, offering his arm. Thorian clasped it.

"Ride swiftly."

Thorian flashed an anxious smile. "Keep safe."

"I will join you soon."

Turisan walked back toward the Silverwash,
where he would have a clear view of the pass. A cold
wind assailed him, and he pulled his cloak close as he
glanced up at the bluff to the north. The guardians
who had stood watch there were gone. He was
alone.

He gazed up at the dark mass of kobalen in the
pass, his heart sinking with dread. He closed his eyes.

Eliani?

Turisan! I have been waiting. What happened?

Kobalen are coming through the pass.

He told her all he had set in motion, all he had
planned. She shared his dismay, and that was comforting.

Are—are you planning to stay and fight?

*I have promised not to. I will leave if it becomes
dangerous to stay at the outpost.*

He sensed her relief, though she did not voice it. He
remained by the river, watching the black mass creep
down the mountain. Night had fallen, making it
harder to discern the kobalen's advance. They moved

slowly, the more so in darkness, for they had not the clarity of vision that blessed the ælven.

Turisan stood watching after Thorian had ridden away, after Josanan's party had crossed the ford and gone up the trail to High Holding. Josanan had left a golden mare for him, along with a water skin and a small pouch of food.

His packs were at High Holding. He had nothing in them that it would grieve him to lose, though he did regret not having his bow. He was glad he had not brought Eliani's veil.

He watched through the night, unable to tear himself away from the sight of the enemy slowly advancing. Toward dawn, he heard the sound of a horse crossing the ford and dragged his gaze away from the kobalen.

A guardian approached, his horse shaking water from its coat as it reached the riverbank. The guardian dismounted, pulling a set of packs from the saddle.

"Lord Turisan? Captain Dirovon sends me with your gear and this message."

He set the packs on the ground at Turisan's feet, then took a folded page from his leather tunic. Turisan accepted the note and swiftly read it.

> The plain before us is now all black, though they have not yet dared to come past the conces. The pass is choked as far as we can see. I feel as if I am standing upon a waterbreak, watching the approach of a flood.
>
>   Go to Glenhallow. There is no more you can do here.

Dirovon had seen him, then. How careless of him to stand in a visible place. Turisan let the note curl back into itself.

"Thank you."

The guardian nodded and handed Turisan his bow and quiver. Turisan glanced at the arrows, wondering if he should send them back to the warriors, who might have greater need of them.

"Do you return to High Holding?"

"Yes, my lord. Do you wish to send a message there?"

He gazed at the guardian. Younger than himself, Turisan was fairly certain. So many very young folk had joined the Guard in response to Jharan's call.

The guardian had braided a falcon's feather into his hair. Turisan suddenly remembered him, remembered a morning not long ago when he had stood on the practice ground before Glenhallow with a hundred others who knew nothing of a guardian's duties or of what they would face at High Holding.

"Dahlaran."

The guardian brightened, a smile flicking across his face. "Yes, my lord."

"Spirits guard you all. That is my message."

"Thank you, my lord."

"If I could, I would stand with you."

Dahlaran's face went grave, but he nodded. "We know that. You walk a higher path."

Turisan shook his head. "Not higher. Only different. No path can be higher than that you walk today."

A horn blew in the distance. Turisan's head turned toward the west, though as yet there was nothing to see save the black stain that had poured down the mountain. He glanced at Dahlaran, whose cheeks paled as he also looked westward. The young guardian met his gaze, and Turisan offered his arm.

As they touched, he felt the jitter of fear in the

other's khi. He gripped Dahlaran's arm tightly until it steadied.

"Help is coming. Ehranan marches from Glenhallow, and Eastfæld is riding hither. You need only stand your ground a little while."

Dahlaran smiled. "We will stand."

Turisan watched him lead his horse back to the river and across it. When the guardian was gone, he hefted his packs and strapped them to his saddle. His heart was heavy, and though he knew he must leave, he looped the mare's reins over a tree branch and hurried up the footpath that climbed the bluff to where the watchers had stood. He wanted a last look at High Holding.

By the time he reached the top, the first flush of dawn had cast a blue light over the mountains. Their hulk was still dark, but Turisan could see the distant glint of metal at High Holding and beyond it the black mass that had spread over the foot of the pass.

Nearer by he saw Dahlaran, mounted, climbing the trail to the work. His flesh tingled with fear for that young soul and for all the others who stood defiant against the kobalen.

He should go. Dirovon was right; he could be no more use here. He should ride, but he could not move. He stood rooted to the watch post as the dawn grew.

High Holding seemed so small, a slender barrier at the foot of the pass. A horn rang out again, its clear note rising with the sun. The sound pierced Turisan's heart, for it was a warning.

He watched as the throng of kobalen twitched like a waking beast, then with a roar surged forward in the growing light. A black wave swept forward, breaking against High Holding, surging and swelling at its foot.

Heart pounding, Turisan scrambled down from the bluff. The mare greeted him with an unhappy whinny. As he freed the reins from the branch, he glanced toward the river and saw a kobalen floating down it, the broken shaft of an arrow protruding from its chest.

He mounted and saw another kobalen drift by, then two more. Looking upstream, he saw the river filled with bobbing black shapes. His gaze rose to the waterfall beside High Holding. The kobalen must be throwing their dead over it.

It made him angry to see the Silverwash so fouled. He wanted to send warning to Glenhallow not to take water from the river, but that would have to wait until he saw Rephanin.

The trade road ran along the west bank of the Silverwash, too close to the fighting for safety. He looked again toward High Holding and saw the flicker of a green and silver pennant atop the work, bright against the sea of blackness.

Swallowing, he turned his mount eastward, making for open plains. As he faced the rising sun, he saw a low-lying cloud of dust, as if a storm were blowing up.

He reined the mare to a halt. No clouds heralded a storm; the sky was clear and windless. He stared at the dust, then let out a sudden whoop of joy.

Riders from the east! More than a hundred, perhaps many more. He did not pause to guess their numbers but started toward them at a gallop.

The mare needed no prodding. Whether it sensed Turisan's urgency or merely wished to flee the grisly sight and smell of the river, it ran with all its heart.

Soon he discerned riders with ribbons of gold and white flowing from bands on their upper arms. They wore no other clan markings and carried no pennants that he could see. Their black hair was bound back from pale faces. Among the foremost Turisan spied the green cloak and fair hair of the Southfæld guardian he had sent to find them.

There were at least three hundred, perhaps four or five. Turisan's heart surged with painful hope. He reined in as he reached them, turning his mount to join them, searching the faces of those near the Greenglen rider. A male whose long black hair was braided with beads of gold and white raised an arm to hail him.

"I am Avhlorin. What news from Midrange?"

"High Holding is under attack. Make haste! If it falls, we must hold the ford and the south road to prevent the enemy's advance."

"Where is the ford?"

"I will lead you there."

"Onward, then!"

Avhlorin waved his arm, and the riders surged forward. Turisan fell in beside the Greenglen rider. Her mount was lathered and laboring, her face set in an expression of grim endurance.

"Rest your horse. No sense in killing it."

She cast him an anguished glance. She had friends at High Holding, no doubt. She eased up and fell back, her mount dropping to a walk.

They rode westward, slowing only as they neared the outpost. Turisan caught his breath as he saw a pillar of smoke rising south of the bluff where High Holding stood. Fire at the foot of the cliff!

He saw fire atop the bluff also, at either end of High Holding. A barrier to the kobalen, to block them from coming around the crumbling ends of the work? But now they had pushed it off the cliff, and the forest was burning.

He saw a line of wagons descending the bluff. Wounded, retreating from the battle.

The trade road out of Alpinon loomed ahead. Turisan led the Eastfælders onto it, following it through the woods to the ford. At the riverbank they halted, and Avhlorin sat gazing in dismay toward High Holding.

"Spirits walking!"

Turisan looked at him. "How many are you?"

A swallow moved Avhlorin's throat. "Five hundred. There are seven hundred more on foot, a day's journey behind us. When your messenger came, we rode ahead."

"There are some three hundred in High Holding. If you can hold this valley for a day or even until nightfall—"

"Yes." Avhlorin nodded, then scowled slightly as he looked at the ford choked with kobalen bodies. "Is this the best crossing?"

"It is. There is another farther down. See where the river curves eastward?"

Avhlorin nodded. "Yes. How deep is it?"

"Deeper than this but passable. This is the better."

Avhlorin met his gaze, steady blue eyes in the fine, chiseled face. Turisan was reminded strongly of Ehranan, somewhat less so of Rephanin.

"Thank you, Avhlorin. I had thought Midrange lost, but you can save it."

He offered his arm, and Avhlorin clasped it. The Ælvanen's khi was clear and steady, and Turisan sensed that he was much older than he had first thought. A look of faint surprise crossed Avhlorin's face as they let go.

"You come with us, yes?"

"N-no. I must ride south, to Glenhallow. Captain Dirovon commands at High Holding. He will welcome you."

"I do not know your name."

"It is Turisan."

Avhlorin's eyes lit with understanding. "Ah." He made a small bow. "I am honored, my lord, but forgive me—you should not ride alone."

Turisan forbore to argue, submitting to the escort of the two riders Avhlorin assigned to him. He led them back through the woods and southward, skirting the band of forest that followed the river.

The forest thinned and the pines faded away, leaving only greenleaf trees, bare-branched and less reliable as cover. The Silverwash narrowed, growing swifter and deeper. Across it the woods diminished, leaving a clear view of the road. A short way up a small ravine, Turisan saw a small mass of kobalen, fifty or more.

"Kobalen!"

He halted, watching in alarm as the kobalen attacked a small line of wagons that were drawn up against a tumble of rock in the foothills. They were the wagons he had seen earlier, bearing wounded from High Holding.

Turisan jumped down from the saddle, going to the river's edge to get a clearer view, ignoring the protests of the two Eastfælders. How had kobalen come so far south? Had High Holding already fallen? He peered northward, but a pall of smoke hung over the valley, obscuring his view of the earthwork.

He stopped behind a mature greenleaf, its trunk wide enough to conceal him. Peering around it, he saw that the wagons were defended by Southfæld guardians, some twenty that he could see, sheltering behind rocks.

The hillside was covered with fallen kobalen and more than a few guardians as well. As he watched, kobalen continued to fall, picked off by archers behind the wagons. The remaining kobalen screamed in rage and hurled darts toward the defenders almost at random. Turisan hoped that few were finding their marks.

He turned to the two Eastfælders. "Those are wounded from High Holding. One of you ride to Avhlorin, tell him to send help!"

The riders exchanged a glance, and one turned her mount north. The other dismounted and joined Turisan.

He turned back to watch the fighting and saw a few kobalen confer and then break off, running down the slope toward him. With a start of fright he drew back behind the tree, then realized he had not been seen. They were making for the road, turning northward. Running to bring reinforcements.

Without further thought he fetched his bow from his saddle and set an arrow to it. The Eastfæld rider protested.

"My lord! You will be seen!"

A kobalen fell, pierced through the heart, and a second lay beside it before its scream faded. Muttering angrily, the Eastfælder took up his own bow. Between them he and Turisan felled kobalen after kobalen until only two remained. Those two turned toward their attackers with a cry of rage and raised their throwing sticks.

Turisan saw one kobalen fall to the Eastfælder's arrow, then heard a grunt. The Eastfælder slumped to the ground, gurgling, a dart lodged in his throat.

Angered, Turisan loosed his arrow. A blow struck his right arm near the shoulder as he stepped behind the tree again.

He had a moment to realize what had happened, then the pain came. He dropped his bow and collapsed against the tree. Sparks of fire jolted down his arm. He slid down the tree trunk to sit heavily on the ground, breathing fast.

Turisan!

He dared to look at his shoulder. The short feathered shaft of a kobalen dart protruded from his leathers, the head sunk deep into his arm. Blood began to seep from around the shaft. A throbbing started in his shoulder, spreading outward.

What happened?!

I—I was careless.

Are you still under attack?

No. I took a dart. Do not worry; it is only in the arm.

I know that!

Through his pain, Turisan smiled. Eliani's annoyance was strangely comforting.

Whiteness filled his mind suddenly, warm and soothing. It was khi, but unlike any khi he had felt before.

Eliani?

Be still. Let it flow.

He let out a long breath. The warmth flooded him, tingling down into the wound, making it hot. Pain ebbed beneath the brightness. His breathing steadied, slowed. His mind cleared somewhat, and he blinked, trying to think what he should do.

The Eastfælder lay still, though he breathed yet. Turisan doubted he could help him, but he pushed himself away from the tree.

Dizziness swept over him. He fell forward, catching himself on his uninjured arm.

Turisan!

He crawled to the Eastfælder's side and sat fighting the resultant nausea. Leaning against a scrub oak, he put a hand on the guardian's shoulder.

Eliani, can you help him?

Oh, love—
Will you try?

She was silent. He waited, and after a moment the whiteness came again. This time it poured through his good arm and into the Eastfælder's shoulder where he touched it. He closed his eyes, not trying to understand, hoping only that it would help.

The whiteness and warmth faded. He opened his eyes, wishing he could see across the river from where he sat.

Tell me what happened. Kobalen?

Yes. They were attacking our wounded, I had to help. He turned his head to peer at the dart. *I cannot pull it. I would break the head.*

No, leave it! Can you ride to Highstone?

The mare was nearby. Turisan thought he could get into the saddle but doubted he could stay in it for long. He swallowed.

Too far.

Are you sure? Heléri could help you—

Let me think.

His best hope was to get the attention of the guardians across the river if they were not still fighting kobalen. He wondered if he had killed the last kobalen or if it had escaped and gone for support. He cautiously rose to his knees and edged back toward the tree where he had sheltered. Dizziness threatened again, and he leaned his good arm against the trunk, gazing toward the river.

Dark shapes lay in the road, tumbled, unmoving. One lay where his attacker had stood. With a sigh of relief, he slumped against the tree.

You were to stay out of danger!

I was. I will explain later.

Turisan—

Hush, love. I must call for help now.

She subsided, though a string of dark thoughts seemed to run through the back of his mind in which words such as "idiot" and "foolhardy" were common. Ignoring these endearments from his beloved, he peered across the river.

As he watched, guardians came out from behind the wagons and rocks, collecting arrows from among the dead kobalen. Turisan saw a face he knew.

"Harathin!" He mustered all his strength to shout again. "Harathin!"

Harathin paused, frowning as he cast his gaze about. Turisan waved with his good arm, then fell back against the tree. Harathin ran to the riverbank, staring across at him.

"Lord Turisan?"

Turisan struggled to his feet, wincing as his movements jostled the dart in his arm. He stood leaning against the tree, head swimming.

"You are wounded! Stay there; we will come!"

Turisan wondered idly where Harathin thought he might go. The pain was returning, interfering with his ability to think. He wanted to sit down again but felt he should remain standing.

Harathin came to the riverbank with a horse and two guardians, one of whom began stripping off cloak and leathers. The other took the cloak from the first, then mounted the horse and rode southward.

"Turisan? Nolanin will cross at the south ford and come to fetch you."

"There is another rider here, wounded. We have horses."

"Good. Now save your strength."

Taking this for permission to relax, Turisan sank to the ground again. The first guardian had stripped to tunic and legs, and he now saw that she was female. She ran north along the riverbank. When she was a good distance upstream she stopped, then jumped into the rushing water. Turisan gasped, for the river was cold and ran dangerously fast here.

The guardian swam with strong strokes and caught herself on a tree root just above where Turisan sat. She scrambled out of the water and hastened toward him, dripping, her wet clothes clinging, braided hair lying heavy against her back. Turisan shivered in sympathy.

She glanced down at the Eastfælder, then stepped past him to Turisan's mare and took his pack and water skin from the saddle. Uncapping the skin, she handed it to him.

"Drink."

The familiar voice made Turisan glance up. He had not recognized her but now saw that it was Filari. Her wet hair was plastered to her head, and her face had fresh cuts in two places—one a nasty gash down the nose—along with the older cut and the bruises Kelevon had given her, now fading.

Turisan took a swallow from the water skin. "Thank you, Filari. You need not have swum the river."

She cast a skeptical glance at him, then dropped to her knees and began to dig in his pack. "Have you a spare tunic in here? Ah, yes."

She pulled it out, but instead of donning it as he had expected, she took out her belt knife and began cutting and tearing the tunic into strips. Turisan leaned back against the tree, watching her destroy his clothing.

The cold of the water seeped into his stomach, making it rumble. He should have eaten something last night, he realized. He had been foolish not to. He felt unwell and leaned his head against the tree trunk, closing his eyes.

Turisan?

Yes, love. I am all right. Help is here.

How were you struck?

He described the skirmish between kobalen and Southfæld's guardians and told of the kobalen he had stopped from running to Midrange. Eliani scolded him for risking himself, as he expected. He listened fondly, waiting until she ran out of abuse.

Eastfæld has come. Five hundred riders.

Ah!

"Turisan? My lord?"

Turisan opened his eyes. Filari was peering at him, looking anxious. She had a pile of torn cloth across her knees.

"I must remove your leathers from this arm."

He nodded and reached up with his left hand to help unfasten them. Filari swatted his hand away and unlaced the bracer from his lower arm. She was gentle, but he winced in pain with each movement.

Filari glanced up at him, then began to work cautiously at the lacings tying the upper armpiece to the shoulder of his leather jerkin. He clenched his teeth and noticed she was doing the same. Her fingers were trembling, the tips blue.

"You are freezing. Take my cloak."

Filari shook her head. "You need it more than I. Nolanin is bringing mine."

She succeeded in untying the lacings, then sat frowning at the dart. "I do not think I can break the shaft without risking breaking the head."

"No."

Kobalen dart heads were made of ebonglass,

wickedly sharp and fragile. Fragments left in wounds were both painful and dangerous.

She bit her lip. "I can try to strip the fletching or just lift the leather far enough on the shaft so that I can see to remove the head."

"Easier to remove without the leather. Strip the fletching."

"All right. Hold still."

She took gentle hold of the shaft, and he hissed, then closed his eyes, determined to make no more sound. Filari did her best to steady the dart, but every tiny movement set up waves of pain. He imagined the barbed head slicing his muscle into shreds.

Whiteness filled his mind again. Eliani, sending her healing. He silently thanked her and, when the jostling stopped, opened his eyes.

Filari had pulled the goose feathers from the dart and was frowning at the bare shaft. He knew she was trying to decide how to remove the leather armpiece.

Grimacing, he slid the fingers of his left hand beneath the leather and gripped the shaft, then nodded. Filari took hold of the armpiece with both hands and pulled it upward while Turisan steadied the shaft. It seemed to take a long time, though it could not have been more than a moment. When the leather left the shaft and the pressure released, he let out a grunt.

"Now let me look."

Shivering, Turisan let his hand fall. The sleeve of his tunic was stained with blood from the seeping wound. Filari cut the cloth away with deft strokes of her knife and peered at the clean slice made by the dart as it had entered, a thin line oozing bright blood, perhaps five times the width of the shaft.

"Can you hold one side? If we pull it open a little, away from the barbs, I can draw the dart straight out."

Turisan nodded. He pressed his fingertips against the skin on one side of the wound, ready to pull. His hand was shaking as badly as Filari's. She set one hand opposite his and wrapped the other around the dart.

"Now."

He pulled, and pain seared into his arm. He felt as if his bone were being drawn out of him. A moment later, wet heat spilled over his fingers. He let out the breath he had not known he was holding, gasping.

"Here, quick."

A blow struck his arm, and he jumped, then realized that Filari had pressed a folded cloth against the wound. He bit back indignant protest.

"Can you hold it? Press hard."

Turisan fumbled his hand over the cloth and pressed. An answering ache rose in his arm. He closed his eyes and leaned his head against the tree, trying to steady his breathing. Eliani was still sending healing, had sent it throughout. He became aware of the tension in his limbs and made an effort to release it. The worst was over, and the pain was already lessening.

He could feel Filari's movements as she bound the wound. He gave himself to Eliani's healing, sinking into the peaceful warmth, letting his hand be moved and replaced over the bandage.

Feeling he should express his gratitude, he opened his eyes. Filari was wiping her knife with a scrap of cloth. He managed a weak murmur.

"Thank you."

Two answered that he was welcome.

◈

Eliani returned to herself to find she was leaning forward in her saddle, left hand pressed to her right shoulder, her horse standing in the center of a circle of riders who were all staring at her. She blinked and looked at Vanorin, who sat his mount before her, eyes filled with concern.

"My lady? Are you well?"

She inhaled and sat up, letting her hand fall. Her muscles were stiff.

"Yes. Where are we?"

She looked around at the forest, vaguely remembering riding through those pines. The party had been following a stream down out of the heights. She spied it after a moment, a few rods away, its murmur a tickle at the edge of her hearing.

Vanorin looked dismayed. "We are in the Steppe Wilds. Do you not remember?"

"Yes, yes. Forgive me. Turisan was hurt, and I was distracted by it. All is well now."

She said this with a silent hope that it was true. Turisan's wound was not dangerous, but she would be glad when he was somewhere safe, well away from the chaos at Midrange.

Luruthin moved his horse up beside hers. "Do you feel able to ride on?"

"Of course." She nodded, but instead of urging her horse forward, she sat staring at the lock of black mane between its ears.

"Eliani?"

Luruthin's voice was gentle. Somehow that broke her determined calm. She felt a tear slide down her cheek as she met his gaze.

"The war at Midrange has begun."

⁊

Hoofbeats, running, intruded upon Turisan's fitful repose. He stirred and was rewarded with a dull stab of pain in his shoulder. Opening his eyes, he saw Filari standing nearby, waving to the approaching rider, a guardian who led a second horse by the reins.

Turisan frowned. He should know who this guardian was. One of his command, and Filari had said his name earlier.

The guardian slowed to a walk and came toward them, tossing a bundled cloak to Filari as he reached them. She caught it and put it on.

Turisan sat up, his movements slow and careful. He was stiff from leaning against the tree. Filari turned and looked at him.

"Ah, good!" She came closer and knelt beside him. "How do you feel?"

"None too well, but better than before."

She smiled, then held up the kobalen dart, turning it to show him all the sides. "See? No chips."

"I am in your debt."

Filari shook her head. "I was in yours."

It was true that she seemed more steady now than she had been in Glenhallow, more vital. Turisan privately doubted he had done her a favor by bringing her here, for the fighting had scarcely begun. At least now the odds were no longer overwhelming.

Filari offered the dart. "Do you want it?"

Turisan took it in his left hand and looked more closely at it, musing. Some guardians kept such things as reminders of their trials or as tokens of good fortune. He twirled it by the shaft, admiring the craft that had gone into the black glass head, its perfect symmetry, the smoky glow of light through its thinnest edges. He then reversed it and smashed the point into a rock that lay beside him. The head shattered, scattering splintered glass.

"Now it will never harm another."

He tossed the shaft away and got to his feet, leaning against the tree for balance. He felt light-headed but thought he could ride. He looked around for his water skin, found it at his feet, and bent to pick it up, then noticed a cloak draped on the ground.

A gold cloak, and beneath it the Eastfælder who had accompanied him. The cloak was drawn up over his face. Turisan looked up sharply at Filari, who shook her head.

Turisan picked up his water skin and straightened, which made his head swim a little. He opened the skin and took two deep swallows, then looked down at the fallen guardian.

The rider had dismounted and now joined them, pausing as he encountered the gold cloak. "Hai—who is this?"

Turisan shook his head. "I do not know his name."

"That is his horse." Filari gestured to the bay that was quietly cropping dry grass. "Do you need help?"

The guardian shook his head, glanced at Turisan, then bent to lift the Ælvanen's body. The cloak draped gracefully as he carried it away.

"Here." Filari picked up a remnant of Turisan's torn tunic, fashioned into a sling. She slipped it over his head, helping him settle his injured arm in it.

"Thank you."

"Do you feel well enough to ride?"

"I think so."

He looked about for his mare, saw it grazing nearby, and went to it. He mounted, wincing as he landed in the saddle and jolted his arm. Gathering the reins in his good hand, he looked across the river.

A pall of cloud hung over the mountains, dark blue-gray, swelling even as he watched. A thin overcast had spread eastward from it, turning the sky overhead a dull white. The sun was hidden and would not appear again this day.

The wagons had come down from the ravine where

the skirmish had been and were now moving south along the road. Guardians on horseback accompanied them.

He gazed northward, though Midrange Valley was hazed with smoke and he could not see High Holding. The sky was darkening, and the rumble of thunder joined the distant sound of the battle. An acrid smell of smoke and death reached him on a cold wind.

"My lord?"

Filari was mounted, waiting with the other guardian. Nolanin, Turisan remembered at last. He was leading the Eastfælder's horse, which bore its master's body. Turisan joined them, and they started south toward the lower ford.

The woods grew more dense, coming into mixed greenleaf and evergreen. Across the Silverwash, the foothills of a ridge descended toward them, defining the south side of Midrange Valley. The ford was just north of it, where the river turned and spread before passing through the mountains' feet.

Nolanin paused and held up his hand. Turisan halted the mare and stifled a sigh of relief. His shoulder had begun to throb again.

Nolanin gestured toward the water. "I will follow."

Filari glanced at Turisan, then clicked her tongue to her horse and made it go into the river. The water came up to its belly near the shore; in the center, it might have to swim.

Turisan patted his mare on the neck, trusting that it would manage. He then urged it into the water, drawing a sharp breath as it scrambled down the bank.

Cold splashed into his face and instantly soaked his legs. The mare struggled beneath him. He laid his hand on its neck, finding its khi through the confusion caused by the water, sending it reassurance.

Forward, only a little way. Almost halfway across.

Two splashes behind him told of Nolanin following. He did not look back.

The mare lurched, losing the riverbed. Turisan quelled its panic, enwrapping its khi with his own, sending it calm.

Forward. Swim.

He was breathing hard, too closely engaged with his frightened mount. He kept his gaze fixed on the western bank. A moment later the mare's hooves scrabbled against rock.

Lurching forward, eager to be out of the water, the horse nearly spilled him into the river, but he clung with both knees and grabbed a handful of mane, the reins still looped around his palm. Ahead, Filari's mount scrambled up the bank and onto the road.

Almost there. He crouched low over the mare's withers, clinging to it. The bank was steep, and the horse faltered going up it, hooves slipping in mud, jolting him painfully. Turisan gasped as stars swam before him, then the mare was up and onto the flat, shaking the water from its coat and jostling him again. Turisan patted the animal, thanking it for bringing him safely across the water.

Behind him, a horse suddenly squealed. He turned and saw Nolanin struggling with the reins of the Eastfælder's horse, which was floundering in deep water, panicked. It thrashed, and Turisan gasped as Nolanin lost his seat and his mount swam on without him.

Nolanin's face showed terror; his arm was tangled in the bay's reins. The horse, burdened with its dead rider, struggled to keep its head above water. In an instant, both the horse and Nolanin were swept down the river.

With a cry of alarm, Turisan put his reins in his

right hand and unlashed a coil of rope from his saddle with his left, pressing with his knees to urge the mare forward. The horse startled into a lope.

Each stride jolted Turisan's arm, but he clenched his teeth and leaned forward as the mare dashed along the riverbank. Nolanin, burdened by his saturated cloak, disappeared beneath the water briefly, then came up sputtering. They were nearing the bend around the foot of a ridge, where the river narrowed and deepened, running swifter.

Turisan drew abreast of Nolanin, then ahead. He would never be closer; he reined in the mare, twined an end of the rope around his wrist, and flung it to Nolanin.

Spirits help us!

A jerk nearly pulled him from the saddle as Nolanin caught hold of the rope. Turisan leaned back, and the mare responded, scrabbling backward at his urging. The rope tightened around his arm, but the handfasting ribbons seemed to protect him somewhat as the pressure increased.

The mare's hooves slipped. Turisan feared he would be pulled from the saddle. He spied a tree close ahead and let the horse go forward.

The rope slackened, and he jumped from the saddle. He just had time to circle the tree once before the rope tightened again. He gasped for breath, his arm caught against the tree trunk by the rope. The tree now took most of the force of Nolanin's weight.

Hoofbeats behind him, and shouting. He did not shift his gaze from Nolanin. The rope stretched between them, the guardian suspended in the middle of the river. The Eastfælder's horse was far downstream; Nolanin must have managed to get free of its reins.

He was not swimming, though. It might be all he could do to hold on.

"Here!"

Filari's voice. She was suddenly beside Turisan, leaping past the tree and grabbing hold of the rope, digging her heels into the bank as she pulled. Other guardians joined her, and Turisan watched with relief as they hauled Nolanin to shore.

The rope slackened from around his arm. He leaned against the tree, gulping deep breaths, fighting a return of dizziness.

Nolanin was dragged up the riverbank and lay coughing, guardians bending over him. Turisan gave silent thanks to whatever spirits had aided them. His legs began to shake, and he clung to the tree to avoid falling.

Turisan, what now?

Ah, we had a mishap fording the river. All is well now.

Filari came to him, pressing her lips together, looking as if she would like to scold him but did not dare. He smiled weakly.

"Thank you for your help. I could not have held much longer."

"You saved his life."

"No more than you did."

"But you—" She glanced northward toward the battle and frowned. "Well, you are wet and cold. Let us get you away from here."

The wagons had moved on and were nearly past the foot of the ridge. While the other guardians helped Nolanin back to his horse, which waited unrepentant in the road, Filari caught Turisan's mare and brought it to him. She regarded him doubtfully.

"Can you mount?"

He pushed away from the tree and took the reins in his left hand, pausing to murmur a word of praise to the mare before hauling himself once more into the saddle. His head swam with weariness. A moment later a gentle flood of white khi flowed into him, less intense than before but every bit as comforting. He gave a sigh of relief as he followed Filari down the road.

Thank you, my love.

Tell me what happened, unless you are about to plunge into another battle.

He told her as he rode southward. Filari rode abreast of him, casting glances at him from time to time. They passed the ridge, leaving the battle behind. The valley beyond seemed oddly peaceful; the mountains blocked more than the noise and smoke. They seemed to block the tormented khi of the battlefield as well.

A rumble of thunder echoed through the peaks. Though it was not yet evening, the sky had darkened and the air grew more chill by the moment. A drizzling sleet began to fall.

Ahead, the wagons had pulled off the road, going up a rise to halt beside a cluster of boulders. Scant shelter from the storm, but better than none. Turisan saw flames leap up from newly kindled fires, orange-gold in the darkening storm. He and Filari turned their mounts toward the makeshift camp.

A driver came to take their horses, shyly offering to tend Turisan's mare. Turisan took his gear from the saddle and yielded the reins, then trudged after Filari toward the fires.

Wounded guardians huddled in the shelter of the wagons and the boulders. Drivers and guardians, some wearing bandages themselves, moved among them, giving water and food to those who could take it, comfort to those who could not. Here and there a quiet moan attested to someone's suffering. Turisan was struck with a sudden sense of his own good fortune, for his wound was nothing compared with some that he saw.

One guardian's face was a ragged mess on one side. Another was heavily bandaged about the throat, a red stain slowly spreading through the bandages. Many had multiple wounds. Turisan walked slowly through the camp, looking at each face.

Eyes turned to him as he passed, seeking reassurance, seeking guidance. A sense of responsibility for their suffering weighed upon him. He had brought them here.

Shaking off the shadow of grief, he made himself stop to speak to those who were conscious, praising their valor and encouraging them to be hopeful as he shared the warmth of their fires. They knew nothing of the arrival of forces from Eastfæld, so he told them of the five hundred who had come and the seven hundred a day away, assuring them the ælven defenses would hold. His doubts he left unsaid.

Filari sought him out. She was clad in her leathers once again and wore a look of stubborn wariness.

"I am going back to Midrange. Nolanin will escort you to Glenhallow."

Turisan restrained an impulse to order her to stay. There was no good reason for it, and she had earned a say in how she was to serve. Better, too, for her to remain away from Glenhallow for now.

He nodded. "Thank you for your help. Spirits go with you."

She smiled briefly, then turned away. Turisan watched her go to her waiting horse and ride down to the road.

The sleet began to fall more steadily. The drivers hastened to make shelters for the wounded out of heavy cloths from the wagons. Turisan drew up the hood of his cloak and continued to walk among them.

Near the upper end of the camp he found Dahlaran, the young recruit who had brought him Dirovon's message, lying with his eyes closed and his cloak drawn up to his neck. He was very pale, and a bloodstain had soaked through the cloak over his thigh.

Turisan knelt beside him and lifted the cloak, swallowing when he saw the blood-drenched legs beneath. Dahlaran's leathers had been removed, and a bandage was bound tightly high around his left thigh, but it seemed to do little to stay the flow of blood.

With only one good hand, Turisan could not tend the wound. He glanced around, looking for one of the drivers.

"Can someone help here?"

"No." Dahlaran's voice was a raspy whisper. "Leave it."

Turisan looked down and saw that the guardian's eyes were open, gazing calmly at him. "You are bleeding."

"I know. That is not the only wound. I fell from High Holding. My back is broken, and there is something wrong inside . . . I am best left as I am."

Turisan felt his throat tightening. He lowered the cloak and sat beside Dahlaran, taking his hand. The young guardian's khi was thin and wavering, like a candle flame near going out.

"I am sorry."

Dahlaran smiled weakly. "Do not be. I will return when the chance offers."

"It will offer. Your sacrifice will not be forgotten."

"Thank you."

They sat in silence, Turisan clasping the cold hand in his. Dahlaran closed his eyes again, and Turisan could feel him fading away. He squeezed his own eyes shut and tears dropped from them, mingling with the sleet.

Eliani?

Yes, love?

Can you help?

A moment.

Turisan waited, breathing deeply. The scent of rain, a smell he had always loved, now filled his senses. Somehow this made him weep the more freely.

All right, love. I have privacy. What is it?

Turisan had no words. Instead he opened his heart to show her Dahlaran's plight.

Oh. Perhaps I can ease him a little.

What should I do?

Be still.

He obeyed and felt powerful heat moving again through his arm and hand, into Dahlaran's. The guardian inhaled sharply in surprise, then relaxed. For a long while they sat still, the glow of healing enveloping both. At last Dahlaran sighed.

"Thank you."

He opened his eyes once more. Turisan saw no more suffering in them, only peace. Dahlaran smiled.

"I am glad to have known you, mindspeaker."

Turisan squeezed his hand. "And I am honored to know you, Dahlaran."

The smile widened, then Dahlaran closed his eyes. Turisan felt him slip away.

The silence he left behind was overwhelming. The hand that a moment before had housed a thread of khi was now empty. Turisan gently laid it down.

He became aware again of his surroundings. The

sleet had changed to snow, and what remained of the daylight was fading. His shoulder no longer ached.

Thank you, Eliani.

Her love enveloped him, warm and tender. Slowly he stood up, collected his belongings, and went to help those who still lived.

⚔ Ebon Mountains ⚑

Shalár strode eagerly at the head of her army, legs protesting and breath laboring at the steepness of the climb as they headed into the Ebons. Tonight they would enter Fireshore.

The route they followed was disused but clear enough, a rocky trail leading into the foothills. To the north and south the peaks rose high and forbidding, but here a gap filled only by lesser mountains, mere hills by comparison, made a natural passage across the Ebons.

Shalár's brows drew together as she thought of what lay beyond the pass. Westgard, where her people had been defeated by two ælven armies, one of which had come through this pass to surprise Clan Darkshore from behind. She had not fought in that battle, had then had no knowledge of fighting. She had been little more than a child.

Her father had fought at Westgard and died there along with many of his followers. Those who survived the battle had fled through the pass into the wilderness of the Westerlands, and the ælven soon drove the rest of her people after them, out of Fireshore. They had almost vanished in the unforgiving lands west of the mountains.

Would have vanished had Shalár not chosen to survive and make her people survive with her. They would return one day, she had promised them, to reclaim their home. Now the day had come.

Her flesh hummed with anticipation, and her mind was alive with speculation. What awaited them beyond the pass?

Ciris had been through it earlier in the year, had crossed into Fireshore and brought her much information about its people and the city of Ghlanhras. The city was walled now. She wondered why the ælven had done it. Ghlanhras had always sent its warriors forth to meet any threat of kobalen, preferring to keep them well away from the city. What else did they fear?

She glanced at Yaras, who walked just behind her on the trail. She might send him forward to learn more, but that would risk betraying their presence to the ælven. Better to keep hidden and fall upon Ghlanhras without giving them time to organize a defense. The city was a fair distance to the north of Westgard. Several nights' march lay ahead of them yet.

Yaras lengthened his stride to come up with her and walked beside her in silence for a time. She knew this meant he wished to ask her a question, for he tended to avoid her company otherwise. She waited, leaving it to him to speak.

"Bright Lady, there is a small village at Westgard."

Shalár nodded. The village had been there before the war, originally founded to watch the pass and give early warning of any kobalen crossing the mountains there. A large field had been cleared to enable the villagers to farm, and it was there that the battle had unfolded.

Afterward the villagers had left, unwilling to live so close to the battleground. For a time the ælven had used the village as an outpost to prevent her people from returning. It had fallen into disuse after a few centuries, the ælven having realized that no threatening masses were about to come through the pass.

Until now. Shalár permitted herself a wry smile.

"Ciris said it was still abandoned."

"I thought we might scout it to make certain of that."

Shalár looked at Yaras. "You wish to go?"

"If it is your will. I would take two or three others."

"You will have to make haste to rejoin us by morning. I will not stop to wait for you."

Yaras nodded. She found his placidity annoying.

"What do you expect to find there? I doubt they will have left swords lying about."

"No, but there are other things they think little of that we might find useful."

A flash of anger burned through Shalár. She felt her shoulders tightening and was tempted to say something sharp but resisted. Yaras was right. Many things the ælven took for granted were long lost to her people. Some of the simplest things—bright colors in cloth or paint, glass beads, certain herbs and ointments—would be precious treasures to her people.

"Go, then. Join the army again when we come through."

"Thank you, Bright Lady."

He fell back, and she heard him talking among the hunters, choosing three to go with him. Soon they passed Shalár, running at a slow jog up the trail. She watched them go and realized the source of her annoyance. It was because she wanted to go with them. Always she had accepted the burden of leading her people. She had not asked for it; she had merely assumed it, and Clan Darkshore was grateful. Without her they had been in danger of descending into savagery and ultimately scattering, dying in small skirmishes with kobalen or falling victim to the westerlands' many dangers, or simply giving up. She had decided Clan Darkshore should survive, and so they had survived.

Why, then, was she suddenly weary of her role? Why now, when they were at last returning to reclaim Fireshore?

She strode on, listening to the footfalls of Yaras and his three hunters, following their khi ahead through the pass. She was lonely and wished for Dareth. She had always turned to him when she felt restless. He had understood that her anger was not directed against him, had been able to listen to it and let it pass him by. She had no one to do that for her now.

Dareth had disapproved of her intention to return to Fireshore.

Well, Dareth was not here. She presumed he was no longer concerned with such worldly matters.

Shalár brushed some small irritant from her eye and lengthened her stride, digging against the rising trail with the long muscles of her thighs. She did not urge her hunters to keep up. They would follow her soon enough. Across this pass lay Fireshore, and she wanted nothing now but to set foot in her homeland again.

Her thoughts flew ahead into the lush forest beyond. The trees there were taller, a mix of greenleaf and sable-boled darkwood trees with their broad leaves and pale blossoms.

Few darkwoods grew west of the Ebons, and Shalár's people had few tools of the quality needed to work that hardest of woods. She prized darkwood almost above all else, for it meant home to her.

Fireshore had vast forests of darkwood. In the north they spread all along the coast and marched right up onto the feet of Firethroat. Burned stumps of darkwood marked where the volcano's wrath had spilled long ago.

The darkwood was her hope for remaining in Fireshore. The trees did not grow in any other part of the ælven lands. If she could take control of Fireshore's forests and keep hold of them, the ælven would have to bargain with her or go without darkwood.

She lifted her head, seeking a glimpse of the familiar tree, but this high only greenleaf and a few stray pines grew. When the trail leveled and she knew she was at the crest of the pass, she eased her pace a little. Her breath burned in her chest from the effort of climbing, and though this pass was not extraordinarily high, she felt light-headed.

She paused to kneel beside a stream that trickled cold water from the mountain to the south. Gasping as she plunged her hands into the flow, she swallowed as much as she could and then splashed more on her face.

Standing, she turned to face eastward again. Though she could not see it from this pass, in her mind she saw the green eastern slopes slanting down to a field that was still barren after centuries. Questing forward with khi, she found Yaras and his three, more spent than she but pressing ahead toward the abandoned village at the edge of the great battleground.

Westgard. She had not been present at the battle, but she had heard of it. The vast destruction and waste of it had burned into her heart. She herself had fled from Ghlanhras, which then had not been sheltered by a wall.

She mused, gazing at the star-strewn sky overhead. The way to defeat the wall was to take it from the city and make it her own. Eyes narrowing, she thought ahead to her arrival there. Her warriors would easily surround the city. The wall itself was not guarded, Ciris had reported. They need only scale it, weapons ready, to take possession of it.

How many hundreds now dwelt in Ghlanhras, though? More important, how many of them would resist?

She must take the wall, then she must take the governor's hall. With Othanin in her control, the people of Ghlanhras would be hesitant to resist.

Shalár mused over the details as she began to walk again. The pass now sloped eastward, gradually at first, then with increasing steepness.

Footsteps on the path, well behind her but within range of her senses, told her the army had caught up with her. She halted them, then stepped forward to address those close enough to hear.

"We are nearing Westgard. Only memories dwell there now, but they are vivid memories. Guard yourselves and do not be distracted by the tauntings of shadows."

A few of them had fought at Westgard, but only a very few. The flesh of the dead had long since gone to dust, but the echoes of their suffering would not fade so quickly.

Her hunters followed her down the lush eastern slopes of the Ebons. When the battlefield came into view, she pulled her thoughts close, curling awareness into herself. Far ahead, she saw Yaras and his hunters. All else was still, and a hushed silence lay like fog over the field. She watched the four hunters, whose course wove strangely now and then as if they ran over ground still littered with bodies. She peered at them in bewilderment, then drew a sharp breath of realization.

There were conces all over the field, hundreds upon hundreds. Shadow-gray, so at first she had not seen them. She swallowed, anger tightening her throat. The ælven had set conces for their dead, but there would be none for her own people, no memorials for the fallen of Clan Darkshore.

Withdrawing her gaze from the conces, she raised it to the village of Westgard huddled on the far edge of the field, then beyond it to the forest. A small trail ran north from there to Ghlanhras and south to Bitterfield, the remains of a road that had been used by the village. She would lead her army along that path, for cutting through the dense and tangled darkwood forest would slow them. They had endured enough of that labor west of the Ebons. Few used the road now, by its appearance, so they should be safe from discovery.

The slope leveled again as the trail gave out onto the field and faded. Behind her the hunters walked in silence. She could feel their surprise even though she held herself close. They were not yet on the battleground, but its presence was already palpable, a pall of heaviness, of anger and grief and dark feelings. The stars overhead seemed dull, though no cloud interfered with the clear cold of night.

She walked on, though she could not keep her steps from slowing. Reluctance to pass among the conces rose in her heart. She denied it and forced her weary legs to lengthen their stride. The sooner she was across this field, the better.

At the field's edge she stepped between two of the

gray pillars, waist-high and carved with the names of ælven warriors long dead. Bitterness filled her. Glancing up toward the village to mark the shortest path thither, she moved forward, not letting her eyes rest on any of the carven names.

She wondered now, as she had not had leisure to wonder when she had first crossed this field, on what part of it her father had fallen. If she were to set a conce for him, where should she put it?

Foolishness. Few of these conces could be on the actual ground where those they commemorated had fallen. Too much labor would have been needed to identify the dead and mark their places. No doubt just burning the bodies and caring for the survivors had required all the effort that could be given.

When Ghlanhras was hers, she would think of the wrongs that had occurred here and make up for the neglect of Darkshore's dead. She would set a conce for her father when Fireshore was back in her hands. A conce of black marble, from the quarries near Ghlanhras, not this gray stone, which must have been taken from somewhere nearby.

She glanced back toward the mountains and spied the sharp lines of a quarry, a scar hollowed into the side of a hill just north of the pass. No effort had been made to conceal it. How unlike the ælven, but then, they would never wish to live here again, so what need for improving the view? The scar was appropriate to the mood of the place.

A figure rose up before her. Shock filled her even as her hands drew her sword. It could not be—an ælven warrior, face wrought with terror and rage, swinging a longsword in reckless unconcern for his own safety.

Shalár brought her sword up to block the blow, and the ælven's blade came down, fading even as it passed through hers. She was left shivering, braced against a phantom blow that would never ring in her flesh, her sword gleaming golden in the cold starlight.

A shade. Shalár struggled to calm her panicked breathing.

Behind her the hunters shouted in fright and warning. She knew without looking that more shades had awakened, disturbed by the feet of living warriors. She flung up a hand.

"Hold! Sheathe your weapons."

She put away her sword. The shades held no physical danger, though those who tried to fight them could injure one another. The danger was in being caught up in the dark khi of these echoes, feeding them with fresh fear, losing hope among the shadows of hopelessness.

Shalár glanced over her shoulder at the army. Wisps of movement rose among the conces, and a few of the hunters swung at them. A sword rasped against the stone of a conce. The sound seemed to sober the army, who fell still, lowering weapons, turning their attention from the shades to Shalár.

"Onward. Do not start at shadows. They cannot touch you."

She turned and moved forward again, hearing the footfalls of the army behind her. Another shade rose to one side, a black-haired female in Ælvanen colors, wielding her longsword one-handed while the stump of a severed shield arm still rose in a useless attempt at defense. Shalár looked away and lengthened her stride, keeping her eyes on the ruins of Westgard village.

There were tokens hanging on some of the conces—wreaths of withered flowers, ribbons, chains wrought by loving hands—new things, left recently. Faint smells of sage and lavender, of rosemary and other herbs, reached her. Not every conce was so honored, but many were.

The Feast of Crossed Spirits had passed recently. These gifts had been brought here by ælven to remember their kin.

Some of the ribbons were of good quality, some of the tokens finely made. These were treasures of the sort that Yaras had gone ahead to seek, but Shalár was not tempted to touch them. A shade could follow such a thing, and she had no desire to be pursued by the troubled echoes of the dead.

None of the ribbons were red and black. There were no remembrances here for Darkshore's fallen.

With that thought another shade appeared before her, one of her own kind this time. A male with white hair and night-black eyes, desperate eyes, and he was running, fleeing. He dropped to his knees before Shalár, felled by a blow from behind, his face contorted with pain and fear. She could not help starting back for an instant; then she deliberately stepped on the ground where the shade had faded.

Perhaps she should not set a conce here. Conces were an ælven custom, and she had not practiced such since she had fled to the west.

Her father had been ælven, though. He had considered himself ælven to the end and had fought for his people's right to stay in their homeland.

She would set no conce. The return of Clan Darkshore to Ghlanhras was remembrance enough for her father.

The crumbling walls of Westgard village rose ahead. Shalár quickened her pace, anxious to be off the battleground, away from the conces and the shades that clung among them. She reached the small circle around which the houses had been built and stopped in its center as the army gathered around her.

"Yaras?"

"Here."

The houses were stone. Their roofs had long since fallen in, leaving only broken walls that ringed the circle in a jagged parapet. Shalár reached the ruined house in which Yaras squatted, sifting the dirt at his feet with long fingers. He looked up at her, eyes glinting in starlight. A wisp of his hair had worked free of his braid and blown across his face.

"Someone camped here not long ago."

Shalár nodded. "Feast of Crossed Spirits. They must have traveled far if they were willing to rest here, even for a night."

Yaras gestured toward the yield of his scavenging, laid out on a large pouch of fine linen that was sticky with the juices of the fruit it once had held: a brooch of metal worked in a simple fretwork design and gilt, the pin of its clasp broken away; a length of dark green ribbon, frayed at the ends; a pottery cup glazed in a wondrous deep blue, slightly chipped on the rim. There were a handful of other such prizes.

"You were right. These are worth the seeking."

He nodded, and knelt to collect his findings. He rolled them up in the linen pouch, then stowed it in his pack.

Shalár led the way out of the house. The circle was now crowded with her army, so closely packed that they had difficulty opening a passage for her and Yaras. She passed out of the village to the ancient road, pausing to look back at her hunters. The hardest part of the journey was behind them; ahead, the test of their mettle.

"This is the way to Ghlanhras." She saw eagerness bloom on their faces and turned, setting foot on the road.

"Come."

❦ Bitterfield ❧

Fireshore looked much the same as the Steppes to Eliani. After descending from Twisted Pine Pass, she and her party had traveled across country, through woodlands where evergreens increasingly gave way to greenleaf trees. They had crossed the river Varindel, with the Great Sleeper looming to the west, and were thereafter in Fireshore, but forest was forest and their journey changed little for several days. When they came to a road running across their path, they rejoiced.

They paused in a glade surrounded by greenleaf trees and occasional twining black trunks of darkwood. Eliani brought out the map she had copied from the records in her father's study. She spread it against her saddle, and Vanorin joined her.

Luruthin peered over her shoulder. "Is it the Bitterfield road?"

"It must be." Vanorin traced a finger along a wavering line below the road. "That is the Varindel. There are no other roads going west."

"How far to Bitterfield? Will we reach it today?"

"We should." Eliani glanced at Vanorin, ready for his denial, but he made none. She looked at her cousin and grinned. "We shall ride until we do."

They mounted and started westward, delighted at

having a road instead of making their way through wilderness. It was smaller than the trade roads, more like the mountain road they had traveled through Alpinon, but plainly in use.

A green canopy rose high overhead, lit with the soft glow of muted sunlight. Vines climbed the sinuous trunks of darkwoods, thick with crimson and yellow flowers that emitted a heavy, sweet scent. A bird somewhere gave a long falling cry.

Eliani looked up but could tell nothing of the sun's position save that it was somewhere to the west. This forest was strange; she felt closed in, cut off from the clear sky. She had been in deep forests in her own realm, but this was different. She knew an urge to climb one of the darkwoods just to catch a glimpse of the sun.

Before long the road widened, and the space beneath the trees grew more open, with here and there an empty place where once a darkwood had stood. She could feel where a tree's khi was missing, which was a strange sensation. It was as if the forest sensed its absence.

The khi of these darkwoods was different from that of any other trees she had known. She was not certain she liked it.

Sunlight slanted through a gap in the canopy ahead, golden with the lateness of the day. Eliani urged her horse forward, hoping it was Bitterfield and not merely a cleared space in the forest. When the dark walls of houses came into view, she looked at Luruthin and smiled.

Bitterfield was the second village to be built here. The first, Fairfield, had been the first ælven settlement ever attacked in force by kobalen raiders. It had happened centuries upon centuries ago, long before the

Bitter Wars. The kobalen had devastated the village, but the survivors had chosen to rebuild. The next time raiders had come, Bitterfield had fought back, thus beginning the ælven's acquaintance with warfare.

Eliani thought on that sadly. Warfare was not in harmony with the creed, yet it seemed they could not escape it. Why the kobalen continued to make war against the ælven when they lost so much by it was beyond her.

Bitterfield had turned its back to the darkwood forest. Houses shouldered close together, leaving no space for raiders to run between, and the road narrowed as it led into the village, passing between stone posts that could be blocked and defended in time of attack. It seemed cold and unfriendly, unlike any ælven settlement Eliani had seen.

As they passed the outer ring of houses, she saw that the front of each house, facing inward to the village, had windows and adornments and a spacious garden. A second circle of houses faced the outermost, and a third, smaller circle had its back to the second. Within the third ring was the village's public circle. By the time they reached it, they had attracted the attention of the citizens.

The folk of Bitterfield looked like Greenglens mostly, though sometimes the fair hair was curly and many of the brown eyes were light in color, not the deep dark brown Eliani knew. A few looked like Steppegards, and one or two had the black hair of Ælvanens. They watched her and her companions in curious silence from doors and windows or looking up from working in their gardens.

Eliani dismounted at the edge of the public circle, thinking it odd that none of the citizens approached.

In Highstone, visitors were surrounded the moment they stepped into the circle, if not before.

A quarter of the way around the circle, a door opened and a male stepped out of one of the larger houses, his long pale hair loose about his shoulders. He wore a light tunic and legs of unadorned gray and soft shoes instead of boots. His eyes were a golden brown that made Eliani think of honey cakes crisp from the oven. Her stomach growled.

The male came toward them, opening his hands in greeting. "I am Dejhonan. I am theyn here."

Eliani nodded and made a slight bow. "I am Eliani of Felisanin, from Highstone in Alpinon, and this is Luruthin, my cousin, who is theyn of Clerestone. We came to visit our kindred."

Dejhonan's brows rose in surprise. "You have kin in Bitterfield?"

"My father's sister, Davhri."

"Davhri . . . of course. Felisanin—yes, I should have realized."

"She dwells here, does she not?"

"She dwells here, yes." Dejhonan nodded, though his smile was somewhat troubled. His gaze passed over the rest of the party. "You are not all kin to Davhri."

"No, these are my . . . companions. This is Vanorin, who hails from Glenhallow."

Dejhonan clasped arms with Vanorin. "You have come a long way."

"Yes."

A brief silence followed, as if Dejhonan waited for elaboration. When none was forthcoming, he looked at Eliani.

"May I offer you and your cousin refreshment before you seek Davhri? My house is just there."

"Thank you, but I am anxious to see her. She is not ill, I hope?"

Dejhonan hesitated before answering. "No. She is not ill. Your companions might like to refresh themselves in the public lodge while you visit her."

He nodded toward the largest building on the circle, and Eliani realized with a start that it was the only house in Bitterfield whose doors stood fully open. All the others had their doors only slightly ajar, the opposite of the custom in both Highstone and Glenhallow, where anyone was welcome in the hearthroom of any house.

"Yes, we would like that, and we should make arrangements with the lodge keeper for our accommodation."

Eliani nodded. "Thank you, Vanorin."

He and the escort started toward the lodge, taking Eliani and Luruthin's horses with them. Eliani turned to Dejhonan, smiling.

"Will you take us to Davhri's house?"

"She lives in the outer ring."

He led them across the circle to one of two other paths that gave onto it. The citizens, seeing them in Dejhonan's company, appeared to lose interest and returned to their pursuits.

Dejhonan led them to the outer row and turned up the narrow street that ran between the facing gardens. Each of them was filled with flowers and herbs, some with kitchen plots, some with vines or waxy-leaved trees heavy with the golden orbs of sunfruit.

The garden before the house to which Dejhonan led them was withered. Eliani saw a kiln there, though it seemed long disused. She recognized some of the flowering plants and shrubs, including a goldenberry bush that seemed yet to cling to life.

Dejhonan led them down the path to the door, which was closed. He knocked on it.

"Davhri. It is Dejhonan. You have visitors from Alpinon."

They waited in silence. No sound came from within. After a few moments Dejhonan knocked again.

"Davhri."

"What happened?"

Dejhonan turned to Eliani with apologetic eyes. "Her partner is missing."

"Missing? Inóran?"

Eliani saw him in memory, the tall, fair-haired smiling one who had stolen Davhri away. She had detested him as a child.

"Yes." Dejhonan spoke quietly, sadly. "He went to Ghlanhras in the spring and has not returned."

"Has no one sought news of him? Has no one else seen him in Ghlanhras?"

Dejhonan gazed at her, his face grave. "We have little traffic with Ghlanhras."

Eliani was about to ask why, but a sound from within the house drew her attention. "Davhri?"

Slow, shuffling footsteps were approaching. Dejhonan took a step back.

The door opened a handspan, and a female peered out. She was clad in a loose gray robe that seemed too large for her. Her brown hair was disheveled, pulled in many wisps from its braid, and her face was lined with worry. The green eyes were dull beneath frowning brows.

Eliani caught her breath, for despite these ravages the face was still known to her, so like her father's. "Davhri?"

The eyes focused on her, frowning in bewilderment. "I know you."

Eliani felt tears starting and frowned to keep them back. "Yes. Yes, it is Eliani."

"Eliani. My brother's child." Davhri's brows lifted, and a glint of life came into her face. "All grown now."

"Yes." Eliani laughed, happy that Davhri knew her, nervous at her unkempt state. "Do you remember Luruthin? Our cousin?"

Luruthin stepped forward, smiling. Davhri opened the door a little wider and stood in it gazing thoughtfully at him, then nodded.

"Yes, I remember you both. Has it been so long? You were a child when I left Highstone."

"I have just reached my majority."

Dejhonan stepped forward. "They have traveled a long way to see you, Davhri. Shall I send Mishri to make a fire and some tea?"

Davhri looked at him and stood a little straighter. "That is most kind of you, Dejhonan. Thank you."

Eliani turned to him. "Yes, thank you."

He nodded, stepping back and glancing from Luruthin to Eliani. "Welcome to Bitterfield. Come to my house when you leave here, if you will."

Eliani watched him walk away, then turned back to Davhri. For a moment they gazed at each other. Luruthin gave a soft cough.

"May we come in?"

"Of course. Yes, come in." Davhri opened the door wide.

The hearthroom was small and dark, the welcoming hearth cold, swept clean though a little ash lingered in its corners. Davhri pulled aside a curtain and stepped into the house, beckoning Eliani to follow. She traded a glance with Luruthin, who drew the outer door closed, leaving it a little ajar.

The house lay in darkness, filled with grief. Feeling stifled, Eliani went to one of the curtained windows.

"May I open this?"

"Oh. If you wish."

Eliani pushed back the drape, letting the late-afternoon sunlight into a room that was clean, almost barren, as if abandoned. A table and four chairs, two more chairs by the empty hearth. Shelves bearing plates and cookware, a few scrolls, and one or two ornaments that had not been moved in some time. Two handfasting ribbons hung above the curtained doorway to the hearthroom, glinting softly.

Apart from this, the house looked as if no one lived there. Eliani grimaced, thinking that though Davhri might dwell here, she was not living much.

Davhri's face had gone dull again, losing the little energy their arrival had brought it. She seemed to be fading before Eliani's eyes. Determined to fight that, Eliani pulled her father's letter from her tunic.

"My father sends you this, along with his fondest love."

She pressed the letter into Davhri's hands. Davhri stared down at it for a moment, then looked up at Eliani. Her face broke into a smile, the first since their arrival.

"Thank you, child! How is Felisan?"

"He is well. Very well. Will you not read it?"

"Yes." Davhri glanced vaguely around the room, then gestured to the table. "Will you sit?"

"Thank you."

Eliani and Luruthin sat on one side of the table. Davhri laid the letter down before a chair across from them. All her movements were slow, deliberate. Eliani wondered if she was actually ill. She watched Davhri sit and pull the letter toward her, turn it over and over in her hands, and finally break the seal. As she read it, a smile grew upon her face, and her eyes lit with laughter.

"Ah, Felisan." She chuckled as she folded the page. "He has not changed, I see."

"Very little. He misses you. We all miss you in Highstone. I have hoped that you were happy in Bitterfield."

Davhri's eyes rose to meet her gaze. "Well, and so I have been. Very happy."

The tinkle of tiny bells came from the hearthroom, followed by a voice calling, "Davhri? It is Mishri."

Before Davhri could move or answer, the curtain was drawn aside and a young female of no more than forty summers came in. She was like enough to Dejhonan in color and feature that Eliani suspected they were close kin. She wore a tunic and legs of soft gray—everyone in Bitterfield seemed to wear gray—and carried a small covered basket, which she set on the end of the table.

"Good day to you, gentles." She smiled at Eliani and Luruthin. "Pay me no mind."

She turned to the hearth, collected a kettle from its hook and an empty copper wood bin, and carried them outside. Though she had said little, the room seemed to fall quiet with her departure.

"Such a kind child. She comes to visit me often and helps me with household chores. It is very good of her. I fear I have little heart for any sort of work of late."

Eliani stretched a hand across the table to her. Davhri clasped it lightly, her fingers cold and strangely small. Davhri had always seemed so strong to her, so vital.

Davhri was a potter, and those fingers had shaped many a beautiful vessel. Her home in Highstone had always been filled with gleaming pots, vases, and bowls and her shelves cluttered with jars of special earth for glazes and scrolls of designs. Glancing around this barren room, Eliani saw one piece of Davhri's making, a wish jar, high on the shelves. No other sign of her work was present.

"Davhri? Tell us about Inóran."

Davhri met Eliani's gaze, and her lips curved in a small, sad smile. "He is gone."

Luruthin stirred, resting his hands on the table. "Dejhonan told us he went to Ghlanhras."

"Three seasons ago." Davhri shook her head slowly, the smile fading. "I do not think he will return."

Eliani frowned. "Why did he go there?"

"He went to trade in Woodrun and sent word from there that he was going on to Ghlanhras. He was hoping to trade for glass, for new windows for my workroom." Her gaze dropped to her hands, which she spread upon the tabletop, withdrawing from Eliani's gentle grasp. "I did not mind it as it is, but he said there should be more light to set off the glazes."

"Why has no one gone to find him?"

Davhri still stared at her hands. She pressed them into the table, fingers splayed, straining against the wood.

"No one cares to go to Ghlanhras."

"But if Inóran is missing—"

"No one *wants* to go there. I would have gone, but I am afraid. Some say the city is cursed."

Eliani sat back, somewhat alarmed. She exchanged a glance with Luruthin.

"Ghlanhras is Fireshore's greatest city."

"Was." Davhri nodded. "It was."

Eliani leaned closer, keeping her voice gentle. "Cursed in what way?"

Davhri raised sad eyes to look at her. "Dark khi. Ill fortune festers there. Some say it is a legacy of the Bitter Wars. The trade caravans will no longer go there. They go no farther than Woodrun."

"Pashani did not mention that."

Eliani glanced at Luruthin. "She may not have known."

"Do you know Governor Pashani?" Davhri looked from one to the other. "Did you visit her in the Steppes?"

"She was at the Ælven Council lately held in Glenhallow."

Davhri blinked. "I did not know there was to be a Council."

"Word of it never reached Fireshore, apparently. That is one of the reasons we are here."

Mishri returned at that moment, carrying the bin, which was now full of firewood with the heavy kettle wobbling on top. She put the wood down by the hearth, hung the kettle on its hook, and set about making a fire. Eliani thought it best to shift the conversation away from her errand in Fireshore for the moment, so she asked Davhri the first question that came into her thoughts.

"I saw the goldenberry bush in your garden. Is that from the cutting you took from Highstone?"

"Yes. I fear I have neglected it of late."

"It is still alive, though. I was not certain you would get one to grow here."

"Inóran cosseted it along. It really does not like the summer heat."

An awkward silence fell. Luruthin made an attempt to fill it.

"This village is unlike any I have seen. So compact. Is it difficult to clear space in the forest?"

"Somewhat difficult." Davhri nodded. "But the village's design is more toward defense against kobalen. They still come over the mountains now and again."

"Have you had much trouble with them of late?"

"No more than usual. I would say less these last few years."

Eliani shifted in her chair, glancing toward the window, where the daylight was fading. Outside, the wasted garden seemed forlorn. She saw one pale yellow berry hanging from the feeble bush Davhri had planted and longed suddenly for Highstone.

A sharp snap from the hearth drew her attention. Mishri's fire had kindled and was sending cheerful light into the room. The logs were some kind of greenleaf, Eliani noted by their bark and pale wood. Darkwood was far too valuable to burn, nor was it the best firewood, she and her party had learned in the last few days. It was reluctant to catch, though once lit, it burned long and steadily.

Mishri came to the table and began taking things from her basket: a small box, two sunfruits, little jars, a loaf that smelled fresh from the oven. Eliani's mouth began instantly to water. She had not tasted soft bread since Althill or sunfruit since the summer.

Davhri bestirred herself. "Tell me about Highstone. How is Lady Heléri?"

Eliani smiled. "She is well. She sends you her blessing."

They talked of family and friends. Eliani chose all the happiest news to give Davhri, who seemed to revive somewhat with remembering her old kindred and clan.

When the kettle boiled, Mishri made tea and served it to them with a platter of bread, sliced sunfruit, and berry preserves. The tea ewer and cups matched, all a pale gray with glints of gleaming copper in the glaze, and Eliani knew from their quality that Davhri had made them. She wrapped both hands around her cup and inhaled the fragrant tea, a blend of tealeaf, sweet grass, and a floral scent she did not recognize.

"You have handfasted." Davhri looked in surprise at the ribbons on Eliani's arm, as if she had just noticed them. "And lately. You still wear your ribbons."

Eliani's heart skipped. Even now she reacted so to the thought that she was bound for life.

"Yes. My partner remains in Southfæld."

"You left before you made your new home together?"

Eliani took a sip of tea, swallowed wrong, and went into a fit of coughing. She glanced at Luruthin, who answered for her.

"She left the morning after the handfasting."

"Only to visit me?"

Davhri looked bewildered, but it was not the vague expression she had worn when they had first arrived. Eliani cleared her throat.

"To visit you, yes. We also have other reasons for coming."

She did not want to distress Davhri by talking of the kobalen at Midrange or the disasters that had befallen those who had tried to bring messages to Fireshore.

Mishri stood up from the hearth, came to the table, and addressed Eliani. "Dejhonan asked me to tell you there is a guest house ready for you both, as your friends have filled the lodge. It is on the public circle, the house with the firevines over the door."

"Thank you." Eliani gestured to the tea and food. "Thank you for all this."

Mishri smiled, then went out. Davhri gazed after her sadly.

"I should offer you my own house, but I fear I would be a poor hostess."

"Hush. That is what guest houses are for."

"You will stay a little longer, though?"

Davhri turned anxious eyes toward her. Eliani felt a deep pity for her, an uncomfortable sensation when she had for so long looked up to Davhri as an example of strength and courage.

"Of course we will stay." Luruthin helped himself to bread and preserves. "We must do justice to this hospitality."

Grateful for the diversion, Eliani took a slice of sunfruit. The sweet, tangy juice filled her mouth.

"Mmm. Delicious. Do sunfruit trees bear all year?"

"Not in winter. Those that are on the trees are the last of this year's fruit. They will rest during the rains. New fruits can be picked in late spring, though they are better come summer. Spring crops often go to making oil."

Eliani reached for another slice. "Sunfruit most of the year. It must be wonderful to live here."

"In some ways it is wonderful."

Luruthin reached for a slice. "This is *more* than wonderful. We are so weary of apples."

"Apples?" Davhri sat up, her face bright with interest. "You have been eating apples?"

Eliani traded a glance with Luruthin, then swallowed a bite of fruit. "Yes, we got them in Althill. They had a very good crop this year."

"Mountain apples!" Davhri sighed. "Oh, what I would give for one! I have not tasted apples in so long."

Eliani wished she had brought her saddle packs, for there were apples tucked into them. She would fetch some for Davhri later on.

"Do no traders bring them?" Luruthin asked.

"Not for years. We see traders seldom enough, and mostly from the Steppes. Our darkwood harvests go to Woodrun. I have thought of going there myself, to see if I can learn anything . . ."

"Davhri." Eliani looked into Davhri's eyes. "We are going on to Ghlanhras. We will seek Inóran there."

Davhri's smile vanished, and she shook her head. "No. Do not go there."

"Well, we must go. I have messages for Governor Othanin."

"Oh. From your father."

"From the Ælven Council."

Davhri looked at Luruthin. "Can you not prevent her?"

He shook his head. "I am pledged to go with her."

Davhri's eyes, no longer vague, now filled with the threat of tears. "I beg you not to go."

Eliani had meant to comfort her by offering to seek Inóran. Seeing her so upset, Eliani turned the subject and very shortly afterward took her leave. Davhri was frail in spirit if not in flesh, and Eliani did not wish to distress her further. Pleading weariness and a desire to bathe, and promising to visit again in the morning, she and Luruthin departed.

Their mood was sober as they walked to the public circle. Evening had fallen, and the darkwood houses seemed wreathed in shadow and suspicion, only narrow glimmers of light escaping through the cracked doors of their hearthrooms. The windows of the public lodge were alight, and a merry fire shone out from its welcoming hearth.

Eliani cast her gaze around the circle, seeking something that could be described as firevine. She concluded it must be the bright scarlet flowers draping the door of one of the houses.

This proved indeed to be their promised guest house, cozy and clean, filled with cheerful ornaments—mostly painted carvings of birds whose colors were unlike any Eliani and Luruthin had seen. Their saddle packs sat in the front room, and a note propped atop a basket of sunfruit on the table bade them come to visit Dejhonan, describing a house with a sheaf of grain carved into the door.

Luruthin dug a comb from one of his packs and worked it through his hair. "Supper first? The smoke from the lodge's kitchens smelled good."

"You just had bread and tea and a plate of sunfruit!"

Luruthin grinned as he braided his hair. "That is not the same as supper."

Eliani frowned at him, then read quickly through the note again. "We had best honor Dejhonan's request first. He may offer us a meal if you truly are hungry."

They found the door carved with wheat standing farther ajar than most, with firelight spilling out of it from the hearthroom. They stepped inside and rang the visitors' chime, and Mishri came to welcome them, smiling as she held a tapestry aside for them to enter a spacious sitting room.

Dejhonan's house was as different as it could be from Davhri's. Here there was light and color everywhere, set off against the darkwood walls. Paintings and weavings covered much of those walls, and the shelves were filled with ornaments. Luruthin smiled, and Eliani guessed he was reminded of the theyn's house in Clerestone where he dwelt amid a similar wealth of gifts from the people of his village.

Dejhonan came forward to welcome them. He had put on a robe of the same subtle gray that he had worn earlier, accented with a sash woven of darker gray and orange. His formality made Eliani wish that she had also troubled to comb her hair.

A quiet female, fair-haired with large gray eyes, joined Dejhonan. He smiled as she made courtesy to the guests.

"Welcome, Lady Eliani, Theyn Luruthin. This is Ghilari, my partner and Mishri's mother."

Eliani returned the courtesy. "Well met."

"Come sit by the hearth and tell us of your journey."

Ghilari led them to wide chairs with thick cushions that felt decadent after so long in the saddle. Mishri poured honey wine for all of them and set a plate of shelled nuts on the table between Eliani and Luruthin's chairs.

"You will join us for supper, I hope?"

Luruthin answered before Eliani could draw breath. "Thank you, yes!"

Mishri smiled, then withdrew to an inner room. Eliani watched her go out.

"She is a good host. Will she be theyn one day?"

Ghilari laughed softly. "Just now her ambition is to become a trader in darkwood. She longs to see the rest of the world."

They talked of pleasantries for a while, then of the journey from Southfæld. Eliani told a hopeful version of their travels, which did not include discovering the slain messengers or being attacked by the cata-mount, or indeed any of the dire tidings she carried to

Othanin. She was trying to gauge Fireshore's mood by that of Bitterfield's theyn, the first official from the realm whom she had met. This was, perhaps, unfair. At last she set down her cup and fixed her gaze on Dejhonan.

"I must thank you for the help you have given Davhri."

He nodded. "She is a valued citizen. We all suffer hardship from time to time."

"Why has no one gone to Ghlanhras to look for Inóran?"

Dejhonan turned his cup in his hands, gazing into it. "I have sent messages. As yet, there has been no reply."

"Messages."

Dejhonan looked up at her. "We do not go into Ghlanhras."

"Why?"

A frown flickered across the theyn's face. "There is much unhappiness there."

Luruthin sipped his wine. "Davhri told us she thinks the city is cursed."

Ghilari nodded. "So it is."

"In what way?"

Dejhonan glanced sharply at his partner, then sat taller in his chair; a small movement, but it gave the sense of convening an audience. "I was not in flesh at the time of the Bitter Wars, but my mother was. She was Greenglen then and fought at Westgard. She told me the worst part of the war was after that battle, when the ælven armies marched on Ghlanhras and drove Clan Darkshore from the city. Many of the Darkshores pleaded to stay and claimed they did not share the alben's hunger, but they were all driven out and across the Ebons.

"Bitterfield escaped that fate. There had been no hunger here, and the citizens were given the choice of following their clan brothers across the mountains or changing their allegiance to the new clan that was forming to govern Fireshore. They chose to join Sunriding. My father said it was the hardest choice of his life."

Dejhonan paused to add another log to the fire. With an iron poker he arranged the coals, coaxing new flames to feed on the fresh fuel. He set the tool aside and turned to face Eliani.

"We do not trade with Ghlanhras. Inóran was the first to go there in several years, and he has not returned. I advise you to keep away from it, my lady."

"I have no choice. I carry messages for Governor Othanin. Or has he removed to Woodrun?"

Dejhonan looked from her to Luruthin. "No, he is still at Ghlanhras. But to go there is to place yourself at risk."

Eliani narrowed her eyes. She suspected what he meant and wanted him to be explicit. He said no more, though. She gazed steadily at him for a moment, then leaned back in her chair, fingers laced across her belly.

"We have lately learned a little about the alben. We have come to believe that their . . . hunger . . . may be a sickness."

Dejhonan was still for a moment, then glanced at Ghilari. "We think so as well. How came you to that conclusion?"

Eliani felt her cheeks grow warm but ignored it. "One Kelevon, a trader from the Steppes, came to the Council at Glenhallow, claiming to represent Fireshore. His claim was false."

Ghilari looked astounded. "Deliberate deception?"

"Yes."

Eliani's gut twisted, remembering the many ways in which Kelevon was false. She had made excuses for him at first, which only made her angrier now.

Luruthin took up the tale. "After Kelevon's deceit was revealed, we learned that he was afflicted with the alben's hunger, though as yet his appearance gave no sign of it. He had been held captive by the alben in the west."

Dejhonan had resumed his seat and was listening intently, his brow creased. "And it was then that he acquired their hunger?"

"So he told us. We learned much from him that was of value, about his affliction and about the alben."

Eliani scowled. "If he is to be believed."

Dejhonan leaned forward in his chair. "Did he tell you *how* he was afflicted?"

Luruthin shook his head. "He had been in close contact with the alben. We thought, if it is indeed a sickness, it might be communicated."

Eliani shifted in her chair and took a few nuts from the dish, disliking this course of conversation. She had fought Kelevon and been cut, and Kelevon had drunk from the wound. Only for an instant, but it was an instant too long. So far she had shown no sign of the alben's curse, but they did not know how long it might take such a sign to manifest.

Dejhonan was silent for a long moment. Eliani glanced up and saw him frowning. At last he leaned back in his chair.

"The alben's affliction has returned to Ghlanhras. That is the curse of which Davhri told you, and that is why no one will venture to Ghlanhras."

Eliani let out her breath. "How long have you known?"

"For several decades now, there have been new

sufferers. We do not know why or how. No alben have come across the mountains that we know of."

She fixed Dejhonan with a hard stare. "Why have we not heard of this?"

"Because the last thing we want, and I hope most sincerely that you share our aversion, is another Bitter War."

All were silent. Luruthin set down his wine cup, and the small click it made against the table seemed to echo.

All at once, Eliani was sharply aware of every detail in the room: the vivid weavings and the black solidity of the darkwood walls behind them, the smell of wine, the small fluttering sound of the fire in the hearth, the strain on the faces of the others. She laced her fingers together, leaning forward, and spoke in a careful tone.

"That decision is not in our hands."

"The decision to avoid it may be." Dejhonan's face was hard as he watched her. "What will you tell the Council?"

"What is being done in Ghlanhras?" Eliani gestured toward the north. "Are those who suffer this curse allowed to feed as they will, in violation of the creed?"

"As they *must*, not as they will." Dejhonan's words seemed angry, but it was grief that showed on his face.

Ghilari turned to Eliani. "Now that the hunger has returned to Ghlanhras, we believe it was true that not all of Clan Darkshore was afflicted. Many souls who bore no stain were unjustly punished."

Eliani shook her head. "That cannot be undone. I am sorry for it, believe me, though not all the Council will feel so. There are those who would be willing to fight the Bitter Wars again."

"They would have no justification to make war upon Ghlanhras. The Lost do not remain in the city."

"The Lost?"

Ghilari nodded. "Governor Minálan, Othanin's predecessor, decreed that they must leave Ghlanhras. They are given supplies and tools with which to survive and sent away, westward."

"And they never return?"

"I have not heard of them doing so."

Dejhonan smiled bitterly. "There have been fewer encroachments of kobalen in Fireshore in recent decades."

Luruthin shifted his feet. "Have the—Lost—joined the alben?"

"I do not know." Dejhonan looked wearily at Eliani. "What will you tell the Council, my lady?"

She ran her hands through her hair, then sat up. "You need not fear retribution. We are already at war."

"What?"

Dejhonan looked alarmed. Luruthin glanced at Eliani, then nodded.

"Kobalen have crossed the mountains at Midrange."

"In force?"

"Thousands. We had just put three hundred guardians into High Holding. More warriors are coming from Southfæld and Eastfæld, but even with their help we are greatly outnumbered."

Dejhonan paled. "This is the news you bring to Othanin."

Eliani nodded. "Two messages were sent to summon Othanin to the Council. Both were intercepted by the alben. It was their leader who sent Kelevon to deceive us into thinking Othanin had received the summons and merely chose not to attend Council."

Dejhonan frowned in bewilderment. "Why?"

Luruthin shrugged. "Kelevon could not tell us why."

"Or would not." Eliani's voice was bitter.

"Is it vengeance?" Dejhonan sounded mystified. "Do the alben seek to divide us from our kindred?"

Eliani sat up abruptly. "Speculation is useless. We none of us want another Bitter War. Agreed?"

Dejhonan nodded. "Agreed."

"Then we must carry out our duty, all of us. For myself and Luruthin, that means continuing to Ghlanhras, delivering our messages to Othanin, and learning what passes there."

"And for me, continuing to guard the interests of Bitterfield." A faint smile crossed Dejhonan's lips. "Accept my apologies for not telling you at once how things stand in Ghlanhras. Perhaps we both trusted each other too little."

Eliani gave a sudden laugh. "My father says trust is a quality in which all the ælven are sadly lacking."

"Does he?" Dejhonan's face relaxed. "I believe I would like to meet Governor Felisan."

"No doubt he would enjoy that. Be assured, we have nothing against Bitterfield."

Luruthin glanced at Eliani, mouth widening in a smile. "In fact, we have a small token we might offer in return for your hospitality."

Eliani looked at him, eyebrows raised. Luruthin grinned, then turned to Dejhonan.

"We understand it has been some time since your village has enjoyed apples."

✑ Fireshore ✑

Shalár sat with her back against a darkwood's mighty trunk, gazing northward toward a landmark she remembered well. As the day's light faded, Firethroat showed it still deserved its name. She could just see it through a gap in the trees to the north, its dull orange glow painting the evening sky.

The great volcano on the northern shore was tall, higher than most of the Ebons, and each night the glow of lava lit its jagged, gaping mouth. Sometimes the lava poured down its broken side and into the sea, raising great clouds of steam that reached as far as Ghlanhras. The city lay in the volcano's shadow, to the east a short way inland from the ocean shore.

She had watched Firethroat often in her youth, fascinated by the mountain's changing moods. It never slept, but it was quiet for great lengths of time, then might suddenly erupt without warning. Once when she was very young, Ghlanhras had been emptied in fear of the volcano's violence. Shalár's face hardened at the memory. That had been the first time she was torn unwilling from her home. The second had been after the Battle of Westgard.

She stood up. It was well past sunset, time for her army to be moving. She went to where Yaras lay resting beneath another darkwood. For a moment she gazed down at him, a dull yearning rousing in her. She had not lain with him for some time. All her energy had gone toward the journey. She wanted Yaras, wanted with sudden sharp desire to relieve her lust, but it was night and she must travel.

The army was becoming hungry. She had no leisure for self-indulgence. She nudged Yaras with her toe, and he opened his eyes.

"Get them up. We are leaving."

Yaras gazed up at her, his face seeming to show an awareness of her recent thoughts. He could not know them, but perhaps he had guessed. Shalár turned away and heard him get to his feet.

While he gathered the army, she strode westward, stretching her senses through the forest. The dark-woods felt familiar, their deep slumber rich with life and seeming to spark at her touch, almost as if they were welcoming her back. She searched as far as the foothills for any sign of kobalen but found none. She turned back toward where her warriors had spent the day, deep in a dense stand of darkwoods.

Shalár led them to the road, searching in all direc-tions for ælven khi before venturing onto it. All was quiet. The day-biding creatures of the forest were settling to sleep, and the night hunters were not yet abroad. Shalár stepped onto the road and turned northward.

She set a fast pace, musing all the while about how to seize Ghlanhras. Ciris had described the wall the ælven had made around the city, built of heavy black basalt taken from Firethroat's slopes. She wished she had him here to ask for more details, but she needed him where he was. By now he would have received her message and sent the kobalen swarming over Midrange

Pass. Shalár allowed herself a small smile of satisfaction.

Near midnight she allowed the army to halt for a brief rest near a stream that trickled down from the mountains. Off the road to the west, she found a spot where a patch of sky could be seen in the space left by a fallen greenleaf tree. The half-rotted trunk lay across the stream with the water chuckling an armspan below it.

Had she been less weary or less burdened with care, Shalár would have leapt onto it and danced across the stream. Instead she went to the bank, drinking deeply, then splashing water on her face. The weight in her belly was deceptive and later she would be all the more hungry for it, but for the moment it gave her the illusion of having fed.

Standing up, she saw Yaras talking with one of the younger hunters, a female whose first hunt had been in the autumn. He was soothing her, Shalár realized. Reassuring her. Telling her that they would reach Ghlanhras soon or that they were certain to find kobalen before long.

Shalár felt a senseless flash of anger. Yaras would never even think of offering comfort to her.

Well, and if he tried, she would like as not laugh in his face. She prided herself on her strength, her endurance. Her people needed her to show no fear. Even when she was weary and hungry, she never let others know it. Only Dareth had ever known it, and he was beyond her reach now.

Feeling restless and annoyed, she strode away northward into the jungle. Perhaps it was the stream that troubled her. Running water always disrupted her perception of her surroundings, and she disliked such a lack of order. Moving away from its unsettling influence, she cast her awareness out through the forest again.

And found kobalen.

For an instant she froze, unsure whether to trust her perception. Then the presence of kobalen came to her senses beyond any doubt, traveling on a wave of fear.

They were hunted. A handful of them, no more than five. Running toward her.

Shalár spun and ran for the army, unwilling to risk losing even one kobalen by trying to hunt them alone. She flew over the leaf-strewn ground, running with a hunter's silent tread. As she reached the army, she sent a burst of khi to warn them into silence. They stopped what they were doing, faces turned toward her.

She halted, breathing fast and short. Yaras took a step forward, and she stopped him with a glance.

"Kobalen." She gestured, keeping her voice a whisper. "Ten of you come with me."

Turning, she sheathed her knife and ran forward into the forest, casting her thoughts ahead of her. Hunters followed. She could feel them at her back. A surge of delight filled her, spiced by the urgency of growing hunger.

There. She found the kobalen again, ahead and to the west, stumbling and crashing through the forest. They had turned toward the mountains.

Shalár paused to signal to her hunters to spread out westward. They formed a line several paces apart and advanced, silent and swift. Shalár directed their movements with gestures and small bursts of khi. She could not afford to spend much but spent what she must. This small catch would at least keep the army moving long enough to reach Ghlanhras, she hoped.

She could smell the kobalen now, taste their fear on

the air. Their progress was marked by heavy running steps, crashing through the forest. The hunters, no longer needing guidance, began to tighten together. Shalár saw the faint glint of a weight from the net in a hunter's hand. She drew her dagger.

A grunt from one of the kobalen as it tripped over a root. Shalár saw the nearest hunter loose her net. A howl of dismay followed, then the hiss of more nets through the air.

The kobalen tumbled to the earth, tangled in nets. Shalár put all her strength into a burst of khi that took hold of them and stilled them. She did not want the nets to be torn.

The hunters lent their aid, and Shalár gave the kobalen over to their control. She gasped for breath. This short hunt had taken all her reserves of strength. Hunger took its place.

She walked forward to where the hunters were untangling their nets. Three kobalen lay unmoving on the forest floor. A small catch, too small, but better than none. She searched the surrounding woods in the hope of finding more. No kobalen, but there was a bright spot of khi!

Without hesitation she plunged forward. Three hunters followed her.

Her prey was solitary but fleet, much more so than kobalen. Ælven! Shalár pushed her pace, knowing that this single ælven must be caught. Her army's presence in Fireshore must not be betrayed, not before they reached Ghlanhras.

Her awareness narrowed to the forest floor, the roots and fallen limbs to avoid, and the prey ahead. The ælven skirted a thicket of thorn berries and stumbled, a fortunate chance for Shalár. She ran faster, ignoring the burning in her lungs and legs.

The prey was in sight now, a female, pale-haired and lightly clad. Shalár became conscious of the burden of her hunting leathers. Sweat ran down inside them and stuck her tunic to her flesh. Still she ran.

She reached to her belt for her net, grasping the cluster of leaf-shaped weights and working it free while she ran. The sharp tines of a leaf bit her hand. She did not slow. When she had the net free she put on a last burst of speed, then threw, aiming at the legs of the fleeing ælven. A startled cry rewarded her.

Gasping and stumbling, she caught up with the ælven, who had tripped on the net but kicked it free and had started to run again. Shalár caught an arm and was struck by the ælven's free hand; then a swirl of flashing leaf weights filled her vision.

The net fell over them both, and they fell struggling to the ground. Angered, Shalár tried to seize the ælven's mind with khi, but the ælven was strong and resisted her. Shalár's arms were entangled in the net, preventing her from drawing her knife. She felt the netting tighten suddenly about her throat.

Shouting. She did not have leisure to pay attention to the words, for she was struggling for breath. She beat and kicked against the ælven, trying to free her hands.

Suddenly the tension on her throat was released. She drew a long, rasping breath.

More shouting, and hands touching her, pulling the net away from her, helping her to sit up. On her knees she gasped, blinking at the ælven still tangled in nets and held firmly by two of her hunters.

"Well done." The words came out as a croak, and she coughed and spat.

Staggering to her feet, she looked around and saw

her net lying nearby. A hunter handed her a water skin and she drank gratefully, with painful swallows.

She gave the skin back and went to retrieve her net, disentangling the leaf weights from the strands of netting. She carried it back toward the others and saw that the hunters had removed their nets from the captive. She stopped and stared in astonishment.

She had thought the female was ælven but now saw that her hair was snow white and her eyes as dark as any Darkshore's. After one sullen glance, the captive averted her gaze.

Shalár searched her face but did not recognize her. She could not have followed the army, not without being noticed. No, she was dressed for this climate, light clothes against the northern heat. Shalár's people had no settlements this far north. Where had she come from?

Shalár took note of the fine quality of the fabric of her clothing, the supple leather of her boots. She looked well fed. She had been hunting the kobalen and by chance had chased them toward Shalár's army. It must have been by chance; why else had she run from Shalár?

"Who are you?"

The captive was silent. Out of patience, Shalár knelt beside her and caught her throat with one hand, not bothering with gentleness. She felt the frantic pulse beneath her palm and smiled. She began to draw upon the female's khi, causing her to utter a startled, strangled cry of alarm.

Strength washed through Shalár's starving flesh. She needed nourishment also, but the khi took the edge off her weariness and gave her the energy to focus her thoughts. She watched the female's face crumple

into an anguished scowl. After a few moments she de-
sisted.

"Did you come across the mountains?"

The female was silent. She lay still, eyes closed and
a frown remaining on her brow though she no longer
suffered.

"Tell me your name."

The female gave no sign of response. Shalár considered using khi to force her, but her own strength was
by no means recovered, and such a struggle was ex-
pensive. She would have a better chance of success
after she fed.

Remembering the catch of kobalen awoke her
hunger again. She got to her feet.

"Bring her."

The hunters she had left with the kobalen had already taken them back to the army. When Shalár arrived, they were gathered near the stream, clustered
around the feet of darkwood trees and along the
stream bank.

The warriors looked up at her arrival. Surprise
came into their faces as they noticed the captive
female.

First they must feed. Three kobalen to be shared
among three hundred hunters. It was pitiful. They
would eat the flesh as well as consume the blood, and
it would still not be nearly enough. Shalár went to
where the kobalen stood under the control of ten
hunters and solemnly drew her knife.

"Three mouthfuls apiece."

Some faces drew into pinched frowns, but no one
uttered a protest. Shalár summoned Yaras to her, then
raised her knife to a kobalen's throat and made a clean
cut. She took one swallow of the hot, heavy blood and
passed the kobalen to Yaras. The army drew closer.

After she had opened the veins of the three kobalen and taken a mouthful from each, she returned to the captive female. The food gave her a small tingle of strength. She regarded the female, frowning, then glanced back toward the feeding.

"Yaras. Come here."

He joined her at the stream bank and gazed in surprise at the captive, then looked at Shalár. "Who is she?"

"I was hoping you might have some notion. She was hunting the kobalen. No doubt it was not her intent to deliver them to us."

The female shot an angry glance toward Shalár, then looked away. Shalár smiled.

"So she does hear. Good." She leaned closer to the captive. "You have been living in the forest, have you not?"

The female gave no reply. Her chest rose and fell with her quick breathing. She was afraid.

"What is your name?"

The female blinked rapidly but remained silent. Shalár tried a push of khi. The captive squeezed her eyes shut, resisting. Shalár could tell that she was not strong enough to conquer this rogue female with khi.

She drew her knife instead and laid the edge of the ebonglass blade against the female's pale throat. The dark eyes met hers then, wide with disbelief.

"Your name."

"V-Vathlani."

An ælven name. Shalár frowned.

"Where do you dwell?"

"In the forest."

"West or east of the Ebons?"

The captive stared up at Shalár, and her breathing slowed. A look of sorrow came into the dark eyes.

Shalár pressed the knife harder, letting her feel the glass blade's bite.

"Answer if you do not wish to share the fate of your prey!"

A slow smile spread across the female's face. She jerked forward suddenly, and the knife sank into her throat. Shalár pulled it back, but too late. Blood welled and ran down from the wound. The female's mouth opened, and more blood gurgled out of it.

Cursing, Shalár stood and backed away. The two hunters holding the captive looked up at her in alarm. Shalár stared angrily down at the female, then swallowed.

"Feed. Do not waste it. Three mouthfuls each."

She turned away, furious at the lost opportunity to learn this female's circumstances. She had not expected the wretch to care more for her privacy than for her life.

She was furious, too, that she was telling her people to feed on ælven blood, which she believed was wrong. She wiped the blood from her knife and sheathed it again.

Yaras came to her. "That female wears clothing of ælven quality."

"Yes."

"Could she have stolen it?"

Shalár frowned. "Possibly. More likely she traded for it."

"One of ours, trading with the ælven?"

"She is not one of ours. She lives here. Lived here." Shalár glanced back to where a new crowd of hunters surrounded the dying female.

"How can that be?"

She turned to look at Yaras, saw the bewilderment

in his eyes. A small comfort, to know he was as puzzled as she.

"A salient question."

She felt tired all at once despite having fed. Glancing back toward the clusters of hunters patiently waiting for their scant feeding, she sighed. The night was old, and by the time the army was done feeding, there would be little point in setting out again.

"We will rest here. Send some of those who have fed to scout nearby for better ground. Then come to me upstream."

"Yes, Bright Lady."

She strode up the stream bank, impatient to be away from the army. The hunters standing nearby gave way before her. She walked swiftly, sorting her thoughts.

The ground began to slope gradually upward toward the mountains, and the darkwoods opened out somewhat. Shalár came to a pair of black boulders, taller than herself and even longer, unusual for this country. Perhaps some ancient flood had carried them here, or perhaps Firethroat had flung them into the sky in one of its fits of fury. She glanced northward at the dull orange glow of the volcano. Homesickness was part of what troubled her, she realized, and to her surprise it was homesickness for Nightsand.

All her planning, all this effort, and now she had doubts? She dismissed the idea with scorn. Fireshore was hers and her people's by right. She had sworn never to rest until she had won it, and though she did not subscribe to the ælven's obsessive devotion to oaths, she meant with all her being to keep this one.

She loosened her leathers, taking off the jerkin and setting it against one of the boulders while she splashed water on her sweat-soaked tunic and sticky flesh. Her fingers slid into her tunic and caught hold of the small pouch she wore over her heart. It held a ring that had belonged to her father, a lock of Dareth's hair—a sentimentality for which she occasionally berated herself.

"Bright Lady?"

Shalár started, opening her eyes. Yaras stood before her, a look of patient resignation on his face. If she had felt desire before, that look quelled it. Anger sparked in her chest.

What angered her most was his honesty. He did not desire her, though he would obey her. She wanted more than mere obedience, she found. She turned away from him, unfastened her leather legs and stripped off her clothing, then stepped into the stream.

It was warmer than the streams near Nightsand, much warmer than the bay, though still cool enough to give relief from the forest's heat. Shalár had not remembered the darkwoods being so oppressive, but then, it had been a long, long time since she had lived here. She squatted to let the water run across her legs and splashed it onto her torso and arms.

After a moment, she heard Yaras stripping as well. He joined her in the water, and she heard him exhale deeply. She ducked her head and scrubbed at her scalp, then sat up and shook the water from her hair. The water was too shallow and too fast for her to lie drifting on it, so she leaned back against the current and watched Yaras bathe. He had unbraided his hair, and its ends floated about his shoulders as he crouched in the stream. Shalár watched him lie back, steadying himself with one arm as he leaned his head into the water. His hair drifted about him like pale moss.

He was strong and comely and would be a fine sire to any child. Shalár pushed away dull resentment at her lack of success in breeding with him. She had failed to breed with any male, and it was not for lack of effort or of variety of partners.

Nor was it affection that was missing. Her affection for Dareth had been deep, as his for her. If affection was necessary, then none of the ælven in the Cliff Hollows would ever have bred, yet some had bred, at first.

Health was the only thing she could think of that might be lacking. Health and strength. Adequate food. Her people had lived in want for centuries despite their constant efforts to hunt and breed enough kobalen for food.

Would health return once Fireshore was theirs again? If not, she feared her people truly were doomed.

She stood up and walked out of the water, then climbed onto the boulder. It was warm after the coolness of the stream. The forest's dampness kept it from being quite dry, but it was comfortable enough. Shalár stretched out on her back and gazed through the darkwood branches overhead. She could see one star flickering in a tiny gap between the boughs of broad green leaves.

She listened to the night sounds: hunters rustling in the undergrowth, a bird calling to its mate, the murmur of the stream, and the quiet splashes of Yaras's movements. A rushing sound told her he had stood, then the stream returned to its quiet flow.

Yaras joined her on the boulder. She looked at him but made no move to touch him. He waited, watching her with eyes darker than the rock on which they rested. At last he lay down beside her, gazing up at the sky.

Faithful, obedient Yaras, whose heart would never be hers. She took his hand, lacing her fingers through his, and felt a single hot tear slide down her cheek. She swallowed and pushed her selfish wishes aside. She would sacrifice them, and Yaras's, and those of all the hunters in her army for the sake of bringing her people home to Fireshore.

◅ The South Road ▻

Turisan sat in the shelter of a tumble of boulders, his arms folded across his updrawn knees, watching the sun rise. The fire beside which he had spent the night had gone to coals, still warm but fast fading. The other campfires were in the same state.

The little column of wounded had made its way slowly southward, taking a full day to cross the valley south of Midrange Valley, the next ridge of mountains, and the valley south of that. Their pace continued to be slow, a source of frustration to Turisan, though he kept it to himself. On the second day they had met the advance force of two hundred riders sent by Ehranan and watched them disappear northward.

Every evening they made camp in what shelter they could find, and those who were fit enough gathered wood for the fires. Every morning what wood remained unburnt went for pyres to burn the bodies of those who had died overnight. One of the wagons now held several forlorn bundles of possessions wrapped in their former owners' cloaks.

The snow continued fitfully, sometimes making the journey difficult for the wagons, even on the road. There was but one wagon of food supplies, all that had been saved in the scramble to get away from High

Holding, and it was dwindling. Turisan knew that the stores it carried were not enough to see them to Glenhallow, not at the pace they were making.

Never had he been in such a precarious position. Never had he led such a vulnerable company through such harsh conditions. He felt each death as a personal failure, yet he knew this was but a small trial compared with what others had suffered. He had only to think of his father and Skyruach to remember it.

My love?

Eliani.

He closed his eyes and laid his head on his arms. He was grateful but also sad and frightened.

Hard night?

I fear so. I have not yet gone to see.

I meant for you.

Her warmth enveloped him, tingling through his limbs. For a startled moment he wondered if he had been colder than he thought, but no. It was just that she knew what he needed and gave without reserve. He relaxed a little.

Are you riding?

Not yet. Eating sunfruit, then we will start.

Sunfruit. Turisan swallowed, hungry at the thought of the sweet, tangy fruit, the color of the summer sun and rich with juice. He had been tired and worried the previous night, and cold dried meat had not been enough to tempt him.

He should get up and talk to the drivers, have them cook the last of the barley from the supply wagon. A hot meal to get the little column moving, and perhaps in the evening those who were fit enough could hunt.

Snow could be melted for water; he did not care to take water from the Silverwash just now. The meal would raise everyone's spirits, but it would require finding more wood.

He felt weary at the thought but made himself stand. Stiff from the cold, he stepped carefully over the cloak-bundled figures lying by the fire and walked toward the wagons.

He found the drivers huddled around a small, fitful fire. When they heard about the prospect of a hot meal, they went to work building it up again. Turisan returned to the camp, rousing the wounded and sending those who were fit enough to help gather wood.

The most severely wounded had been left in the wagons and covered over with tenting. With some dread he visited each one and found to his relief that none had died overnight. Some seemed unlikely to survive the entire journey, but at least this day they would have to build no pyres.

He was returning to the supply wagon when he heard a distant rumbling, as of many feet moving. His heart quickened with fear, and he looked northward across the valley toward the ridge they had crossed, dreading to see kobalen.

All was quiet to the north. Turning south, he saw a black horse at the head of a column of guardians in Southfæld cloaks. He let out a soft cry of relief. Ehranan and the Southfæld Guard had come.

He hurried to where the horses were picketed and found his little mare. Not bothering to saddle her, he rode her bareback down the slope to meet Ehranan, guiding her with his knees and his good hand in her mane, the other still in its sling.

Ehranan raised a hand to hail him but did not halt the column. Turisan fell in beside him.

"Greetings, Ehranan. Your coming is most welcome."

The commander cast a grim look at him. "Midrange is fallen, then?"

"Not when I left the valley. Eastfæld's riders arrived in time to make a stand there."

"Eastfæld!" He smiled with pride. "They came quickly."

"Yes."

Ehranan frowned at the sling Turisan wore. "You are wounded?"

Turisan felt the heat of a flush sting his cold cheeks. "A dart to the arm. It is not serious."

"Tell me."

Turisan related all that had occurred while he was at Midrange. Ehranan listened, nodding now and then, his expression grave. When Turisan spoke of the retreating wounded under his command, Ehranan glanced up toward the little camp, then toward Midrange.

"You came only this far?"

"Alas, we cannot travel quickly."

"You are but halfway to Glenhallow."

Turisan nodded. "Thereabouts."

"Are you supplied?"

Turisan shook his head. "We are almost out of stores. We can hunt, but we have few arrows."

"I will give you wagons with food enough to see you through the march and fifty arrows for each of you who is fit enough to hunt. Will that do?"

Hope woke in Turisan's chest, but he hesitated. "I do not wish to deprive the Guard who are facing battle."

Ehranan waved his reservations aside. "We have enough to spare and can send for more from Glenhallow. I will have Rephanin relay a request."

"How does Rephanin?" Turisan glanced behind him but did not see the magelord. Guardians five abreast were crossing the ridge to the south.

"Well enough. You will wish to give him messages for Glenhallow. Ride back along the column and you will find him in our midst."

"Thank you."

Ehranan smiled. "You have done well, son of Jharan."

Surprised and honored, Turisan bowed before turning to find Rephanin. He had almost reached the foot of the ridge when he saw a cluster of horses come over it, a figure cloaked in dull gold at its center. Rephanin rode with his hood pulled forward, obscuring his face, surrounded by guardians. Turisan hailed him.

"Good morrow, Lord Rephanin! I trust you are well."

The hooded head lifted and turned his way, and he glimpsed Rephanin's startled face. The guardians parted as Turisan rode up and fell in with Rephanin's horse. The magelord gave a subdued nod of greeting.

"What happened to your arm?"

"A kobalen dart."

"Thorian did not mention it when we met yesterday eve."

"It happened after he left Midrange. Is Thorian well?"

Rephanin nodded. "Making better progress since the snow stopped. The road is clearer to the south."

"Thank the spirits for that! We are moving at a crawl as it is."

" 'We'?"

"A small group of wounded, bound for Glenhallow. Will you ask Thorian to tell my father?"

"Of course. Should I mention your own wound?"

Turisan pressed his lips together. Best to inform Jharan of that at once rather than risk his hearing it by chance.

"Please tell him I am *slightly* wounded and in no danger."

A wry smile twitched the magelord's lips. "Poor Thorian. I would not wish to bring Jharan such news."

"Give him my apologies and assure him that my father will not eat him."

That drew a small laugh from Rephanin. He turned his head to look at Turisan, gray eyes glinting with humor.

"Very well."

Turisan thanked him and left the column to return to his camp. The fires were burning brightly, and the drivers were moving among the wounded, dishing out hot barley into bowls or onto camp plates, whatever each guardian happened to have. Some shared plates, and most ate with their fingers. All seemed glad for the hot meal, simple as it was.

A driver looked up at Turisan as he dismounted. "Some barley, my lord?"

"Yes, in a moment."

He turned the mare out with the other horses and went to the fire where his pack lay. The smell of the barley had awakened his hunger, and he hastened to dig his wooden plate out of the pack.

A driver spooned some food onto the plate for him. The barley steamed in the cold air.

"Thank you for cooking. I know it is not your usual duty."

The driver glanced up. "Glad to be of service, especially to these. I saw . . ."

His face went grim, and he fell silent, eyes apologetic. Turisan smiled to reassure him.

"Thank you."

He had forgotten his spoon, so he balanced the bowl on his right hand in the sling and scooped up hot pinches of barley with his fingers, eating as he strolled through the camp. Faces turned toward him, most with brave smiles. Some of the less seriously wounded had gone to the wagons to feed those who could not feed themselves. Turisan was moved by their courage and thankful for it. They would need it to reach Glenhallow.

❧

Rephanin felt the battle before the column reached the outskirts of Midrange Valley. A deep discord echoed through the khi of all life ahead. He closed his awareness, guarding himself from the distressing sensation, and wondered how he would manage to serve as Ehranan demanded.

Thorian?

There was no answer. Rephanin tried the query signal as well, without result. As distance separated them, it had become apparent that it was Thorian who must speak first. Rephanin was, so far, unable to initiate contact, though he continued to try.

The day was well advanced, however, and they had agreed that they would always speak at sunset. Rephanin hoped Thorian would speak to him soon, for he expected that Midrange was about to engage his full attention.

The sun had retreated behind an overcast of cloud, becoming a sullen, misty globe. The mountain peaks were shrouded, the road muddy with snowmelt. Rephanin shivered, less from actual cold than from dread. The guardians around him became alert, watching the ridge they were approaching with wary eyes. The horses, more sensitive to khi in some ways than ælven, grew restless despite their weariness.

A bloom of warmth touched his brow. He drew a grateful breath.

Thorian.

Yes, my lord. We have halted for the night. Have you?

No. We are nearing Midrange. You remember all the messages for Jharan?

I have written them down.

How close are you to Glenhallow?

I am not quite certain, but I should be there tomorrow, I think.

Rephanin swallowed, wondering if he would ever return to the city that had become his home. He felt suddenly lonely for it, for the magehall and his circle. Most of all for Thorian.

He now understood as he had never done before the ballads that told of mindspeakers' yearning. It was not simply that he and Thorian were separated—they were close in spirit, after all, and spoke daily—but that they were both close and far apart, which created a peculiar longing.

Give my best regards to the governor and to all at the magehall.

I shall. And I will speak to you again in the morning.

I may not be able to answer you. I think we are about to—to begin.

Thorian was silent briefly and subdued when he spoke again. *Be careful, Rephanin.*

The magelord smiled. *Have no fear. I was not made to be heroic.*

He did not want to end his conversation with

Thorian, but a change of movement ahead drew his attention to a rider trotting back along the column. Rephanin knew there could only be one reason. His heart sank.

I must leave you now. I expect I will not be at liberty to speak to you for a while. Try in the morning, though.

Spirits guard you.

And you.

The rider reached Rephanin's escort and bowed in the saddle. "Lord Rephanin, the commander desires your presence at the head of the column."

Unable to make himself answer, Rephanin nodded. Still surrounding him, his mounted escort moved off the road, leaving it to the companies that were on foot.

Rephanin clung to the saddle unashamed as they hastened forward. He was no expert rider and had nothing to prove. Were it not that he knew he was fated for this service, he would have preferred to be elsewhere.

The head of the column had paused at a rise where the road crossed the foot of another ridge. Though he had never traveled this road before, Rephanin knew that beyond that ridge lay Midrange. The darkness he felt from there must be affecting everyone in the column, but still they marched on.

Ehranan hailed him as he drew near. Rephanin acknowledged the commander with a nod, seeing in his face a strange mixture of grim determination and excitement. Could he actually be looking forward to this conflict? Rephanin could not pretend to understand a warrior's feelings and had no desire to.

"Midrange Valley lies ahead. Would it be best for you to speak to the Guard before we enter it?"

"That might be best, yes." Rephanin was dismayed to hear a tremor in his own voice.

"Please do so, then. When you are ready, I will give them greeting."

Rephanin glanced at the ridge to the west. "The mountains may prevent me from being heard once we move forward. I could speak now but lose contact as we pass this ridge."

Ehranan frowned up at the mass of stone. "Even in the open air?"

"Possibly. I think it likely."

"Well, speak now and I will greet the army, then speak again when all have crossed this narrow."

"Very well. I need a moment."

Rephanin closed his eyes and cautiously opened his awareness. Dark turmoil to the north filled his mind, and he had to fight not to recoil from it. He faced it and saw that it ran on two levels: a high, clear flow of khi that came from hundreds of ælven and the dark, heavy, and much greater mass of khi from countless kobalen.

A third and much weaker element was the khi of all other living things in the valley, trees and plants and the few animals that had not fled, mostly carrion eaters. Rephanin shuddered.

He began building barriers in his mind, as he had lately learned so well to do. First he blocked all the lower, denser khi: the kobalen and lesser beings. That alone relieved him to a great extent. Next he divided himself and the Southfæld Guard from the other ælven ahead in the valley. Ehranan might wish him to speak to them all eventually, but for now he would touch only those who were prepared for it.

Finally, he made a shield around his own awareness, a cloud to filter out the feelings of the hundreds of ælven around him. His escort of guardians, assigned by Ehranan to the sole duty of protecting him, would keep his flesh safe, but it was for him to guard his own heart.

Thus sheltered, he opened his eyes and gazed back southward. The Guard had gathered in the valley, waiting to cross into Midrange. He swallowed and, though he did not need it to speak, drew a deep breath.

Guardians of Southfæld, pray attend to your commander.

The khi of hundreds smote him; a bright confusion of eagerness, dread, and courage. He shifted his mental shield to block it, then looked to Ehranan. The commander nodded in silent thanks, then faced the army.

We are at the threshold of battle. For your pledge of service, I thank you on behalf of all ælven realms. Remember that you stand between your loved ones and this threat.

Rephanin retreated to the shelter he had made for himself, not needing to hear Ehranan's words of encouragement. They were meant not for him but for those who were about to risk their lives.

A corner of his awareness he reserved to tend to his flesh, to keep himself from falling off his horse. Beyond that his escort would see to his safety.

He turned his private thoughts away from the madness ahead. He thought of Thorian, Glenhallow, and his magehall, all of which increased his longing but at least distracted him from Midrange.

Heléri came sudden into his thoughts. Heléri, for whom he also yearned though he had lately had little leisure to think of her. He was close to her now and also impossibly distant; she was a short ride away, but Midrange lay between them. He felt a sudden surge of desire that manifested itself most intensely in his flesh. That seemed to him incongruous with his surroundings, and the thought brought his awareness forward.

The column was moving. He had crossed the ridge and was now descending into Midrange Valley. As he had expected, he sensed interference from the mountains, but the guardians who were nearby could still hear Ehranan through him. The commander's voice in thought was ceaseless, giving guidance and encouragement.

It was cold here. Rephanin's fingers pulled numbly at his cloak, drawing it closer around him. His hood was drawn forward as was his custom, and it blocked the sight of the battlefield, but he could hear the fighting, a constant crashing, growling sound of mingled anger and despair. He recoiled, instinct urging him to block all of it, everything, and for a moment he could not help but do so.

Ehranan's face turned toward him, questioning, alarmed. Rephanin regained his balance and opened to Ehranan again, though it cost him unexpected effort. The instinct to preserve himself against the chaos flowing through this valley was much stronger than he had anticipated.

Maintaining contact with the Guard had been simple when everyone's feelings had been calm for the most part. Here, emotions shot like lightning through them: anger, fear, horror, elation. Rephanin could not begin to understand them. He focused his attention on Ehranan's voice, on lending it the strength to reach all the Southfæld Guard in the valley.

He became aware of a rushing movement. Ehranan's force was advancing to join the battle. He himself had stopped moving; he was aware of his escort surrounding him and Ehranan not far away, though he could not have said in which direction he stood. Confused, he gave attention to the sense of Ehranan's words.

Lashiri, take your company to the left—there is a thinning of the shield wall there. Archers to the left as well, behind Lashiri's company—array yourselves on the slope and send your arrows over our line.

His instructions were to specific captains, but all the Guard heard them. Rephanin saw that practicing this technique in Glenhallow had been well worthwhile; the Guard did not answer, having been trained not to do so, but they heard and were able to avoid impeding the companies being ordered to move.

Rephanin dared to raise his head and look at the valley from within the shelter of his hood. He was appalled by what he saw.

A line of ælven stood across it, at the west extending up into the hills until it came against a sharp cliff, steep and unscalable. At the east it descended to the banks of the Silverwash, which was choked with dead kobalen, actually overrunning its banks and sending fouled icy water over the road in one place.

High Holding had fallen, then. Inevitable, but still a source of grief.

The line holding back the kobalen seemed tiny and frail. Beyond it they seethed and roiled, roaring with fury as they flung themselves against the ælven's shields without seeming sense or order.

Rephanin shut his eyes and concentrated on Ehranan's commands. As the Southfæld guardians reached the shield line, the tone of their khi changed, sparking with fear, pain, eagerness, weariness, grief. Blending with that of the Ælvanen warriors holding the line.

He could no longer keep Ehranan's messages back

from the Ælvanen now that the Southfæld Guard was among them, and their surprise rang a new note through the khi of the ælven in the valley. A few Southfælders who stood with the defenders reacted with joy. These must be the guardians who had gone ahead to High Holding, but so few! So few.

Rephanin pushed aside his own shock and stayed with Ehranan's voice, constant now though not always giving commands; a flow of words that soothed and steadied. He felt admiration growing in him, and fondness for the commander who would do this for his guardians, who gave them this gift of reassurance. Ehranan's voice was a beacon in the midst of the storm, and Rephanin felt as grateful for it as any warrior.

The Ælvanen were beginning to retire now, retreating toward the south side of the valley, coming near to where Rephanin stood. The bright strength of the Southfæld Guard had lifted the spirits of all, and the shield line seemed less fragile now even as the Eastfælders left it.

"My lord?"

The spoken voice startled him; looking up, he saw one of his guardians standing beside his horse. He became aware of others moving nearby.

"If you care to dismount, we are establishing a camp for you here."

Rephanin nodded, unwilling to add the complication of voicing a reply while his mind was still engaged with Ehranan. He slid from the saddle, noting the stiffness of his muscles, grateful to be standing on the ground.

A guardian took his horse's reins and led it away. Others were erecting a tent, building a fire. The ground where they had stopped sloped upward behind them, toward the ridge that marked the southern side of Midrange Valley.

Rephanin gazed at the battle line, confused at how distant it actually was from where he stood. In his mind it was immediate, and if he allowed it he could hear the roar of the battle through the awareness of the army.

Ehranan fell silent. The Southfæld forces were all in place now, and Rephanin sensed that Ehranan was talking with the commander of Eastfæld's forces.

"If it please you, my lord, we have made a place for you to rest until the tent is ready."

Blinking as he shifted his attention to the guardian who had spoken, Rephanin saw her gesture toward a makeshift couch of baggage covered with blankets. He followed her to it and settled upon it, murmuring a word of thanks.

Something was clawing at him. Panic shot through him, though he was in no physical danger. He was safe, apart from the battle, surrounded by his escort of guardians.

Seeking elsewhere for the cause of his unrest, he came to realize it was beyond the barriers he had built around his mind, muted by them, distant. It was the pain and fear of guardians who were dying.

He could feel their surprise at being shorn of their flesh, could feel their thoughts of loved ones they would not see again. He tried to shut out the anguish but could not block it entirely. He was trapped with it, for he must serve as he had pledged to do, and this would not cease.

He must feel their crossing, resist joining them, and lend his gift to Ehranan's voice with no end in view. Even though he was distanced from the sensations of his flesh, he knew tears were running down his face.

❧ Ghlanhras ❧

Eliani and her party reined in before Ghlanhras and sat frowning at the high wall surrounding the city. Black basalt, roughly cut and unpolished, a rod or more in height, it was a wall of function but no beauty. Glenhallow's masons—even Highstone's—would have been ashamed to call such work finished.

The gates, made of darkwood, were closed. Eliani had never seen an ælven community that did not offer welcome to all visitors. Glenhallow was the only other walled city she had seen, but its walls were finer and its gates stood open. This felt wrong.

A space two rods wide was cut between the wall and the forest, all the way around, so that the city was ringed in sunlight despite being in the midst of deep forest. Beyond that circle, the woods grew so densely that she doubted any could pass through save by chopping a path as they went. Darkwoods twined in the midst of the tangle, their limbs interweaving, making it difficult to discern to which tree the branches belonged.

Luruthin's horse sidled. "It appears no one is watching for visitors. Shall I knock?"

Vanorin shook his head. "That is not your place. You are an ambassador here. Taharan, if you will."

A Stonereach rider dismounted and went to the heavy darkwood gates. He pounded with a gloved fist, the sound falling deadened in the quiet. Somewhere beyond the gates a child squealed, then was quickly silenced.

This city, this forest, felt forbidding. Eliani wished to be anywhere but here. She rolled her shoulders, trying to rid them of tension.

Hurried steps sounded beyond the gates, followed by several heavy clunks, then one side of the gate swung slowly open. A male looked out, dressed in a dark gray tunic and legs that had seen much service. By his coloring he might have been Greenglen save that his face was hardened and his eyes were wary, a look Eliani was beginning to associate with Clan Sunriding.

He gazed at her in astonishment, making no gesture of welcome. She felt a surge of impatience and sat taller in the saddle.

"I am Lady Eliani of Felisanin, come to bring messages to Governor Othanin."

This news did not appear to give the gatekeeper any pleasure, but he stepped back, opening the gate wider to let them in. Eliani nudged her mount forward, riding through at a walk with Vanorin close behind.

A long avenue stretched before them. To either side, a street curved away from it on which houses built of darkwood stood shoulder to shoulder much like those Eliani had seen in both Bitterfield and Woodrun. When the last rider had come through the gate, the keeper swung it shut.

"Pardon my caution. Visitors seldom come to Ghlanhras. Darkwood Hall is this way."

Eliani and the others followed him down the avenue. The dull clopping of the horses' hooves against packed dirt echoed from the houses, sharp sounds reflected by the hard darkwood. No faces appeared at the windows of the houses.

They crossed a broad, silent street, then another. Ghlanhras was laid out in concentric circles like Bitterfield, but on a much larger scale. They passed seven sets of circles, but not until they reached the public circle did Eliani see another soul: a fair-haired child of no more than twenty years rolling a hoop in the street, who stopped and stared at the strangers.

Eliani smiled at him. A female came out of a house, caught the child up, and hurried back inside, hushing his protests.

Eliani realized that none of the doors stood open, not even slightly ajar as they had been in both Bitterfield and Woodrun. If there were hearthrooms in these houses, none welcomed visitors, not now, in any case. That alone bespoke the city's deep unhappiness.

The public circle was larger than Highstone's, smaller than Glenhallow's, and cobbled in dark polished stones on which the horses' hooves clattered. If Ghlanhras held a market, it was not meeting today.

On the north side of the circle stood a sprawling hall, much larger than any other structure in Ghlanhras. Its wide, low wings seemed to embrace the circle, and rooftops of varying levels were all flat, with deep overhangs creating shade. It was at least twice the size of Felisanin Hall and all black, built entirely of darkwood. Eliani concluded that this must be Darkwood Hall, the governor's residence.

She inhaled sharply at the thought of so much darkwood in a single structure. The wood was prized and rare in Alpinon, used sparingly where its strength and endurance were most needed. The fact that most of the buildings she had seen in Fireshore were built partly or entirely of darkwood made this realm seem extraordinarily prosperous.

Nowhere had she seen darkwood used on such a grand scale as in Darkwood Hall, however. The beams of its roofs were massive, and she had by now seen enough darkwood trees to know that such large pieces of straight wood were rare and must have come from the boles of very old trees. This hall rivaled Hallowhall, she thought, though its grandeur was of a different style. Where Hallowhall was all golden lightness, this place was all shadow.

Its doors stood open, however; an encouraging sign, although no fire gleamed forward from the welcoming hearth. The warmth of the climate might account for that, though custom called for the token flame of a candle or lantern if there was no fire.

Customs were different here, Eliani thought with a grimace. She dismounted and looked around the circle, noting that no other doors stood open.

Railings stood at the edge of the public circle along with water troughs for horses, implying that there were markets, or at least had been. The gatekeeper indicated that they might tie their horses.

"Do all of you go in to the governor?"

Vanorin glanced at Eliani. "We need not all go. If you will show us your public lodge, some of us will wait there."

The Sunriding looked confounded. "The lodge?"

"Yes. You do have a public lodge?"

"Y-yes." The male frowned. "Stay a moment, if you will."

Without waiting for an answer, he strode into Darkwood Hall. Eliani stared after him, astonished at being left alone. She was no stickler for formality, but even in the casual ambience of Highstone visitors were never abandoned in the public circle.

Luruthin cast a wry glance at Vanorin. "Mayhap the lodge has not been in use much of late."

"You must be right."

The gatekeeper returned, bringing with him a tall, sharp-featured male with the black hair of an Ælvanen, dressed predictably in gray. He kept wary eyes on Eliani as the gatekeeper introduced him.

"This is Tenahran, steward of Darkwood Hall. He will take you to Governor Othanin, and I will show the rest of your party to the lodge. We have no lodge keeper, I fear, but you may make yourselves at home there."

Eliani hid her surprise at this lack and nodded in acknowledgment of Tenahran's bow. The steward glanced at the gatekeeper as he straightened.

"The kitchens at Darkwood Hall will send a meal to the lodge. How many of you go there?"

Vanorin turned to the guardians. "Hathranen, Rovhiran, you will accompany us. The rest may retire to the lodge."

Eliani watched ten guardians follow the gatekeeper away across the circle, leading their horses. She, Luruthin, Vanorin, and the two others tied their own mounts at the railings, where she noted that the troughs were dry. It appeared they would have to come back to tend the animals, for she began to suspect that no one from Ghlanhras would do so.

Tenahran invited them with a gesture to follow him into Darkwood Hall. The hearthroom was large, though the hearth itself was small and looked as if it had not held a fire in a long time. There were few ornaments, and the darkwood walls made the room feel close despite its size.

The steward pushed aside a curtain of gray silk, revealing a wide corridor. Near the ceiling were windows, wide but no more than two handspans high, covered in a latticework carved of darkwood. The light they cast was filtered, dappled against the walls. Closed doors and smaller passages branched off on either side, but the steward led them down the long corridor before them. Their footsteps echoed in the otherwise silent hall.

At the far end of the corridor, Tenahran swung open a pair of tall, ornately carved darkwood doors, revealing what looked to be a vast audience chamber. The ceiling here was high, the full height of the building, and more of the lattice-covered windows ran all around the top of the walls. Five large chairs of darkwood, ornately carved and cushioned with orange velvet, stood upon a dais that ran the length of the far wall.

The steward led them through the audience chamber to a passage that opened from the right-hand wall beside the dais and down it to a door that stood ajar about midway along its length. He turned to Eliani.

"Pray wait here a moment while I announce you to the governor."

He opened the door and stepped through, drawing it closed behind him. An exchange of murmurs followed, a soft voice responding to Tenahran's, then the steward opened the door wide.

"Please come in."

The room they entered was small and windowless, a personal workroom. Eliani and her companions filled most of its open space.

The floor was softened by a carpet woven in intricate patterns in shades of gray. A three-lobed copper lamp hung from the ceiling, illuminating a darkwood table at which sat a male in robes of gray silk trimmed at the throat and cuffs with a narrow band of orange. Tenahran stepped beside the table.

"My lord governor, allow me to present Lady Eliani of Felisanin and her companions."

The governor stood. His hair was as black as an Ælvanen's, and his eyes as dark and rich as Turisan's, though they showed more care. Lines of worry had etched his face, but he smiled as he stepped past Tenahran to greet Eliani.

"I am Othanin. Welcome to Ghlanhras."

Eliani made a formal bow, compelled perhaps by the knowledge that her messages were from Jharan and the Council. "Thank you, my lord governor. This is my cousin Luruthin, theyn of Clerestone, and our friends Vanorin, Rovhiran, and Hathranen."

"Welcome to you all."

Vanorin bowed to him, then turned to Eliani. "With your permission, my lady, we will attend to the horses."

She smiled. "Thank you."

He and the other two guardians stepped out, relieving the crowding in the room. Othanin turned to Eliani.

"House Felisanin, you say? You are kin to Governor Felisan?"

"I am his daughter."

"Ah. I am honored to meet you, my lady. Please be seated. Tenahran, if you would bring some refreshment?"

The steward, who had moved two chairs forward, bowed and left the room. Eliani and Luruthin sat in the wide, low-backed chairs of darkwood, which proved more comfortable than they looked.

Anxious to discharge her duty, Eliani drew two letters from within her leather jerkin, one sealed with ribbons of silver and pale green, the other with all the colors of the Council. Both were a trifle worn at the corners. She laid them on the table before Othanin.

"I bring you these missives, my lord governor."

He gazed at them, then glanced up at her. "You carried them here yourself. Most would have sent them on from Woodrun."

"I was charged to lay them in your hands. Two other envoys have failed to reach you."

Othanin looked startled. "I am sorry to hear it. I assure you they were not turned back from Fireshore."

"They never reached Fireshore. They—well, read these, and then I will explain." Eliani gestured to the letters.

He gazed at her for a moment, the outer corners of his eyes pinched with concern. He picked up the Council's letter but paused before breaking the seal, and met Eliani's gaze.

"Tell me this. Are we at war?"

Eliani drew a breath, then nodded. "We are at war with kobalen, at Midrange."

Othanin's eyes widened. He broke the seal and spread open the Council's letter. Eliani watched him read, the frown deepening on his brow. At one point he gave a soft exclamation of alarm but read on. He finished the Council's letter and pushed it aside, reaching for Jharan's. He read it quickly, then let it fall to the table and looked up at Eliani.

"I cannot send help to Midrange."

"We gathered as much."

Luruthin's tone was wry. Eliani glanced at him,

then laid a hand on the table and leaned toward Oth-anin.

"Why have you not informed the other realms of the state of things in Fireshore?"

A bitter smile touched Othanin's lips. "Sunriding has no wish to share Darkshore's fate. When I asked about war, I meant that, not kobalen. I am very sorry to hear of the threat at Midrange."

"No longer just a threat. Since those letters were written, the kobalen have come across the mountains. Eastfæld has sent support and we are holding the valley, but the outcome is by no means decided."

Othanin closed his eyes briefly. "I wish I could help."

Tenahran returned with a tray. All were silent as he poured golden wine into small goblets, then offered a plate of light bread. Eliani took a piece and bit into it, her hunger waking with sudden fierceness. It was sweet and crisp and melted easily in her mouth, leaving her wanting more. Luruthin helped himself to two slices and leaned back in his chair, munching.

"Close the door, please, Tenahran."

The steward looked surprised, glanced at Eliani, then complied. Othanin put his elbows on the table, hands clasped before him.

"What of this alben who posed as a messenger from me? What has been done with him?"

Eliani's pulse jumped with anxiety. She took another sip of wine before answering, then cleared her throat.

"I regret to tell you that since then he has escaped. We suspect he will either head west of the mountains or seek refuge in the Steppes."

"And your first envoy, those with whom he was captured. Will you seek to free them?"

Eliani's mouth dropped open in surprise. She closed

it, feeling color rise to her cheeks. "To be honest, we assumed they were lost to us."

"You are probably right. Even if they live, they may well have succumbed to the curse by now."

Eliani set her goblet on the table. "What can you tell us of this affliction? Have you learned its cause?"

Othanin gave a slight shrug. "Would that we had. We know only that it most often befalls those who spend considerable time in the darkwood forest."

Eliani caught her breath and traded a glance with Luruthin. They had ridden through Fireshore's forests for days.

"That is why you walled the city?"

Othanin nodded. "Though I cannot say whether it has made much difference. We must go into the forest to harvest darkwood. Those who go sometimes succumb."

"Bitterfield has not suffered this affliction, and they are surrounded by forest."

"True. They harvest darkwood near their village, as do the people of Woodrun. So far neither has suffered as Ghlanhras has. Our darkwood is taken from camps deep in the forest."

Luruthin shifted in his chair. "From the look of the city, I am surprised you are able to harvest."

Othanin glanced at him sharply but nodded. "I understand your thinking so. Many of our folk have left, though there are still enough to harvest darkwood. It is taken to Woodrun for trade."

"Why do you remain in Ghlanhras at all?"

Othanin gazed at Eliani, his eyes deep wells of sadness. "Clan Sunriding was charged with holding Fireshore. Ghlanhras is Fireshore's chief city."

Luruthin reached for the ewer and helped himself to more wine. "Ghlanhras is dying, by the looks of it."

"Yes. I have sought a remedy but found none. I will remain until the others have all left."

"That is folly." Eliani set her cup on the table. "Forgive me, Lord Othanin, but it seems to me you should seek help from the Council."

He looked at her, a small, mirthless smile on his lips. "Summon a Council to Ghlanhras? They would not come."

"It need not be Ghlanhras."

"And what help could the Ælven Council give, when all its efforts are bent toward Midrange?" Othanin shook his head. "What help could they give in any case?"

"Fireshore was repopulated after the Bitter Wars. It can be done again."

"I would not ask any of our kindred from other realms to come and dwell here. It would be to place themselves at risk. The good theyn is right: Ghlanhras as it once was is dying. I have thought, when enough are gone, that the city might be given to the exiles."

"What! To the alben?" Eliani could not conceal her outrage.

"Not the alben."

Luruthin coughed slightly. "The Lost?"

Othanin leaned back in his chair, and a wary look came into his eyes. "You have heard of the Lost?"

"Bitterfield's theyn and his lady told us."

Othanin nodded, his gaze growing distant. "My father made a decree when the hunger first returned. Those who suffered and did not choose to leave flesh were offered peaceful exile and given what they needed to survive. They send us word from time to time, messages for their kin. We have even traded with them."

Luruthin sat up and leaned forward, frowning. "You trade with those who will not keep the creed?"

"They *do* keep the creed in all but the one respect, and even in that they follow our customs."

Eliani felt a flash of outrage. "Customs? We have no customs for the drinking of kobalen blood!"

"We have customs for hunting. Practices according to the creed, to avoid cruelty and to offer atonement."

"That applies to game beasts, not to creatures of intelligence!"

"Yet we slay those intelligent creatures outright."

Othanin's voice remained calm. He spread the fingers of his hand upon the table and gazed at them. "The Lost cannot help the demands of their affliction."

"You would welcome them back into Ghlanhras?"

Othanin looked up at Eliani, his eyes hardening. "If others will not dwell here, they might as well do so. They could harvest darkwood. The forests around Ghlanhras are rich and produce the highest-quality wood in all the realm. If the Lost returned to work these stands, then none others need be at risk, and we would all benefit from the harvest."

"But that would be a reversal of the Council's decree against Darkshore!"

"We are not Clan Darkshore, nor are the Lost. They uphold the creed in every way they can."

Lurùthin looked skeptical. "How can you be sure of that?"

Othanin was silent for a long moment. "I know it because my lady is with them."

Eliani caught her breath. Othanin heard, for he turned to face her.

"She has kept the creed faithfully all her life." A tremor of grief crossed his face. "She almost chose to leave flesh when the hunger came over her. I begged her to stay. I could not bear to lose her as well."

"As well?"

Othanin met Eliani's gaze. "My father faced the same choice. A few years after he decreed the Lost must leave Fireshore, he fell victim to the hunger."

He lowered his gaze, seeing memories. His voice dropped so that Eliani had to lean forward to hear him.

"There is a place not far from here, on the northern shore in the shadow of Firethroat. The currents there are swift and strong. It has become customary for those who are afflicted with the hunger and desire to cross into spirit to go there and give their flesh to the waters. My father handed the governorship of Fireshore to me, and the next day we went together to the shore. I watched him walk into the sea."

Eliani was stricken with pity. "I am so sorry."

"Thank you." Othanin smiled sadly. "It has been . . . very hard. I have walked to the shore with many of my friends and kindred. Every time I wonder if I shall someday take that path myself."

"I hope not."

Luruthin stirred. "What of your lady? You say she chose to remain in flesh?"

"Yes. I have not seen her since she joined the Lost, but we have exchanged messages." Othanin gave a small smile. "Most of those who still dwell in Ghlanhras remain because they have loved ones among the Lost."

Eliani closed her eyes, overwhelmed by sadness. She began to feel that Ghlanhras truly was a cursed place. Perhaps the ælven should never have settled there, but that could not be undone now.

Luruthin's voice roused her from these thoughts. "Eliani and I have kin in Bitterfield—Davhri, the potter. Her partner, Inóran, came to Ghlanhras this past spring and has not been heard of again."

Othanin frowned. "Inóran?"

"Yes." Eliani cleared her throat, reaching for her goblet. "He was seeking to trade for glass, she said."

"Oh. Yes, we have a master glassworker, Ranohran. One of the few skilled crafters who have remained in Ghlanhras."

Eliani met his gaze. "He has kin with the Lost?"

Othanin nodded, smiling sadly. "I will send a message to him if you wish, asking if Inóran came to see him."

"Thank you, yes."

Eliani fell silent. What she had learned of Ghlanhras was disheartening, and she wished to consult Turisan about its troubles. Thinking of him made her realize that her task was done; she might now return to him. A quiet shimmer of joy went through her.

Othanin straightened in his chair. "Allow me to amend an omission. You have traveled long to reach me and must desire to refresh yourselves. May I offer you rooms and hot water? I would be honored to continue our discussion over dinner."

Eliani looked up at him with a grateful smile. "Yes. Thank you."

The governor stood and stepped to the door. Reaching outside it, he rang a sonorous chime, then returned to stand beside Eliani's chair. By the time she and Luruthin had risen, Tenahran had come in answer to the chime.

"Please show our guests to chambers."

The steward bowed and led them away, back through the audience chamber and the broad main corridor. The afternoon had passed while they had been closeted with Othanin, and the light filtering through the high windows was tinted with gold. Rush torches augmented it, casting an orange glow that did not quite illuminate all the main corridor. Eliani saw chandeliers hanging at intervals from the high ceiling, but they were dark.

Tenahran took one of the torches in hand to light their way as he turned into a lesser hallway. Save for the fading daylight coming through the latticed windows, this passage was unlit. He turned a corner and after a short distance threw open two adjacent doors, revealing guest chambers that had plainly not been used in some time. Though clean, they were still and silent, hushed with the absence of khi.

"Water will be brought you." He kindled a lamp in the first chamber from his torch. The smell of spice-scented oil arose as he turned to Eliani. "Is there aught else you need?"

"Our saddle packs."

"Ah, yes. My apologies for not having them here."

"Tenahran, how many attendants are there in Darkwood Hall at present?"

He hesitated. "Only myself and my daughter at present, my lady. Governor Othanin's demands are few."

"He has no kindred, no counselors dwelling here?"

Tenahran shook his head, then turned to Luruthin. "This next chamber is yours, Theyn Luruthin."

They stepped out into the passage, leaving Eliani to look about at the ornate hangings in her room and on the bed, similar in style to the latticework and the rugs she had seen. Intricate knotwork seemed to be the fashion in Fireshore. Oddly appropriate, for matters here were certainly in a tangle.

❧

Shalár stood just within the forest's edge at the end of the road from Westgard, gazing at the high wall of basalt that surrounded Ghlanhras. The damp warmth made her uncomfortable and the tickle of hunger still plagued her, but she paid no heed to either.

The musty smell of wet darkwood sparked memories, many disturbing, unhappy. She put them aside as well. She was here at last, though her home looked nothing like she remembered and, to her surprise, she felt no pleasure in returning. The pleasure would come later, perhaps, when she walked in the hall that had been her father's.

She turned to Yaras. "I want a volunteer to scale the wall. Someone small, less likely to be seen."

"Yes, Bright Lady."

She listened to his receding footfalls, confident in the plan she was already weaving. Depending on what the hunter who scaled the wall saw, she would send one or more of the pack down into the city near the gate. If it was guarded, they would capture or kill the guards. If not, they would simply open the gate to the rest of the army. It seemed almost too easy.

Yaras returned, bringing with him Benavh, a female who had gone on the recent Grand Hunt. It seemed long ago, though only one turn of seasons had passed since then. Shalár quickly told Benavh her wishes, and she nodded.

"Yes, Bright Lady."

"Do not let yourself be seen or heard."

The hunter flashed a grin, then crossed the space between the forest and the wall in five silent strides. Shalár watched her climb, clinging to the rocks. She hauled herself onto the top of the wall and lay flat upon it, still and silent, peering down into the city.

Shalár's skin tingled in anticipation of fighting. She almost wished she had scaled the wall herself.

Benavh crawled along the wall toward the gate,

then rose onto her elbows, peering toward the city's center. At last she slid toward the outside of the wall again, carefully lowering herself to the ground. She darted back to Shalár, grinning.

"There is a light in one house by the gate. All the others near the wall are dark, as far as I could see. The only other lights are in the middle of the city."

"Around the public circle. Well done." Shalár looked to Yaras. "Five will go in. Choose the swiftest and lightest of foot."

"May I go?" Benavh's eyes shone with excitement.

"Are you prepared to kill ælven?"

She looked shocked for a fleeting moment, then set her chin. "Yes, Bright Lady. I will slay any who stand in your way."

Shalár glanced at Yaras and gave a tiny shrug, leaving the decision to him. Yaras looked at Benavh.

"Very well. Wait here while I bring the others."

He slipped away into the forest. Shalár stood gazing at the gate. Benavh fidgeted beside her, clearly looking forward to scaling the wall again.

"Soon." Shalár's whisper was only partly to Benavh. "Very soon."

◅◦▻

Luruthin picked up his wine goblet and leaned back in his chair of ornately carved darkwood, sated as he had not been for days. He and Eliani were both dressed in borrowed silks provided by Tenahran, who had taken away their travel clothing to be washed. Luruthin reveled in the luxury of being clean and well fed.

On the table between himself, Othanin, and Eliani lay the remains of a feast that would have made even Lord Jharan proud. Pheasants roasted and glazed with a sweet sunfruit sauce; myriad vegetables, some of which he had never before encountered; rice flavored with delicate spices; rich sauces; and breads light and moist, hot from the oven.

Luruthin raised his goblet in salute. "A most excellent meal. Thank you, Governor."

"I am glad to be able to offer my hospitality, and I may tell you that Ghenari, our cook, was overjoyed. She rarely has the chance to exercise her talent nowadays."

"And a rare talent it is. May she always prosper."

Othanin smiled, though trouble never quite left his face. "Were things not as they are, I would ask you to stay a few days. I suspect you will want to leave tomorrow, though."

Eliani nodded. "Yes. I am anxious to return—to Glenhallow."

She had been about to say "home," Luruthin thought. Except just now, where was her home? Highstone, but also Glenhallow. Her home was wherever Turisan was.

Feeling a sudden sharp pang of longing for Jhinani, Luruthin nodded. "I, too."

Othanin poured more wine into their goblets. "I will write letters for Jharan and Felisan tonight. The Council has disbanded, you said?"

"Yes. They plan to reconvene on the first of spring, in Highstone."

Luruthin drained his cup and set it down. "If the fighting at Midrange is not over by then, there will likely be no Council at all."

The others were silent. Perhaps that was too grim a prediction.

Othanin shifted in his chair. "You—you did not

encounter one of our exiles on your way here, did you? She would have resembled an alben."

"No." Eliani shook her head. "We have seen no alben."

"It is just that she has not returned—from hunting—for some days now. My lady is becoming concerned."

"Do the Lost never choose to leave flesh?" Eliani asked quietly.

"None have done so. That choice was made when they left Ghlanhras. They are dedicated to surviving, to continuing to dwell in harmony and mutual support, and to living by the creed as much as their affliction allows."

Eliani frowned, as if she still doubted the feasibility of this. Luruthin looked at Othanin.

"Have they made a village?"

"Not so far, but that is under discussion. Some of them are growing weary of living as wanderers. Kobalen prefer it, but the ælven want a home."

The ælven. Luruthin returned a half smile to show he did not disapprove, though he was not sure he agreed that Ghlanhras's Lost were still ælven. By the Council's ruling, they were alben, but that Council had met centuries ago, at a time when fear was high and no one understood the nature of this affliction. It was poorly understood now, but at least they were making an effort to learn about it instead of merely slaying or banishing those unfortunate enough to suffer it.

Eliani spoke softly. "I hope they find a home. I hope we can come to a better understanding of this hunger. If it is indeed a sickness, perhaps it can be healed."

Othanin leaned back and folded his hands over his stomach. "There are records—letters and journals—from before the Bitter Wars. Many were burned in the purging of Fireshore, but a few were preserved. They mention efforts at healing, none of which were successful."

"But it is worth pursuing. They may not have had sufficient skill or sufficient time for a healing to be effective."

"All avenues of hope are worth pursuing." Othanin gazed at Eliani. "You are correct, my lady, when you say that to give Ghlanhras to the Lost would, in essence, reverse the decree that followed the Bitter Wars. I believe that would be a boon to us all."

Eliani looked up at him, plainly dismayed by his words. Othanin seemed to wish to embrace those who fed upon kobalen, to welcome them back as brethren of the ælven. Luruthin's instinct was to object, for he knew the Council would take strong exception to this proposal, but he held his peace.

Othanin looked from Eliani to him, then back. "Would it not be better to admit that decree was a mistake than to compound it by continuing to punish our own kindred for what cannot be helped?"

Eliani's brow knit in a worried frown. "This is a matter for the current Council to decide."

"And I will gladly plead my cause before them."

Luruthin nodded. "That alone should go far toward reassuring the other realms of Fireshore's goodwill."

Eliani glanced at him, then looked back at Othanin. "Fireshore is not alone, Governor. It is not isolated, or should not be. This will be resolved."

"Thank you."

Othanin smiled, though the trouble did not leave his eyes. Perhaps it never would.

They fell silent. Luruthin thought Eliani looked tired and possibly upset. He turned to the governor.

"I think we should retire, perhaps."

Eliani bestirred herself. "Yes. Thank you for your kind hospitality, Lord Othanin. We shall see you again in the morning."

"Very well. Perhaps I will ride with you a little way toward Woodrun. Tenahran is forever urging me to get out of this gloomy manse, as he calls it."

As they all rose from the table, Othanin offered his arm to Eliani, then to Luruthin. His clasp was light, almost hesitant, but Luruthin could feel strength in his flesh and in his khi.

"May you rest sweetly, my new friends. Thank you for the hope you have brought me."

Bidding him good night, they left the hall and made their way to their chambers. Eliani was pensive, and Luruthin refrained from interrupting her thoughts. They would have plenty of time and more privacy to discuss Ghlanhras as they rode tomorrow. Meanwhile, a night beneath a solid roof would do them both good.

He bade Eliani rest well and retired to his room, glancing up at the narrow lattice-covered window that ran the width of the room at the top of the far wall. No glass, but a thin screen of tissue to mute the sun's light and keep out insects and other unwanted visitors. Starlight now cast the faintest glow through it. He could feel the forest breathing beyond.

His saddle pack lay on a small darkwood table beside the bed. Folded neatly beside it were his clothes: two sets of tunic and legs, now clean and smelling faintly of sunfruit.

He stretched out on top of the bed in his borrowed silks, having no desire for more covering. Night in northern Fireshore was no cooler than day.

He closed his eyes, seeking to still his thoughts. He centered his awareness in his flesh, then slowly let it expand to the room and beyond, taking in the small sounds of night-biding creatures within and without the house. There were few, very few.

And that was wrong.

Suddenly alert, Luruthin opened his eyes, listening and seeking with khi for the sounds of a normal evening. Though this land was strange to him, there should not be silence.

He sat up slowly, preserving his own silence. His flesh prickled with tension. He stood and walked with noiseless steps to the door, laying hands and forehead against it. Cautiously he explored the corridor with khi, following it back to the center of the house. There he found movement. Silent movement, of many feet.

Recoiling from the door, he stared at it. Could Othanin have been deceiving them? He disbelieved it but dreaded what he thought was walking in the governor's house.

He opened the door a crack and peered down the corridor. Nothing moved there, but beyond it he felt shadows stirring.

For a moment he was still, pondering what to do. He must warn Eliani; they should leave this place. By stealth? But what of Othanin? If he was innocent and unaware, did he not also deserve warning?

A scrape of leather against stone from down the corridor told him it was too late to reach the governor. They were coming.

"Eliani! Arm yourself!"

He ducked into his room and caught up his sword. The bow would have been better, but he had left it on his saddle and it had not been brought to his chamber.

Stepping back into the corridor, he saw a figure at the far end of it opening a door with cautious stealth. The figure was male, dressed in black leathers, with snowy hair caught back in a braid from a face paler than a Greenglen's.

Luruthin's breath came short and swift. No sign of movement from Eliani's chamber. He could not now summon her without attracting the attention of the male in black. The best Luruthin could think of was to try to distract him while giving warning to Eliani. He gripped his sword and started forward, drawing a deep breath to shout both accusation and warning.

"Alben!"

◄ Darkwood Hall ►

Eliani sat up, startled by Luruthin's cry. It took a moment to remember where she was, so deeply entwined with Turisan she had been.

Something is happening. I must go.

Let me follow.

He had sensed her fear. No time to argue; she leapt up from the bed, scrabbling her feet into borrowed slippers. The silk tunic and legs whispered softly as she moved.

There was noise in the corridor outside. Luruthin had shouted something—she had not quite caught it. She went to the door and stood listening.

"A sword!" The voice was unfamiliar. "This one is armed! Bring a sword!"

Eliani needed no more prompting. They wanted a sword? She would bring hers.

She drew it silently, then opened the door a crack and looked out. Luruthin stood a few paces down the passage with his back to her, sword in hand. Beyond him were three warriors in black leather, eyes black and wide, hair and flesh as white as sun-bleached bone.

Alben! That was what he had shouted!

A shiver of fear went through her. She inhaled, flung open the door, and strode forward.

One of the alben threw something toward her, a black shadow that spread as it flew. She parried with her sword. Torchlight flashed on metal, and a high-pitched ringing followed as her blade deflected the thing. She glimpsed a tangle of black cord and bits of metal—a net.

Poorly armed. She took heart as she joined Luruthin. The alben retreated before them, but she heard the voices of more beyond, in the heart of the manse.

Othanin! Spirits, were they here to capture him? Or could these be his Lost? No, they would have no reason to attack.

Luruthin glanced at her, green eyes bright beneath a frown of concentration. "Get out. I will hold them!"

"No! We stand together."

Luruthin parried another net, and Eliani dodged clear of his blade. There really was not room for them both to swing in this passage.

"There are too many of them," Luruthin gasped as he swung at an alben, who jumped back from the arc of his sword. "You must get away!"

"No, I—"

"Your *gift*!" He turned his head to glare at her. "Find a way out! I will follow."

He was right, but she hated to run from a fight. She was no coward, though her heart was thundering.

More alben appeared, coming down the passage from the audience hall. That was the only way out that she knew of, but behind her the corridor extended toward the back of Darkwood Hall.

Luruthin stepped forward, menacing the nearest alben, who hastily drew back. Another net was thrown and tangled for a moment around Luruthin's sword arm. He took the sword in his other hand and shook the net off.

"*Go!*"

He was right. Eliani stepped backward, felt a net beneath her foot, and flinched. Muttering a curse, she turned and ran down the passage.

Shouting pursued her. The passage turned right, toward the center of the hall. Eliani tried the nearest door and found that it opened on another bedchamber.

A shout of challenge sounded behind her, then the clash of sword blades. Glancing back around the corner, she saw Luruthin engaged with an alben, swords glinting in torchlight, feet scuffling. Beyond them, the passage was filled with more alben.

With a cry of frustration, she ran down the corridor. The doors on either side all looked the same. The passage ended in a smaller door; she wrenched it open to find a storage closet, no exit.

She started back, trying doors on either side, frantically searching for a way out. All led to bedchambers, those on the left with higher ceilings than those on the right. She gave up and ran back to the turning.

Luruthin had taken down the alben with the sword. She could see the blade lying on the floor where he had kicked it out of his opponents' reach. She would fight beside him, then, until they were both taken. There was no other choice.

She started forward just as a shout went up from the many alben. Suddenly the air between them and Luruthin was filled with flying nets. He dodged, but there were too many to evade. One tangled around his sword; another caught at his legs. He stumbled, and a third net wrapped itself around his head.

"*No!*"

Even as Eliani screamed, the alben shouted in triumph. More nets flew, and Luruthin disappeared beneath the tangle of black. Three alben fell upon him, and others scrambled past. One caught up the abandoned sword and started toward Eliani.

She turned and fled, sobbing with anger. She ran into a bedchamber, slammed the door behind her, and pushed a table against it. Not enough.

Her glance fell upon a tall wardrobe of darkwood. She tossed her sword onto the bedstead, then pulled at the wardrobe, tugging it away from the wall. Though empty, it was heavy. She toppled it and wedged it between the table and the bed.

The door handle moved, then the door banged against the table. Eliani gave a small, startled cry. She was trapped, cornered like a cat in its lair. They would take her, but not without a fight. She retrieved her sword and held it before her in trembling hands, watching as the door shook beneath repeated blows.

A small sob escaped her. She wondered if they had killed Luruthin. The thought tore at her heart, and she gasped.

"Oh, spirits!"

Eliani!

Oh, love! Alben—

I know. Do not give up. I am with you.

Warmth flooded her, Turisan's love, lending her strength. It steadied her. Wiping at her eyes, she looked desperately around the room for something, anything to give her an advantage. There was nothing in it but the table, a chair, the bed, and the wardrobe. Nothing hanging on the walls and only a small unlit lamp suspended from the ceiling by a slender chain.

She could make a weapon of that, perhaps. If there was oil in it, maybe she could set a fire. Only if she got out to the passage and could reach one of the torches.

The door shuddered as heavier, regular blows began to hammer against it. Eliani scrambled onto the wardrobe and caught at the lamp's chain. She tugged, but it was hung from a metal loop embedded in the darkwood ceiling. She pulled harder, sobbing with anger and frustration. The chain broke, and the lamp fell to the floor with a clatter.

Useless. It was useless. She had only her sword and could not stand against the many alben now shouting outside the door.

Gasping, she looked wildly around. Her gaze fell on the filigree latticework covering the high window. The panel was narrow, but she might be able to squeeze through.

Yes. Try it.

She jumped down from the wardrobe and dragged the chair over to the wall beneath the window. Standing on the chair, she could just reach the panel and saw that it was hinged at the bottom and secured by two small latches at its top edge. She pushed them aside, and the top of the panel dropped toward her, a small chain at either side supporting it.

It was carved into filigree, but it was still darkwood. She hoped that it was yet strong enough to support her and that the hinges would not give beneath her weight.

A loud splintering told her the table was breaking. The door opened a crack, and the shouting beyond it grew louder.

Eliani fetched her sword, shoved it through the open panel onto the roof, and grabbed at the carved wood, her fingers breaking through the fragile fabric behind it. She hauled herself up, scrabbling to get a leg onto the panel. It creaked with her weight.

The hammering at the door increased. Eliani's foot slipped on the darkwood. She kicked off her slipper and tried again, bare toes clinging to the wood. Pulling with both arms and one leg, she managed to scramble onto the panel and then roll out of the window and onto the roof.

She stood on a strange terraced landscape of gentle slopes and filigreed panels. Many were dark, but some glowed with light, and uneven torchlight flickered behind others.

The shouts and hammering below her were strangely muted. Over them she could hear the furtive sounds of the forest.

Hurry, love. They will not be far behind.

Yes.

She caught up her sword, kicked off her remaining slipper, and ran lightly along the roof. Slate tiles were cool underfoot despite the warm night. She followed the row of filigreed panels that defined the bedchamber she had escaped from and its neighbors. Above, a higher row of larger panels glowed with light. She slowed, remembering the shape of the audience hall. Someone was there now, and she doubted it was Othanin.

"Oh, spirits."

Eliani—

I have to see.

She climbed onto the next tier of the roof and silently approached the nearest large panel. She put her ear to it to listen and heard many voices, murmuring here rather than shouting. Slowly, cautiously, she worked at the silk covering, which time and exposure had made fragile, making a small hole through which she could see the chamber below. What she saw chilled her blood, and she almost cried out.

The chamber was now lit by bright torchlight, and alben stood within, a hundred or more, with their hair glowing pale against the darkwood. Near the five

chairs of state stood a female cloaked in black and
red, Darkshore colors.

Shalár!

What?

The alben leader. Kelevon told me of her.

Eliani gazed down at the female, whose face was
cold and stern. Her white hair was pulled back into a
hunter's braid. At her feet, bound with black nets,
were several ælven.

Luruthin! Oh, spirits!

He was there, on his knees, alive if somewhat battered. His head was bowed, and his arms were bound
behind him. Sprawled beside him, apparently unconscious, was Othanin.

Eliani bit her lip to keep from calling out to them.
She wanted to scream with frustration.

You cannot help them. Not alone.

I will not leave them!

Get to Vanorin. He and the others will help you.

Eliani stifled a sob. The alben leader, Shalár, reached
down and caught Luruthin's chin in her hand, forcing
his head up. A cruel smile formed on her lips, and
Eliani could scarcely contain her rage.

Get away, Eliani. Get to safety.

She gasped as she tore herself away from the window. She could hear shouting again from the wing
where she had crawled onto the roof and more somewhere out in the city. Slinking low, she darted east,
away from the guest chambers and from the exposed
public circle. She dropped down one tier of the roof,
then another.

Reaching the eastern edge of the hall, she saw that
an avenue ran between it and the nearest houses. The
distance was too great for her to jump across. There

were gardens, though. One house had its private garden bordered with trellises of grapevines and berry canes. She glanced behind her, hearing sounds of pursuit on the roof.

She tossed her sword down into the garden, then leapt after it, landing hard and rolling to lessen the impact. She got to her feet and picked up the sword, then hurried toward a small archway between the house and its neighbor. She passed through and out into the street beyond.

There were no lighted windows that she could see. She had no time to wonder if Vanorin, too, had been captured or to search for citizens who might have escaped the alben. She had to get out of the city at once. She paused, struggling to catch her breath and to think through the panic that gripped her.

Get away from there, Eliani. I will come to you.

She laughed under her breath. *It is a trifle far, my love.*

I will come.

The devotion behind that ludicrous pledge steadied her. She looked up and down the street, and when certain it was empty she ran across and between the next row of houses. The city gate was likely to be watched, but perhaps the alben had not had time to set a guard all along the wall.

Anger and sorrow welled within her. She fought them back, striving to think clearly. A pity she had no idea where Othanin's stables were. She pressed on, crossing street after street on her way toward the black wall.

◅

Turisan watched helplessly through Eliani's eyes as she darted through the streets of Ghlanhras. His face was molded in a scowl of concentration, and he scarcely dared to breathe. So present was he in Ghlan-hras that the sensations of his own flesh were muted, distant. It was some moments before he came to the hazy realization that someone was talking to him.

"Please, my lord!"

Turisan opened his eyes, blinking at the wavering firelight of the camp. The nearest fire had fallen to coals, its heat barely reaching him as he leaned against the cliff wall. Willow Bend was a haven his little column had been glad to reach. It meant they were but three or four days from Glenhallow.

"Not now."

"But my lord, the wagons have come!"

"Wagons?"

Eliani had ducked behind a large building, a crafthall, perhaps. She must have seen or heard something and gone into hiding. Turisan wanted to stay with her, but the driver would not leave him alone.

"—from Glenhallow, my lord! Please, I was sent to bring you at once."

"Where is he?" A more strident voice reached them from downhill.

Turisan looked up. "Father?"

He let Eliani go for the moment. Jharan came striding toward him, dressed for riding, eyes intense and his hasty footsteps grinding against the sandy packed earth of the camp. Turisan struggled to his feet, just in time to be caught in his father's tight embrace.

"W-what are you doing here?"

Jharan held him at arm's length, gazing at him with eyes filled with concern. "I have brought wagons to carry your wounded back to Glenhallow."

"But—"

"When I heard you were wounded, I could no

longer stay." Jharan lowered his voice. "I could not wait patiently in Hallowhall while you struggled homeward."

"It is only a scratch. Thorian was to tell you so."

"He did." Jharan lifted his hand from Turisan's right shoulder, laid it gently over the sling for a moment, then touched Turisan's cheek. "I used to rail against Turon for risking himself and all his nextkin at Skyruach instead of staying in Glenhallow. Now I know why he did it. Staying behind is much harder."

Turisan felt an echo of the feeling behind his father's words. The burden of responsibility was writ all through Jharan's khi. Ordinarily he did not let it show, but the care and worry in his face betrayed feelings he usually kept hidden.

"You are safe now." Jharan smiled softly. "At first light we shall start for Glenhallow."

"Not I, Father. I ride north."

Jharan's smile faded. "Do not be foolish. You can do nothing at Midrange."

"Not to Midrange. To Fireshore. Eliani needs me."

"She has her escort—"

"No, Father."

Turisan closed his eyes briefly to see where Eliani was. She had emerged from hiding and was once more prowling through Ghlanhras. He opened his eyes again and looked at his father, who was frowning. He frowned back.

"She is alone. The escort—I have much to tell you. Let us take counsel together now, and in the morning I will ride. I need only a fresh horse and a satchel of food."

"My son—"

"Hear what I have to say."

Jharan gazed at him, dark eyes troubled, frowning in concern. "What has happened?"

Turisan glanced at the driver, who was waiting a few paces away. Beyond him the rest of the camp was also watching. He leaned close to his father, placing his good hand on Jharan's shoulder, and whispered in his ear.

"The alben have returned to Fireshore."

◆

Rephanin had become the battle. His memories of himself were distant, vague, hidden beyond the barrier that kept him from feeling the anguish that churned in Midrange Valley. He had no thoughts save for the commands that passed through him and the occasional pleas for aid that came back from some desperate captain watching his warriors fall and die.

Death was merely an ache to Rephanin now. The army was his body, and when Ehranan told him to move an arm, he did so. A hundred warriors shifting to fill a gap in the shield line. Two hundred rested guardians returning, taking the place of others who were spent.

Some died, an ache, a discomfort to the body, but the body lived on. The constant shifting and reacting to the flow of the battle were natural to him now, easy to understand and even to anticipate. With the omniscience of khi he saw a weakness developing near the river, where water lapped at the feet of the ælven on the shield line.

He had abandoned words—he now understood Davharin's difficulty with them—but he focused a pulse of bright khi toward Ehranan and drew his attention to the trouble. Ehranan responded at once.

Forunan, move your company to the right! Avhlorin,

send some of your reserves to clear that blockage in the river—stop the flooding.

Those blockages were made by heaps upon heaps of grisly corpses. Most were kobalen, but some were not.

There was no time to grieve. Grief was a luxury, one that could not be afforded now. Later there would be leisure for grief.

Often in the evening when the fighting slackened there was a danger of thinking too much about what was happening here, but tonight there had been no slackening. If anything, the fighting had intensified. Rephanin sensed the change but did not understand it. He saw little difference in the orders that Ehranan sent through him. They were the same as went out every evening, save that the warriors being taken off the line were not dismissed to rest but instead gathered south of the fighting, along the river's edge.

Rephanin felt whispers of their thoughts: weariness, curiosity, anticipation. Every ælven on the field was a part of his awareness, and the ripples of mood that washed through their ranks overbore his own feelings. They were his body, and he was their heart.

Rephanin. Look at me.

Look? How shall I look? With whose eyes?

Rephanin.

A shaking sensation, dimly felt. His own flesh, not the living mass of the army. Not the horse's movements either; the horse had been dispensed with a day or two after his arrival, when it was found that he had no need to move about the field. His flesh lay in his tent, with his escort nearby to protect him.

Rephanin, open your eyes.

The shaking continued, drawing his presence back

to his flesh. He shifted the focus of his thoughts there, away from the ælven army. Ah, yes, someone was shaking him by the shoulders. Enough of that.

He opened his eyes, blinking at Ehranan as awareness of the army receded. Ehranan released his shoulders, letting him lie back against the jumble of packs and blankets that pillowed him.

Crouched beside him in the tent, the commander looked the worse for several days' fighting. A gash along Ehranan's jaw told where a kobalen dart had just missed him.

"What is it?" Rephanin's voice came out a dry croak.

"I want your counsel."

Ehranan handed him a half-filled water skin. Rephanin pushed himself upright and drank greedily, then gasped for air. His flesh was hungry, beginning to suffer from neglect.

"What counsel can I give you here?" Rephanin gestured toward the battleground. "You know more of this than I."

"You know what they are feeling." Ehranan set a wooden plate beside him. "Here, try to eat something."

Dried fruit, dried meat. Rephanin picked up a shriveled pear but could not bring himself to bite it. He let his hand drop into his lap and sat frowning, trying to overcome disorientation. His fingers turned the pear over and over.

Ehranan spoke in a low, tense voice. "Have they the heart for a fight?"

Rephanin met his gaze and knew he meant the army. "They will fight on."

"But will they attack if I ask it?"

"Attack?"

Rephanin stared at him, bewildered. What good would an attack do? They could not drive the kobalen back through the pass. The snow had blocked it, snow that continued intermittently, along with the persistent cold. In some places the flooding water had frozen into treacherous patches of ice. The only comfort in the weather was that the kobalen liked it even less than the ælven did.

"I think we can end it if we make an attack tonight. It means no rest, though."

No rest until the task is done. Rephanin had resigned himself to that days ago.

"They trust you. They will follow you."

Ehranan's blue eyes gazed at him from beneath frowning brows. Ice eyes, black frown. Fearsome unless one knew the heart beneath, as Rephanin now did. They had been in close contact for so long that he could not help feeling kinship with Ehranan, who bore such a burden for his people.

Kinship and more, like his feelings for Thorian. Rephanin wondered idly if the mindspeaker had tried to contact him. He doubted he would have heard.

"I have one more thing to ask of you. Can you gauge the kobalen? Can you sense their mood?"

Rephanin's parched lips fell open. Ehranan was asking him to touch the kobalen, whom he had so carefully blocked from his awareness. Asking him to tear down one of his own defenses.

"I need to know if they are losing heart. Have they any leaders, or do they fight only because they know no other choice? Can you tell me, Rephanin?"

Rephanin swallowed. The difficulty of it reminded him of his thirst, and he reached for the water skin again.

Enormous weariness descended on him. He knew it was in part a reluctance to do as Ehranan asked. He drank, feeling the cold pour down through his chest, into his belly. Setting the skin aside, he closed his eyes.

I will try.

Kobalen. He let the fear and repulsion that accompanied the thought echo away. Summoning calm in its place, he turned his attention to the barriers he had built against distraction.

One held kobalen rage away. He moved toward it, then within it, a breath away from passing through. The barrier was strong but also fragile. It might shatter, and he did not know what he would do if that happened.

Flesh moved, distracting. He paused to identify the change and felt a warm strength against his palm. Ehranan had taken hold of his hand.

Gratitude. He let the sensation hang for a moment so that Ehranan would perceive it. Then, encouraged by Ehranan's support, he opened a thought toward the kobalen.

Rage, fear, betrayal, dark and heavy anger. A promise made that could not now be kept. Pain, hunger; hunger a rage unto itself. No food here, no hunting! But the promise would not be kept, the reward would not be given, if they did not fight.

Bewildered, Rephanin withdrew from the chaos, though he maintained a tenuous contact. What promise? Whose?

A familiar gnawing sensation grew upon him, the deaths eating away at the body, only now it was kobalen deaths as well as ælven, and the kobalen died much more rapidly, much more often. Killing one another, dying together, souls fleeing flesh both kobalen and ælven. Confused and appalled, Rephanin curled into himself, seeking to escape the horror of mutual destruction.

There was a line somewhere, a shelter, a place of safety, but he had lost it. He heard only the death cries of tens of ælven, hundreds of kobalen, more and more every moment. Felt their pain, rage, fear—

Rephanin!

Whose voice? The voice that commanded him. But there was no controlling this, no more control.

Rephanin, stop. Come back. Now!

Shaking again. Suddenly he was aware of his own flesh, very much alive as yet. He did not like being shaken in this way but could do nothing to stop it. The flight of souls all around had drained him of the will to act.

No more!

Sudden silence stunned him. The voices of the dying were gone. So, too, were the dark throngs of kobalen, the hundreds of heartbeats of the ælven. There was only one voice, one presence that filled his mind. Slowly he opened his eyes.

Ehranan's hands gripped his head on both sides. Ehranan's eyes locked onto his. Somehow the commander had separated him from the battle. A trace of fear passed out of the blue eyes as Rephanin relaxed. How pleasant, this silence.

"Forgive me." Ehranan released him. "I should not have asked it of you."

Rephanin inhaled somewhat shakily. His body was curled almost into a ball, as if he had been trying to protect himself. He sat up and looked around vaguely but could not find the water skin. No matter.

"My lords? Is all well?"

The voice came from the tent's door. Rephanin

smiled wryly as Ehranan called back a reassurance. Could it be that they missed the voice of their leader in mindspeech, so constant in the past few days? How quickly one became accustomed to the strangest things.

Rephanin coughed and drew a careful breath. His fleshly voice was ragged. "The kobalen are losing the will to fight, Ehranan. They were promised something and now begin to doubt they will receive it."

Ehranan frowned. "Promised something? In return for attacking us?"

Rephanin nodded. "I do not know what or by whom. I—cannot try again."

"No!" Alarm crossed Ehranan's face. "No, do not. I should not have asked it. You have given so much, and all I do is demand more."

Rephanin closed his eyes briefly, touched by this acknowledgment. In truth, he would willingly do whatever Ehranan asked.

Oh.

Looking at Ehranan again, his heart jumped with ecstatic hesitance. Was he fickle, or was it just that he saw so much to love in those close to him?

Perhaps he was unable to separate admiration and affection. Perhaps the strain of this unspeakable situation and the constant contact with Ehranan had made him susceptible.

I am a fool.

"Rest now. You have gone far too long without proper rest and food. I will have something hot brought to you."

"Wait."

Ehranan paused on one knee, halfway to standing. Rephanin gazed at him, filled with admiration. If Ehranan had demanded much of him, the commander had demanded even more of himself. He risked his own flesh even as he guided the army and planned its movements. His courage was a banner for all to follow.

"You think you can end this with an attack to-night?"

"Possibly."

"Then please do. I will be glad to have it finished."

Ehranan sat back, a frown of concern on his face. "Will you be all right?"

Rephanin smiled and nodded. "Thanks to you."

"To me?" Ehranan scoffed. "I am the cause of your suffering. When we set out I did not realize the cost . . ."

Ehranan looked at him with haunted eyes. It only made Rephanin love him more.

"Let us finish this. Then we can move on."

Ehranan held his gaze for a long time, then nodded. He reached out his arm. Rephanin clasped it formally, briefly, ignoring the fire that even this small contact sent racing along his nerves. If Ehranan felt anything like it, he gave no sign. He let go and gazed abstractedly at the tent wall for a moment, then stood up.

"When you are ready, Lord Rephanin."

Rephanin leaned back against his makeshift couch and closed his eyes. Drawing breath, he turned his thought to the ælven again. They were there, anxiously awaiting him. He paused to make certain it was only the ælven he touched now.

The kobalen were shut away again behind the barrier that spared him their anguish. Though he could never forget it, it would not distract him now. Hesitantly, he opened his heart to the ælven army once more.

I am here.

His mind lit with awareness of them—hundreds of ælven, weary and frightened, yet filled with painfu hope as he spoke to them. Ehranan joined him, addressing the army through mindspeech, and now the fire Rephanin had felt ran not only through his flesh but through his soul.

There was no hiding it, not in this strange union to which they had become so accustomed. Ehranan must be aware but again showed no sign. He gave orders, and through Rephanin they went out to all the ælven.

Ehranan the mind, Rephanin the heart, and hundreds of ælven the body. Together they were one being moving with a single purpose, and that purpose now shifted. No longer did they merely stand and hold at bay the reckless, disorganized attacks of the kobalen. Now they moved as one to end the agony of this conflict.

The new force continued to form behind the shield line. All the ælven not currently holding the line joined it. Ehranan went there in flesh as well and was met with cheering.

Rephanin shut away the dread he felt for Ehranan's personal safety. A leader must lead, and Ehranan knew how best to inspire his weary army.

We will cross the river. Strike north along the far bank, then cross again at the north ford.

Most of the kobalen were south of there now, hurling themselves against the shield line. Rephanin slowly realized that their numbers were not infinite. What had seemed an incalculable swarm of kobalen had dwindled, if that word could be applied to a force that was yet many times larger than the ælven army.

The kobalen are leaderless. When we fall upon them from behind, they will scatter and flee. They will cross the snowbound mountains or die trying, and we will hunt them down until Midrange is free again and the Silverwash flows clear.

Cheers rose again into the night. As Ehranan led his force across the Silverwash, its bitter cold stinging their flesh, the sky seemed to clear.

Through hundreds of eyes, Rephanin saw stars glimmering in a dome of cold velvet, bright almost beyond bearing. Some of the stars seemed alive.

He knew, even before the warriors had finished crossing the river, that Ehranan was right. This would break the kobalen, shatter what was left of their will. Whatever they had been promised would not keep them fighting against the determination of the ælven army. He knew, and as the battle began to take new shape, he smiled.

☙ Fireshore ❧

Darkwood Hall was hers. Ghlanhras was hers. Before long, if all went well, the rest of Fireshore would be hers. Clan Darkshore had reclaimed its own.

Shalár glowed with satisfaction as she looked over the audience hall, where a steady stream of captive ælven was being brought before her. She sat in a chair that had been pulled forward from the wall and hastily draped in black to cover the usurpers' orange. Very little red was to be found in Ghlanhras, but she would soon amend that.

She was pleased with her army's success in capturing the city. It had to be admitted that the ease of the seizure was due in part to the surprising lack of numbers dwelling in Ghlanhras, but those few had resisted, and the pack had dealt efficiently with some challenging situations.

Three of her hunters had been killed and seven wounded by the sword-wielding Stonereach who had been taken in the guest quarters. The so-called governor had submitted without resistance in his chambers, chambers that were even now being prepared for Shalár's residence. The worst loss had been at a house on the public circle, which had proved to be filled with Stonereaches and Greenglens, all armed. Some of them

had escaped, but some had not. Shalár expected to find
them a source of useful information.

Yaras approached and paused a few paces from her
chair to bow. Shalár smiled, knowing this gesture was
largely for the benefit of the captives, for Yaras was
not ordinarily so formal. He came closer and knelt
before her, resting a knee on the cushion placed for
that purpose.

"Bright Lady. You sent for me."

"Yes. What is your progress?"

"We have searched more than half of the city and
are going through the outermost rows now. Those
seem to be entirely unoccupied. Many of the houses
are empty."

"What of the female with the sword?"

Yaras's eyes flicked downward. "No sign of her.
Yet." He raised his head. "She will not pass the gate."

Shalár regarded him in silence, then decided not to
remark. If the female was not found when all the city
had been searched, then would be the time for repri-
mands.

"Have you found any more swords? Other weapons?
Tools?"

Yaras shook his head. "Not in the outer parts of the
city. All that were found have been brought here."

Twenty-two swords had been captured, along with
a number of bows. Shalár had hoped for more, but at
least she could now arm more of her army. She
frowned.

"Make careful note of any useful supplies."

"We are doing so. We have not found much—a few
trade goods and a store of lamp oil. No darkwood."

"It goes straight from cutting to trade."

Or it had when she had lived here, so far as she
remembered. She had paid little attention to the

darkwood trade, though she had visited the cutting fields with her father on occasion. So many things to which she should have paid better attention, but she had been young and heedless.

"I want any records you find brought here."

"Yes, Bright Lady."

"Thank you, Yaras. You have done well tonight."

He met her gaze, his expression watchful. It had been too long since she had enjoyed fleshly pleasures. Perhaps Yaras would accompany her to her new quarters when the night was done.

Much as she enjoyed savoring such thoughts, there were two major tasks yet to be addressed. First and most pressing, she must send out hunters to catch kobalen. Her army needed to feed, and she preferred not to feed them on the ælven.

She must then prepare to defend the city. The distraction at Midrange would not hold the ælven's attention once word of Darkshore's return reached them.

She turned to Yaras. "Choose twenty to hunt. Pick them a good leader."

"I would gladly lead—"

"No, I have need of you here. Send them out at once and tell them to bring their first catch back tomorrow night."

"Yes, Bright Lady."

Yaras bowed, then moved to stand. Shalár stayed him with a gesture and rose from her chair. Her silken cloak, the best mark of Darkshore's authority she possessed, whispered about her as she stepped close to him.

"When you have set them hunting, return here. I would take counsel with you in my quarters."

Yaras gazed up at her for a moment, then stood and met her eye to eye. "We have taken the city. We have accomplished your goal. I have done all I can to aid you in the effort, and that is all I pledged to do."

His voice was low but rang with emotion. Shalár found herself wishing he felt so intensely toward her, but she knew where his desires lay and knew his meaning.

She stared back at him, appraising his mood. She had been able to command his arousal before and was certain she could do so again, whatever reluctance he might feel. His personal ideas of loyalty were tiresome. She was inclined to be annoyed with him.

"Do you still wish to be steward in Nightsand? Or would you care to consider a higher place?"

Yaras's eyes stared flatly, betraying no change of heart. She stepped closer still, resting her hands lightly on his shoulders and feeling the tingle of his khi along her flesh. All in the hall were watching, she knew.

"You could be my companion. You have earned a place of honor."

"Stewardship of Nightsand is honor enough for me, Bright Lady."

She stepped back and gazed at him. Part of her wanted to send him to his knees, but though that might inspire respect for her in the rest of the army, it would not make Yaras inclined to serve her. Gratitude would make him far more useful to her than enforced submission, especially at the distance of Nightsand.

"When you have sent the hunters forth, return here." A flash of resentment crossed his face, but she smiled wryly. "I will give you messages to carry to Nightsand. You will leave before dawn and take three hunters with you."

Fire lit his eyes now, where earlier she had seen blank resistance. "I can travel faster alone."

"You will take three with you and be careful to avoid

any ælven you may encounter. Do not risk yourself or the letters I will give you. I will not lose my steward through needless misadventure."

A smile of sheer joy crossed Yaras's face, then he bowed deeply. "Thank you, Bright Lady. I will not forget your kindness."

Kindness? She was rarely accused of that.

She watched him back away, then straighten and stride out of the hall. Nightsand would benefit under his guidance, and her people there would benefit, too, from the summons she would send with him. She would welcome all her people to come to Fireshore and settle there to help her reclaim their rightful home.

Yaras passed out of the audience chamber, following the broad corridor that led to the front of Darkwood Hall, and Shalár turned away. A pity Islir had such a hold on him.

She returned to her chair, gesturing to a waiting hunter to bring forward his captives for her perusal. There was much yet to be done this night and much pleasure to be taken when the night's labors were finished.

❧

Luruthin stumbled into the small, empty room, pushed by ungentle hands. He managed to keep his feet and turned to face his captors.

"Unbind my hands."

The two alben laughed at him, and one cocked her head. "And have you trying to claw your way out of here? I think not."

She slammed the door shut, and he heard something being done to it. Securing it, no doubt. Shuffling and more slamming followed. At least one other captive was put in a neighboring room.

Luruthin waited until the alben voices and footsteps

had receded, then silently went to the door. His hands were tightly bound behind him, with cord now instead of the nets. With his back to the door he fumbled at the handle, succeeded in turning it, and pulled but could not open the door. Discouraged, he slid down to sit on the floor.

His arms ached already from the awkward position in which they were bound, and he knew it would only get worse. He was battered and bruised from the fighting. His only hope was that Eliani had escaped. He had not seen her among the other ælven brought into the audience hall.

"Spirits help her."

"Who is there?"

He had only whispered, but the answerer had heard. Luruthin's head shot up, and he turned an ear to the gap beneath the door.

"Othanin?"

He had seen the governor in the audience hall, though they had not had opportunity to do more than exchange a glance. They had been brought before the alben leader, the one they all called Bright Lady. Bright she was—white as sunlight—and also cruel. He had seen it in her eyes and in what she had done to Othanin.

After a long pause, Othanin answered. "Yes."

"It is Luruthin."

He heard Othanin sigh. "I am sorry."

"Is Eliani here?"

"I have not heard her nor seen her."

Luruthin felt a flood of relief. He looked around the small room where he was trapped. Patterns of dust on the floor showed where furniture had stood, but it was empty now, and dim. Faint light came under the door from the passage outside. There was no window in the room.

"Where are we?"

"These are the rooms where the hall's attendants dwell, those who choose to live here."

"Are you bound?"

"Yes."

Luruthin closed his eyes. Little hope of escape, then. He wondered what the alben would do with them. Hold them as guarantee against the ælven's retaliation, most likely. Their presence would discourage attacks upon Ghlanhras.

"Tell me about Darkwood Hall, my lord. I did not get to see all of it."

He hoped Othanin would understand that he was most interested to know about the hall's entrances, how many and where they were. Othanin began in a lackluster voice to describe the structure, which it seemed was much larger than Luruthin had guessed. Not only did it sprawl along a good portion of Ghlanhras's public circle, it extended deeply into the city's north side and included vast enclosed gardens and several smaller courtyards. Any of them might be an avenue of escape, and being surrounded by the hall, they might not be guarded closely. Luruthin began to be hopeful.

Footsteps sounded down the passage, approaching. Othanin fell silent, and Luruthin did the same, fearing what might happen next as he listened. At least two were approaching. Their steps stopped nearby, and Luruthin heard the sounds of a door being opened.

"Come along."

Shuffling and dragging sounds, the door being closed, the footsteps receding. Luruthin waited until they were gone.

"Othanin? Governor?"

Silence. The faint hope Luruthin had felt drained away.

"Othanin?"

They had taken him. To what fate?

"Anyone? Can anyone hear me?"

Silence stretched through the darkness. He was alone.

✿

Eliani crouched between two unoccupied houses, staring at the city's outer wall. She had been there for some time, watching and listening for any sign that the wall was patrolled. All was still.

She looked over the few items at her feet, things she had scrounged as she came through the deserted city: an ax shaft, two lengths of rope, and a broken-handled ewer she had filled with water from a well in one of the many gardens she had crossed. She would have given much for a water skin, but the ewer was the only vessel she had found.

She would have given even more for a scabbard for her sword. Carrying the blade was awkward, but she dared not abandon her only weapon. She used it to cut a length from the shorter rope and fashioned a crude sword belt, the bare blade hanging from a cradle of knots about its hilt. She would have to take care if it became necessary to draw the sword lest she cut both the rope and her clothing.

She twined the rest of that rope around the ewer and the ax shaft, making a rough net that she could sling over her shoulder along with the remaining rope. She settled everything against her back, slopping a little of the water. It made a cool spot down her right side.

She was ready. Reluctant to leave her shelter, she sent a query to Turisan.

I am here, love.

I am about to climb the wall.

Are you near the gate?

No. On the east side.

Be careful.

Yes.

Eliani closed her eyes. Her heart was already
pounding with fear.

*Turisan—if something should happen, remember
all that you must tell your father.*

He is here.

What?

*He came to meet us. I have told him about the al-
ben and about what you learned from Othanin.*

Oh.

She felt relieved and realized it was because she had
feared for Turisan's safety. Also that what they had
learned of Fireshore would be lost if they both suffered
misfortune. Now Jharan knew it as well, and he would
see that the news went to all the ælven realms.

Give Jharan my fond regards.

*He sends you his as well. He has many questions
for you, of course.*

Eliani smiled. *Of course.*

So you must take care, love. Take every caution.

She felt the tremor of fear in his khi. She did not answer, shaken by her own helpless dread as she thought
of those she was leaving behind. Luruthin, her beloved
cousin. Othanin, so gentle and patient. Vanorin and
the escort and others she had not met who had suffered much already and were now suffering worse as
captives of the alben.

"Spirits help them." She scarcely dared to whisper,
fearing discovery. "And spirits help me."

I am going.

Turisan stayed with her, a silent observer. She felt
his presence at the edge of her awareness and was
grateful. It was a comfort not to be alone.

She stood, steadying her sword at her hip with one hand. With the other she settled her makeshift pack. Looking up and down the narrow space that ran along the inside of the wall behind the outer row of houses, she saw no movement. She stepped out of her shelter and across to the wall, then began to climb slowly and carefully, trying not to let the sword clatter.

The rocks were rough volcanic stone, easy to find holds upon but sharp against her flesh. By the time she had reached the top, her hands and bare feet were bleeding from scrapes and cuts. She paused, raised her head just above the top edge of the wall, and looked toward the gate.

No one stood outside it. If there were alben inside, they were blocked from her view by houses. She began to pull herself up cautiously, listening with every small movement. The sword made a tiny clank, and she froze for a moment, then climbed onto the top of the wall. More water spilled from the ewer, soaking her back. She hoped at least a couple of mouthfuls would remain, for she did not know when she would find more. She crouched atop the wall and paused to listen again, but no sounds of alarm troubled the night.

Outside, the forest waited, dense and gloomy. The space between it and the wall seemed terribly exposed, but Eliani knew that only a few paces would take her across it. She shifted her position and began to lower herself down the outside of the wall, limbs trembling with the strain of moving slowly.

Perhaps she should have waited until daylight for this. The alben could not tolerate the sun. The forest blocked much of its light, though, and they might care more about capturing her than about their own safety. No, it was best to be gone from Ghlanhras as quickly as possible.

Her feet touched bare earth, and she sighed as she let go of the wall. She stood for a moment, trying to calm her breathing, wishing she could stop shaking.

All she need do was elude any alben who might be watching the outer wall and get to the road without being seen. She would go to Woodrun, summon help from there. It would take days, but it was the best she could do. She could not reconquer Ghlanhras alone.

She put a hand on her sword's hilt and in three quick strides crossed the open space to the forest. Wedging herself through a tangle of vines, she stood just inside the woods, listening. No sounds of imminent pursuit came to her.

Good. Forward, then.

Within a few moments she realized the futility of trying to push through the undergrowth. It was so dense that she could not make her way through it. The ax shaft was useless. Only her sword would let her make any progress, and the sound of someone hacking through the woods would no doubt attract unwanted attention.

The ground was uneven, root-covered and vine-tangled and full of dangers to her bare feet. She was forced to conclude this was not the way to get to Woodrun.

She turned and for a moment panicked, for she could not see the wall. Even this little way into the forest she was close to becoming lost. Taking deep, deliberate breaths, she noted the displaced vines and broken twigs that marked her passage and followed them back to the edge of the clearing.

I must take the road. It means passing the gate.
Wait until daylight.
Yes.

Was it merely hopefulness, or had the sky brightened a little? She could see clear sky above the wall, and though stars still gleamed to the west, she thought perhaps the night was no longer fully dark.

She unslung her rope pack and took a swallow of water from the ewer, which was less than half-full. The silks she wore were now torn and damp and clung uncomfortably. She worked her way a little farther into the woods and leaned against the trunk of a young darkwood tree. She could still see the wall through a gap in the foliage but felt confident she would not be visible to a casual observer.

She sighed, trying to relax. Patience had never been one of her strengths.

Turisan?

Yes, my heart?

I am afraid for them. Luruthin and the others.

I know, love.

She felt tears gathering at the corners of her eyes and brushed at them angrily. This was no time for self-indulgence. Luruthin had given up his own freedom to preserve hers. She must use that gift to bring back help. She must stay alert.

Something crawled over her right foot. She gasped, jerked her foot away, and gasped again as she stepped on something sharp.

"Who is there?"

Eliani froze. Quiet footsteps came hurrying toward her from the direction of the gate.

A pale figure in dark leathers appeared, hurrying along the foot of the wall. Eliani shrank against the tree and tried to blend her khi with that of the forest, but these plants were strange to her and the darkwood's khi was rather heavy and impenetrable. The alben stopped and turned, then returned a few paces, frowning as her gaze searched the woods. She lifted her head as if scenting the air, and a sharpness came into her eyes.

Dark, dark eyes. Darker than Turisan's and far colder. They traveled straight to Eliani, and the nostrils below them flared. Smelling blood.

Eliani swallowed as their gazes met, silently cursing the wall that had cut her hands and feet. For a moment they stared at each other, as if each disbelieved what she saw, then Eliani pushed away from the tree.

She stumbled toward the alben, trying to get clear of the woods so that she could draw her sword. The alben stepped back and reached to her belt.

No time for the sword. Eliani plunged forward, out of the trees and straight at the alben, who threw her net, but too late. It thumped half-unfurled into Eliani's chest, and she carried it with her as she charged the alben.

The alben lost her footing and fell. Eliani landed heavily on top of her. Water splashed up her back from the ewer.

Eliani pushed herself up and grabbed at the net, shoving part of it into the alben's mouth as she opened it to shout. One of the alben's hands was caught in the net, pinned under Eliani's weight. Eliani grabbed the other hand and tangled more net around it, then put her knee over both and fumbled at the alben's belt.

The alben kicked. A crunch and wetness down her back, then Eliani's hand found what she had glimpsed and sought. She pulled the dagger from its sheath, putting the point to the alben's neck.

"Be still."

The alben blinked several times but ceased struggling. Eliani sat up with a small clatter of broken pottery. She shrugged the tangled ropes off her shoulder, letting them fall to the ground.

The alben's eyes were furious. She would fight. The easiest and safest course would be to kill her, but Eliani rebelled at that thought. There had been too much killing already. Taking life without absolute need was against the creed, and the creed was what separated her from this angry female. One of the things that separated them.

Eliani swallowed, leaned back, and with her free hand carefully drew her sword. The alben's eyes widened with fear as Eliani laid the blade against her neck opposite the dagger.

"Do not move or I will kill you."

The alben was still. Watching her, Eliani slowly got to her feet, keeping the sword blade at the other's throat. Her flesh prickled with fear that at any moment another alben would come along.

"Turn over."

The alben rolled awkwardly onto her stomach, the little leaf-shaped metal weights of the net tinkling together. Eliani frowned, wondering what to do next. She mistrusted the alben, and if she tried to control her, they might end up struggling again. Biting her lip, she bent and withdrew the ax shaft from her tangled ropes.

"I am sorry for this."

She aimed a blow at the back of the alben's head. A soft grunt followed, and the alben went limp. Eliani knelt to examine her, hoping she had not struck too hard.

Heat rose in Eliani's hands as she touched the alben, startling her. No time for a healing, though she knew through the glow in her hands that the alben was not badly hurt. The female's khi felt peculiar, an uncomfortable prickling sensation, but Eliani did not pause to explore it.

She rolled the alben onto her back and pulled the net out of her mouth, then quickly bound her hands with a length of rope. The alben did not wake. Eliani unbuckled the black leather belt and put it on over her silks, sheathing the dagger again. The belt also held a small flask that gave a reassuring splashing sound. She considered it her rightful prize after losing the ewer.

Boots. She pulled the soft leather footwear off the alben's feet and onto her own, wincing a little. They were slightly too large, but it was better than going barefoot.

Perhaps she should take the leather armor as well. No, it would be too difficult to strip the unconscious alben, and the leathers would be no use as conceal-ment, for her dark hair would betray her. Better to move fast and light.

Eliani glanced toward the gate, listening, fearing some friend of the alben's would come looking for her. She had been on patrol, walking the city's perime-ter, and no doubt would be missed before long.

Eliani no longer had the choice of waiting for sunrise. She picked up her ropes, shook pieces of the broken ewer out of them, coiled them, and tucked them into her belt.

The net. Take it.

I cannot throw it.

It might be of use, though. Take it anyway.

Eliani picked up the net, frowning as she gathered it into an awkward bundle and shoved it through the belt. She shoved the ax shaft through it, too, begin-ning to feel rather bulky about the middle. Her sword she kept in hand. She might have to run, and it would be less awkward running with it in her hands than having it bounce about her legs.

She stood back, looking at the alben. She had struck this female, injured her, and taken her possessions. All against the creed. She would have to find some way of atoning.

Her heart suffered a pang as she realized that this enemy was yet an honored being in her view. This was the first alben she had been near, and she had felt no overriding horror. They were kin; that was obvious. There must be a way out of the strife between their people.

Eliani—

Yes. I am going.

Keeping close to the wall, she started toward the gate. She walked slowly, cautiously searching both before and behind her with khi. No one came in pursuit.

Ahead, she saw a figure above the wall. She froze.

A male alben, alone, a dark silhouette against the night. He seemed to be watching the road. Eliani saw that she was not far from the gate, twenty paces, perhaps.

Oh, for a bow. But that would mean killing or wounding the watcher. She preferred not to do that.

What had come over her? She had killed countless kobalen with no more thought than a few words of regret and atonement. The alben were enemies only because they, too, killed kobalen, albeit for different reasons.

Eliani gritted her teeth. She was beginning to think the Bitter Wars had been a terrible mistake, one for which she and her kindred were now having to atone.

She edged forward, staying close to the wall and moving silently. Ten paces from the gate, she dared go no farther, fearing to attract the watcher's attention. The road was only a few paces away but beyond her reach.

Distract the watcher? She wished she had kept a piece of the broken ewer to throw over the wall. The path before her was beaten earth and clear of any loose rock. All she had were ropes and the net and the ax shaft. She was not about to part with her sword or the alben's dagger.

The ax shaft, then. She drew it out of her belt with careful slowness, watching the alben all the while.

A sudden burst of shouting made her tense. She flattened herself against the wall.

Blows, more shouting—the clash of swords. A fight, just inside the city gates! Some citizens of Ghlanhras seeking escape?

"Mihlaran! To me!"

Eliani gasped. Vanorin's voice!

The watcher on the wall had raised a bow. Eliani drew a sharp breath, then flung the ax shaft at his head. It struck him a glancing blow and fell with a clatter onto the slate tiles of a nearby rooftop, but it was enough to distract him. His head turned toward Eliani.

She ran.

Just before reaching the gate, she flung herself against the wall, peering upward. Stars in a velvet sky above the pale-headed alben watcher. She saw him raise his bow again, taking aim. Clenching her teeth, she fixed her khi on the bow and closed her eyes, reaching into the slender wood, setting a spark there, willing it to grow.

A cry of alarm indicated her success. She glanced up in time to see the alben fling the flaming bow away from him.

Pleased, she looked for something else to burn. The watcher had disappeared, gone to join the fray below. Eliani laid a hand on the darkwood of the gate, wondering if she might burn it, but no. Too hard to set alight, and her folk were trying to come out this way.

Eliani—

I know, but I must help them!

The hinges of the gate stood out from the wall. She stepped on the lowest one and hauled herself up, climbing swiftly. Clinging to the topmost hinge, she raised her head to look over the wall.

Vanorin and several others stood in a small cluster, swords outward, surrounded by a circle of alben, twenty or more of them. Three had swords; the rest held nets or bows.

One of the sword wielders stood before Vanorin. The Greenglen lunged toward his opponent, sweeping his blade in an arc that clipped the alben's sword arm. With a cry the alben dropped the weapon and stepped back. His neighbor lifted the sword.

Eliani dragged her eyes from the fighting. She could not watch; she had to help them somehow. The alben outnumbered Vanorin and the others, and more were coming, running down the avenue from the center of Ghlanhras.

The alben had mostly nets and a few bows. She knew the bows would burn.

She unfocused her gaze, concentrating on the khi of the nets. She put a hand to the net at her hip, feeling its fibre, then searched the circle of alben below for the same fibre.

Yes. She had it. The nets felt soft, faint whispers of khi from the plants that had gone into them, with hard glints of metal from the leaf-shaped weights. An alben threw one, and Eliani had a strange, vague sensation of floating. She shook it off, narrowing her focus to one thought.

Burn.

Voices rose in shouts of alarm. Her gaze was unfixed, but she saw spots of gold suddenly flame upward in an uneven ring. At its center, her escort. They stood still for a moment, then as one they dashed for the gate, pushing through the fiery circle.

Cries of pain filled the air. Some of the nets were in the belts of the alben, burning—

Eliani turned her mind to the bows. She fixed her gaze on one, capturing the essence of its fibre—light wood, a breed unknown to her, the same as the watcher's bow had been—and sought out all the similar khi she could find. Drawing khi from the very air around her, she sent heat flooding out into the wood.

More fire. More cries of distress.

A heavy thunk vibrated through the gate and the hinge beneath her feet. She scrambled downward, felt the hinges begin to shift, and jumped to the ground.

One gate swung inward. Cærshari dashed out of it, followed by the others. Eliani ran to join them, falling in beside Sunahran, who gave her a startled glance.

"Eliani!"

"Keep running!"

She had no breath for more. She felt light-headed and focused all her strength on keeping her feet and getting away down the road. Shouting continued behind her but quickly faded. She dared to hope the alben would not pursue.

An arrow whipped past her head, breaking that hope.

"To the right!"

Vanorin's command heartened her. She turned with the others and skittered to a halt at the side of the road, hard against the dark wall of the forest.

Gasping for breath, Eliani looked northward, surprised at how short a distance they had come. The gate of Ghlanhras stood ajar, and within she saw flame. Without, dark figures were advancing.

An arrow crashed into the forest above her head. She flinched.

"Bows!" Vanorin's voice was hoarse. "Answer them!"

Only five of the escort had bows. All of them stood forth, aiming arrows toward the alben.

Arrows would burn.

Eliani frowned in concentration. She did not want to set the bows of her friends alight, nor did she trust herself to alter more than one arrow at a time. She chose the arrow nearest her and, when Mærani loosed it, twisted the khi of the slender shaft into a flame that sped away toward the alben.

A scream rose from the north. Eliani lit two more arrows as they flew, then called to Vanorin.

"Run!"

They ran. Eliani's side began to ache. The alben's boots were slightly loose and threatened to trip her. She began to think she must stop, then a bridge rose before them, one that crossed a small stream she remembered from their journey in.

Their feet thundered across the darkwood. On the far side Vanorin halted them. He returned to the bridge, standing in the center of its slight rise, facing north.

Eliani dropped to the ground, gasping for breath. Her throat was dry, and she reached for the skin at her belt, then frowned at it.

An alben had drunk from it. Was there danger of passing the curse that way?

She flung the skin away into the woods.

Vanorin turned. "They are not pursuing."

Eliani scrambled down the stream bank beside the bridge. She splashed cold water on her face and drank deeply. Vanorin joined her.

"My lady—forgive me—"

"Vanorin, if you call me that again, so help me—"

"I failed you."

Eliani stood, ignoring the mud on the knees of her now torn and sodden silks, and gestured toward the others in the road. "You brought these guardians out alive. That is no failure."

He glanced toward the escort. "I did not bring them all."

"Enough, though."

He looked back at her, frowning in grief. "We saw you running across the rooftops. We tried to follow but lost you in the city."

"I came over the wall."

"It was you who set the alben's nets alight."

"Yes."

A look of troubled wonder crossed his face. "I would never have thought of that."

Eliani climbed the stream bank, muscles complaining, and faced the handful of guardians that remained of her valiant escort. Eight of them and Vanorin. All turned weary eyes to her.

"We must go back."

Vanorin protested. "We must get you to Woodrun, m—Eliani. We can send help from there."

"Luruthin is in Darkwood Hall. And Governor Othanin. We must get them out."

"That is folly. There are hundreds of alben."

"So we wait until morning."

Vanorin leaned back, his eyes full of dread. She saw a swallow move his throat and continued her plea.

"In daylight, they cannot follow us. We go in the way I came out—over the wall and across the palace roofs. There are high windows all through Darkwood Hall. All we need do is open them, and the alben will not be able to pass through the light they let in."

Eliani looked at the faces of her guardians. Stonereach and Greenglen, but that mattered little now. They had a common foe.

"We bring Luruthin and Othanin out of the palace. Then we go to Woodrun."

Eliani—

Luruthin helped me escape. Now I must help him.

Vanorin was staring at her, doubt and admiration warring in his eyes. At last he nodded.

"Very well. Tenahran and Jæthali, stand watch. Alert us of any movement beyond the bridge. We go in at dawn." He bent to pick up a twig from the side of the road and offered it to Eliani. "In the meantime, show us the shape of Darkwood Hall."

Grinning, surrounded by her bedraggled guardians, Eliani squatted to scratch her battle plan in the dirt.